SUE H

Other Avon Books by
Sue Harrison

MOTHER EARTH FATHER SKY
MY SISTER THE MOON

SUE HARRISON

Brother Wind

AVON BOOKS  NEW YORK

AVON BOOKS
A division of
The Hearst Corporation
1350 Avenue of the Americas
New York, New York 10019

Published in hardcover by William Morrow and Company, Inc.; for information address Permissions Department, William Morrow and Company, Inc., 1350 Avenue of the Americas, New York, New York 10019.

First Avon Books Printing: September 1995

AVON TRADEMARK REG. U.S. PAT. OFF. AND IN OTHER COUNTRIES, MARCA REGISTRADA, HECHO EN U.S.A.

Printed in the U.S.A.

RA   10   9   8   7   6   5   4   3   2   1

Again, for Neil
And for our sisters and brothers

ACKNOWLEDGMENTS

UPON COMPLETION OF *BROTHER WIND*, THE FINAL book of the trilogy which includes *Mother Earth Father Sky* and *My Sister the Moon*, I must leave my characters who, during the past seventeen years, have been a very real part of my life. But though I am leaving "old friends," I have acquired many new friends, and to these new friends—my readers—I extend my most sincere appreciation. I find constant delight in your curiosity, your intelligence, and your enthusiasm.

My heartfelt thanks go to all the members of my family who have been so supportive—especially my husband, Neil, and our children, Neil and Krystal, and to my parents, Bob and Pat McHaney, and my grandfather Bob McHaney, Sr. I also much appreciate all those relatives, friends, and booksellers who have formed a network of support for my work across the United States and Canada and throughout the world.

Once again, I thank Dr. William Laughlin and his daughter Sarah. This trilogy could not have been written without their generosity in sharing their expertise and research findings.

My gratitude to Mike and Rayna Livingston, Mark McDonald, Gary Kiracofe, Dr. Richard Ganzhorn, and those previously acknowledged in *Mother Earth Father Sky* and *My Sister the Moon* for their contributions of time and knowledge.

Others who have recently lent me books from their personal libraries or shared their expertise include Bob Mecoy, Ann Chandonnet, Mr. and Mrs. James Waybrant, Mr. and Mrs. Bob

Blanz, Abi Dickson, Denise Wartes, Warren St. John, Bonnie Chamberlain, Larry Kyle, Ross Blanchard, Roger and Annette McHaney, and Patricia Walker. My sincere thanks to all of you, and also to Forbes McDonald for sharing his experiences fishing Alaskan waters.

My appreciation to those who again waded through cumbersome pages of the *Brother Wind* manuscript in various drafts: my husband, my daughter, my parents, my sister Patricia Walker, and my friend Linda Hudson. Thank you all!

Thanks also to Sandy Benson for typing my research notes, and to my husband for his computer work on the map and genealogy.

I would be remiss if I did not acknowledge the Alaska Native Language Center, located at the Fairbanks campus of the University of Alaska. The materials it has published on native Indian, Aleut, and Eskimo languages of Alaska are truly a gift to the world.

I respect and esteem the many authors whose books and articles—from the early writings of Veniaminov to recent papers yet awaiting publication—have been the foundation on which I constructed my stories. Though the names number well into the hundreds, space permits me to mention only a few: Lydia Black, Raymond Hudson, William S. Laughlin, Steve J. Langdon, George Dyson, George L. Snyder, George D. Fraser, David W. Zimmerly, F. Krause, Derek C. Hutchinson, Otis T. Mason, Patricia H. Partnow, Waldemar Jochelson, Alés Hrdlicka, Margaret Lantis, Ivan Veniaminov, Ethel Ross Oliver, Farley Mowat, Richard K. Nelson, Frances Kelso Graham, Barry Lopez, John McPhee, Howard Norman, Edna Wilder, James Kari, Knut Bergsland, Moses Dirks, and Lael Morgan.

Any historical or scientific errors in my fiction are solely my own and not the fault of the researchers and writers whose work I have cited.

And finally, all my gratitude to my agent, Rhoda Weyr, and to my editors, Bob Mecoy and Ellen Edwards, who all have the ability to smooth out rough roads and round off jagged edges. Their enthusiasm, insight, and professionalism make them a delight to work with.

GLOSSARY OF
NATIVE AMERICAN WORDS

AKA: (Aleut) up; straight out there.

ALANANASIKA: (Aleut) chief whale hunter

AMGIGH: (Aleut—pronounced with undefined vowel syllable between *m* and *g* and unvoiced ending) blood.

ASXAHMAAGIKUG: (Atkan Aleut) I am lonesome.

ATAL: (Aleut) burn, flame.

BABICHE: lacing made from rawhide. Probably from the Cree word *assababish*, a diminutive of *assabab*, thread.

CHAGAK: (Aleut—also *chagagh*) obsidian. (In the Atkan Aleut dialect, red cedar.)

CHIGADAX: (Aleut—ending unvoiced) waterproof, watertight parka made of sea lion or bear intestines, esophagus of seal or sea lion, or the tongue skin of a whale. The hood had a drawstring and the sleeves were tied at the wrist for sea travel. These knee-length garments were often decorated with feathers and pieces of colored esophagus.

DYENEN: (Ahtna Athabaskan) shaman, medicine person.

IK: (Aleut) open-top skin boat.

IKYAK, pl. **IKYAN:** (Aleut—also *iqyax, iqyas*) canoe-shaped boat made of skins stretched around a wooden frame with an opening in the top for the occupant; a kayak.

KAYUGH: (Aleut—also *Kayux*) strength of muscle; power.

KIIN: (Aleut—pronounced "kēēn") who?

QAKAN: (Aleut) the one out there.

SAGHANI: (Ahtna Athabascan) raven.

SAGHANI S'UZE' DILAEN: (Ahtna Athabascan) My name is Raven.

SAMIQ: (Ancient Aleut) stone dagger or knife.

SHUGANAN: (Origin and exact meaning obscure) relating to an ancient people.

SHUKU: (Ancient Tlingit—pronounced "shoe-KOO") first.

SUK: (Aleut—also *sugh*; ending unvoiced) calf-length, hoodless parka with a standing collar. These garments were often made of birdskins and could be worn inside out (with the feathers on the inside) for warmth.

TAKHA: (Ancient Tlingit—pronounced "tawk-HAW") second.

TUGIDAQ: (Aleut) moon.

TUGIX: (Aleut) aorta, large blood vessel.

UGHELI: (Ahtna Athabascan; predicate adjective) a good thing. It is good.

UGYUUN: (Aleut) cow parsnip or wild celery (Poochki, Russian). A plant useful for food, dyes, or medicine. The peeled stalks when cooked taste somewhat like rutabaga. The stalk's outer layer contains a chemical that can cause skin irritation.

ULAKIDAQ: (Aleut) multitude of ulas; group of houses.

ULAQ, pl. ULAS: (Aleut—also *ulax*) dwelling dug into the side of a hill, raftered with driftwood and/or whale jawbones, and thatched with sod and grass.

UTSULA' C'EZGHOT: (Ahtna Athabascan) His/her tongue is crooked. He/she lies.

WAXTAL: (Aleut) desire; pity.

The native words listed here are defined according to their uses in *Brother Wind*. As with many Native languages that were recorded by Europeans, there are multiple spellings of almost every word as well as dialectical differences.

FIRST MEN

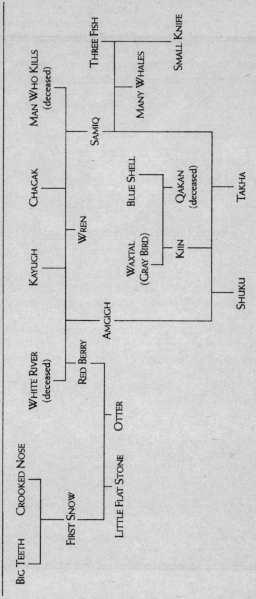

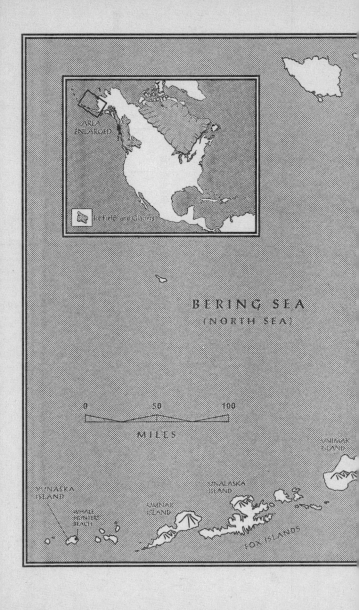

AREA
ENLARGED

Ice Field and Glaciers

BERING SEA
(NORTH SEA)

0   50   100

MILES

UNIMAK
ISLAND

YUNASKA
ISLAND

UNALASKA
ISLAND

WHALE
HUNTERS
BEACH

UMNAK
ISLAND

FOX ISLANDS

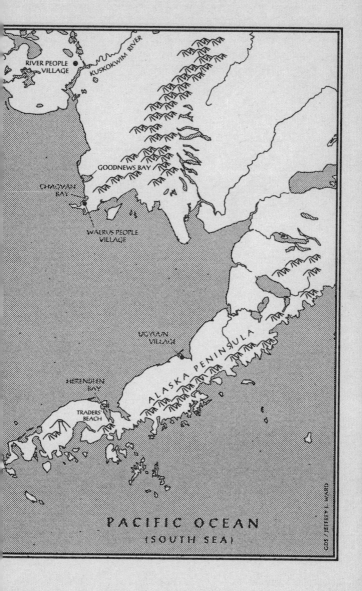

RIVER PEOPLE
VILLAGE

KUSKOKWIM RIVER

GOODNEWS BAY

CHAGVAN
BAY

WALRUS PEOPLE
VILLAGE

UGYUUN
VILLAGE

ALASKA PENINSULA

HERENDEEN
BAY

TRADERS'
BEACH

PACIFIC OCEAN
(SOUTH SEA)

CDS / JEFFREY L. WARD

Brother Wind

PROLOGUE

SUMMER
7038 B.C.

THE FIRST MEN

Herendeen Bay, the Alaska Peninsula

KIIN PUT AWAY HER CARVING TOOLS. THE GRAY light of early morning squeezed through the smokehole and met the glow of the seal oil lamp.

Sometime during the night, a mist had begun to fall. It had soaked through the skin walls and mats of their shelter into their sleeping robes and clothing until Kiin thought she would never get its chill out of her bones.

We are safe here, my babies and I, Kiin thought. But the cold that enveloped her body came from more than the rain. I should not have let my husband bring me here. My babies and I were safer in the village with our people than we are in this tiny shelter with Three Fish. Even if traders have come to our people looking for wives, they will not bother me.

"No, stay here," Kiin's spirit voice said. "You are wife. You must do what your husband tells you to do. Stay here with Three Fish until Amgigh comes for you."

Kiin took a long breath, but still could not rid herself of the heaviness that seemed to settle over her. She looked across the sodden sleeping robes at Three Fish. The woman was just waking up. She smiled at Kiin, showing the broken corners of her front teeth.

"I am hungry," Three Fish said. "We should go out and get food." Her voice was heavy with the accent of her people, the Whale Hunters. "I know where there are crowberries."

"It is too soon. The berries will not be ripe yet," Kiin said.

3

Three Fish shrugged. "Then we will gather crowberry stems for medicine," she said.

"Yes, good," said Kiin. "We can go now."

But Three Fish made no move toward the door flap. "There was a trader looking for medicine for his eyes," she said. "If I make crowberry stem medicine, he might trade meat or oil for it."

"Yes," said Kiin, "you could do that. We can go now."

But Three Fish continued talking, telling Kiin about the medicines her mother used to make from fireweed and ugyuun root, and about the bitterroot bulbs that grew so well on the Whale Hunters' island.

As she listened, a tightness grew in Kiin's throat. This woman is Samiq's wife, Kiin thought. This woman has been in Samiq's arms, has shared Samiq's sleeping place.

But Kiin's inside spirit voice whispered: "You had the joy of Samiq for one night. Be glad for that."

And I have Takha, Kiin thought. Because of that night I have Takha, this son who looks so much like his father. She laid her hands against the bulge under her fur suk where Takha lay, held against her chest by his carrying strap. She moved her hand to her other son—Shuku, twin to Takha—also strapped to her chest.

"But remember," Kiin's spirit voice whispered. "Amgigh is your husband."

Yes, Kiin thought. Amgigh. He is a good husband. What woman could want better? And Amgigh gave me Shuku. Who, seeing Shuku, could doubt he was Amgigh's son?

"Amgigh also gave you the night you spent with Samiq," Kiin's spirit voice reminded her. "It was his choice to share you with his brother."

"I am glad to be Amgigh's wife," Kiin said. "You know that."

But her spirit answered, "Who can explain the difference between something chosen by the mind and something decided by the heart? Words are not kelp string. They cannot bind pain into neat packs to be stored away like food in a cache."

Kiin wrapped her arms around her upraised knees, cradling Takha and Shuku between her chest and legs. Three Fish was still talking, her words as steady as the wind. Kiin closed her eyes and tried to think of something other than husbands and babies, something besides the rain and Three Fish's loud voice. But the thoughts that came to her were again worrying thoughts, and a strange unrest beset her feet and hands.

"It is this shelter," her spirit voice whispered. "The walls are too close. The oil lamp light is too dim. Turn your mind toward sky and sea, toward high mountains and long grass."

Then there was a pause in Three Fish's talking, and Kiin realized that the woman had asked her a question. Did Kiin like to sew birdskins more than sealskins?

What did it matter, birdskins or sealskins? Kiin thought, but she said, "Birdskins."

"Birdskins?" Three Fish said. "But they tear so easily and it takes so many to make one suk."

"Yes, you are right," Kiin answered, but wished Three Fish would stop talking. Kiin pulled Takha from his carrying strap. Maybe if Three Fish were holding him, she would be quiet.

Kiin wrapped the baby in one of the few dry furs from her bed and handed him to Three Fish. He opened his eyes, looked solemnly at Kiin, then turned his head toward Three Fish and smiled. Three Fish laughed and again began to babble, this time to the baby.

Kiin sighed and looked down inside her suk at Shuku. He was asleep. Suddenly she heard what Three Fish was saying to Takha: "Your father will fight and you will be safe. Do not worry. He is strong."

Kiin pushed herself across the bedding to Three Fish and clasped the woman by both arms. "What did you say?" Kiin asked.

"Only what Amgigh told me, that we must stay here because there are men on the beach who want to trade for women."

Kiin's heart moved up to pound at the base of her throat. "And Amgigh will fight them?" she asked Three Fish.

Three Fish pulled away from Kiin's hands and scooted back against the damp wall of their shelter. "He said he might," she answered. "All I know is that I saw one of them. A man with a black blanket over his shoulders. Even his face was black. I think Samiq and Amgigh were afraid he would want us."

"The Raven," Kiin said. "My brother Qakan sold me to him. I was his wife at the Walrus People's village. He has come to take me back.'' Her voice cracked, and the sound was like a scattering of words broken away from a mourning song.

Three Fish stared at her as though she did not understand what Kiin had said.

"Amgigh cannot win a fight against him," Kiin whispered. The Raven was too strong, too cunning.

Amgigh would die unless Kiin went with the Raven, and if she went back with the Raven, back to the Walrus People, what would happen to her sons? One would die. Woman of the Sky and Woman of the Sun, those two old ones—the Grandmother and the Aunt—they would tell the whole village about the curse.

"No child can bring death to a village," Kiin's spirit voice said, and the voice no longer whispered, but spoke in anger. "Woman of the Sun and Woman of the Sky know nothing but fear."

My sons are good, Kiin thought. They carry no curse, but because they are twins and because my brother Qakan used me as wife when they were in my womb, the Walrus People think they are cursed. How can I protect two babies against a whole village?

Kiin pressed her lips together and looked at Three Fish, but Three Fish was still talking to Takha, her face close to Takha's face, both woman and child smiling.

Kiin watched them, and an ache began to build at the center of her chest. She lifted her thoughts to the wind spirits, to the spirits of the mountains that protected the Traders' Beach. I will be content to be Amgigh's wife, she told them. Just let him live. She clasped the amulet at her neck. If he is safe and my sons are safe, she thought, I will ask nothing more.

She crawled over to sit beside Three Fish and said, "Our husbands Amgigh and Samiq are brothers, just as my babies Takha and Shuku are brothers."

Though Kiin wanted to hurry, she forced her words out slowly, gently, so Three Fish would understand. "Our husbands are brothers, so we are sisters."

"Yes," said Three Fish.

"I have to go to the beach now, Three Fish," said Kiin, "but you should stay here with Takha. Keep him from crying as long as you can. If he sleeps, that is good. But finally when he is crying so hard you cannot stop him, then take him to

Samiq's sister Red Berry. She has milk. She will feed him.''

Then Kiin untied the string of babiche that held the carving Samiq's mother Chagak had given Kiin and handed it to Three Fish.

''A gift for you,'' Kiin said. Three Fish cupped the carving of man, woman, and child in her hand.

''Samiq told me about this,'' Three Fish said. ''The great shaman Shuganan made it. I cannot take it.''

But Kiin said, ''You must. We are sisters. You cannot refuse my gift. The one who wears the carving receives the gift of being a good mother.''

For a moment Three Fish sat very still, then she tied the string of babiche around her neck. She clasped the carving tightly in both hands.

Kiin unwrapped the walrus tusk ikyak that she had carved during the long night when sleep would not come. After she had finished carving it, she had cut the ikyak crosswise into two pieces. Had not Woman of the Sun said that Kiin's sons, being twins, shared one spirit and so must live as one man? Had not Woman of the Sky told Kiin that Shuku and Takha must share one ikyak, one lodge, one wife? Someday, Kiin would make carvings of a lodge and a woman also, and split each, giving one half to each son. With her carvings, they could live without the curse of being twins, each one building his own life as a man.

She hung the ikyak halves on braided sinew cords, fastened one cord around Takha's neck, the other around Shuku's.

''This is my blessing to my sons,'' she said to Three Fish.

Takha clasped the ikyak and lifted it to his mouth. Shuku slept.

For a moment Kiin watched her sons, then she turned away to roll up her sleeping skins.

''Why are you going to the beach?'' Three Fish asked as Kiin worked. ''Amgigh told us to stay here.''

''I must go,'' Kiin said. Again she sat down beside Three Fish. She reached out to stroke Takha's cheek. The baby turned his face toward her hand, opened his mouth. ''While I am away, you must be mother to Takha,'' Kiin told Three Fish. ''He is son to Amgigh, but also to Samiq. See,'' she said, gathering Takha's hand into her own, spreading her son's fingers, "he has Samiq's wide hands." She brushed the top of his head. "He has Samiq's thick hair."

Three Fish lifted the baby and laid him against her chest, tucking his head up under her chin. "I will be a good mother to him," she said.

Kiin looked away, then leaned forward to pick up her carving tools. She slipped them into her sleeping furs, strapped the bundle to her back, then crawled to the door flap.

"Be sure Red Berry feeds him," Kiin said. Then, though she had not meant to go back, Kiin turned. She held her hands out toward Takha.

Three Fish handed Kiin the baby, and Kiin lifted him from his fur wrappings. She stroked her hands down his fat legs and arms, over his soft belly. She pressed him against her face, smelled the good oil smell of his skin. Then she handed him back to Three Fish and slipped out of the shelter into the rain.

"I will see my son again tonight," Kiin said to the wind and waited for an answer, but there was nothing. No answer, no whisper to pull away her doubts.

Kiin stroked the carving that hung at her waist, the whale tooth she had made into a shell—her first carving, a sign of the gift the spirits had given her. Then she tucked her arms around Shuku, alone in his carrying strap under her suk, and walked toward the beach.

THE WHALE HUNTERS

Yunaska Island, the Aleutian Chain

FOUR HUNTERS' IKYAN HAD LEFT THE BEACH. Three returned. Kukutux, eyes gifted to see beyond what others saw, blinked once, twice, and looked again. Only three.

She glanced at the other Whale Hunter women around her, saw their grim faces.

"You see them, Kukutux?" Speckled Basket asked. The woman leaned against the stick her husband had carved, which allowed her to walk in spite of a foot crushed last spring when the mountains destroyed the Whale Hunter village.

"I see ikyan," Kukutux said slowly, her words heavy with the weight of her fear.

"How many?" asked Fish Eater's third wife, a young woman, too young to belong to the one-eyed Fish Eater, a man nearly too old to hunt.

Kukutux shook her head, lifted her shoulders in a shrug. She had seen hunters return before, knew that the ikyan seemed to lift themselves over the horizon, as though the sea curved down under the weight of the ice that bordered that far edge of the earth. Sometimes when she sighted only one or two ikyan, others would suddenly appear—thin dark lines coming up from the water, as though they had been visiting those undersea villages owned by seal and whale.

She waited, saying nothing, until some of the other women began to point, able themselves to see the first of the three ikyan coming back toward the Whale Hunter beach. "Kukutux," Flowers-in-her-hair said, "how many? Do they bring a whale?"

"No," Kukutux answered. "No whale."

"How many?" asked Speckled Basket, her voice whining with anxiety.

"Three," Kukutux finally said, and suddenly felt the need for tears, as though the word made true what her eyes had known. "Only three."

Several women raised their voices in a thin, high mourning chant, but Old Goose Woman hushed them, hissing that their mourning would call spirits. Who could say, she told them, perhaps the last hunter was coming still, towing seal or sea lion, the animal buoyed with breath-filled sealskins. Who could say? Perhaps there would be meat and oil for everyone tonight. Why curse a blessing? Had not those mountains—Aka and Okmok—brought enough curses to the Whale Hunters? Did the women themselves need to add to the curse of fire and ash and darkness?

And though Kukutux clung to Old Goose Woman's words of hope, fixing her eyes on the woman's thin and matted hair, the dark and grease-stained fur of her ankle-length suk, she heard the mourning chant in her head as though the women still sang it.

It is for your son, Kukutux told herself. The mourning chant is for your son, that strong, dark-haired baby, gone now three moons, his breath stolen by the mountain's ash that still covers the beach and the hills behind the village. You mourn him.

The chant is for him. The spirits would not take another of the Whale Hunter men. They would not. Too many men have died, in hunt after hunt. How can the village survive if more men die? The mountain has taken enough. And this spring, the whales did not come. Even the beach geese—those winter-breaking birds, their voices loud enough to scare away the snow—have passed the Whale Hunters' island, the geese flying so high that the women's bird nets, the men's bird spears, could not hope to take them.

Kukutux scraped at the beach gravel with her feet and did not let herself look at the sea. Perhaps her own eyes were the curse. Perhaps if she did not look, the fourth ikyak would appear. But then she heard the women's voices lift in questions, their words edged with the hard sharpness of fear, and she could not keep her eyes from looking.

Finally Old Goose Woman said, "Tell us, Kukutux. It is better to know than to be caught between hope and fear."

So Kukutux said, "There are three, only three, and the first two ikyan are tied together. Something lies over their decks."

"A seal?" Speckled Basket asked and reached up to clasp a strand of her hair taken by the wind.

"A man," Kukutux said. Then the ikyan drew near, and she felt all strength leave her knees so that they folded and let her drop to the ground.

"Who?" came a woman's voice, then another, all calling her, as though they did not notice she had fallen. The words, like sharp-nailed fingers, picked at her suk, her hair, her skin, until Kukutux closed her eyes, cursed their far-seeing in her heart, and whispered the name: "White Stone."

She tried to begin a mourning chant, tried but could not remember the words. The women's voices were only a rush in her ears, like wind roaring; and lifted above all other sounds was her own voice crying out, "White Stone, my husband, my husband White Stone."

PART ONE

SUMMER
7038 B.C.

ONE

THE FIRST MEN

Herendeen Bay, the Alaska Peninsula

KIIN PUSHED HER WAY THROUGH THE CIRCLE OF men gathered on the beach. When she reached open ground, she saw the Raven. His chest was bare, his skin glazed with sweat, flecked with blood. He lifted a long-bladed obsidian knife as though to greet her. It was Amgigh's knife, one Amgigh had made, and the blade dripped blood.

The Raven sucked in his cheeks, let the lids of his eyes nearly close. "Your carvings, wife," he said. "They gave me power."

He pointed, and Kiin looked back at the edge of open ground, where a line of her carvings divided those men who watched from those who fought. The carvings were the ones she had made and traded for meat and oil so the First Men could live through the winter.

"Where . . ." she began, then shook her head and said to the Raven, "I am not your wife."

The Raven snorted. "Go then to him." He raised the knife, used it to point, and Kiin let herself look where she did not want to look, let her eyes see what she did not want to see: Amgigh lying in the sand, Samiq kneeling beside him. Then Kiin, too, was beside Amgigh, her arms over Amgigh's chest, her hair turning red with Amgigh's blood. She clasped her amulet, rubbed it over Amgigh's forehead, over his cheeks.

"Do not die, Amgigh," she whispered. "Do not die, oh Amgigh. Do not die."

Amgigh took one long breath, tried to speak, but his words were lost in the blood that bubbled from his mouth. He took another breath, choked. Then his eyes rolled back, widened to release his spirit. Kiin moved to cradle Amgigh's head in her arms, and began the soft words of a song, something that came to her as she held him, something that asked spirits to act, something that begged her husband's forgiveness, that cursed the animals she had carved.

When the song was finished, Kiin stood, wiped one hand over her eyes. "I should have come sooner," she said. "I should have known he would fight the Raven. It is my fault. I . . ."

But Samiq came to her, pressed his fingers against her lips. "You could not have stopped him," he said. "You are my wife now. I will not let Raven take you."

Kiin looked into Samiq's eyes, saw how much of him was still a boy, and how little he knew about the kind of fighting that had nothing to do with knives. "No, Samiq," she said. "You do not have the power to kill him."

Samiq's jaw tightened; he shook his head. "A knife," he said and turned to the men gathered around him.

Someone handed him a knife, poorly made, the edge blunt, but Samiq grabbed it.

The Raven clenched his teeth, screamed in the Walrus tongue, "You, a boy, will fight me? You, a child? You learned nothing from that one there, that dead boy in the sand?"

"The Raven does not want to fight you," Kiin said, her breath coming in sobs. "Samiq, please. You are not strong enough. He will kill you."

But Samiq pushed Kiin aside, lunged forward, wrist cocked with the longest edge of the blade toward the Raven. The Raven crouched, and Kiin could hear him mumbling—shaman's words, chants and curses, prayers to the carvings she had made. She ran to her carved animals, knelt among them, heaped sand over them.

She looked up, saw Samiq slash his knife in an arc toward the Raven. The blade caught the back of the Raven's hand, ripped the skin open, drew blood. But the Raven did not move.

"Kiin," the Raven called out, "this man, he is your 'Yellow-hair,' is he not?"

And Kiin, remembering the Raven's love for his dead wife Yellow-hair, said, "Do not kill him. I will be your wife, only please do not kill him."

The Raven moved, his movement like the dark blur of a

bird flying. The long blade of his knife bit into Samiq's flesh, into the place where wrist joins hand. Then Kiin was running across the sand, through blood from the first fight, to stand between Samiq and the Raven. Small Knife, Samiq's adopted son, was there also, gripping Samiq's arms.

"You cannot win," Small Knife said. "Look at your hand."

Samiq glanced down, but said, "I have to fight. I cannot let him take Kiin."

"Do not fight," Kiin said. "You have Small Knife. He is your son now. You have Three Fish. She is a good wife. Someday you will have the power to fight the Raven and win. Until then I will stay with him. I am not strong enough to stand against him, but I am strong enough to wait for you. I have lived in the Walrus village this past year. They are good people. Come for me when you are ready."

Then Ice Hunter, a man from the Walrus village, was beside Kiin. He reached for Samiq's arm, wrapped a strip of seal hide around the wound, pulled it tight to stop the blood. "You have no reason to fight," Ice Hunter said. "The first fight was fair. The spirits decided."

Kiin looked into Samiq's eyes, saw the emptiness of his defeat. She pulled off the shell bead necklace he had given her the night of her woman's ceremony. Slowly she placed it over Samiq's head. "Someday you will fight him," she said. "You will fight him, and then you will give this necklace back to me."

She turned to the Raven. "If I am to go with you, I must go now," she said, and she spoke in the First Men's language, then repeated the words in the Walrus tongue.

"Where are our sons?" the Raven asked.

"Shuku is here," Kiin answered, and raised her suk so he could see the child. "But I gave Takha to the wind spirits as the Grandmother and the Aunt said I must." Kiin took Shuku from his carrying sling. "This is your son," she said to the Raven, "but he is no longer Shuku. He is Amgigh."

Kiin saw the Raven's anger, the clouding of the Raven's eyes, but she did not look away, did not flinch, even when he raised his hand as though to strike her.

"Hit me," Kiin said to the Raven. "Show these people that a shaman has only the power of anger against his wife, the power of his hands, the power of his knife." She dropped her voice to a whisper. "A man does not need a strong spirit when he has a large knife, a knife stolen from someone else."

The Raven threw the obsidian knife to the ground. Kiin picked it up, walked back to Samiq, placed it in his left hand. Her eyes met Samiq's eyes. "Always," she said, "I am your wife."

The Raven gestured toward Ice Hunter, toward the other Walrus men who had come with him. One picked up Kiin's carvings, another brought the Raven's ik to the water.

"We will not return to this beach," the Raven said.

But Kiin bent down and picked up a handful of pebbles from the sand. She waited as her mother brought Shuku's cradle and a bundle of Kiin's belongings from the ulaq.

Once more Kiin looked at Samiq, tried to press the image of his face into her mind, then she turned and followed the Raven to his ik.

TWO

THE WALRUS PEOPLE

The Bering Sea

HE HEARD NOTHING. NOT THE FULL ROUND VOICE of the wind nor the high, curling cries of oyster catcher and gull, not the dip and splash of paddles nor the soft throat purr of Shuku nursing. But the silence was as sharp as obsidian, as dark as old blood. Even Kiin's spirit was still, so quiet that if she had not felt its ache in her chest, she would have believed it was gone—passed on to Three Fish along with the gift of Kiin's son Takha, along with that carving of man, woman, and child made long ago by the great shaman Shuganan.

She had not offered to paddle, nor had she looked back at the

Raven, nor at the ikyan that skirted the Raven's trading ik.

Kiin pulled herself away from what her eyes were seeing, what her ears were hearing, until there was nothing but the throb of her spirit, pulsing like a wound. At first, its rhythm was the sound of her loss: Amgigh, Takha, Samiq; Amgigh, Takha, Samiq. But now there was silence, and Kiin wondered if she and the Raven and the Walrus People traders were no longer a part of the seen world, but instead had paddled into some world of story or song. Perhaps even now they were carried in the mind of a storyteller, alive only when words fell from the storyteller's mouth into the ears of those who listened.

When the Raven finally spoke, Kiin did not hear him, but instead, in a rush as harsh as storm wind, heard the noise of the sea. Then she felt the cold of spray against her cheeks, and she knew the choice she had made was not merely a story to be told on winter nights, but something so real that it could separate her mind from her spirit until the emptiness was complete.

So as the Raven called to his men, pointing with his paddle toward an inlet that broke the gray line of the shore, Kiin called to her spirit, until she heard the thin whispers of her spirit voice, its first word, a name—"Takha."

And Kiin answered, "No, Shuku."

Then the Raven's ik touched shore, and Kiin, arms careful of Shuku asleep in his carrying sling under her suk, leaped ashore. She gathered driftwood and watched as the men made a beach fire, and when Ice Hunter handed out pieces of dried fish, Kiin did not ask or wait, but took fish as though she were one of the traders.

Ice Hunter did not speak, but raised eyebrows at her, so that Kiin, biting into the firm, smoky meat, said, "I carve," and before he passed on to another, she reached out for a second piece.

They used the ik for shelter, tipping it to lie with its broad bottom toward the wind. The Raven hung the rectangle of wood that was Shuku's cradle from the ik ribs, then motioned for Kiin to pull off her suk. Kiin looked hard into the Raven's eyes and did as he asked, but she did not put Shuku into his cradle. He would be warmer strapped against her chest.

The Raven pulled off his parka and pushed Kiin into the shelter of the ik's bow. Kiin turned so her face was toward

the ik, her back to the Raven. He lay down beside her, draped
his feather cape over them, and pressed his body against hers.

Kiin waited, her flesh prickling with the touch of his skin.
She laid one hand over Shuku, the other against her belly, and
remembered when she had carried both her sons warm and
safe under her heart. Then she felt the push of the Raven's
man part, hard against her back, and she lay very still, scarcely
allowing herself to breathe. But he did not try to enter her, to
claim her as wife. Finally, he relaxed, his arm heavy against
her ribs, and the rhythm of his breathing smoothed into sleep.

The Raven's warmth softened the darkness, until the night,
like fingers weaving, twined dreams into Kiin's thoughts. But
then Kiin's spirit spoke, jerking her awake with a voice as
shrill as an oyster catcher's cry. "Amgigh, Amgigh, Amgigh." A mourning song.

Kiin let the sorrow fill her until it pushed tears from her
eyes. Once again, she saw Amgigh dead on the beach, but she
also pictured Samiq, Takha in his arms, the two safe with
Three Fish in the shelter of Samiq's ulaq.

Kiin took a long breath and wiped her cheeks with the back
of her hand. "I am strong," she told her spirit. "They are
safe, and I am strong."

Turning her head in the direction of the Traders' Beach,
where the mound of Samiq's ulaq rose from the earth, she
whispered the same words to the night wind.

Who could say? Perhaps the wind would carry the words
to Samiq. Perhaps someday it would bring his words to her.

THREE

KIIN GUIDED HER SON'S HEAD TO HER BREAST. HE
drew the nipple into his mouth and sucked, bringing a twinge
of pain and then the release of milk. Shuku's body relaxed
against her own.

Though she had awakened to the words of a mourning song, Kiin had held those words within until she and the Raven had launched the ik. Now the song filled her mouth and she sang. She rocked, and her rocking joined the rhythm of the Raven's paddle, the swell of waves.

"I hope you mourn our son," the Raven called to her.

A sharp thrust of anger pierced Kiin's pain, and she turned to face him.

"You would tell me to mourn?" she said, spitting the words out toward the man. "You would have allowed two old women to kill our sons. You tell me to mourn?"

The hood of the Raven's chigadax covered his dark hair, and the wooden visor he wore against the glare and spray of water shaded his eyes, but Kiin saw the tight working of his jaw.

"Our son Takha is dead," the Raven said. "You were the one who gave him to the wind spirits!"

Kiin clamped her teeth together to hold in her words.

"Why did you go with your brother?" the Raven asked. "He stole you from your father. He tried to sell you as slave. Why trust him after he had done those things to you? I told you I would let you go back to your First Men husband if you left Shuku and Takha with me. Instead you chose to kill Takha. Now you have lost both son and husband. Did you also help your brother kill my Yellow-hair?"

Kiin's anger filled the emptiness left by her grief. "You were going to kill my sons. You had chosen to believe the Grandmother and the Aunt. You had decided your power could not stand against their curse. You are no shaman!"

"You fool, Kiin!" the Raven hissed. "Why would I kill our sons? I am a shaman. I need their power."

"See!" Kiin said, her arms tightening around Shuku. "You do not care about them except for yourself, for your own power. When the Grandmother and the Aunt made you believe my children could bring a curse to your lodge . . ."

"Who told you I would kill our sons?"

"My brother Qakan."

The Raven's face twisted. "When did Qakan ever speak the

truth?'' he snarled. ''If a man uses his sister like a wife, can
he do anything but lie?''

The Raven's words moved over Kiin like the dense wetness
of fog. So the Raven knew about Qakan, knew that Qakan
had forced himself on her. Perhaps that was why he had never
taken Kiin into his bed even though he called her wife.

Kiin pressed her hands into tight fists. ''He told the truth
to save his sons,'' she said. Her words were quiet, so that
the Raven leaned forward, and for a moment stopped paddling.

''He believed the babies were his?''

''Yes.''

The Raven dug his paddle down into the water and for a
long time did not speak.

Finally Kiin said, ''I did not know Qakan killed Yellow-
hair. I did not know she was dead until I saw you and Qakan
fighting on the beach, until I heard you accuse him as he
died.''

''You were there on that beach?'' the Raven asked.

Grief closed Kiin's throat. If the Raven had found her, he
would have taken her back to the Walrus People. There would
have been no fight at the Traders' Beach, and Amgigh would
still be alive.

Then her spirit whispered, ''But perhaps one of your sons
would be dead.''

''So you believed Qakan,'' the Raven said. ''But if you left
me in order to save our sons, why did you give Takha to the
wind?''

''His spirit is with his own people,'' Kiin said, ''with the
First Men. He does not belong to the Walrus People. I have
saved one son, and if the Grandmother and the Aunt were
right, if their visions and dreams were true, my people do not
have to fear a curse, nor do yours.''

The Raven only grunted, then pointed with his chin toward
a paddle that lay in the bottom of the ik. Kiin picked up the
paddle, turned around, and plunged the blade into the water.

''Be thankful I did not leave you with the First Men hunter
Samiq,'' the Raven said. ''The wound he carries—I have seen
such wounds before. The hand is useless. He will never throw
a spear again. He will not be able to hunt. His wives and
children will starve.''

The Raven's words made Kiin's throat ache in sorrow, but she did not answer him. Instead she paddled until she felt Shuku stop nursing. She laid her paddle in the bottom of the ik and looked inside her suk. Shuku was asleep. She watched his gentle breathing, then moved her amulet so it would lie close to his head. She had placed the few bits of gravel and sand she had taken from the Traders' Beach inside the amulet. A promise to return to Samiq. Even if he could not hunt.

"We will not stay with the Walrus People forever," she said to her son, but she spoke quietly so the wind that cut in across the bow of the ik would not take her words to the Raven's ears.

But her spirit said, "Can you risk a return? Can you chance that the Raven will follow you, will see Takha, recognize him as your son? What if he fights Samiq again? If Samiq cannot hunt, how can he fight?"

"In several years, the Raven will not be able to tell Takha from any other small boy," Kiin answered. "Men do not see babies in the same way women do."

But her spirit said, "Do not let your anger make you believe the Raven is stupid. There is not so much difference between women and men as you might think."

Kiin picked up her paddle, and as she thrust its blade against the waves, the Raven said, "I would not have killed our sons, Kiin."

And when he said the words, Kiin knew he spoke the truth. She set her paddle across the top of the ik and looked back over her shoulder at him. "There are so many ways a child can die," she replied.

"I am strong enough," the Raven said. "Takha would have been safe."

"Better that his death be a gift to the spirits than something done in hate," Kiin said. Stroking the front of her suk, the bulge that was Shuku, she said, "We have this son."

The Raven nodded, but said, "You cannot call him Amgigh. His name is Shuku."

Kiin raised her head and, calling back to the Raven, she said, "The part of my son that is Walrus People will be Shuku. His spirit name is Amgigh."

Kiin waited for the Raven's answer, but he said nothing.

She picked up her paddle and looked toward the sun. Its path across the sky grew lower each day.

"Too soon the sun turns toward winter," her spirit said.

"We have lived through other winters," Kiin answered, and paddled in silence.

FOUR

THE WALRUS PEOPLE

Chagvan Bay, Alaska

THE WALRUS PEOPLE'S VILLAGE HAD NOT changed, and though Kiin had been gone nearly four moons, it suddenly seemed as though she had left only the day before. The gray beach shale, the thick smell of oil-lamp smoke coming from the lodges, the dark red strips of walrus meat drying on racks at the edge of the village, women in groups repairing willow-withe fish traps—all were the same.

Men gathered to help the traders pull iks and ikyan ashore. Young boys reached into the boats, prying at bundles of trade goods. Kiin felt a small edge of her sorrow lift as she watched Ice Hunter's ineffective attempts to stop so many quick brown hands. She did not want to see the questions in the eyes of the Walrus People women, so she pushed her way through the crowd and up the rise of the beach toward the long earth-and-walrus-hide lodges.

She crawled through the entrance tunnel of the Raven's lodge. Most Walrus lodges had sod walls, stacked and braced with logs. Each roof was a peaked double layer of walrus skins over willow poles, the walrus skins yellow in the glow of day.

But the Raven's lodge, though long and narrow like other Walrus lodges, had a sod-and-driftwood roof, like the roofs of First Men ulas. Raven's lodge was warmer than the other Walrus lodges, but always dark, without even a roof hole, such as First Men ulas had, to let in light.

As she came out of the entrance tunnel, Kiin braced herself for the giggling questions of Grass Ears' two wives, but their portion of the lodge was empty.

"Perhaps Lemming Tail, too, is not here," said Kiin's spirit voice. Kiin carried that hope with her as she stepped through the walrus hide dividing curtains into the Raven's side of the lodge.

"So you have come back," Lemming Tail said without even the politeness of a greeting. She made a face and turned away from Kiin to paw through the storage cache.

Kiin set down her walking stick and carried the pack she had brought from the ik to her sleeping platform. Shuku's cradle was strapped to the top of the pack. Kiin untied the cradle and stepped up onto her platform bed to hang the cradle from the lodgepoles.

Lemming Tail turned to point at the Raven's sleeping platform. "Hang it there," she said. "I do not share his bed." She patted her belly, and chortled. "You cannot tell yet, but I carry his son."

"A son?" Kiin said.

Lemming Tail shrugged. "Or daughter," she answered.

For a moment Kiin paused, looked into Lemming Tail's round and beautiful face, then she said, "You and I will share this bed. I will not move to his until he tells me to."

She hung the cradle, then lifted her suk to pull Shuku from his carrying strap. She laid him on the sleeping platform and loosened the soiled sealskin wrapped between his legs. During the days of travel from the Traders' Beach, she had not been able to clean him well, and his buttocks were red with rash.

Kiin went to the food cache and, reaching in over Lemming Tail's arms, pulled out a seal stomach container of oil.

"You do not ask, you take?" Lemming Tail said, sitting back on her heels to stare at Kiin. When Kiin did not answer, Lemming Tail stood, glanced over at Shuku, and asked, "Where is Takha?"

"At the Dancing Lights with his grandfathers," Kiin said. "Given to the wind." She pulled out the ivory plug that blocked the end of the seal stomach, dipped her middle finger into the oil, then smoothed it over Shuku's legs and buttocks.

Lemming Tail walked over to stand beside Kiin. She watched for a moment, then reached for the oil. "It is mine," she said and grabbed the container, lifting it so that the soft sides of the seal stomach squeezed in against the oil. Oil squirted out the top opening and onto the bedding furs.

Kiin dipped her hands into the spilled oil and continued to clean Shuku. Lemming Tail carried the container over to the storage cache and squatted there with it between her legs.

Kiin wrapped Shuku in clean strips of sealskin, then she spoke to him, waiting for his eyes to catch her eyes, but he turned away from her to stare at his hands. "He misses his brother," Kiin's spirit whispered, and Kiin, pain again rising in her chest, closed her eyes and pushed away her spirit's words.

Kiin lifted Shuku into his cradle and tried not to remember when Takha's cradle hung beside Shuku's, when Takha's body was a warm bundle stretching the soft sealskin sling of his cradle as Shuku's did now. Kiin gave the cradle a push so it swung gently from the lodgepoles. She walked back to her pack and picked up her walking stick. She ran her hands down the water-worn smoothness of the wood, then held the stick so Lemming Tail could see its pointed end.

"This is more than a walking stick, Lemming Tail," she said.

Lemming Tail dipped one finger into the oil container and looked up at Kiin. She smirked and said, "You are telling me it is something sacred, an amulet or a spirit caller?" She licked the oil from her finger.

"No," said Kiin, "it is a spear. For months before the Raven found me, I lived alone. But I did not go hungry. I was all things on that beach where I lived. I was hunter and I was trader. I was mother and I was grandmother. I was carver and I was shaman. I was chief of my own village." Kiin braced her legs, standing with feet far apart. She lifted the spear and pointed it at the top of Lemming Tail's nose, in the narrow place between Lemming Tail's eyes.

"Do not ever take anything away from me again," Kiin said.

Lemming Tail's mouth opened, but she said nothing. Slowly, she pushed the ivory plug back into the seal stomach container. She kept her eyes on Kiin and wiped her fingers over the black tattoo lines on her lower legs. "The oil is yours, my sister," said Lemming Tail in a small voice.

"Good," Kiin said, then added, "I give half to you. Perhaps you should use it to fill our lamp. It smokes."

Kiin spent the rest of that day repairing her suk and unpacking bundles that Ice Hunter had left in the Raven's lodge. At first Lemming Tail hovered over Kiin as she untied each bundle, but finally the woman sighed and said, "He cares for no one but himself. He promised me necklaces and furs, but see, there is only food, oil, and carvings."

Kiin did not answer, but worked until everything was put away, then, seeing that Shuku still slept, she picked up a small bladder of oil she had saved from one of the trade packs and said to Lemming Tail, "I go to see the Grandmother and the Aunt. I will be back soon. Watch Shuku."

Kiin took the long way, walking behind lodges and up around the village refuse pile, so she would not have to talk to other women. Let their questions wait for another day when Kiin's tears were not so close to her eyes.

She used a branch to scratch at the woven grass door flap of the old women's lodge.

"You did as we told you," called out Woman of the Sky, her voice high and thin.

A chill raised bumps on Kiin's arms and scalp. How did Woman of the Sky know it was her? Kiin crawled into the lodge and stood. She straightened her suk then walked between stacks of death mats to squat before the old women.

Woman of the Sky's hands stopped their work on the death mat she and her sister were weaving, but Woman of the Sun still wove, and as she wove, she swayed, eyes closed, so that Kiin was not sure she was listening.

"Yes," Kiin answered. "I gave my son Takha to the wind spirits."

Woman of the Sky leaned forward, pressed her fingers to Kiin's lips. "Do not say his name," she said. "It may bring him here, back to us."

Kiin stood up. Perhaps she had been foolish to visit the old women so soon after returning to the village. Already she could feel her spirit's frantic need to leave their lodge. What good would it do to stay here and listen to the old women and their talk of curses?

"Your brother is dead?" Woman of the Sky asked.

"Yes, the Raven killed Qakan and I buried him."

"Tugidaq," the old woman said, using Kiin's spirit name, "why do you say his name? Why take chances with the spirits? He has cursed you enough. What brother should use a sister like a wife? What brother forces a sister to do what only a wife should do?

"But now that your son is with the wind spirits, we are safe; this village is safe. You are a strong woman, Tugidaq."

Kiin looked long into Woman of the Sky's face. "Yes, Grandmother, I am strong," she said. She handed the woman the oil bladder. "My husband brings you oil from the Traders' Beach," Kiin said.

Woman of the Sky took the bladder and smiled. "Ice Hunter brought us oil, too," she said and set the bladder down beside her. She began weaving again, and Kiin looked over at Woman of the Sun. Woman of the Sun's eyes opened. She smiled at Kiin but said nothing. Kiin sat down beside the old women and for a time watched as their hands, small like children's hands, wove split grass into the death mat. They did not speak, nor did Kiin, and finally the silence seemed to fasten itself to the ache in Kiin's chest, enlarging the pain of her loss.

"I am leaving now," Kiin finally said and stood. Woman of the Sky continued to weave, but Woman of the Sun followed Kiin through the entrance tunnel. As they stood outside, the wind from the bay blowing cold, the old woman reached out, clasped Kiin's arm, looked deep into Kiin's eyes.

"Sometimes my dreams are a curse," Woman of the Sun said. "Sometimes I wish I did not know those secrets the spirits choose to tell me." She sighed, looked out toward the bay. Finally she said, "What you have done, you have done. My sister does not know and I will not tell her, even if Raven blames us for Takha's death. I know what it is to have a son. I hold no anger toward you."

Kiin's hands clasped over her suk, but her suk was empty, no baby suckling her breasts.

"He is not the one," Woman of the Sun said, and gestured toward Kiin's suk as though Shuku were tucked inside. "He holds no curse. It is the other, Takha, but perhaps he is far enough away for us to be safe.''

For a moment, Kiin saw Takha, cradled in Three Fish's arms, and Kiin's need for him was like a point of ice piercing through skin and muscle to lodge itself at the center of her heart.

"You are wrong, Aunt," Kiin said. "I gave him to the wind spirits. He is dead." And Kiin turned away, walked back to the Raven's lodge.

FIVE

LEMMING TAIL SQUATTED AND DUG HER FINGERS into the bowl of meat. She looked up at Raven and spoke through the food in her mouth. "It is good, husband. Did you bring me gifts?"

Raven frowned. "The meat is not gift enough?" he asked, but as Lemming Tail pinched her mouth into a frown, Raven squatted beside one of his trade packs and loosened the strings. He pulled out a necklace, something strung with beads of bird-bone and shells. He tossed the necklace to Lemming Tail, then reached again into his pack for a second necklace.

"For you," he said to Kiin and carried it to her, dropping it over her head. It glistened against the bare skin of her chest, drooping into a long loop between her breasts.

Kiin lifted the necklace and studied the beads. Each was a circle cut from whale jawbone. Each circle was drilled with a hole and etched with fine lines. It was beautiful, almost as beautiful as the shell bead necklace Samiq had made her, but the Raven's necklace felt cold and heavy against her skin.

"Thank you," she said.

"I see you no longer have your other necklaces," he said.

"I gave them as gifts."

The Raven's eyes hardened. "You should have kept the carving," he said.

No, Kiin thought, though she did not answer him. I am glad I gave it to Three Fish. It will give her power to be a good mother to Takha.

"That carving could bring us enough meat for the whole winter," the Raven said.

Kiin lowered her head, and the Raven turned away. She went to the sealskin boiling bag that hung above the oil lamp and dipped out a bowlful of meat. She handed the bowl to the Raven, then filled one for herself and went back to squat beside her sleeping platform. Lemming Tail slid over to sit beside Kiin. She studied her own necklace, then looked over at Kiin's, and her bottom lip thrust out into a pout.

Kiin did not look at the woman, but suddenly the Raven was standing beside them, a sealskin sewing case in his hands. He gave the case to Lemming Tail and said to her, "Another gift. Keep it or trade it. Perhaps Shale Thrower has a necklace she will give you for it."

Lemming Tail smiled and, looking at Kiin from the sides of her eyes, slid her tongue over her teeth.

"We brought back other trade goods," the Raven said to Lemming Tail. "If you go now, you will be first to see what other wives have. You will get the best trades."

Lemming Tail scooped the rest of her food into her mouth and scurried into the basket corner. She set the sewing case in the bottom of a large basket, then covered it with several fox pelts and a grass mat. She pulled on her parka and, with another smile at Kiin, left the lodge.

The Raven finished eating, then held his bowl out toward Kiin. He looked at her through slitted eyes, and Kiin's heart hammered in her chest. She knew he wanted something more than food, but she took his bowl, started toward the boiling bag.

The Raven caught the back panel of Kiin's woven grass apron. "Not yet," he said and pulled her toward him.

Kiin set the bowls on the floor and waited as the Raven stood and stretched his arms over his head. He pulled off his parka and caribou skin leggings, then moved to stand in front of Kiin. He untied the band that held his apron, letting it fall to the floor.

Kiin looked back over her shoulder toward Shuku's cradle. But her spirit whispered: "Do not look to your son to help you. You must be his strength. When you left the Traders' Beach, you knew you would have to be wife to the Raven. If you resist him now, what chance will Shuku have? The Raven might decide to treat him as slave instead of son.''

The Raven reached over, untied Kiin's apron, let it fall. For a moment Kiin lowered her head, bit the insides of her cheeks, then she made herself look up into the Raven's face. The centers of his eyes opened, and in the blackness, Kiin saw a reflection of herself, the sharp, clear image of her face, the wide forehead, the small full mouth, but in the hollows above her cheekbones where her eyes should be, she saw only darkness, darker even than the black of the Raven's eyes. "See," her spirit told her, "you are the strong one."

She followed the Raven to his sleeping platform, to the jumbled mound of furs and woven bedding mats. And as though no time had passed, she saw the Raven and Yellow-hair, remembered the afternoons she had found them together in this bed, even after the Raven had given the woman to Qakan as wife. With the vision of Yellow-hair came the echo of laughter, but death had taken Yellow-hair's voice, and so it was Lemming Tail's laugh that Kiin remembered, and then the image of the Raven and Lemming Tail during the nights they rolled themselves together in the furs and bed mats.

Kiin sat down on the platform, moved back to make room for the Raven. He reached out, lightly traced the rise of her nipples. He cupped a breast in his hand. Kiin looked down at his fingers, and suddenly did not see the Raven's hand, but that of her father. She remembered the times her father had sold her to a trader for the night, how she would fight with nails and teeth against the trader's touch. Even as the Raven moved over her, Kiin's muscles seemed suddenly sore with remembered injuries. But she lay down, opened her arms and legs for the Raven's embrace. He was heavy against her chest, and she shifted slightly under him so his weight did not rest on the tender fullness of her breasts.

The Raven raised up, pushed himself inside her, began the rhythm of man with woman. Kiin closed her eyes, pulled her thoughts away from him and back to the one night she had spent with Samiq.

Almost, she could believe she was with Samiq, and for a brief moment her mind filled with the contentment of Samiq holding her, the joy of their union. The Raven thrust himself against her and moaned, and Kiin's need for Samiq was suddenly like some sickness inside her, spreading pain from stomach to heart to throat.

"Each time it will be easier," Kiin's spirit said, singing the words like a mother comforting her child. "Each time you will feel less pain."

SIX

THE FIRST MEN

Herendeen Bay, the Alaska Peninsula

SAMIQ SAT ALONE BESIDE HIS IKYAK. THE LONG arms of land around the bay sheltered the Traders' Beach from the north wind, but the sky was heavy with dark clouds. Samiq wore two parkas, one over the other for warmth.

He unwrapped the sealskin strips from his right hand. During the moon since Amgigh's death, the wound had healed well. His mother Chagak's tiny stitches had pulled the skin tightly together so the scar was only a thin pink line on his dark wrist. But the wound had been more than the slicing of skin and muscle. Somehow the knife had cut through into the hand's spirit, and destroyed its strength. Samiq could tighten his hand into a fist, but could not stretch it out, straight and flat.

He pried back his fingers and fitted them over his long flat throwing stick. His smallest finger curled up over the edge of the stick as it should, but his first finger, the one that must lie flat against the bottom of the stick and point back over Samiq's shoulder when he cocked his arm to thrust the spear, that finger would not stay straight. The curl of the finger tilted the throwing stick, and each time Samiq threw his spear, the spear made a short arc into the ground. If he tried to adjust his aim, the spear flew high like a boy's bird dart, then came down straight from the sky.

Samiq stood up, pulled the throwing stick from his right hand, and, clasping the stick with his left, flung it as far as he could. He squatted beside the ikyak and closed his eyes.

What is a man if he cannot hunt? he asked himself. Would Kiin have left Takha with me if she had known I could not hunt? Better for him to have Raven as father.

"You have no more respect for your grandfather's throwing stick than that?"

The question startled Samiq, and he looked up to see his father Kayugh. Kayugh squatted beside him and placed the throwing stick at Samiq's feet.

"What good is it to me?" Samiq asked. He held out his right hand, fingers curled like a bird's claw. "How will I feed my family? How can I teach Takha to hunt? Why should Three Fish call me husband if I cannot bring meat for her and our sons?"

"So what then?" Kayugh asked. "Will you take Takha to Raven? Will you send Small Knife back to the Whale Hunters?"

Samiq looked at his father, saw the anger in Kayugh's eyes. "What good am I to Small Knife or to Takha?" he murmured.

Kayugh shrugged. "Then I will keep your throwing stick," he said. "Your grandfather Shuganan did not make it so that you could throw it away. Your foolishness will curse your hunting far more than the wound on your hand. You can paddle your ikyak, can you not? But I will go now and tell Small Knife that he no longer has a father. Perhaps he will decide to take Takha back to the Whale Hunters with him. Then you will not have to worry about either son. It is good that Kiin and Shuku went back with Raven. At least you have no concern about them." Kayugh stood, then said, "Or perhaps your worries about yourself are so large there is no space to think about others."

Samiq jumped to his feet and faced his father. "You have never cared about me. You cared only for Amgigh. I would give my life to bring him back. But I cannot. I promised myself I would raise Kiin's son, train him as Amgigh would have. That is all I can do for Amgigh, but now how will I do that?"

"Do not ever think that Amgigh was closer to my heart

than you," Kayugh said. "Perhaps you are not son of my
flesh, but you are son of my spirit."

Kayugh walked away then, back toward the low earth-and-
grass mounds that were the First Men's ulas. Samiq turned
and watched him go. Though now a grandfather, Kayugh still
carried himself with the sure and powerful walk of a hunter.
Then Kayugh, as though knowing that Samiq watched him,
turned back and called, "There is more to being a hunter than
the skill of arms and hands. Do not forget the spirit. Do not
forget the heart."

Then he left Samiq alone on the beach.

SEVEN

CHAGAK LOOKED UP FROM HER SEWING AS
Kayugh came down the climbing log into the ulaq. "You
found him?" she asked.

"He is on the beach." Kayugh went to his weapons corner.
He sorted through a basket filled with spearpoints and took
out a fine obsidian blade, black and nearly translucent, one of
Amgigh's best. Kayugh held it for a moment against his cheek.

Chagak had carried the pain of Amgigh's death like a stone
in her chest for this long moon, and now as she saw the sorrow
in Kayugh's face, her throat tightened and tears burned her
eyes.

Kayugh spoke from the weapons corner, his voice thin, almost like a boy's. "Do you think, wife, in raising our sons
that I favored Amgigh over Samiq?" he asked.

The pain in his words reached into Chagak's chest,
squeezed her heart, so that for a moment she could not answer.
She wiped the palms of her hands over her cheeks and closed
her eyes until she stopped her tears, then she walked over to
Kayugh, leaned against his back, placed her hands on his
shoulders.

"There is no better father than you," she said. "Ask your

children. Ask Red Berry, ask Wren. Wren is still only a child, but she knows. You were fair to both sons, but they were different, as all people are. You did not favor one son or the other just because you treated them differently.''

"Samiq thinks . . .''

"Whatever Samiq says, remember he has lost more than any of us. Not only a brother, but Kiin and her son Shuku, and the use of his hand. You know that sorrow not only twists the heart, but also dims the eyes. Only the very wise can see good in the earth when they are grieving.''

Kayugh nodded, laid the spearpoint back in the basket. He stood and pulled Chagak into his arms, held her tightly against his chest.

In a small voice Chagak asked, "Do you think he will hunt again?''

"Samiq?'' Kayugh asked, his mouth close to Chagak's ear. She nodded.

"Yes,'' Kayugh said. "I do not know how, but he will.'' Kayugh pulled away, looked down at his wife. "Do not doubt your son,'' he said. "He is just like you. He will not give up until he has found a way.''

"Samiq?''

Samiq took a long breath. It was Three Fish. Why must she treat him as though he were a boy who needed watching?

He stood. "I am here.''

Three Fish smiled. "I brought you food,'' she said and held out a basket of dried fish.

Samiq sat down cross-legged on the ground as though he were Whale Hunter, not First Men. "I am not hungry, Three Fish.''

"How will you hunt if you do not eat?'' Three Fish asked, and she squatted beside him. "Eat,'' she said again, and held a piece of fish out toward him. "Eat, then I will tell you something that will make you happy.''

Samiq reached for the fish she offered, realizing too late that he had reached with his right hand. He looked up into the sky, ground his teeth to hold in his anger. But Three Fish merely took his hand in hers, laid it on her thigh, and put the fish into his left hand.

"You will hunt soon?'' she asked, studying his fingers.

Samiq snorted. "How?"

Three Fish looked at him, eyebrows raised. "You ask me?" she said. "I am a woman. I do not hunt. If you have a question about sewing or cooking, ask that. Then I will tell you."

Samiq bit into the fish. "You spend too much time with my mother," he said. "You begin to talk like her."

Three Fish laughed. "Good."

She turned his right hand one way, then another, took a fish from the basket, and ate it still studying his hand. "The fingers hold tight?" she asked.

"Yes."

"Then what is the problem? Your arm still works, you can still throw the spear."

"Look," Samiq said. He picked up his throwing stick, pressed it into his right hand, and showed her the curled finger that lay against the bottom of the stick.

"It must lie straight?" Three Fish asked.

"Yes, or I cannot aim, and the throwing stick wobbles."

Three Fish continued to eat, and finally when she had finished the last piece of fish, she said, "Wait. I will be back."

She took two running steps toward the ulas, then turned and picked up the empty food basket. "Are you still hungry?" she asked.

Samiq held a smile inside his cheek. Three Fish had eaten all the food, except for the piece of fish still in Samiq's left hand. He held it up for her to see. "I have food," he answered, then watched as she left. Three Fish was as wide as any of the First Men hunters, nearly as tall as Big Teeth, and she ran slowly and awkwardly in the sand of the Traders' Beach.

Samiq took a bite of fish. He stood and stretched, then walked the length of the beach. It was good that their ulas were protected from the North Sea by the arms of the bay, but sometimes he wished he could see the open water. Better to tell if whales or seals were swimming. But now what did it matter? How would he teach the men to hunt whale with his hand crippled as it was?

Now that Amgigh was dead and Samiq could no longer hunt, what did the First Men have? Three hunters—Kayugh and Big Teeth, nearly old men—and First Snow, Red Berry's husband. Red Berry's two sons were still only babies, and who could count Kiin's father Waxtal as a hunter, the man now bringing in only two, three seals a season? Small Knife, though still a boy, was better with the harpoon.

Perhaps Hard Rock and the Whale Hunters had been right when they blamed the curse of Aka's fire and ash on Samiq. Perhaps he had brought curses to the First Men as well, so finally they would have no hunters and be forced to live on the fish and berries the women brought in.

And what about Kiin? he asked himself. She will be waiting for me to come for her. What will she think when I do not come?

He pulled the throwing stick from his hand and held his fist up toward the gray of the sky. "What about this?" he cried into the wind. "How can I hunt with this? What good am I if I cannot bring meat for my people?"

Suddenly Three Fish was beside him. "Look," she said, her round flat face creased with a smile. "Look, Samiq, this." She waved a narrow piece of birdbone before his eyes and pulled his hand toward her. She straightened his forefinger, then tied the bone to it with thin strings of twisted sinew.

"See," she said, then turned toward the ikyak rack. "Where is your spear?"

"Wait," Samiq said, holding her back. Who could say what curse would come to a weapon if it were touched by a woman? He picked up his throwing stick and ran to the racks where he had left his spear. He fitted the stick into his hand and set the butt end of the spear into the ivory hook at the top of the throwing stick. He pulled his arm back, made a strong sidearm throw. It was not a perfect throw, but the spear flew straight, no short awkward arc, no high erratic path.

"Three Fish!" Samiq called, his voice lifting into a shout.

He ran to her, squeezed her against his chest. Three Fish pulled away, but Samiq said, "I do not care who sees."

Three Fish, her face flushed, looked down. "You will crush your sons."

Samiq stopped, eyes wide.

"Takha is here," she said, stroking the bulge of the baby under her suk. "Your other son is here," and she patted her belly.

EIGHT

WAXTAL STARED AT THE CHUNK OF DRIFTWOOD.
"It has not been a good year for carvers," he said and threw
the driftwood down in disgust. "If I had ivory I could carve
all winter, then go to our daughter's husband Raven. He would
trade for my carvings. Look what he gave for the poor animals
Kiin made."

Blue Shell looked up at him from where she sat sorting
grass beside the oil lamp. "Take the day, go up the beach to
the North Sea," she said. "Who can say what you will find?
Perhaps the spirits will see your need and send a walrus tusk."

Waxtal looked up at her and scowled. "A woman thinks it
is easy to walk to the North Sea. A woman says, 'Take the
day. You will find a walrus tusk.' Any hunter knows even in
an ikyak it is not an easy trip. There are strong currents and
hard winds. What other hunter would go with me? They see
little value in walrus tusks. No spirit has opened their eyes to
what a carver's knife can do."

Blue Shell bent her head over her work.

"Besides," Waxtal said, "no one could expect me to go
out in this wind with this suk. I need a parka. It is colder here
than on our island. I should dress like the Walrus People do,
with a hood to cover my head and fur leggings. Kayugh and
Samiq have parkas, but my woman is too stupid to make one."

"If you want a parka, I will make one," Blue Shell said
quietly, "but I cannot make a parka from birdskins. Kayugh
and Samiq have furs from Kiin's trading, but we do not. You
will have to hunt. You will have to bring us fur seal skins or
caribou hides."

"A woman thinks it is easy to hunt . . ." Waxtal began.

Blue Shell took a long breath and continued to sort her
grass.

Samiq laid the feathered practice spears at his feet. He had
sharpened the tip of each shaft and hardened the points with

fire. He picked up the nearest spear and set it into his throwing stick, but before he threw, he turned to Three Fish. "When will the baby come?" he asked.

"I have missed two bleedings," Three Fish said.

Samiq nodded and threw the spear. It was a good throw, but short. "I am glad Takha will have a brother or sister," he said. He did not give voice to his fears: the child would be born in early spring, a hard time for all people, especially mothers with new babies.

Two sons, he thought—Small Knife and Takha. No, three. Shuku was his. If Three Fish had a son, he would have four.

Samiq reached out, brushed fingers over Three Fish's cheek. "You are a good mother to Takha and to Small Knife. You will be a good mother to this new baby."

Three Fish smiled, her lips pressed together over her teeth.

"I will hunt," Samiq said to her. "Even if I have to start again and learn like a boy. Our children will not starve."

He did not let himself think about their meager supply of seal oil and dried meat. Instead he reminded himself that their bay was full of fish. The women caught pogy in the kelp beds each day. There were sea animals also, harbor seals and otters. Besides, the women had put in a good supply of roots and berries. Kiin's carvings had brought them furs for winter clothing. Their ulas were strong. They would not have to burn much oil to stay warm this winter.

"It will not be an easy winter," he said to Three Fish, "but we will live." He set another of his practice spears into his throwing stick. "Watch," he said. "See the clump of ryegrass there?" He threw. The spear flew without wobbling and struck the grass.

"Another whale," Three Fish said.

But Samiq, afraid some spirit might think he was proud, said, "Perhaps a harbor seal. Whatever animal takes pity on men who need meat."

NINE

SAMIQ LAY AWAKE LONG INTO THE NIGHT. THE joy he had felt earlier that day when Three Fish told him she carried a child seemed somehow bound to the light. When the sun set and night closed over the ulas, the fears he had pushed to the back of his mind claimed his thoughts, and he saw Three Fish, Takha, and the new baby sick and dying for need of food.

"You are leader, chief hunter of this village," some spirit whispered in the darkness of his sleeping place. "You are responsible for your people's needs."

Samiq tried to form plans for hunting and fishing, but ideas slipped away from him like half-remembered dreams.

"In the morning," he finally told himself, whispering aloud so bothering spirits would hear and let him sleep, "then I will go out in my ikyak and let the wind and sea tell me what I should do."

Still, though, he did not sleep, and near morning he finally got up, pulled on leggings, parka, and chigadax, and left the ulaq. The sun was new, gold and orange in a sky nearly free of clouds. He felt his spirit lift as he guided his ikyak through the length of the bay and into an inlet near its mouth. There he could see over the tide flats out to the North Sea, where the water rose in swells, then foamed into whitecaps as each wave crossed the sandbar shallows near the bay.

The auklets were gathering, flocks riding the wind currents, dark flashing to sudden white as they turned their breasts toward the sun. In early winter the whole auklet tribe gathered, then flew away and did not return until the snow was melting in late spring. Samiq wondered where they went. Did they have winter villages on other beaches?

He closed his eyes and imagined the joy of wings.

"Like an ikyak when a hunter paddles with the wind," some spirit whispered, and Samiq opened his eyes to see the auklets rise again, then fly close, turning just before they reached him. Samiq raised his paddle to them, then held out his left hand, open and empty.

"Brothers," he called. "I am a friend. I have no knife."

Then with the wind and the sun clearing his mind, the fears of the night dimmed, and he knew what he would do.

Samiq went to Kayugh first and asked him if everyone—men, women, and children—could eat together that night in Kayugh's ulaq. Kayugh lifted his head to look at Samiq from under lowered eyelids. It was a look that Samiq remembered from the days of his childhood, a look that asked a question but did not demand an answer.

"After we have eaten, we will plan for winter," Samiq told him.

"And does everyone eat from my cache?" Kayugh asked.

"No, no, they will all bring food," Samiq said, then added quickly, "I have a good reason."

"A good reason to meet in my ulaq?"

"Yes."

"To save your lamp oil? To keep Waxtal out of your food cache?" Kayugh asked.

Samiq opened his mouth to explain that his own ulaq was small, that he wanted the women at this meeting as well as the men, but then he understood that his father only teased him, saw that Kayugh's belly shook with silent laughter. Samiq let himself smile.

Kayugh laughed out loud and slapped a large hand against Samiq's shoulder, then handed him a bowl. Chagak had made a good stew.

That night after everyone had eaten, the men settled in a circle close to the largest oil lamp, and the women gathered behind them. Samiq planned to ask the women questions—how much food was in each cache, how long that food would last. Perhaps his questions would make them uncomfortable—usually in village meetings only the men spoke. But how could he plan hunting trips if he did not know how much meat was needed?

When he began to speak, Samiq said, "The Whale Hunters have ways that are not our ways. Sometimes, during that year

I lived with them, I thought they were foolish. Sometimes I thought they were wise. But I learned much. In Whale Hunter meetings, when plans are being made for hunts and winter storage, their women speak out.'' Samiq looked over the men's heads to the women. "We men know most about hunting. You women know most about food. Why should I make decisions without using what knowledge is available to me? So tell us," he said to the women, "how much food do we have?"

But Waxtal curled his lip and said, "Women? You ask women? Since when have women had any great wisdom?"

Samiq pretended he did not hear Waxtal, and listened as Crooked Nose—Big Teeth's wife—and Samiq's mother Chagak told how much food was in their storage caches. Then Three Fish spoke, telling of the egg cache Kiin had made during the spring, the eggs stored in sand high above tide lines.

"You have seen the eggs?" Waxtal asked.

Samiq held his breath, afraid that Three Fish would tell the man where the eggs were, but she only nodded and lowered her eyes in the manner of First Men women, then looked slyly from under her lashes, showing Samiq she understood his fears.

"Blue Shell," Samiq said, "your cache?"

But before Blue Shell could answer, Waxtal shouted, "We have nothing. This woman is lazy. She does not fish enough. She does not set enough bird snares."

Samiq's face grew hot in anger, but before he could speak, Big Teeth said, "So then, Waxtal, you have no food to share. Yet you expect us to share with you?"

Waxtal stood up, lifted the walking stick he always kept at his side, and turned to point it at Blue Shell. "She should be the one who does not eat," he said.

"Ah, yes," said Kayugh. "She is the one who sits and carves all day and does not go out with the hunters after seals. She is the one who eats in other men's ulas and never invites anyone to eat in her ulaq."

Waxtal drew back his lips. The hair that hung in a thin string from his chin quivered. He walked through the circle of men, in rudeness walked between them and the oil lamp. He grabbed a handful of Blue Shell's hair and pulled the woman to her feet. Samiq stood, but his father's hand held him back.

"Wait," Kayugh said to Samiq, the word a quietness in the ulaq.

Blue Shell grabbed her husband's wrist, twisted the hand down to her mouth, and bit. Waxtal jerked his hand away and drew it back to slap her, but Blue Shell blocked the blow with her arm.

"Do not touch me," she hissed. "You cannot stop me. I will tell Samiq what he needs to know." She turned to Samiq and said, "Besides the fish I caught today, we have four seal-skins of fat and two sea lion bellies of rendered oil. We have three bellies of dried fish and a sealskin of puffins, whole. I have three baskets of bitterroot bulbs and one, not large, of dried seal meat."

Samiq closed his eyes in despair. Waxtal had only enough oil for one, perhaps two moons. Did the man think he could live forever on other men's hunting? He glanced at his father, but Kayugh's eyes were lowered.

"Well then," Big Teeth said, "we must hunt."

"I hunt," Waxtal said. "I would have as much in my food cache as any man if my wife did not waste what I bring in."

Blue Shell began to laugh. Waxtal lifted his walking stick, but she brushed past him and left the ulaq without looking back.

The next day, Samiq sent First Snow and Small Knife to hunt seals and otters—whatever they could find in the inlets of the bay. He asked Kayugh and Big Teeth if they would be willing to go inland to hunt caribou. "Last summer, traders said there were caribou living on the tundra, one, two days' walk from this beach," Samiq said to the men. "We have never hunted caribou before, but . . ." He paused when he saw light come into his father's eyes.

"Once when I was a boy, my father took me caribou hunting," Kayugh said. "I am willing to try again."

"If you want, take Waxtal," said Samiq and smiled at his father's grimace.

But that morning as all the men left the village, Waxtal was with Kayugh and Big Teeth, the three with throwing spears and seal flipper boots, walking inland toward the mountains.

The women went out in Chagak's ik to fish for cod with handlines. After they left, Samiq went to his ulaq and painted his face red with ocher and seal fat, in the manner of the Whale Hunters. He did not go out to hunt. How could he hunt whales with his hand as it was? Perhaps someday he would hunt seals or sea lions, but even with Three Fish's birdbone straightening his finger, he would never have the quickness to hunt whales. He would be a retriever—one who followed the whale once it was harpooned, and helped bring it back to the village after it died. But first he must ask the whale spirits to choose another alananasika, a man to be chief whale hunter of the village, someone for Samiq to teach what he had learned from the Whale Hunters.

He took his ikyak out into the bay and began a Whale Hunters' song, a song he had learned from his grandfather Many Whales, once alananasika of the Whale Hunter tribe. When the song was finished, Samiq sang his own words, a plea to the whale spirits. "We do not hunt so men will honor us with songs. We do not hunt so women will praise us. We hunt to live. If you choose a hunter from our village, we will treat you with honor. Any whale who gives himself to us, we will honor. We will fill his mouth with fresh water. We will give his heart back to the sea. We will do all those things that honor whales."

He waited then, hoping to feel the power of the whale spirits, to know in his heart that the whale spirits understood his people's needs. But he felt only emptiness under the high gray dome of the sky, and in his heart the same emptiness.

He looked down for a moment at his right hand, clamped tightly around the paddle, and as he turned his ikyak back toward the village, he asked himself why he had thought the whale spirits would listen to him. He was no hunter.

"You knew," some spirit voice told him. "You knew. Why else did you go alone, without the others? The whale spirits, they do not see you as a hunter. The whale spirits, they see that your power is gone."

First Snow and Small Knife came back to the village looking like old men, faces lined, backs bent. They had seen nothing, heard nothing, had had no chance even to unlash harpoons from ikyan decks.

"Tomorrow," Samiq told them. "A hunter does not expect to bring back meat each time he hunts." But even as he said the words, Samiq felt a chill at the center of his chest. What if they did not bring back meat? What if some curse had driven the animals from the Traders' Beach?

They went out again the next day, and the next, and Samiq, too, went out, paddled his ikyak to the mouth of the bay and spoke to the whale spirits. Both days the men brought back nothing. Both days, in his prayers and in his songs, Samiq felt only the emptiness of sky and sea.

On the fourth day, Kayugh, Big Teeth, and Waxtal returned from their hunting trip. They, too, brought back nothing.

The women made a meal of fish and served it in Kayugh's ulaq, and Samiq watched as the men sat with heads hung low, eyes dark and sunken with the need for sleep. After they had eaten, there was no conversation, only the heaviness of each man's thoughts filling the inside of the ulaq, until finally Kayugh said, "We need rest, then we will go again."

"You think I will go, spend four days walking, for nothing?" said Waxtal, his face flushed, his eyes narrowed into dark slits. "I could have been home in my own ulaq, carving something that I could trade for oil and meat. Go again if you want. I will not."

Samiq met Waxtal's eyes. "You do not hunt. You do not eat," he said.

Waxtal pointed his walking stick at Samiq's right hand. "And you?" Waxtal asked and laughed. "I am not afraid to live off what I can get for my carvings. Will you live off what you bring in with your harpoon?"

TEN

LOW TIDE. WAXTAL STOOPED TO PICK UP A PIECE of driftwood. It was rotten, so soft that he could gouge it with a flick of his thumbnail. But what could he expect? The sea seldom brought gifts for his carving knife into this shallow bay. Even the driftwood was worthless. He tossed the wood aside and continued his walk down the beach.

He pressed his teeth together, ground them in irritation. He should have stayed in the ulaq, but at least he had not taken Blue Shell's advice. Stupid woman! She had wanted him to travel all the way to the North Sea. He could have done what she suggested—spent a cold day in the ikyak, made the long trip to the mouth of the bay—and found the same there, nothing worth his efforts.

As it was, he had been following the inlet beach for so long that when he looked up at the sky, he could see the pattern of the beach sand on the gray of the clouds. He rubbed his eyes, then scanned the surface of the bay.

At first he thought he was seeing Samiq's ikyak. For days, Samiq had been throwing practice spears, and this morning, Waxtal had seen him take his ikyak out and fling spear after spear at an inflated seal bladder.

Waxtal had watched, laughing. Did Samiq think the sea animals would give themselves to a hunter marked with deformity? Samiq was better off to go with the women to pick berries.

For a moment Waxtal let himself imagine the pleasure it would have given his son Qakan to see Samiq's awkwardness with weapons. But Qakan was dead, killed by Kiin's husband, Raven. Waxtal sighed. Was there no honor in the world that a man would kill his wife's brother?

Waxtal stopped and turned back toward the water, hoping to see Samiq make a poor throw, or even better, overturn his ikyak. Then Waxtal realized he was not seeing Samiq's ikyak but an ik paddled by two men. Waxtal waited, his hands gripping his walking stick, until the ik was close enough to see the bow markings: the yellow lines and red circles of a trader's ik. Excitement filled Waxtal's chest, puffing up his ribs and belly as though he had swallowed a great mouthful of air.

He ran to Kayugh's ulaq, scrambled up the sod that layered roof and sides, then called down through the smokehole, "Kayugh, traders have come!"

Kayugh climbed up from the ulaq, shaded his eyes with his hand, and looked out toward the water. "Traders, this time of year?" he asked.

Waxtal shrugged.

"Get Big Teeth," Kayugh said. "Find Samiq."

Waxtal curled his lip. Who was Kayugh to tell him what to

do? Instead, Waxtal walked back to the beach, waved to the traders until they followed him to the low place where waves gentled to allow easy landing at ebb tide.

"Traders?" he called, and waded out to help them beach their ik. The men were young, scarcely older than boys, and alike enough to make Waxtal believe they were brothers.

"Yes, we are traders," the one in the bow of the ik answered. His words came from deep in his throat, in the manner of Walrus People, but he spoke in the First Men tongue.

The traders climbed from the ik, and Waxtal helped them pull it ashore. When the ik was beyond reach of the waves, Waxtal held his hands out palm up in traditional greeting. "I am a friend. I have no knife."

The traders nodded and repeated the greeting. Waxtal looked back toward the ulas and saw that Kayugh was coming with Big Teeth and First Snow. Waxtal pointed toward them with his chin. "You see those men," he said to the traders. "They are good hunters." Then, smoothing his hands over the front of his suk, he said, "I am chief hunter and shaman. Welcome to our village."

Chagak frowned as Waxtal sat in the honored place between the traders, but she hid her irritation in the quickness of her hands as she prepared food.

When the politeness of introduction was complete, the traders removed their parkas, and Chagak, hearing Three Fish gasp, turned to see that both men wore many necklaces. The jumble of bear claws, shells, bone beads, and seal teeth made Chagak wonder how the men could stand straight under the weight of them.

But, Chagak thought, there is wisdom in a man's wearing what he has to offer in trade. How do people know what they want if they do not see what they might have?

The women made a feast and served the food on mats inside Kayugh's ulaq. Chagak did not let herself think about the emptiness of the village's caches. What family would refuse to feed guests? What hunter would not share what was given as gift to his spear?

While the men ate, Chagak fed Wren leftover bits of meat and dried berries, scraps not good enough to give to guests. And as she fed Wren, she watched the traders. They were young, both with narrow faces, small hands and feet. They wore fur leggings and hooded parkas like the Walrus People, and their words, too, came harshly from their throats, like Walrus People.

The one who spoke the most had thick dense brows that met over his nose. The other had markings on his face, thin dark lines across his cheeks, much like the Whale Hunter lines that marked Samiq's chin.

When the men had finished eating, they gathered near the largest oil lamp to talk. The women ate, helped Chagak clean bowls and put away food, then left.

Chagak took Wren to sit near her sleeping place and put a sheaf of dried ryegrass on the floor beside them. She pulled Wren to her lap and showed the girl how to split each blade of grass with her thumbnail so the grass would coil easily and could be used to weave small baskets.

Wren pinched her face into a frown and slowly split a strand. Chagak bent to whisper praise into her ear, then laid the split pieces on a mat. "Flat and straight so they will not tangle," she whispered to Wren. She sat Wren on the floor beside her and handed her several blades of grass, then picked up a bundle for herself, laying it across her lap.

As she worked, Chagak let herself listen to the men's conversation. . . . At first they spoke of weather, tides, and currents, so that Chagak would rather hear Wren's prattle than the men's words, but then one of the traders said, "We plan to go to the Whale Hunters' village."

"Now before winter?" Kayugh asked.

Chagak took a long breath. The Whale Hunters' village. Who would be so foolish as to try to make a trip to the Whale Hunters' island this close to winter?

"There will be storms," Big Teeth said.

"Yes," said one of the traders, the smaller one, the one who appeared to be the older of the two. "But we have survived storms before."

"If there were more of you, it would be better. You could lash your iks together if a storm came while you were at sea," Samiq said, and Chagak noticed that her son kept his right hand down by his side, out of sight. She felt a catch of sorrow under her breastbone and forced her thoughts from Samiq back to Wren, who was using her front teeth to split the grass.

"No," Chagak whispered to her daughter. "Your teeth are too thick. The grass will fray."

Wren sighed, but pursed her lips and picked up another piece of grass. Chagak reached over to stroke a hand down the length of Wren's dark hair. It did not seem so long ago that she was teaching Kayugh's oldest daughter Red Berry to split grass. And now Red Berry had two sons of her own.

And soon I will be grandmother again, Chagak thought. She smiled as she remembered Three Fish's excitement. Chagak had been afraid that Samiq would find no joy in Three Fish's pregnancy. But he had come to her with eyes shining, and with questions, worry edging his words as he asked once again about food supplies in Kayugh's ulaq.

Three Fish will have a large, strong baby, Chagak had told Samiq. Then you will have three children, she had said, and saw the brief darkening of her son's eyes, and knew that he was thinking of Kiin and Shuku.

But three children were enough for any hunter to feed. At least Small Knife, the son Samiq had adopted from the Whale Hunters, was old enough to bring meat for himself and others. Chagak thought of Takha, the baby now beginning to smile, to make small sounds that Samiq claimed to be words, and she tried not to think of Shuku, Amgigh's son.

Amgigh. Chagak had fought so hard to keep him alive, first as a baby when Kayugh had come to them, his wife dead, Kayugh's newborn baby starving. Then when Amgigh was a young man, he had nearly drowned in a whale hunt. At least he had lived long enough to make a son, even if that son was being raised by Raven.

Chagak looked across the ulaq through the lamp haze at her son Samiq. He was growing strong again. At first, after Kiin left, it had seemed that Samiq had not wanted to live, and Chagak had begun to think that each day some part of his spirit slipped away, perhaps to follow Kiin over the North Sea, to settle inside Kiin's body and there live side by side with Kiin's spirit.

But now Samiq was nearly Samiq again, learning, in spite of his injury, to paddle his ikyak, to throw his harpoon. Still, there was the darkness of grief in his eyes.

Then Chagak heard the voice of the sea otter, its whisper

close in her mind. "Is that not true for all of you?" the otter asked. "You all mourn Amgigh. You wish Kiin and Shuku were with you. Do you not mourn your own beach and Aka, that sacred mountain, as well? So many things left behind. So many things lost during these few months since the mountains' anger forced the First Men from their island."

Chagak took a long breath to lift the heaviness from her chest and said to the otter, "Yes, we all mourn." She bent her head over her work, tried to turn her thoughts away from her sorrow. From the corners of her eyes she saw Waxtal leave the circle of men. She shook her head at his rudeness. Kayugh was talking, but Waxtal behaved like a child, giving no attention to politeness.

"All of us mourn except Waxtal," Chagak told the otter. "He thinks only of himself."

Waxtal turned his back to the men and began sorting through a pile of the traders' goods. Now and again, he held up a piece of ivory, turning it in the light that spilled from one of the oil lamps. The traders kept looking at Waxtal, and the oldest lifted a hand toward him, opened his mouth as though to speak, but then turned back to the circle of men.

Why not speak out? Chagak thought. What trader wanted a stranger going through his trade goods? Waxtal was not some shaman to be feared or respected.

"Yes, Waxtal thinks only of himself," the sea otter said. "Of himself and of his carving."

Chagak's mind was drawn to the baskets of carvings that were tucked in the corner of her sleeping place. Shuganan's work. She remembered how the old man had taken her in after the massacre of her people. How he had called her granddaughter and claimed her son Samiq as grandson, though Samiq was the child of one of those men who had killed her family.

By his caring and through his love, Shuganan had given Chagak the courage to live again. Who could not see the same caring in the lines of each ivory animal and the driftwood people he had carved?

Then she thought of Kiin's carvings, so different from Shuganan's, but full of grace and movement, as if she caught the spirit of each thing she carved.

Waxtal's hands on the traders' ivory suddenly made Chagak

angry. "The smallness of Waxtal's soul comes out through his knife," she told the sea otter. "He does not carve ivory; he destroys it."

But the otter was quiet, saying nothing, as though Chagak's anger had stopped the animal's words. Chagak sighed. "Enough, Wren," she said to her daughter. "The men will talk all night. You and I, we need to sleep."

ELEVEN

WAXTAL CLAMPED HIS TEETH TOGETHER TO KEEP them from chattering. Walrus tusks, some longer than a man's arm, thicker than a man's wrist, were bundled together in the bow of the traders' ik.

Waxtal leaned into the ik and stroked his hand down the length of one.

"Good, eh?"

The voice startled him and he jerked upright, catching his hand on one of the ik's wooden thwarts. A sharp sliver of wood tore his skin. Waxtal raised the hand to his mouth and sucked the blood welling from the cut, then turned and looked at the trader standing beside him. Waxtal shrugged his shoulders. "I have seen better," he said.

The trader's eyes widened, then he laughed. "Where?"

Waxtal pretended interest in his injured hand. The bleeding slowed, and he picked at the sliver sticking up from the wound. "I am a trader," Waxtal said. "My son was a trader— before he was killed by someone who stole his trade goods."

"So . . ." said the trader, and he leaned down to touch the ivory, "you might like to have these tusks for your next trading trip."

"I am also a carver," Waxtal said. It would not hurt to let the trader know he was dealing with a man of many talents.

The trader coughed and looked down, hiding his mouth with his hand, but not before Waxtal saw his smile, a smile that said the trader knew the value Waxtal would put on ivory.

"I have seen better," Waxtal said again, then turned and walked back toward the ulas. Let the man smile. The ivory itself wanted Waxtal. Its spirit would long for the joy of Waxtal's knife. What chance did a trader have against the power of the ivory's spirit?

Waxtal raised his upper lip in derision. Yes, let the trader hide a smile behind his hand. Waxtal would be the one laughing. He puffed out his chest, walked with shoulders high, back straight, but when he reached the leeward side of his ulaq, Waxtal suddenly felt as if all power had been taken from his body. He leaned against the ulaq and closed his eyes. It was the ivory, its spirit. It was dealing with the trader even now, bending the trader's thoughts, and it needed Waxtal's strength.

Even here, out of sight of the traders' ik, Waxtal felt power leave his hands and flow with the cold beach wind to settle into the walrus tusks. He could hear the voices of the men and animals who lived in the yellow hardness of the ivory. They pulled at his hands as waves pull at the blade of an ikyak paddle. Waxtal held his hands out, saw that they trembled like those of an old man.

"That much power," he whispered. "That much power, and I, of all the men here, am the only one who understands. The others, they will see the furs and the oil, the dried fish and caribou meat, and they will not know that those things are nothing compared to what I can do with the walrus tusks."

But what did he have to trade for the ivory? He had lost so much in the move from Tugix's island. A foolish move, he thought. He had told Kayugh it was a foolish move. All mountains have times of anger, but those times pass. What man did not know that? It was Samiq's fault. Samiq wanted to move so he could find Kiin. Kiin. She had always been a problem. What father had ever lost more because of one daughter?

Waxtal sighed. Of course, he must remember that the traders themselves did not truly know the value of the ivory they carried. Perhaps they would take oil in exchange. Perhaps not for all the tusks, but for a few, and a few would be enough.

Kayugh, Big Teeth, Samiq, First Snow, and Small Knife left the next morning to hunt. The traders stayed, talking long with Three Fish and Chagak about the Whale Hunters, and Waxtal curled his lips at men so weak that they would find worth in women's words. It was good, though, because they gathered in Big Teeth's ulaq, leaving Kayugh's and Samiq's ulas empty.

Waxtal took unused sea lion stomach containers from his own food cache, rolled them, and tucked them under his suk. Outside, he walked between the ulas, staying out of sight of the water. Who could say whether one of the hunters would look back and see him? He crawled to the top of Kayugh's ulaq and called down. When there was no answer, he went inside. He was cautious at first, peering into all the curtained sleeping places, but there was no one, not even Kayugh's little daughter Wren.

Waxtal laughed, then went to the food cache. He pulled one of the rolled sea lion stomachs from beneath his suk and took a stomach of seal oil from the cache. He pulled what he had carved the night before from his sleeve. Yes, he thought and laughed again: a narrow end made to fit loosely into the opening of the empty seal stomach container and a wide end to channel the oil from the full container into the empty one.

He worked quickly, forcing the oil from one container to the other with gentle squeezes. He emptied only a part of the container, slipped in the stopper, then pulled out another container. He poured portions of oil from each storage belly, filling four empty stomachs from the ten and seven in Kayugh's cache. Then, one at a time, he carried the containers from Kayugh's ulaq. Waxtal's heart pumped hard each time he left the ulaq with a full sea lion stomach in his hands, but no one came, no one saw him.

He took the containers into his sleeping place, covered them with pelts and skins and grass mats. Four sea lion stomachs of rendered oil, perhaps enough for two tusks, he thought, perhaps enough for three if he also traded some of his carvings. And if by some chance he could take oil from Samiq or Big Teeth . . .

When Blue Shell came back, Waxtal was sorting through his basket of wood carvings. She said nothing to him, only went to the food cache and brought out a handful of dried meat, put it on a mat, and set it beside him. He grunted and pointed at the water bladder hanging over him.

She handed him the bladder. He took a swallow of water

and wiped his mouth with the back of his hand. "I have made prayers to spirits," he said to his wife. "I have made promises. Stay out of my sleeping place so you do not curse me."

Blue Shell shrugged and nodded.

Waxtal held a bit of the dried meat over an oil lamp flame, and when the meat had softened, he used his sleeve knife to cut off a chunk. He put the meat in his mouth and watched Blue Shell as he chewed. Who would believe she had once been beautiful? If he had known what she would become, as thin and dried-up as the skin of a smoked fish, he would have chosen a different wife.

Ah, well, he thought, at least she understands the power of my walking stick. Waxtal chuckled. Wisdom never comes without pain.

TWELVE

"THESE THREE CARVINGS AND A SEA LION STOM-ach of oil," Waxtal said.

The older trader, the one with black tattoo lines across his cheeks, picked up one of Waxtal's carvings and turned it in his hands. "You made this?" he asked.

Waxtal nodded.

"Someone told us that your daughter carves."

Waxtal snorted. Who else but Samiq would tell them that? he thought. Samiq was a fool. He should forget about Kiin. Better for Kiin to be Raven's wife than to belong to Samiq, especially now that Samiq's hand was crippled. But perhaps the traders had visited Raven's village sometime in the past and seen her there.

"She is wife to a shaman—Raven of the Walrus People," Waxtal said. "You have visited his village?"

"Perhaps," said the trader.

Waxtal cleared his throat and tried to remember the traders' names. Every man liked to hear his name spoken. The older was Owl, yes, and the younger was also named for something about birds.

"These are not her carvings but your own?" the younger trader asked.

Heat spread up from Waxtal's throat and burned across his cheeks. "They are my carvings," he said, trying to keep his voice even.

Owl walked over to his ik and, sorting through several packs, finally pulled out a driftwood carving. It was a seal. The carving flowed with the wood's grain, and Waxtal could see no knife marks on it—as though the sea itself had formed it.

"Your daughter is Kiin?"

Waxtal nodded.

The trader extended his hand, the carving on his palm. "This is one of hers," he said.

Waxtal reached for it, but when his fingers touched the carving, the wood seemed hot. He drew back his hand.

The trader raised his eyebrows. "Here," he said. "You can hold it if you want."

The pulse of Waxtal's heart suddenly beat hard at one side of his head, at the insides of his wrists and knees. There was some spirit here that he did not understand. Something in the wood of that carving. He turned his head to spit, but his mouth was dry, so instead he coughed. He turned back to Owl and said, "I have seen my daughter's work before. Who do you think taught her?"

The trader shrugged and placed the carving back in his pack. "We are going to the Whale Hunters."

"So you have said," Waxtal replied.

"Then you know we do not need seal oil except for our own use. Whatever seal oil the Whale Hunters need for food, they take from seals they kill themselves, and who burns seal oil when they have whale oil?"

"Whale Hunters like carvings."

"Why trade for your carvings," the trader asked, picking up one of Waxtal's wooden animals, "when they can have your daughter's?"

Waxtal laughed. "You think they would take something made by a woman above something a hunter carved, Owl?"

''Who will tell them a woman made it?'' the younger trader asked and smiled.

''Three carvings and two stomachs of oil,'' Waxtal said, his voice a growl.

''Someone might think that is not enough,'' Owl said, and before Waxtal could make another offer, both men walked away.

THIRTEEN

WHO COULD TRUST THE MAN? KAYUGH THOUGHT. But what harm was there in doing what he asked? Now that Amgigh was dead, they needed someone to make their spear-heads and knives. Better to have Waxtal making weapons than carving. What harm to lend him the basket that held Amgigh's andesite points?

''I will give them back,'' Waxtal said. ''But I will learn more quickly if I have these to study.'' He paused, then raised his eyes to look into Kayugh's face. ''You know I will never be as good as your son.''

For once there was an honesty in Waxtal's eyes that Kayugh could respect. ''Perhaps his gift will come to you from these stones,'' Kayugh said and handed Waxtal the basket.

''Three carvings, two sea lion stomachs of oil, and this,'' Waxtal said. He handed Owl the basket of spearheads. The man sorted through them, occasionally holding one up for his brother to see. ''They are good,'' the trader finally said, then quickly added, ''but the Whale Hunters might have better.''

Waxtal shook his head. ''They do not, nor will you find more like them. The man who made these was once my daugh-ter's husband.''

''She left him for the shaman?''

''No,'' he said.

''So then he sold her to the shaman?''

''So then,'' Waxtal said, ''he is dead.''

The trader raised his eyebrows. "You would trade these?"

"For three tusks," Waxtal said.

"One."

Waxtal reached for the basket. The trader's fingers tightened.

"Five stomachs of oil, four carvings, and the basket of spearpoints for two," the trader said and set his mouth into a firm line.

"For three."

"Two," the trader said.

It was the last offer. Waxtal could not doubt the hardness he saw in the man's face. He had the four bellies of oil from Kayugh's cache, and if he took one from his own food cache . . . He thought of the winter, long and without enough food. We have no babies, he told himself. And I will hunt yet before winter comes. Blue Shell can fish. We will have enough.

"I will bring the oil," Waxtal said.

FOURTEEN

CHAGAK PULLED THE SEA LION STOMACH FROM the storage cache. It had been three days since the traders left, and all the men, even Waxtal, were hunting. Today perhaps they would return. And bring sea lions, she prayed, then lifted her head so her breath took the prayers up out of the ulaq. Perhaps the wind would take those words the many days' journey to the sacred mountain Aka. Or to Tugix, if Aka had no power after pouring out its anger in smoke and fire.

She picked up the sea lion stomach, then realized that her hands were covered with oil, not just the little that always seemed to coat the outsides of stomach containers, but enough so that it dripped from her fingers. She pulled out another container of oil and another.

She heard someone at the top of the ulaq and turned to see Kayugh's daughter Red Berry descending the climbing log.

Red Berry's baby son was a bulge under her suk; the other boy, now with more than two summers, straddled her hip.

"Mother, what are you doing?" Red Berry asked as she set Little Flat Stone on the floor.

Chagak reached into a basket of dried cod and handed the boy a chunk of fish. "Wren is in her sleeping place," she said. "Go and share your food with her."

The boy scooted into Wren's sleeping place, and Chagak smiled at Red Berry as they heard the children begin to chatter.

"What a mess," Chagak said and held up her hands dripping with oil.

Red Berry pulled off her suk and laid her baby on it on the floor. "Did one of the oil containers split?" she asked.

"I think so," Chagak said and leaned into the cache to pull out another container. "Not a good year for this to happen," she said. "We have so little."

"The traders, they probably gave us poor containers," Red Berry said. She squatted beside Chagak and picked up one of the seal stomachs. "This one is not full, Mother," she said. "Look. But it is sealed well." She ran her hands over the sides of the container. "No splits. It is good. But they did not give full measure."

She set it down and watched as Chagak picked up another. "Red Berry," Chagak said slowly, "this one is not full either, and it is one I filled myself."

One after another, they lifted the containers. Finally Red Berry found the one that was leaking. It had a split stopper. "But none are full," Red Berry said. "Do you think the traders took what we would not trade?"

"They were never here alone."

"Who then?"

Chagak shook her head. Who? Then the sea otter voice came, something soft and pulling at Chagak's mind. "Waxtal," the sea otter said. "Who else is foolish enough to steal what is already his?"

Chagak closed her eyes and waited until she could speak past her anger. "It was Waxtal," she finally said. "Blue Shell told me that he wanted those ivory tusks the traders had lashed in the bottom of their ik. He must have stolen our oil and traded it for the tusks." She bit at her lip, and for a long time sat without speaking. Finally in a quiet voice she said, "Kayugh gave him your brother's greenstone spearheads."

"Amgigh's?" Red Berry asked.

Chagak nodded. In her mind, she was suddenly once more a young woman. The softness of Amgigh's baby breath was against her skin. Then the years moved and she saw him as a boy running, and then as a young man, head bent over the beautiful spearpoints he knapped. And in that moment, she felt the loss of those spearpoints more keenly than any amount of oil.

The men returned from their hunt that day. After speaking to Chagak, Kayugh sought out Samiq and his son Small Knife, Big Teeth and his son First Snow. So few hunters for a village, Kayugh thought. And now they would be without Waxtal. But what man could be allowed to stay in a village where he had stolen another hunter's oil? Then Kayugh remembered Big Teeth's words: "Waxtal eats more than he brings in."

"What about Blue Shell?" Samiq asked after the men had heard Chagak's story. Kayugh was proud of his son. A leader must think of all things, not only the punishment, but also the consequences of that punishment. Would it be fair to hurt a wife for what a husband had done?

"Wait," Big Teeth said. He left the lee of the ikyak racks where the hunters squatted out of the wind.

Kayugh saw him go into his own ulaq. While Big Teeth was gone the other men said nothing, each keeping to his own thoughts.

When Big Teeth returned, he squatted beside Kayugh, flexing his long-boned arms, cracking the knuckles of both hands. Samiq asked his question again: "What about Blue Shell?"

"I will take her," Big Teeth said.

"She is welcome in your lodge?" Samiq asked.

"Yes."

"Who will go with me then?" asked Samiq.

Kayugh stood, then Big Teeth, and according to age, First Snow and Small Knife. Samiq looked at Small Knife, then glanced at his father Kayugh. Kayugh saw the question in his son's eyes. Was Small Knife too young to be a part of this? But boy or man, he was a hunter, bringing in seals and sea lions. How many times had Kayugh held praise thoughts for this young man whom Samiq had brought from the Whale Hunters? Kayugh caught Samiq's eyes and nodded his head.

"Then we will all go," Samiq said.

They went to Waxtal's ulaq. At first, Blue Shell tried to bring them food, but when they refused, she huddled into her storage corner, stacks of baskets and mats pulled close around her as though she were a child playing the hiding game. And thus they sat, no one speaking, no one eating, all with eyes on the flames of the oil lamp as they waited for Waxtal.

When he finally came in, his clothes brought with him the outside smell of wind and grass. He looked at them, first in surprise, then with a sudden flicker of fear. But he stood straight, eyes searching the ulaq until he found Blue Shell. "You gave them no food?" he asked in a high voice. He went over to where she crouched, gripped his walking stick with both hands, and lifted it over her head. Blue Shell covered her face with one raised arm, but Big Teeth stood, grabbed the stick as Waxtal swung, and twisted it from the man's hands.

"No!" Big Teeth said.

Samiq stood and said to Waxtal, "You have spearheads that belonged to one who is dead. I need them for my hunting. Bring them here, now."

It was a good beginning, Kayugh thought. If Samiq had asked for the oil, Waxtal could laugh, blame Chagak, even his own wife. But no one had the spearheads except Waxtal himself.

Waxtal drew in a long breath, and Kayugh saw that the man's hands trembled. "Why would I have your brother's spearheads?" he asked.

"You borrowed them. You wanted to learn to knap stone," Kayugh said.

Waxtal licked his lips, then sucked in his cheeks. "Oh, yes," Waxtal said. "Yes, I gave them back."

"No," Kayugh said, looking over at Samiq. "He did not."

"Yes . . ." Waxtal began, but Big Teeth cut in, his words hard. "You say Kayugh lies?"

"No, no. I gave them to Chagak."

Kayugh pressed his lips together. He did not want to bring Chagak here. "She would have told me," he said.

Waxtal shrugged. "She does not like me," he answered, his voice a whine. "She is still ashamed that she was once wife of a Short One. She is ashamed that she gave herself to the ones who killed her own people.'' He laughed, a harsh sound. ''And she is ashamed that she bore . . .''

Then both Kayugh and Samiq were beside the man. Samiq's clawed hand was twisted into Waxtal's hair, his fist at Waxtal's face. ''Kayugh calls me son,'' Samiq said, and his words squeezed out from clenched teeth into a whisper that made Kayugh's skin rise in bumps along his arms. ''I need nothing more than that. Nor does my mother. Where are the spear-points?''

''He traded them.''

Then all the men were looking at Blue Shell, the woman standing now in the midst of her baskets and grass mats. ''He traded them,'' she said again. ''The spearpoints and oil and some of his carvings.''

''Woman!'' Waxtal bellowed. He jerked from Samiq's grasp and lunged toward his wife, but Kayugh and First Snow were beside him, and Big Teeth went to stand next to Blue Shell.

''For what?'' Samiq asked, his words coming between breaths as though he had been running.

Blue Shell moved from her corner and went into Waxtal's sleeping place. She came out holding a walrus tusk that was nearly as long as she was tall. ''This and another,'' she said.

''You have broken my vow,'' Waxtal said. ''You went into my sleeping place when I was not here and broke promises to the spirits. Now what will I carve? You have cursed the ivory with your hands.''

''You have cursed it with your lies,'' Big Teeth said to Waxtal.

Then Samiq said, ''You are no longer part of this village. You are not First Men. Take your ikyak and leave us.''

Waxtal looked into Samiq's face, pursed his lips as if to spit, but Kayugh opened his fingers to show he held a sleeve knife, point out, in his hand. ''Take your boots and hunter's lamp. Take your walking stick. Nothing more.''

''Food?'' Waxtal asked.

''You traded your food for the tusks,'' Samiq said. ''Take the tusks. Eat them. You would let us starve for them. You starve instead.''

Kayugh released Waxtal, and the man scurried into his

sleeping place to bring out the other tusk. "Wife," he said as he bound the tusks together with a length of braided kelp, "get my boots and lamp. Get your suk and sleeping furs."

"No," Big Teeth said. "She does not die for what you have done. She is my wife now."

Blue Shell's eyes widened, but she stepped closer to Big Teeth.

Waxtal's lips quivered. "I will die," he said.

"We might all die," Samiq answered. "You should have thought of that when you traded our oil."

For a long time Waxtal said nothing. Then he looked up at Big Teeth and said, "Make her get my boots and lamp. I do not know where she puts them."

Big Teeth shook his head. "Any man with eyes can see where they are," he said, and he reached up into the ulaq rafters, pulled down boots and a hunter's lamp. He handed them to Waxtal.

"You are a woman now, doing a woman's chores?" Waxtal asked as he took the boots and lamp from Big Teeth's hands, but Blue Shell pushed between the two men, leaned forward, and slapped Waxtal.

"Be careful how you speak to my husband," she told him.

Waxtal raised his hand, and for a moment Kayugh thought he would strike Blue Shell, but then Waxtal dropped his arm, and when he turned to leave the ulaq, the mark of Blue Shell's fingers was still red on his face.

FIFTEEN

WAXTAL PADDLED HIS IKYAK TOWARD SHORE. HE looked back the length of the bay. The village was too far away to see, but a white smudge of smoke from the roof holes lightened the sky. Waves from the North Sea pushed in from the mouth of the bay and slapped against the sides of the ikyak.

"Tonight I stay here," he said aloud, so the spirits lurking near would know that he was not afraid to live alone. But his voice sounded small in the noise of waves and wind.

He pulled out his hunter's lamp. They had given him no oil, but there was a thin ridge of hardened tallow at the center of the lamp. He scraped some loose with his thumbnail. "They think they gave me nothing to eat," he said, and forced out a laugh. He licked his thumbnail and reached inside the sleeve of his suk, where he had hidden several pieces of dried fish. He ate the smallest piece, then carried his ikyak up into the grass that grew long at the high edge of the beach.

He recognized a stand of tall, healthy ryegrass. Yes, this was where Blue Shell and the other women came to cut basket grass. Curling his lips and biting the insides of his cheeks, he pulled the grass out by the roots, handful after handful, until an area as wide and long as a ulaq was bare. Let them come next summer to look for grass, he thought.

He gathered armfuls and carried it to his ikyak. He laid the grass on the ground, making a thick pad. He used a braided kelp fiber rope from inside his ikyak to tie the boat on its side, then he lay down in its lee. For a long time he looked up, watched as the sky darkened into night. He had put the walrus tusks in the bottom of his ikyak, and now he reached in through the ikyak hole, moved his fingers until they found the smooth cool surface of the ivory.

Tomorrow, he thought, I will carve. He stroked one of the tusks, and it seemed as though he felt the voice of that carving, vibrating like a whisper beneath his fingertips.

"Waxtal will not go far," Samiq said, and he looked at the men sitting in a close circle around the one oil lamp burning in Kayugh's ulaq. "We must be sure he does not come back to steal food and oil."

"So, do we go after the traders?" First Snow asked. "Perhaps they would give us back some of the oil Waxtal stole."

"Why should they?" Kayugh asked. "Besides, it would take us too many days to find them. Perhaps a whole moon, and by that time they may have traded everything away. We are better off to spend our days hunting."

"So we have lost some oil," said Big Teeth. "What does it matter? We are hunters. We will bring in enough seals and sea lions to fill our food caches.'' He stretched his long arms out in front of him and cracked his knuckles. It was a gesture Samiq had often seen, and it always meant Big Teeth was worried.

''What other tribe hunts better that we do?'' asked First Snow. ''We bring in more seals. And Samiq hunts whales. Among all men Samiq is the greatest hunter. Who can equal him?''

Samiq opened his mouth to protest First Snow's praise, but caught his father's quick headshake, the warning in his father's eyes. It was not the time to deny ability. The men needed the confidence of praise. So instead Samiq raised his voice above the murmuring agreement that met First Snow's words and said, ''I seem to remember a day when someone brought in three sea lions. I seem to remember the praise songs the women sang that day.''

Now it was First Snow's turn to drop his eyes, acknowledge Samiq's praise as Big Teeth and Kayugh reached over to slap First Snow's shoulders while Small Knife watched smiling.

But the laughter faded. Kayugh and First Snow sat staring at the oil lamp, as though the flame could give them answers to the problems they faced. Big Teeth smoothed a spear shaft with a lava rock, and Small Knife hummed a song, something Samiq had heard often when he lived with the Whale Hunters.

The five of us, then, Samiq thought. Five men to bring meat for our four women and our babies: Wren, First Snow's two sons, and my Takha. How much oil do we need? Nine, ten sea lion bellies for each person? And it takes the fat of at least four seals, even five, to fill one belly.

Then some spirit, its voice coming from the darkness behind Samiq's eyes, whispered: ''Where will you find that many seals this time of year? And if you do find them, how will you hunt them?''

Samiq glanced down at his hand and then away. Yes, he was throwing better, but still, he needed more practice.

''You were the one who brought your people here,'' the same badgering spirit said. ''Your father wanted to stay in the islands. He stepped aside, let you take your place as chief hunter, and now in your first winter as leader, you will see your people starve.''

First Snow's laughter brought Samiq back from his

thoughts, and he realized that Big Teeth was telling jokes again, this one about a hunter and two women, and though Samiq was glad to see the others laughing, he could not even smile.

"Tomorrow, then," Kayugh said.

Chagak watched the men leave the ulaq. Her eyes lingered on her son Samiq. Kayugh turned to her, and his smile faded. But she said, "You lead them well."

"Samiq leads them," Kayugh said.

Chagak shrugged. "And when your own son leads, you think you have nothing to do with that?"

Kayugh squatted beside her, but Chagak was careful not to touch him. Sea animals were sometimes jealous of wives. A woman's scent on a hunter's hands might make an animal angry. And who could say how a man's ikyak might feel, outside in the cold while the hunter enjoyed the warmth of his wife's bed? The night before a hunting trip, it was better for a man to sleep alone.

"It will not be an easy winter," Kayugh said.

"We have had hard winters before," Chagak answered. "Remember when Samiq and his brother had six summers? That was not a good winter."

Kayugh nodded. "But we did not starve," he said.

"No," Chagak answered. "We did not starve."

Kayugh stood. "I will sleep now. Tell the women to be ready for meat tomorrow night."

He smiled, but Chagak could tell the smile did not come from his heart. She watched him as he went to his sleeping place. She heard the soft sounds of grass mats and bedding furs as he lay down.

Meat tomorrow, she thought. She remembered times when her arms had been weary from scraping seal hides, when her eyes burned with the smoke of drying fires. She wished she could again be so blessed.

The knife slipped, and Waxtal looked up into the clouded morning sky to snarl his anger. He threw the blade down, then stood and stretched, turning so his eyes fell on the ryegrass he had pulled the night before. He frowned, then nodded his head. He had to leave this place. The grass spirits were angry, and they pushed against his knife as he cut.

He put away his carving tools and ignored the rumbling of his stomach. He tied the tusk at the bottom of his ikyak, securing it to the chines of the hull.

It is a good ikyak, this one, Waxtal thought. He ran his hands over the taut sea lion hides that covered the frame. He had built the ikyak soon after they came to the Traders' Beach. He had shaped the hull in the manner of the Whale Hunters. He had asked Samiq for advice, but had made the ikyak himself, with help from no one except Blue Shell, who did the woman's work of sewing the sea lion hide covering.

He laughed now as he remembered the angry comments Kayugh and Big Teeth had made as they were left to build the remaining ulas. What had Waxtal cared? His ulaq, built first, was finished. He and his wife were warm. Besides, he had been in mourning over Qakan, his only son. What sorrow could be greater than that?

Not even this present sorrow—loss of village and wife— could compare. But every carver had to sacrifice a portion of his life for his carving. Every gift had to be earned.

"My choice was the best choice," Waxtal said out loud. "Now I have no ulaq, but I have the ivory, and I have this fine ikyak. Perhaps even the knowledge of that—building an ikyak in the manner of the Whale Hunters—will be enough to bring food for the winter." But as soon as he had said the words, a chill tightened the muscles of his back, as though the spirits watching laughed, knowing more than he knew.

He thought he heard a whispering then, perhaps something brought to him on the wind, perhaps something that came from his ikyak or his ivory: "You have no food, no oil. What will you eat? You have no village, no ulaq. Where will you go?"

"To Kiin," he said, but the words were like something dead in his mouth. Her husband was shaman, powerful enough to make the Walrus People let Waxtal stay in their village. But what if Kiin did not want him? Waxtal closed his eyes against a sudden image of his daughter as she crouched before him while he swung his walking stick against her back. "She was not a good daughter," Waxtal said to the wind, to the ivory tusks. "She would never have become a shaman's wife if I had not beaten the stubbornness from her."

Perhaps it was best not to go to Kiin. Waxtal did not have enough food to travel more than one day in any direction. It was many days to the Walrus People village, especially if a man did not cut across the North Sea. And a hunter alone would be a fool not to stay within sight of the shore.

Waxtal looked west, the way the traders had taken. There were First Men villages only a few days' west of the Traders' Bay. If he did not catch up with the traders, perhaps he could find a new home with people who would appreciate his skills.

The hunters left before sunrise, each ikyak weighted with ballast stones, each carrying bladders of oil for hunter's lamps, and seal fat to patch holes or gaping seams in ikyak covers. Tied to the top of each ikyak were extra paddles, sealskin floats, coils of kelp twine, and harpoon shafts.

Samiq wore two parkas, and over the parkas a watertight, hooded chigadax of sea lion esophagus and a slope-brimmed wooden whaler's hat. It was not the hat he had received during his whaler's ceremony—that had been left at the Whale Hunters' island—but one he had made himself after returning to his own people. It was not as beautiful as his first hat. It carried no markings, red and black, had no thin ivory strip where wood met wood at the back of the head, but it kept wind and water from his eyes.

The journey from the village beach to the end of the bay was a long one, and during that time, the sun rose. It brought little heat, and the clouds were so low that it seemed to Samiq he could reach up with his paddle and pierce their bellies.

As he watched the sky, voices came to Samiq, small spirits bringing doubts.

How could the First Men hunters expect to find sea lions at this time of year, so close to winter?

How would they live without meat and oil?

Would Red Berry have enough milk to nurse both her own baby and Takha?

The hunters began a sealing song, but still Samiq heard the spirit voices. Their questions pounded until Samiq's head ached with their noise, so that he finally said to them, "We will live if we have to eat grass. Three Fish will not starve, even if I have to give her my own flesh to eat. If Red Berry cannot feed Takha, then I will take him back to the Raven. It is better for him to be raised a Walrus People than to starve.''

"You cannot take Takha back to the Walrus People," one of the spirits whispered. "They will kill him. Have you forgotten what Kiin told you about the babies' curse?''

"Kiin took Shuku back with her," Samiq answered. "If she thought he might be harmed, she would have left him also.''

"But she told Raven Takha was dead. You heard her tell him. Why would she do that except to protect Takha?''

"To give me my son, something to bind us together while we live in separate villages.''

Samiq waited for the spirit voices to reply, to laugh at his words, but they said nothing, and as Samiq paddled into the North Sea, he decided that he had left them behind in the gentler waters of the bay.

Samiq smelled the stink of the rookery long before he saw the beach, and he began to allow himself to hope, to think with a smile tucked in his cheek of the women's faces as the men brought home sea lions buoyed with floats and trailing the ikyan. He thought of what he would tell those troublesome spirits back at the Traders' Bay.

Huge rocks protected the rookery beach. Squinting, Samiq thought he saw sea lions on the rocks, thought he saw movement, and he slowed his ikyak. Then he realized that he heard no sound of animals calling. Even the gulls and cliff birds were gone, the beach silent in its preparation for the wind and snow of winter.

He watched as the other men's shoulders slumped, as their paddling became listless, without rhythm or purpose. The sea lions were gone.

"We will find them," Kayugh cried out, and Samiq opened his mouth to agree, but found he could say nothing. Why lie? It would not bring the sea animals to them. Better to look for seals, even otters. Eating otter meat was worse than eating dirt, some men said, but meat was meat, and what was warmer than an otter pelt? So he continued to paddle, following the shore. And turning, he saw that the others followed him.

They returned with one harbor seal, which First Snow had taken at the mouth of their bay. The women, when they saw, were at first silent, then Chagak began a praise song. The high trilling made Samiq forget that they had brought back so little, and for one brief moment he saw himself as hunter. Then, as though he had suddenly become a child, tears burned his eyes.

Am I a boy, he asked himself, that I must cry at any disappointment? We eat for one day, two days. That is better than not eating. Looking up, he saw that all the men watched him from their ikyan; the women watched from the shore.

Samiq took a long breath, wished again he was not leader. How much easier to have some other hunter tell him what to do, what to hope for. But he smiled at his people. "We need food, fish, sea urchins, whatever you have brought in today," he told the women. Then he turned to the men. "Tonight we will feast. Tomorrow each hunter should do what he wants: sleep, repair weapons, fish, hunt. It is each man's decision."

Samiq paddled ashore, placed his ikyak on the rack, then went to his ulaq to prepare himself for what he would do.

He began when the sky lightened, even before the first edge of the sun showed itself. Samiq made a shelter of old mats and sealskins, layering them over willow poles, tying everything in place with kelp twine. He had brought only a bladder of water and a hunter's lamp, a little oil from his ulaq. Nothing more. No food. No sleeping furs. When the shelter was finished, he sat outside, facing east, waiting for the sun. After sunrise, he went into the shelter, trimmed the wick of his lamp, and began the days and nights of songs to whale spirits.

It was the fourth day when Samiq finally heard the voice. First he thought it was his father coming to bring him back to the village, back to take his place among the First Men, but then he realized that the voice came from within, and it was not a voice of strength but one of whining, a child's voice crying for food, crying for sleep.

So this is who I am, Samiq thought. Only yet a child, thinking more of myself than of others, demanding to eat, demanding the comfort of a warm sleeping place. What right do I have to lead my people? What have I given them except a strange place to live, with mountains we do not know and animals we do not understand?

He started another song, something to cover that child's voice, but his throat was raw from days of singing, and each word was like lava rock scraping against his flesh. While his inside voice was the mewling voice of a child, the outside voice—the sounds that came to Samiq's ears—carried the words of an old man, hoarse and broken.

Finally he decided to allow himself the strong medicine of sleep. He prayed for dreams, but his spirit longed for peace, and a part of him hoped no dreams would come.

What came was the smooth, cool wood of a paddle in his hands, the oil-and-hide smell of an ikyak. Then sight also came, and hearing. And he realized that he did not dream. Somehow he was in his ikyak, in the middle of the bay.

He did not remember taking his ikyak out. One moment he was lost in the strange thoughts that come to a hunter fasting, and then he was paddling, cold in the wind, wearing only his woven grass apron and Kiin's shell bead necklace, no chigadax, no whaler's hat, no seal flipper boots. He was againp at the mouth of the bay, and in his confusion he could not find the sun beneath the clouds that hung as thick as otter fur over the sky.

The water was gray, and Samiq, looking into its depths, knew that if some sea animal, angry at Samiq for his nakedness, bit a hole in the bottom of the ikyak, the water's cold would seep quickly through his body to stop his heart.

"I have done nothing except work for my people," Samiq said, whispering the words to the small waves lapping at his ikyak. "I hunted this summer as much as I could." He held his crippled hand up, the paddle still clenched tightly in the bent fingers. "Until this. Now I cannot hunt. Waxtal took what was not his to take, but I have done what I could do. I have worked hard." His voice was small under the wide dome of the sky, and his words were taken by the wind as soon as they left his mouth.

Suddenly, instead of the sea, instead of the translucent sea lion skins of his ikyak, he saw the faces of his people. Then the cold did not matter, and it did not matter that he was tired, that he was hungry. Three Fish and Takha and Small Knife, they were more important than the tight ache of his belly. Kayugh and Chagak, First Snow and Red Berry, Crooked Nose and Big Teeth, Samiq's sister Wren, his nephews Little Flat Stone and the baby, Otter. Kiin's mother, Blue Shell.

They were more important than the cold that wrapped him as closely as a puffin feather suk.

Samiq stretched his arms up, raised his paddle in the air, and when he called out, his voice was the strong voice of a hunter. "What does it matter if I cannot hunt? What does it matter who I am? I will pick berries with the women if it will help my people. I will walk the beach like an old man and gather sea urchins. It does not matter about me. But do not let my people starve. Do not give them a winter of pain and cold. Protect them from the sickness that comes to body and mind when there is no food."

For a moment his words seemed strong enough to fill the sky. But then, like rain, they fell, and there was nothing. No sound except the waves, no color but the gray of beach and water and clouds.

The whale spirits do not hear me, Samiq thought. Still, once more, with paddle lowered, head bent in grief, Samiq said, "Please save my people."

The next night Kayugh and Big Teeth returned from another hunting trip. They brought a caribou, the meat wrapped in two bundles, each man bowed beneath the weight of his load.

"There is another caribou cached," Kayugh called to the women over the trills of their praise songs.

That night, Samiq returned, his face drawn in like the face of an old man, so that Kayugh knew his son had been fasting.

Kayugh felt a sudden guilt for the fullness of his own belly, for the taste of caribou meat that still clung to his teeth, the smell of the caribou fat he had rubbed into his hands. But as he helped his son beach the ikyak, Kayugh saw that Samiq's arms were strong, that his hands did not shake. And when the ikyak was ashore, Samiq reached out, wiped two fingers over the back of Kayugh's hand, raised those fingers to his mouth, then looked up at his father, questions in his eyes, a smile coming slowly to his lips.

"Caribou," Kayugh said and began to laugh. "Big Teeth took one and I took another."

Samiq whooped and grabbed his father in a sudden embrace. Kayugh, surprised, started to pull away, but then, still laughing, threw his arms around his son.

"You prayed?" Kayugh asked Samiq. "You fasted?"

Samiq replied, "The skill is with the hunter. Whose spear is stronger than Kayugh's spear?"

Kayugh opened his mouth to praise Samiq, but his throat was so tight he could not speak. Again, he hugged his son, then he picked up Samiq's ikyak and carried it to the racks, placing it carefully where it would get a light wind so the ikyak skin would dry. Then they walked to the ulas where their wives waited.

That night in his sleeping place, his belly full, Samiq lay still as Three Fish rubbed the muscles of his back.

Sleep pulled against his eyelids, and he relaxed as his wife's strong fingers pressed against his skin. Samiq's thoughts returned to the small shelter where he had fasted. He thought of the need that had driven him, while he was still lost in sleep, to take his ikyak into the bay.

Samiq raised his head from his crossed arms and asked Three Fish, "Do you think there is some spirit, something that is greater than whale spirits? Something that joins animal and man in understanding?"

Three Fish reached out to place her fingers over Samiq's mouth and whispered into the darkness of his sleeping place, "Husband, there is nothing greater than whale spirits. Why ask such a thing? Be quiet. Go to sleep."

SIXTEEN

THE WHALE HUNTERS

Yunaska Island, the Aleutian Chain

KUKUTUX SPREAD A PASTE OF MASHED UGYUUN root over the scars on her forearms. She had slashed her arms and cut her hair in mourning. What reason did she have to be beautiful? Why should she care if her hair was short like a boy's? She had no husband to please. What should it matter if scars were added to her arms? Her left arm was already marked with three long scars from the night her father's ulaq roof had collapsed on her and her family.

Kukutux's left arm had been badly cut, and the elbow broken, but that pain had been small compared with the loss of her father, mother, and sisters.

Even with the help of Old Goose Woman and others skilled in chants and medicines, the elbow had healed poorly. Now Kukutux could not straighten her arm, and it ached always in cold, in rain.

Her belly had been big then with her son—White Stone's baby—and that night as the Whale Hunter people huddled together in fear under the rain of ash, as their prayers helped them endure the shaking of the earth, the collapse of ulas, her son was born. When he burst forth from her body, his cries were as loud as the cries of the Whale Hunters lamenting their dead.

It was as Old Goose Woman said: he understood his mother's sorrow and sang his own mourning songs.

That same night, before the earthquake, Kukutux's husband, White Stone, had been with the hunters, celebrating the coming of whales with dances and chants. He came to Kukutux after the baby was born, told her to name the boy He-has-courage in honor of Kukutux's dead father.

He-has-courage always cried, night and day, no matter what Kukutux did. And Kukutux knew that because of his crying, the baby breathed in the angry spirits that lived in the falling ash. Each day, as Kukutux watched, prayed, wept, he grew thinner. His lips became dark, nearly blue, and finally He-has-courage died.

Soon after, Kukutux's brother—the only one left of her family—had drowned while hunting. And now White Stone was also dead. Perhaps their chief hunter, Hard Rock, was right. There was a curse. Somehow the Whale Hunters had angered the spirits.

Now Kukutux had only this ulaq—something she and White Stone had built together using rocks and rafters from her father's ulaq. The food cache was full enough to get her through the winter if she ate carefully, if she did not burn too much oil. And then—who could say? Perhaps some hunter would take her as wife. But many men had been killed during the past few months. In a village without enough hunters, what man needed another wife to feed?

Kukutux went to the corner where she kept her basket supplies, next to the woven grass curtains that separated her sleeping place from the rest of the ulaq. In a small basket with a sealskin drawstring top, she kept a piece of her son's fur wrapping blanket. She opened the basket and pulled out the strip of fur, held it, soft and cool, against her cheek.

Sometimes, when she was just drifting into sleep, Kukutux could feel her son once again in her arms, the weight of him, his hard, round head against her shoulder, the softness of his hair against her cheek. Tears burned in her eyes, and her throat tightened.

She tucked the strip of fur seal skin back into the basket and clasped the basket to her chest, then she went to her husband's sleeping place, stood before the curtained door.

"He is not dead," she told herself, saying the words aloud in the empty ulaq. "He is only away hunting, and I must clean his sleeping place. The heather on the floor is old. It will soon begin to stink."

And so she gathered courage to do what she had not done since White Stone's death. She went inside his sleeping place.

White Stone had been a large man, slow and careful in his words, strong and sure in his hunting, gentle in his lovemaking. A feather-stuffed otter skin still showed the imprint of his head; furs were thrown back as though he had just left his bed.

Kukutux set down the basket she carried, knelt in White Stone's bedding furs, began folding and sorting, piling the furs according to size and type. She took a bit of heather from the floor, tucked it into the drawstring basket. She saw a single strand of White Stone's dark hair, curled it around her fingers, and put it into the basket.

Then she began to gather the heather that covered the mud-and-stone floor. When she had an armful, she threw it out into the ulaq's main room.

"There, see," she said aloud to herself, "this is not so terrible. You are stronger than you thought."

Again, she gathered an armful of heather, threw it out of White Stone's sleeping place. Later, she would cut fresh heather, spread it over the floor. What was better than a ulaq filled with the smell of crowberry heath?

Kukutux turned back to gather the last of the old heather, but in stooping she saw a yellow-and-brown bear claw wedged in a crack between floor and wall. Suddenly her sorrow came fresh and new, as sharp as the knife she had used to cut her arms. And the memories came alive in her mind: White Stone—his large calloused hands touching her gently, moving up to tangle in her long black hair. He had laughed and begun to tickle her. Kukutux had laughed, too, but in pushing him away had caught her hand on his bear-claw necklace. The necklace broke, scattering bear claws around them, but White Stone had pulled Kukutux to him, had whispered that there would be time to find the claws and repair the necklace—later.

The next morning, Kukutux had gathered the claws, and White Stone had restrung him. This was the bear claw Kukutux had not been able to find. And now the necklace was buried with White Stone and White Stone's ikyak under the rocks that were a Whale Hunter's burial mound.

Kukutux began to cry, hard shaking sobs. And she wondered where those tears had been hiding. Had she not already cried all the tears in the earth?

SEVENTEEN

THE WALRUS PEOPLE

Chagvan Bay, Alaska

"NEXT SPRING," RAVEN SAID. "PLAN TO BE GONE two, even three moons."

Ice Hunter shook his head. "No," he said. "Someone has to stay here and hunt."

Raven smiled and moved his eyes toward Ice Hunter's young wife. "Some men get caught in a woman's bed."

"Some men do," Ice Hunter said. "Others live for years alone, without a woman, until they find the right one for their lodge."

Raven smiled. "You think your son might go with me?"

"Which one?"

"Either. They both speak the River People language."

Ice Hunter shrugged. His wife padded softly to his side and handed him a bowl of dried seal meat. Ice Hunter held the bowl toward Raven and waited while the man took three good-sized chunks. Ice Hunter set the bowl on the floor between them and took a piece of meat, cut a slice from it with his sleeve knife, and put the slice into his mouth, moving it to rest between his right cheek and teeth.

"I cannot answer for either of my sons," said Ice Hunter.

"If they go with me," Raven said, "they can have a double share of the trade goods. I go more for learning than for trade. I have heard stories of the River People shamans. I want to understand their ways." He took a large bite from one piece of seal meat and tucked the other two pieces up inside his sleeve.

Ice Hunter stuck a finger in his mouth, fished the softened meat from his cheek, and began to chew.

Raven pointed with his chin toward Ice Hunter's jaw. "I gave you medicine," he said.

Ice Hunter shrugged.

Raven mumbled something, scooped the rest of the seal meat from the bowl on the floor, then stood. At the entrance tunnel of the lodge he turned back and said, "Ask your sons if they will go with me."

Ice Hunter nodded, but said nothing until Raven had left the lodge. Then, looking at his wife, he said, "If he is such a great shaman, why does he steal our food?"

Ice Hunter's wife crouched beside him and placed a bowl of broth into his hands. Ice Hunter drank the broth quickly, leaving the last of the warm liquid in his mouth, his left cheek bulging with it.

"If he is such a great shaman," his wife said, "why do your teeth still ache?"

*   *   *

"I have hunters coming soon," the Raven said to Kiin. "Where is Lemming Tail?"

"With Shale Thrower," Kiin said. "Do you want me to get her?"

"No. She is better there," the Raven said. "Her mouth is forever full of words."

Kiin kept her smile hidden. The Walrus language, spoken as the people of the Raven's village spoke it, always put strange pictures in her mind.

The Raven pointed at Kiin with one long finger. "Whatever you hear today—say nothing."

"If my mouth fills with words," Kiin answered, "I will swallow them." She could not keep a smile from her lips.

The Raven frowned and looked at her from narrowed eyes, but Kiin busied herself at the food cache, taking out meat that would please whatever men would come to the lodge.

Finally, the Raven broke the silence, said to her, "I plan a spring trading trip to the River People. They have many villages north of here."

Kiin nodded, but asked no questions.

"We will leave as soon as the ice is out."

Again Kiin nodded.

"They have furs from inland animals: caribou, bear, wolf, and others." He paused as if waiting for Kiin to answer him, and when she said nothing, the Raven asked, "Is there something I can bring you?"

"Animal teeth for carving, and . . ." For a moment Kiin paused, unable to remember the word she wanted.

"Yes?"

"I have heard they have . . . trees." She stopped, thought for a moment. "Yes, trees." She lifted one hand up above her head. "Tall, very tall. They grow like the willow and alders that are here, but the wood is stronger."

"Lemming Tail has told you this?"

"Yes."

"Against she is wrong. There are places like that, with many kinds of trees, but the River People's trees are like ours."

Kiin shrugged. "Well, if you see any different kind of wood, bring it. Only small pieces—to carve."

The Raven grunted, nodded his head, and again Kiin went

back to setting out food, chopping hardened fat into dried berries, mixing in sandwort greens she had cooked and allowed
to sour.

It seemed strange to Kiin that at one time she had carved
only because she could get goods in trade for her carvings.
Now the carving was a need, something as important as her
songs—something that brought peace to her, so that she could
lose herself in the work, as though she slipped into a world
apart from that of Lemming Tail, the Raven, and the Walrus
People.

A scratch at the dividing curtain called Kiin from her
thoughts, and she looked up to see White Fox, Ice Hunter's
oldest son, enter their side of the lodge. He carried a cooking
bag that filled the lodge with the rich smell of ground squirrel
stew.

Kiin took the bag from White Fox and hung it from the
lodge rafters over the oil lamp so the food inside the bag
would stay warm.

The Raven smiled at the man. "Tell your wife I will bring
her something in my next trading trip," the Raven said. He
motioned to the sleeping platform where he sat, and White
Fox sat down beside him.

Kiin filled two bowls with stew and handed them to the
men. They ate without speaking.

When his bowl was empty, the Raven wiped his mouth with
the back of his hand. Kiin lifted the dripping caribou-scapula
ladle from the cooking bag and raised her eyebrows. The
Raven nodded. She took his bowl and filled it again. She
looked at White Fox, but he shook his head, settling his empty
bowl into his lap.

The Raven tilted his bowl and used his fingers to push meat
into his mouth.

"I plan to trade with the River People, those who live in
that village at the mouth of the Great River," he said as he
chewed. He licked his fingers, and when White Fox said nothing, he continued, "I need men to go with me. Your brother
says he will go."

"He speaks their language," White Fox said.

The Raven shrugged. "So do I."

White Fox frowned, and the scar that curved from his eye
to his chin pulled taut.

"But not as well as your brother does," the Raven added.

"We will get a share of the trade goods?"

"Everything except what I get for my wife's carvings."

White Fox nodded. "How long will we be gone?"

"Only two moons, maybe less," the Raven said. "It is not far to the River People."

"You say my brother plans to go with you?"

"Yes."

"My father?"

The Raven shrugged. "Who can say? He has a new wife. His bed holds more interest than trade goods."

White Fox smiled. "If my brother is going, then I will go," he said.

"Good." The Raven held out his bowl, and again Kiin filled it. White Fox nodded toward his bowl, and she filled his as well. Then she went to her basket corner and sat twisting sinew until White Fox had eaten and left the lodge.

"Your brother White Fox is going with me," the Raven said to Bird Sings.

Bird Sings, Ice Hunter's younger son, had come to the Raven's lodge after White Fox left. He also brought food—a thick fish soup that often earned his wife praise in the village.

Bird Sings raised his eyebrows and frowned. "To the River People?" he asked.

The Raven nodded and held his bowl out to Kiin. She filled it again with the soup.

Bird Sings pointed toward the bowl. "Blackfish—fresh," he said. "My wife catches them all winter, you know."

The Raven nodded and raised the bowl to his mouth.

"I will come if I can bring my wife," Bird Sings said.

"Would she prepare our food?" the Raven asked and belched his appreciation of the soup.

"Yes."

"Bring her."

"Then I will go."

"Good, I will tell your brother."

When Bird Sings left the lodge, the Raven went, too. Then Kiin helped herself to the fish soup. Shuku woke from his nap, crying and cross. Kiin took him down from his cradle, settled him on her lap, and used her finger to scoop some of the soup into his mouth. He bit down hard on her finger, and Kiin snapped her thumb against his lips. His chin quivered, and Kiin hugged him to her until he pulled back to smile. He pointed at her basket corner and began to babble in baby words.

"The Raven had hunters come," Kiin said, speaking to her son in the First Men language. She gave Shuku several more mouthfuls of soup, then sat on the edge of Lemming Tail's bed and turned Shuku toward her to nurse.

"He tricked them, but that is how he does all things," she said aloud to Shuku. Then Kiin remembered her promise to the Raven to swallow her words, and so she said nothing more to her son. But she could not keep herself from wondering why the Raven would plan a trading trip in early spring, when people had less food, less oil to trade. And why would the trip have such importance that he would lie to White Fox and Bird Sings to get them to go with him?

Then came the whispering of her spirit's voice: "Whatever his reason, the Raven does nothing to help anyone except himself."

And even with Shuku warm against her, dread settled like ice in Kiin's heart. She wrapped her arms more tightly around her son and rocked him as he nursed.

EIGHTEEN

THE WHALE HUNTERS

Yunaska Island, the Aleutian Chain

KUKUTUX WOKE FROM HER SLEEP AND KNEW IT was morning. Men and women were outside, greeting the sun. Their greeting songs should be to the mountains, Kukutux thought. Did they think the sun was stronger than the mountains? How could they forget that the mountains' ash had hidden both sun and moon, had even blanketed the sea?

The women of the village had laughed at her, at the little woven grass apron Kukutux had made to cover her nose and mouth when the ash was still falling. They laughed, yet they wore grass aprons to cover their genitals, a protection against those spirits of disease that enter through the openings of the body. They laughed, but now, even after much of the ash on beach and rock had been taken by wind and sea, they were still coughing, as though they could rid their chests of the spirits they had breathed in. And how many children, how many babies, had died from the ash? Even Kukutux's son had died, though she had covered his face as much as she could.

"Kukutux!" The voice broke into her thoughts. "Wake up!"

The sleeping place curtain was thrust aside, and She Cries bent over her, pulled against her left arm, so that Kukutux was forced to her feet.

"Just because your husband is dead, do you think you can spend your days in bed?" She Cries asked.

Kukutux jerked her arm from She Cries' grasp.

"You did not see me sleeping my days away after your brother died, did you?" She Cries asked. "I was left alone, without husband or children, just like you. And I had my mother to worry about. What good is an old woman to bring in meat or oil? You are better off than I was, but still I did not waste my days sleeping. I found myself another husband."

She Cries continued criticizing until finally Kukutux raised her voice to ask, "What do you want, She Cries? Why are you here?"

"Wind Chaser asked me to come and tell you good news."

Kukutux walked over to the food cache and pulled out a grass bag filled with dried fish. She offered a piece to She Cries. The woman settled herself cross-legged on a floor mat near the oil lamp, and Kukutux squatted on her heels beside her.

"You should eat some," She Cries said, holding out the piece of fish Kukutux had given her.

Kukutux shook her head.

"I do not pity you, Kukutux," said She Cries. "Every woman in this village has lost husband or children, mother or father. Yet you are the one who carries the scars of mourn-

ing.'' She pointed with her chin at Kukutux's arms, then tilted
her head and said, ''You should not have cut your hair. How
do you think you will get another husband now that you are
so ugly? And with your arm, too.''

''I am strong enough,'' Kukutux said. She cupped her left
elbow with her right hand. ''And my hair will grow back. I
had a good husband. I have chosen to honor him. I do not
care what you think, or what anyone thinks.''

She Cries snorted. She took several bites of fish, then said,
''How can we help you if you do nothing for yourself?''

''I did not ask for your help,'' Kukutux said.

She Cries blinked, lifted her chin, and said, ''I did not come
to argue with you. Wind Chaser told me to tell you that
something good has finally happened to this village.'' She patted her belly. ''I carry a child. A son, I am sure.''

Kukutux made herself smile. Almost she opened her mouth
to ask if it was Wind Chaser's child. Who did not know that
She Cries, in trying to find a husband to replace Kukutux's
dead brother, had slept with nearly every hunter in the village?
But why exchange rudeness for rudeness?

''I am glad for you and for Wind Chaser,'' Kukutux said.
''I will hope with you that the baby is a son, if that is what
you want.''

She Cries raised her eyebrows. ''You know his other wife
has given him only daughters, and all of them but Snow-in-
her-hair are dead. I have promised him a son. Snow-in-her-
hair will be a good help. She is nearly old enough to marry.
Wind Chaser says Red Feet's youngest son wants her.''

''He is still a boy,'' said Kukutux.

She Cries shrugged. ''Old enough to hunt. And Wind
Chaser says he will make the boy come live with us. Then we
will have two hunters in our ulaq.''

''Good,'' said Kukutux. ''You will not want for meat.''

She Cries drew herself up to sit very straight. She was a
small woman with tiny round eyes and thin legs. She reminded
Kukutux of a kittiwake, that quick and sharp-beaked bird.

''Even if that happens, do not think we can help you,'' said
She Cries. ''Wind Chaser says that since your brother is dead,
you are no longer my sister. He says we owe you nothing, but
Wind Chaser is a good man. He says you may still fish with
me in my ik, and also that he will give you a widow's share—

double portion—from his next sea lion. But do not ask for more than that.'' Again she patted her belly. ''I must have enough food to keep this son strong and healthy.''

Kukutux wanted to tell She Cries to leave her ulaq, that she did not need meat from Wind Chaser's next sea lion, but then she remembered something her mother had once told her: ''The foolish woman cuts off her own thumb to punish her hand.'' And so, Kukutux thanked She Cries, then sat and listened in politeness as the woman berated her for all her many faults.

NINETEEN

THE FIRST MEN

Herendeen Bay, the Alaska Peninsula

THE SOUND BROUGHT SAMIQ OUT OF HIS DREAMS, and for a moment he did not know where he was. Then he felt Three Fish's gentle breathing, saw the bulk of her body in the shadows of the sleeping place. The sound came again, a calling, a sadness in the voice, and Samiq did not know whether it was animal or spirit. He pulled on his parka and climbed from the ulaq to stand on top of the sod roof.

Again it came—a long cry like a woman's mourning song. The moon was round in the sky, giving light that let Samiq see as though it were day. The voice called again, and Kayugh, Big Teeth, and First Snow came from their ulas.

A second and a third voice joined the first, blending and turning, twisting the calls into one song.

''It does not come from the sea,'' First Snow said.

Kayugh pointed toward the hills behind the ulas. ''Wolves,'' he said. ''I have not heard them since I was a young man.''

Then Samiq saw the wolves lined against the sky, faces

pointed up, noses like long seal snouts. "Wolves," he whispered.

"They are big," First Snow said.

"Some grow to be nearly as large as a man," said Kayugh, turning toward Samiq as he spoke, and Samiq remembered the stories his father had told him as a child, Walrus People stories, of wolves who were wiser than the wisest hunter.

"Why have they come?" First Snow asked.

"Perhaps to show us where to hunt," Kayugh said.

"Perhaps to follow us and take a portion of the caribou we cached," said Big Teeth.

But Samiq said, "Who can know why they are here? Perhaps for many different reasons, a different reason for each one of us." Then he sat down on his ulaq roof and watched the wolves, listened to their crying, until the moon moved across the sky and made room for the early sun.

It seemed strange that Three Fish was the one to see them. She was on the beach, the other women in their ik fishing, the men atop ulas watching sky and sea and sometimes turning to study the hills where the wolves had been the night before.

"Whales!" she called, and at first Samiq was angry.

"What foolishness is this, wife?" he called out, standing to give his words strength. "There are no whales in this shallow bay." But as he stood, he, too, saw what Three Fish had seen. Whales, three of them, bowheads, with their double spouts, one already tipped sideways on a bar of gravel in the shallow center of the bay.

He called to the other men, called as he ran, called as he pulled on his chigadax. He grabbed his ikyak from the storage racks, pushed it out into the sea, and pulled himself in, fastening the chigadax to the ikyak coaming even as he began to paddle.

Fumbling with kelp lines and floats, he started toward the nearest whale. His anger rose against his right hand, useless except to hold his paddle as he tied knots with his left hand and his teeth.

Then Kayugh and Small Knife were beside him in their ikyan, both watching Samiq, doing what Samiq did, tying floats to harpoon lines.

"Be ready to turn your ikyan," Samiq said. He stopped to

pry his paddle from his right hand and replace it with his throwing stick, but he dropped the stick into the sea and nearly upset his ikyak trying to retrieve it. Finally he threw his whale harpoon with his left hand.

The harpoon fell short. He coiled the harpoon line in toward himself, drawing the weapon back to his ikyak. He flipped the harpoon up from the water to the deck of the ikyak, then watched as his father and Small Knife threw their seal harpoons. Both harpoons lodged in the side of the whale, but they were small and carried no poison. The whale turned but could not dive in the shallow bay.

Samiq pulled the obsidian tip from his barbed whalebone harpoon head, took a pouch from around his neck, and smeared aconite poison under the tip. He paddled close to Kayugh and handed his father the harpoon. "You throw it," he said.

Kayugh fitted the butt of the harpoon shaft into his throwing stick, pulled back his arm, and threw hard. The harpoon hit just under the whale's flipper.

"He is ours," Small Knife said.

Samiq drew in his breath against his son's words, but said nothing. If the whales were offended, they were offended. There was no way to take back the boy's boast.

They paddled away from the whale, then Samiq heard Big Teeth's cry, saw the man point his paddle toward the second whale, saw Big Teeth's harpoon embedded in the whale's side. Samiq patted the pouch at his neck. "You used poison?" he called to Big Teeth.

The man held up a pouch.

First Snow's harpoon took the third whale, then the hunters separated, staying at a distance, but watching the whales.

"There is a good chance they will wash up on our beach," Small Knife said to Samiq, but Samiq did not answer the boy, did not let the boy know he had heard. Why anger the whale spirits by telling them what should happen?

Then Kayugh brought his ikyak near and called to Samiq, a father's praise.

"My harpoon took no whale," Samiq called back, but there was only light in his heart. If they had meat and oil enough for the winter, what did it matter whose harpoon made the kill?

"Go now, be alananasika," Kayugh said. "Become the whale as you told me the alananasika must. Let the whales know we have need of their meat and that we honor their spirits. You called them. Your power brought them to us."

Samiq nodded and turned his ikyak toward the shore. As he paddled he remembered his grandfather Many Whales telling him the same thing when he had lived with the Whale Hunters. That summer had been a summer of whales, more whales than the hunters had ever seen before. "My people believe your power brought the whales to us," Many Whales had told him. But they had also believed his power had called Aka's fire to move the earth and destroy the Whale Hunter village.

"No," Samiq said, as though his words could go back through months and death to his grandfather, the old man now with the spirits at the Dancing Lights. "I do not have that kind of power," Samiq whispered, and his voice was as quiet as his breathing. "My only strength is my concern for my people. What power does that hold except the power to bring tears to a man's eyes, to lay sorrow over his heart? What strength does that carry except the strength of hope?"

TWENTY

The Bering Sea

WAXTAL'S ARMS ACHED FROM PADDLING, AND the muscles in his chest were so tight that he could scarcely breathe. It had been seven days since he left the village. He should have caught up with the traders by now. An ikyak was faster than an ik. But there were two of them, and they were young, strong.

"Besides," he said aloud, "I do not have food." He rested his paddle across the top of his ikyak and looked out at the North Sea. "Do you hear that?" he called. "You spirits out there, do you hear that? I am a hunter and a carver, yet they sent me away without food. They gave me no oil. It was Samiq, the crippled one. If you have a curse to give, curse him. If you have a blessing, bless me. I am a hunter and a carver. I honor all sea animals. Help me find the traders.''

Waxtal moved his foot to touch the walrus tusks lying at the bottom of his ikyak. He felt power flow up from the tusks to warm him, and the warmth eased his fears.

Even if I do not find the traders, I will soon come to a village, Waxtal told himself. He remembered one village from trading trips—a First Men village usually about five days' travel from the Traders' Bay. It was not a place he would choose to stay for the winter—the women were ugly—but better to stay there, with roof, bed, and oil lamps, than alone with only his ikyak.

His throat was dry. He drew his cheeks together to pull spit into his mouth. He was thirsty, but he needed food even more. His belly ground against itself with emptiness.

He dipped his paddle back into the waves and looked up at the sky. It was nearing sunset. He needed to find a beach for the night. If he remembered his journey from Tugix's island to the Traders' Bay, there was a good place not far ahead. He squinted toward shore, then frowned. No, not yet, but there was something . . .

At first he thought it was a rock, long and low just above the waves, but then he knew, and his heart tightened in joy. It was not a rock, but an ik, a trader's ik dark against the water.

Suddenly his arms were strong, the paddle sure in his hands. He sped toward the ik, calling out even though he knew he was too far away to be heard. Soon he was close enough to see the men in the ik. Yes, they were the two brothers who had come to the Traders' Beach.

As the ik turned toward shore, the younger brother stopped paddling and pointed toward Waxtal. Waxtal called again and paddled harder, his breath coming in gasps. But when he drew close, he saw that they faced him with spears and spear throwers in their hands.

"I am Waxtal," he called to them. He dug in his mind for the traders' names. Bird names . . . the older brother was Owl. "Remember me, Owl?" Waxtal called. "I am Waxtal. I am the one who traded for the walrus tusks."

They lowered their spears, but kept their hands tight on their spear throwers. "Why do you follow us?" Owl called to him.

"Do not ask us to take the tusks back," said the younger brother.

"I want to come with you," Waxtal called. He moved his ikyak closer to the ik, then remembered the younger brother's name. "Spotted Egg," he called, "let me come with you."

The traders spoke to one another in the Caribou tongue, so though their words came clearly to Waxtal over the water, he did not understand what they said.

"Why?" the older brother asked Waxtal.

"I want to see my brothers, the Whale Hunters."

"You are a Whale Hunter?"

Waxtal felt the beginning of a lie in his mouth. It built until it bulged large against his tongue, but he was not a fool. What Whale Hunter would claim him as brother? "No," he called out, but then said, "Remember what Kayugh told you? Before the mountain Aka grew angry, we lived on an island close to the Whale Hunters' island. We often traded with each other."

"So you have been to their village before?"

"Yes. I know the chief, Hard Rock."

The brothers bent their heads together and spoke.

Owl looked up at Waxtal and asked, "You will not expect to have a portion of our trades?"

"No."

"Our food?"

Waxtal swallowed. "Our village is poor," he began. "How could I take food from my wife for this trip?"

"You traded oil for the tusks," the younger said.

"And I will carve the tusks, trade at least one of them to the Whale Hunters for whale oil, much whale oil. Then I will pay you for my food. Besides, I am a hunter. I will help by taking seals as you paddle your ik. It is easier to hunt from an ikyak than from that." He pointed his paddle toward the large, open-topped ik.

"You have the tusks?" Owl asked.

"Yes, here," Waxtal said, laying his hand against the top of his ikyak.

The brothers looked at each other, and the younger shrugged. The older called to Waxtal, "Come then, go ahead and find a bay for us, a place to make camp. Look," and he pointed toward the west, toward a shimmering darkness in the clouds, "a storm is coming."

A shiver of fear ran down Waxtal's back as he studied the sky. He should have noticed. If he had not found the traders, he would have paddled into the throat of that storm. He had never worried much about reading the sky. Kayugh and Big Teeth were better at such things, just as he was better at carving. They left the carving to him; why not leave the sky watching to them?

"When?" Waxtal asked, nodding toward the clouds.

"It will come tonight," Spotted Egg answered.

Waxtal plunged his paddle into the water. "I will find a place," he said.

It did not take long until they came to the beach Waxtal remembered. It was sheltered by rocks, so that the storm in passing only rattled against their upturned boats and dripped through the beach grass they had cut to pack around their legs as they sat huddled in their chigadax.

The next morning the tide flats were strewn with cod that the storm had blown in from the sea. The traders sent Waxtal to gather the fish. "Women's work," Waxtal said, so hovering spirits would see how he was being treated. Still, it was food. Better to gather fish than to starve, he thought.

Waxtal laughed. "Samiq believes I am dead," he said to the spirits. "He thinks I have starved or drowned. He does not understand that you are with me. When I am a shaman and known for my carving, then I will go back. Blue Shell will plead to be my wife, but I will find someone young and beautiful, someone who can make me sons, and I will force Samiq to leave our village as he once forced me."

He picked up a cod and used his thumbnail to scoop out its eyes. He sucked the eyes into his mouth, felt them pop between his teeth.

It had been a long time since he had eaten fish eyes. They

were usually saved as a treat for children. He remembered a riddle grandmothers ask:

> *What is better than fish eyes?*
> *Your eyes, smiling at me.*

"What is better than fish eyes?" Waxtal called out to the spirits, then answered, "Samiq's eyes, open in death!" And he laughed at his own cleverness.

PART TWO

EARLY SPRING
7037 B.C.

TWENTY-ONE

THE WALRUS PEOPLE

Chagvan Bay, Alaska

LEMMING TAIL SCREAMED AND GRABBED A HAND-
ful of Kiin's hair. Kiin pried the woman's fingers loose and
wrapped them around the rope that hung from the birthing
lodge rafters. "Pull," she said. "When the pain comes, pull."

Lemming Tail, squatting on her heels, closed her eyes and
blew out a long breath of air. She pulled hard against the rope,
then relaxed and leaned back against Shale Thrower.

"Do you have something you can give her?" Kiin asked
Woman of the Sun. The old woman, squatting beside the oil
lamp, looked up from her sewing. She rose slowly to her feet,
then shuffled to Lemming Tail's side and leaned over, pressing
with the flats of her hands against the woman's belly.

"She needs nothing," Woman of the Sun said. "She does
not even need this rope." She flipped the loop of braided
walrus hide from Lemming Tail's hands, and Lemming Tail
rose up on her knees to grab it. She hugged it against her
chest, her lips thrust out in a pout. "Your pain is nothing,"
Woman of the Sun said, and bent down so her face was only
a handbreadth from Lemming Tail's face. "It has barely
started yet."

Lemming Tail's eyes snapped, and she hissed at Woman of
the Sun. "What do you know of pain, old woman? You have
no children."

"Pah!" said Woman of the Sun. "I know pain. I birthed
four and lost four. I know pain." She turned her back on
Lemming Tail and walked in slow, careful steps to the oil
lamp. She settled herself on a grass mat, picked up her sewing,
then lifted her head to say, "Because something happened

91

before you were born does not mean it did not happen. Do you think the spirits made this world just for you?''

But Lemming Tail, her forehead furrowed against another pain, did not answer, only leaned against the rope and pulled, this time screaming out with words against her husband Raven.

Kiin clamped her hand over Lemming Tail's mouth. ''Are you a fool to curse your husband when you are giving birth? Shut your mouth. Spirits will hear you and take your child, perhaps take you.''

Lemming Tail pursed her lips, pulling in, so that Kiin knew she was gathering spit from the insides of her cheeks.

''You spit at me and we will leave you,'' Kiin said. ''Then you can have this child alone—you and whatever spirits you have called here with your curses.''

Lemming Tail's eyes widened, and she clamped her teeth together, swallowed. ''It is the pain,'' she said weakly. ''It is the pain speaking.''

''Then see you do not let it use your mouth again, Lemming Tail,'' Kiin answered.

For a time then Lemming Tail was silent, but there was anger in the woman's eyes, and she kept her lids half closed like a child sulking. By the middle of the day, she began to whimper, and soon, with each pain, she screamed, the screams filling the lodge so full that Kiin knew the sound would seep through the walls and into the Walrus People's village. She was ashamed of her sister wife. What woman let her pain come out in cursing and shouts? Perhaps the last push, that tearing thrust, would make a woman scream, but why during the small pains, those no worse than what a girl-woman suffers in the first day of her first bleeding, why during those pains would Lemming Tail give voice to her discomfort?

''Get her something for her mouth,'' Woman of the Sun said to Kiin.

Kiin nodded and sorted through her supplies until she found a stout piece of driftwood about the length of her hand. She brought it to Woman of the Sun, and with the next pain, when Lemming Tail opened her mouth to scream, Woman of the Sun thrust the stick between Lemming Tail's teeth.

''Bite, bite hard,'' she said to Lemming Tail. ''The biting takes away pain.''

Lemming Tail clamped her teeth down on the wood, and finally the screams ended. In the sudden silence the lodge seemed larger, as if a crowd of people had left after a long time of arguing.

The day turned to night, and the night passed slowly. Woman of the Sun left the lodge, and after a time came back, a cup in her hand.

"What is it?" Kiin asked, leaning over the cup to sniff at what was inside.

"Only water, boiled with a few dried berries and a bit of willow bark."

"It will help her pain?" Kiin asked.

Woman of the Sun shrugged. "If she thinks it will." She went to Lemming Tail, who had wrapped the walrus hide rope around her forearms. The biting stick lay on the floor at her feet.

"It is morning," Woman of the Sun said. She bent over Lemming Tail, laying a hand on her belly. "A good time for babies to be born."

Lemming Tail did not answer, but Woman of the Sun held the cup to her lips. "Drink," she said. "It will help the pain."

Lemming Tail sucked in a mouthful of liquid and swallowed it, then took another. Woman of the Sun stroked Lemming Tail's head, and squatting beside her, slipped one hand under Lemming Tail's grass apron. Lemming Tail groaned.

Woman of the Sun wiped her fingers on the grass mat at Lemming Tail's feet and stood. She clicked her tongue at Shale Thrower, who had spent the night sitting behind Lemming Tail, bracing the woman's back with each pain. Woman of the Sun turned to Kiin with a smile on her face. "He is ready to be born," she said.

Lemming Tail suddenly screeched, and Kiin hurried to her side. "One more push, one more," Kiin said, and she clasped Lemming Tail's wrists, steadying her grip on the rope.

Shale Thrower braced her feet against the floor and leaned against Lemming Tail, the two women back to back. Lemming Tail screamed again, then rose up, crouching on the balls of her feet.

"The baby comes!" Kiin said.

Woman of the Sun pressed her hand gently against Kiin's

shoulder. "Be quiet or you will frighten the child back up into its mother," the old woman said.

Kiin nodded, then reached forward to turn the baby as the dark head emerged from the birth canal. Another pain and the shoulders came out, then the child slid into Kiin's hands.

"A boy!" Kiin said and laughed. "A boy, Lemming Tail. You have given us a hunter!"

Lemming Tail moaned as the afterbirth slid from the birth canal, then she loosened her grip on the rope and eased herself back to lie on the floor.

"Three necklaces," she said, panting to catch her breath. "Tell Raven I want three necklaces. And puffin feathers for my parka. A son is worth at least that much."

Kiin tied off the baby's cord and wiped him clean, then held him out to Lemming Tail, but Lemming Tail waved him away. "I will feed him later," she said, and let her hands flutter at her neck. "Three necklaces," Kiin heard her whisper. Lemming Tail smiled and closed her eyes.

Kiin glanced at Shale Thrower. Shale Thrower shrugged her shoulders and said, "You nurse him. I will burn the afterbirth."

Woman of the Sun snorted and left the lodge. Kiin squatted on the floor, the baby in her arms. She held Lemming Tail's baby to her breast. He opened his mouth and after several tries closed his lips and sucked.

He was a well-formed baby with fat arms and legs and a thick thatch of black hair. His sucking was strong, and when Kiin stroked his cheek with her finger, he did not pause at her touch, but only sucked harder. Something about his face, the tilt of his brows, reminded Kiin of Takha, and for a moment she had to close her eyes against tears.

"You have the wrong son," some troublesome spirit seemed to whisper.

"Shuku is in his cradle," Kiin answered.

But the spirit said, "Takha, Takha. Where is Takha?"

And afraid the spirit might tell her secret to one of the Walrus People, Kiin said, "He is dead. Let the dead nurse him."

TWENTY-TWO

THE FIRST MEN

Herendeen Bay, the Alaska Peninsula

"YOUR MOTHER," THREE FISH SAID. "PLEASE, please get your mother."

Samiq opened his eyes to see Three Fish squatting beside him in his sleeping place. She moaned and pressed her hands against her belly. Her breath came in short puffs from circled lips.

Samiq shook his head to pull himself from his dreams.

"Your mother, go get your mother," Three Fish said again.

Samiq slipped from the warmth of his sleeping robes and pulled on his parka. His hand caught in the parka sleeve, and he held his arm out toward Three Fish. "Pull my hand through," he said, but Three Fish, her face drawn into a grimace, only shook her head at him.

He caught the end of his sleeve with his teeth and pulled it taut until he had worked his hand out. "I will be back," he said, then stopped. "Should I help you to the birthing lodge?" he asked.

"I cannot. I cannot," Three Fish gasped. "The pain is too great. But take your weapons so there will be no curse."

Samiq realized that his wife's hands were red with blood. He pulled spears and harpoons from the weapons corner, forcing open the fingers of his right hand to clasp them as he climbed to the roof hole. He ran to his father's ulaq, called down for his mother.

Chagak came, her face so pale that it looked like a moon rising from the darkness of the lodge.

"Three Fish is bleeding. The baby is coming," Samiq said.

"It is too soon," Chagak mumbled—as though she spoke

to someone, not Samiq, but Samiq heard the words and felt the beginning of fear like a sharp pain at the center of his heart.

He followed his mother to his ulaq, but waited outside. It was not good for a man to be present during a birth. Woman's blood was a strong curse against hunting. He climbed to the top of the ulaq, squatted down beside the roof hole. He could hear the murmur of his mother's voice, a soothing sound, but could not make out her words. He looked out toward the bay, and while he waited, he made himself think of the whales that had come to them last fall.

Those whales had given enough meat and oil to get the First Men through the winter, with some left for the starving moons that come before the birds and seals return in spring.

Would whales have shown themselves first to a woman who would soon die? No.

Samiq lifted prayers to the whale spirits, asked them to remember the Whale Hunter woman who was his wife. He remembered the questions that had come to him in his last fasting. Here near the North Sea whales were more powerful than any other animal, but to the Caribou People, in the land where they lived, caribou must be more powerful. Did they, then, pray to some other spirit, not the spirits of whales? His father had told him that the Walrus People said there were places without mountains, where a man could see only land or sea, stretching to the edge of the sky. How could the people there pray to mountain spirits? Was there some spirit greater than all? Greater than whale or mountain?

Almost, he lifted prayers to that spirit; almost he asked the help of that one. But suddenly he was afraid. Was he shaman to call a spirit unknown to his people? So instead he turned his thoughts back to the whale spirits, to their powers, and he asked them to give strength to his wife, a Whale Hunter woman, and to the Whale Hunter child she carried.

Three Fish's face reddened and she screwed her eyes shut, pressed her lips into a thin line over the jagged edges of her teeth.

Those teeth, Chagak thought. Those sad teeth. They had been the first thing she had noticed about Three Fish when Samiq had brought the woman back with him from the Whale

Hunters. Three Fish had been boisterous, loud. Even that first day, Chagak had realized that Samiq was embarrassed by his wife, that he held no feelings of pride or joy toward her.

I would have gladly sent her back to the Whale Hunters then, Chagak thought.

"And now?" The voice was the sea otter's voice, pushing into her thoughts.

"I love her," Chagak said simply. She blinked away tears. What did it matter if a woman's teeth were broken, if her words were sometimes too loud? What did those things matter when you knew that her soul was large and filled with goodness?

Three Fish moaned. The bleeding had stopped, but the baby was too early. It would be too small to live.

Then the otter voice said: "Sometimes small babies live. Remember Amgigh. His arms and legs were so thin you could see the blood pulse beneath his skin. And he lived."

Yes, Chagak thought. Amgigh had grown into a strong man. Lived to give Kiin a son. She turned toward the west, toward the sacred mountain of her long-ago village. She meant to pray, to beg for the child's life, but her prayer was a command, as though she were a shaman or village chief. "This baby will live," she told Aka. "It will be strong." She waited for the otter to scold her, to remind her of the proper way to offer prayers. But then she heard the otter's voice, and the otter repeated her words.

Samiq walked to the pile of driftwood he had set up as a target and picked up his practice spears. An ache in his belly reminded him that he had not eaten, but he walked back to his place in the gray beach sand, turned, and threw again. He had started by counting: five practice spears thrown once, five thrown twice. He had kept count up to ten and two, but now could not remember the times he had thrown. Four tens, perhaps five.

He threw his spears again. After the fifth throw, he pried the throwing board from his hand. His fingers had stiffened, almost without his notice, during the months since his injury, and now it was difficult for him to force the hand flat. Only the one finger, splinted to direct his throwing board, was still flexible.

"At night," he said aloud to his hand, to the spirits that directed his spears, "at night I will have Three Fish splint each finger." But when he said his wife's name, the sound of it came to his ears like a wail of mourning. "Three Fish," he said again, this time a whisper. He crouched on the gravel, looked out toward the bay. Women died giving birth, and Three Fish had been bleeding.

"Do not die, Three Fish," Samiq said. He clasped Kiin's shell-bead necklace as though it were an amulet. "I have lost Kiin. I cannot lose you. I do not care if you give me a son. Just do not die."

He began chants to the whale spirits, but felt his prayers drawn up toward something stronger, perhaps some mountain, perhaps the sun. Perhaps some spirit not bound to earth or flesh, some spirit that lived as mystery beyond the thoughts of men.

Three Fish's labor lasted through the night. When the sun rose, Chagak went outside, faced the east, and welcomed the light. The welcoming was something she had learned as a child from her Whale Hunter mother, something she had lost in the years since the massacre of her father's village.

She closed her eyes and saw the brightness of the sun as a glow of orange through her eyelids.

Chagak heard Three Fish groan, and so went back into the smoky darkness of the ulaq. She knelt beside Three Fish. She was crouched in the center of the ulaq, clasping a kelp rope that hung in a long loop from the rafters.

Chagak pulled aside Three Fish's woven apron and ran her hands over the woman's belly. "The baby is almost here, Three Fish. Almost here," she said. "Push. Push hard."

Three Fish clamped her mouth shut and strained.

"I see the head, daughter," Chagak said. "There is hair, much hair. Push."

Then the baby came, in one rush so fast that Chagak nearly let the child drop to the floor. "A boy," Chagak said.

"Will he live?" Three Fish asked, her voice as rough as lava rock.

"He is small," Chagak answered. She laid the baby on the finely woven grass mat she had made and dipped a soft strip of sealskin into a wooden bowl filled with warm water. She wiped away the birth blood from her grandson's eyes and mouth as she waited for the cord to stop pulsing.

Three Fish suddenly groaned, and Chagak laid a hand against the woman's knee. "It is only the afterbirth. Only that. It comes quickly and is easy to pass."

Chagak tied and cut the birth cord, then stuck a finger down inside the baby's mouth. He was limp in her arms. Fear, hard as ice, lay against Chagak's heart. She pulled a string of mucus from the baby's throat, then flipped him over her arm.

"The baby, he does not cry," Three Fish said. She leaned forward and reached for the child, sending a gush of blood from between her legs.

"Lie back, be still," Chagak said to Three Fish, then she rubbed the baby's back. "Breathe, little one," she whispered.

The baby's face was gray, his lips blue. Chagak snapped her fingers against the bottoms of his feet. Suddenly he pulled in a long breath of air and let out a jerking wail.

Chagak laughed, and the laughter, coming from her throat, caught itself on her tears, so she could not speak. She held the baby until she was sure his breathing was steady. Then she handed him to Three Fish.

Three Fish turned to her side and cradled the baby in one arm. "Should I feed him?" she asked.

"Sometimes the small ones do not suck," Chagak said. She waited as Three Fish gently opened the baby's mouth with her fingers and pressed his head close to her breast. The baby turned his head away. Three Fish tried again, and this time, Chagak clasped the baby's head, held it still. "Rub your nipple over his lips," she said to Three Fish.

The baby opened his mouth, uttered a short cry, then clamped his lips over Three Fish's nipple and began to nurse.

Chagak shook her head and smiled. "He is small, but he is strong," she said. "Your husband will be glad."

"Yes," said Three Fish. "Now he has three sons. What man could want more?"

Chagak nodded, but thought of Kiin and Shuku and said nothing.

TWENTY-THREE

THE WALRUS PEOPLE

Chagvan Bay, Alaska

"CARVE," THE RAVEN SAID TO KIIN. "NOTHING else—do not sew. Do not make baskets. Just carve. The more carvings you finish, the more I will get in trade from the River People, and some of what I get I will give to you."

He turned to Lemming Tail. "You," he said and flicked his long fingers toward her, "I need another pair of leggings."

Lemming Tail crossed her arms and stood up to face the Raven, her jaw tight, teeth clenched. "You think I have nothing to do but sew leggings?" she asked.

"You would rather spend your time in other men's lodges and shame your husband," the Raven answered.

"I have a new son," Lemming Tail said. "You think after staying up all night with him, I can work all day for you?"

The Raven reached out and clasped a fistful of Lemming Tail's black hair. "You do not want me to go?" the Raven asked. "You do not want me to bring back necklaces and caribou hides?" He pulled his fingers out through her hair, jerked his hand when his fingers caught in tangles near her ears.

Lemming Tail winced and grabbed his wrist, sinking her fingernails into his skin.

The Raven pulled his hand away. "You are my wife; you will do what I say."

"And if I do not?"

"I will take you with me and trade you to the River People."

"You will trade your son, then?" Lemming Tail asked, her top lip curled to show her teeth.

"Why would I trade my son?" the Raven asked and shook a knot of Lemming Tail's hair from his fingers. "Kiin has milk. She can feed him. Kiin is a better mother than you."

Kiin's breath hissed in over her teeth. What good would it do to set Lemming Tail against her, especially when the Raven would soon leave on his spring trading trip?

Lemming Tail screamed and, arching her hands into claws, went for the Raven's eyes. He caught her wrists and twisted her arms, forcing her to her knees. Lemming Tail's baby, nestled in a cradle hung from the lodge rafters, began to cry.

"I would rather belong to the River People than to you!" Lemming Tail screeched, her words carrying over the wails of her son. "At least they treat their wives well."

"What do you know about River People?" the Raven asked, and Kiin heard the anger under his words.

"More than some," Lemming Tail answered.

"You sleep in their traders' beds, so you think you know them. How much does a woman have to know to spread her legs for a man?"

Kiin turned her back on them, went to the corner where she stored her carvings. She had heard Lemming Tail and the Raven argue too many times. Why listen now? She squatted near the oil lamp, opened the drawstring top of her carving basket.

At first when she had returned to the Walrus village, Kiin had carved nothing more than stoppers for seal belly containers or fishhooks from mussel shells.

How could she forget that her carvings had given strength to the Raven when he fought against Amgigh? Perhaps if she had not carved those animals, Amgigh would still be alive, and she would be living with her own people, not as wife to Samiq, but at least close enough to see him each day, to hear his laughter, to pray for his safety during each hunting trip. And she would have her son Takha.

Besides, each time she picked up a piece of wood or a chunk of ivory—even though she saw the small animal within, the ikyak or the flower, the man or woman—she also heard some voice telling her she was not strong enough to release that delicate spirit from the wood or ivory. And sometimes she was not. Sometimes what she carved was a mixture of spirits: animal and man, ikyak and plant, growing out of one another, as though she had not listened hard enough to know what her knife should bring forth. She hid those poor carvings in a basket near her sleeping platform, and sometimes she would bring them out and sing soft songs asking forgiveness from the spirits wounded by her knife.

Then she had come to realize that carving was a part of her, a way to express her joy and her sorrow. So when the emptiness of her loss pulled at her spirit, she would carve, forcing her mind to break away from the pain.

Kiin reached into her basket and took out an otter carving. She turned it in her fingers, but suddenly felt the Raven's hand on her head.

"No," he said and reached down into the basket to pull out a walrus carving. "Finish this one first." He stroked his hand down the length of her hair and left the lodge.

Lemming Tail, her face still flushed with anger, was sitting with a caribou skin spread over her lap. She took a strand of twisted sinew from a bundle she kept in her sewing basket and held it between her teeth, then pulled an awl and a needle from her ivory needle case.

"You will never have my son," she said to Kiin, her words garbled by the sinew.

"I do not want your son," Kiin answered.

Lemming Tail looked down at her baby, now quietly sucking at her left breast. "He is better than your son. He will be a better hunter."

Kiin shrugged. Who was she to say what would be? Why take the chance of angering those spirits that decided such things?

"I hope they are both strong hunters," Kiin said, knowing her words were the truth. Who did not benefit when a village had many strong hunters?

She held the walrus carving up to the light. Once it had been a whale tooth, like the shell carving she wore at her waist, Kiin's first carving.

Kiin had found that whale tooth herself, but the Raven had given her this one. It was blunt, water-worn, and when Kiin held it in her hands, she felt the walrus hidden within the ivory. Now the walrus was nearly free. She tucked her hair behind her ears and bent over her work. She moved her knife in small circles to make the eyes, then held the walrus up, turned it slowly in the oil lamp light.

Lemming Tail flipped the caribou skin from her lap, spat out the sinew in her mouth, and stood up. She walked over to Kiin.

"You think you are stronger than me because you carve," Lemming Tail said. "You think our husband cares more for you because you carve. My birth bleeding has stopped. Soon I will go back to Raven's bed. Then he will forget you. I am first wife. While Raven is on his trading trip, you must do what I say. Perhaps I will decide I do not want you in this lodge. Perhaps I will decide I want to live alone."

"There are places I can stay," Kiin said. "But are you sure you want to cook and clean for yourself?"

Lemming Tail went back to her sewing, but as she passed Shuku's cradle, she reached up and slapped her hand against the wooden side. Shuku began to cry.

Kiin stood and took the baby from the cradle, held him tightly against her until he stopped crying. "Have you forgotten my walking stick?" Kiin asked Lemming Tail.

Lemming Tail smiled and, looking at Shuku, said, "You think you can watch him always? You think he can protect himself?"

"I protected him against animals and spirits," Kiin said. "I can protect him against you." She waited until Lemming Tail was once more working on the leggings, then Kiin sat down beside the oil lamp and began to carve.

When the Raven returned to the lodge, he found his wives each with a baby at her breast, each working.

TWENTY-FOUR

THE WHALE HUNTERS

Yunaska Island, the Aleutian Chain

THE WIND WAS COLD ON KUKUTUX'S BARE SKIN AS she ran down the mud path that led to the river. The snow had melted back from the gray soil of the riverbank. Each day the sun rose higher in the sky.

Kukutux broke the thin ice at the river's edge with her heels, then slid her feet down into the water. It was so cold that it numbed her ankles until her bones ached, but she reached cupped hands below the surface and, squatting, splashed water between her legs, then up to her shoulders, neck, and face. She waded ashore and wiped her skin dry with the edges of her hands, then pulled on her suk.

She shivered and crossed her arms over her breasts until the suk drew the heat from the center of her body to warm her skin. She flexed her arms, then winced at the throbbing in her left elbow.

There are others with greater pain than mine, Kukutux told herself. What about Speckled Basket, whose foot had been crushed? And the old man, Fish Eater, who had lost an eye? What about Fat Wife, who was dead, and Three Fish and Small Knife, who had never been found? Better to have a stiff elbow than to be buried with ash and angry spirits beneath a heap of crumbled stone and dirt.

But then she wondered: Better to be a woman with no husband, no children?

"Others besides me have lost husbands and babies," Kukutux said aloud and shook the discontent from her head.

But as she thought of going back to her ulaq, her chest was suddenly empty and aching. She rubbed one hand against the

104

bulge of the whaleskin amulet that hung under her suk, and she took a long breath.

"Baskets today," she said, loud enough for the sun to hear. The sun should know that she filled her days with work, that there was no laziness in her hands or in her mind.

"Kukutux! Kukutux!"

She recognized Hard Rock's voice, and her heart suddenly pumped hard, pressing into her ribs. There had been talk among the women that this man, their chief, would soon take his fifth wife.

Kukutux had tried not to let herself hope for such an honor. Fifth wife! she had scolded herself. You were first wife to a good hunter. Now you hope for fifth?

But with so few men left among the Whale Hunters, what woman would not be happy with fifth wife? Even a fifth wife had hope of being a mother to sons. And if food were scarce, the fifth wife's portion would be no smaller than what Kukutux received now—bits given from women who pitied her.

So she took a long breath and walked to Hard Rock.

"Is there something you need?" she asked, with a politeness that again sent her heart in quick shudders against her ribs. At the same time she said to herself, Remember, he is often angry. What woman wants a husband who is always burning? Still, her heart trembled with hope.

"You have good sight," he said. "Better than most."

Kukutux raised her chin. Yes, since she was a child, that gift had been hers, to see eagles where others saw only sky.

"Look out there. What do you see?"

Kukutux shaded her eyes with her hands, ignoring the twist of pain in her left elbow as she raised her arms. "Two ikyan," she finally said.

Hard Rock nodded.

"No," Kukutux said, squinting to see more clearly. "One ik, one ikyak."

Hard Rock locked his hands around his walking stick. Kukutux looked up into his eyes. They were hard and flat, like black stone, and she could read nothing in them.

"Watch until you see any markings," he said.

Again Kukutux shaded her eyes. Finally she said, "The ik carries yellow and red markings."

"A trader," Hard Rock mumbled under his breath. "You

have baskets?'' he asked. ''Do the women have baskets they can trade or seal bellies of dried fish, any grass curtains?''

''Some,'' Kukutux said.

''What do you do with your days? You no longer have husbands to care for.''

''How do you expect us to weave?'' Kukutux asked. ''The ash ruined most of our basket grass.''

Hard Rock walked away from her, muttering something about the laziness of women.

''And so what are you going to tell those traders, Hard Rock?'' Kukutux asked, allowing her anger to speak though she knew the man was too far away to hear her words. ''That the Whale Hunters took no whales this year? That the Whale Hunters are a tribe of women?''

Waxtal moved his foot so he could feel the partially carved tusk lying at the bottom of his ikyak. He had wanted to finish it before they reached the Whale Hunter village, but winter had been filled with women's work: mending parkas, catching and preparing fish, caring for oil lamps. What man could spend an evening carving after a day of doing women's work? But he had kept his complaints inside his mouth. He had food and a place to live. He could have been alone, starving.

There would be time for carving, and then, when he had finished the tusks, his power would be complete, and Owl and Spotted Egg would do their own women's work.

Even though storms had kept the traders from reaching the Whale Hunter island before winter, they had had enough oil, and had taken sea lions and seals, fish and birds for meat. They spent the winter on a sheltered island, its caves warmed from within by mountain spirits. Waxtal had heard stories of such places and now knew those stories were true. So he and the traders had had a good winter, safe and with food.

Now at last it was spring, and they were at the Whale Hunters' island. Waxtal scanned the beach, pointed with his paddle toward the rise of ulas at the back of the beach. ''See?'' he called to Owl and Spotted Egg. ''The village.''

He guided his ikyak toward shore, ahead of the ik, to show the traders where to land. He stepped from his ikyak and waited as the traders beached their ik.

''I told you I was here before,'' Waxtal called out, but then he saw the frown on Owl's face, the man's sudden narrowing of eyes.

"You said it was a strong village," Owl said to Waxtal.

Waxtal turned, his eyes following the trader's gaze, and he saw that several of the ulas were without roofs, rafters broken and rotting through the sod. Spotted Egg pointed at the ikyak racks. There were only three ikyan on the beach.

"What has happened here?" Owl asked.

A sudden heaviness in the air seemed to push against Waxtal's chest. He rubbed his amulet with one hand and squatted down to grope inside his ikyak until he found one of the walrus tusks. The surface of the tusk was cool, and a calm spread from his hand to arm and chest, moving his heart into a steady rhythm.

Then from between the ulas he saw a man. Someone old, he thought at first, because of the slowness of the man's walking, the hunch of his shoulders, but as the man drew near, Waxtal saw the face, and knew it was Hard Rock.

Waxtal held out his hands. "I am a friend, I have no knife," he said. "I am Waxtal of the First Men, once from Shuganan's beach."

Hard Rock stopped and frowned.

"Remember?" Waxtal said. "We came to your village and helped you fight the Short Ones. Remember, I was the one who saved you. I was the one who thought to put two climbing logs in each ulaq's roof hole so hunters could go up back to back to fight."

"Gray Bird?" Hard Rock said.

Waxtal smiled. "Yes, then I was Gray Bird," he answered. "I have taken the name Waxtal in mourning for my son."

Hard Rock nodded, then looked past Waxtal at the traders.

"I have brought you traders," Waxtal said.

"We cannot feed you," said Hard Rock.

"We came to trade, not to eat," Owl said.

Hard Rock shrugged. "We will share what we have, trade what we can," he answered.

"Whales will be coming soon," said Waxtal, his words a rush.

Hard Rock looked at him, raised his eyebrows. "You think you understand the ways of whales?" he asked.

Waxtal turned away, his face red with the heat of Hard Rock's words.

"We are cursed," Hard Rock said. He stepped close to Waxtal, pressed a finger against Waxtal's chest. "Yes, you Seal Hunters saved us. But then one of you cursed us. See what we have become. If you think you can take what we have—our women, our food—you will find that we still know how to fight."

Waxtal felt a lump of anger rise into his throat, but looking back at the traders, he said, "Hard Rock, the Whale Hunters and Seal Hunters have always been brothers. Why do you say we cursed you?"

Hard Rock stared into Waxtal's eyes. "It was our fault as much as yours. That one who cursed us was grandson to the old man who was our chief."

Many Whales, Waxtal thought. The old chief Many Whales.

"At least he who cursed us, the one who called fire from Aka and then Okmok, he is dead also. Soon he will choose to rise to the Dancing Lights so he can be there with others like himself, and the curse will lift."

Waxtal's mind cleared, and he realized that Hard Rock spoke of Samiq.

Samiq! Waxtal thought. So that is why Samiq left the Whale Hunters. And these people think he is dead.

Waxtal opened his mouth to speak, to tell Hard Rock the truth, but then said nothing. Better to wait, to see what Hard Rock would give for such knowledge. A good way to spend the nights, deciding how to punish Samiq for taking Waxtal's ulaq, his food, his wife. Suddenly laughter bubbled into Waxtal's mouth so that he had to lower his head and press one hand across his lips.

Owl stepped forward and said to Hard Rock, "We bring no curses, only strength, the power of amulets and shaman blessings, fair trades."

And Waxtal, head still bowed, followed the traders as Hard Rock led them into the village.

TWENTY-FIVE

HARD ROCK HANDED WAXTAL THE HARPOON head. After four days of waiting, four days of politeness, Waxtal had finally been invited into Hard Rock's ulaq. Waxtal had not minded the wait. He had needed the time to plan, and he had planned well.

Now the trading begins, Waxtal thought as he studied the harpoon head. It was made of whalebone, barbed on both sides, and as long as Waxtal's outstretched hand. The end was blunt and slotted to hold poison under a small triangular obsidian tip. The harpoon head was old, the bone yellowed, and one of the four barbs, one near the tip, was broken off. The workmanship was good, but Waxtal had seen better. Whose harpoon heads could compare with those made by Amgigh?

He looked into Hard Rock's face. How many years since the last time Waxtal had seen him? Three, four years? In some ways, Hard Rock had not changed since then. He was a powerful man, short, with thick arms and legs, his wrists nearly as wide as Waxtal's ankles. His teeth were straight and even. His coarse black hair lay in a fringe over his forehead; at sides and back it hung to his shoulders. His eyes were cold, flat. A man could not look into those eyes and see Hard Rock's thoughts, but a good trader had many ways of knowing what another man felt. Who could hide anger under a slack jaw? What man could keep desire from showing itself in a twist of lips, the quick blink of an eyelid?

Waxtal closed his fist over the harpoon head. "You have more?" he asked. At other villages, trading with other men, Waxtal would have thrown the harpoon head to the floor in feigned disgust, but there was something about the way that Hard Rock sat, his shoulders drawn in toward each other, his arms crossed, his hands clasping his elbows, that made Waxtal decide to treat Hard Rock's first offer as something to be considered.

"A few," Hard Rock said.

"For this and three more like it I will give you a seal belly of oil," Waxtal said.

Hard Rock straightened. He raised one eyebrow, looked into Waxtal's eyes.

Waxtal understood. What man, watching, would not think Waxtal offered the oil in pity? Though Hard Rock had told Waxtal and the traders that most of his men were away hunting, anyone could see that there were few hunters. Ulas stood unrepaired, good rafters left to rot. In the four days since he and the traders had come to this island, Waxtal had seen more people crippled in some way—hand, eye, foot, leg—than he had in all the years of his life.

How could anyone doubt that the Whale Hunters were cursed? Waxtal saw these things and felt the beginning of fear. He needed Hard Rock to be strong. But he reminded himself that a man's strength is more than the favor of spirits. A man's strength—and his weakness—is what he believes it to be. Waxtal made himself remember Hard Rock's hatred for Samiq, and smiled. Yes, it would happen as he planned, but until then, he must try to keep Owl and Spotted Egg away from Hard Rock. Waxtal did not want them to fear the curse Samiq had put on the Whale Hunters' village.

Waxtal was glad that Hard Rock had given Owl and Spotted Egg each a woman for nights spent on the Whale Hunters' island. Waxtal had held his smile inside his cheek when he saw the wanting in the traders' eyes, and he told himself, as he often did, that young men should not be traders. They thought too much of quick pleasures and let the pull of their loins block out wisdom. Still, he hoped Owl and Spotted Egg would enjoy their days with the Whale Hunter women. Perhaps they would leave sons to grow into hunters, children who would give strength back to these people who understood the secrets of whales. Even now both traders were with their women rather than seeking out good trades. But though Waxtal would complain to the men later, he was glad. It was better for him to be alone with Hard Rock in this ulaq, alone and trading without interference.

He looked again at Hard Rock's face, saw the flush of the man's anger, the tension of jaw and brow. Waxtal reminded himself that Hard Rock was not a foolish man. If Hard Rock took Waxtal's oil, he was admitting his village's need. Yet how could Hard Rock refuse? Most Whale Hunter children were as thin as blades of grass, the women worse.

Waxtal leaned forward, lowered his voice. "You think I am a foolish trader," he said, then allowed himself to smile slowly. "You think I do not know that my oil is worth more than four harpoon heads?" He leaned back, flexed his shoulders. "In other villages, yes," he said. "But this is the Whale Hunter village. The Whale Hunters must stay close to their island during the trading months. They must be prepared for whales, so they cannot send traders out except to the closest Seal Hunter villages. You do not know what those Seal Hunters do with the harpoon heads they receive from you. You do not know that the River People will give two women for each Whale Hunter harpoon head. The Caribou People, who live almost at the edge of the world, they will give parkas and boots, well sewn and decorated with teeth and colored sinew. All for only one or two Whale Hunter harpoon heads. You do not know this, and the traders will not tell you. Why tell when they can get so much for so little?"

Waxtal watched Hard Rock as he spoke, watched as Hard Rock raised his eyes to stare into Waxtal's face—as if he could know the truth of Waxtal's words by seeing them as they came from Waxtal's mouth.

"If this is true," Hard Rock finally said, "why do you tell me? Why not take what you can get and leave as other traders do?" He stopped, his words broken by a cough, then asked again, "So why do you tell me?"

"Because we are brothers," Waxtal said.

Hard Rock narrowed his eyes and leaned toward Waxtal. "You are not my brother."

"I am a Seal Hunter, of the First Men," Waxtal said. "You are a Whale Hunter, also of the First Men." He paused, watched as Hard Rock leaned back, sucked in his cheeks, tilted his head. "The Whale Hunters and the Seal Hunters have always been brothers," said Waxtal. "Our long-ago grandfathers are the same. They live together now in the Dancing Lights. We marry your women; you marry ours."

Hard Rock nodded.

"Those men I am with," Waxtal said, pointing with his chin toward the top of the ulaq, "those men are Caribou Peo-

ple. They do not think as I think. They do not see as I see.
We are together only for this trip, then I will go alone or with
some First Men trader. How can I let men who are not my
brothers cheat someone who is a brother?" Waxtal met Hard
Rock's eyes and did not look away.

Slowly Hard Rock smiled; slowly he said, "Tell me then
why those people, those who name themselves Caribou and
River, why do they want our harpoon heads? Do they hope to
hunt whales?"

Waxtal laughed. "They will never hunt whales. Some live
away from the sea, so far away that they cannot even hear its
voice. But they visit the sea. They have seen whales. They are
skilled hunters, taking caribou and bears, so they have some
understanding of the power it takes to hunt on the sea." Waxtal leaned far forward. "You kill whales. What man has more
power than that?"

For a moment, Waxtal looked away, then he held up the
broken harpoon head. "This," Waxtal said, "you think they
will use it as a weapon?" He laughed. "No." He rubbed his
fingers over the broken barb. "This harpoon head has been
used against a whale. Some hunter will have it as an amulet."
Waxtal smiled and slipped the harpoon head into a pouch at
his waist. "Perhaps I will keep it myself."

"Ho!" Hard Rock said. "Two seal bellies of oil, then!"

And though he had expected the man to make such an offer,
Waxtal raised his eyebrows to show surprise. For a moment,
he chewed at his bottom lip. He patted the pouch. "For this
and three others," he said.

"Yes."

"Two seal bellies then, but also a woman for my bed tonight."

"Done!" said Hard Rock.

Waxtal stood, but Hard Rock reached out, pointed to a food
cache dug into the wall of the ulaq. "A good trade should end
with eating," he said.

Waxtal waited while the man sorted through sea lion belly
containers. Finally Hard Rock brought out dried fish and whale
meat. When he saw the whale meat, Waxtal thought of his
son Qakan. Qakan had liked whale meat. How good if Qakan
could be here to watch his father trade.

In his mind, Waxtal spoke to Qakan, as though Qakan were

beside him in this Whale Hunter ulaq: ''The secret to a good trade is knowing what is truly wanted—not the oil, the meat, the weapons. Those are outward things. They are only symbols of what a man really wants. A good trader sees through these things as though he were looking through water. A man like Hard Rock, one who has lost his pride, is the easiest of all men to understand. He wants that pride back, and to get it, he must first have power, then revenge, and in his old age, honor. Remember what I tell you, Qakan. Perhaps someday you will be a trader at the Dancing Lights. Who knows what a trader can get there?''

Then Hard Rock gave Waxtal a piece of dried meat. Waxtal used his sleeve knife to cut off a chunk. Smiling at Hard Rock, he held the meat up as though he passed it to invisible hands.

TWENTY-SIX

USING THE CURVED BLADE OF HER WOMAN'S knife, Kukutux slit the belly of the cod she had just caught and cut out a portion of the gut to use as bait. She handed a strip to Many Babies and wrapped some around her own hook.

''He was a big man, not like the three traders now in our village,'' Many Babies said. ''He wanted me and told Hard Rock he would give me anything for sharing his sleeping place.'' The woman laughed. ''That was how I got this fish-hook and also my seal tooth necklace. But I worked hard. He was wanting it all night long.''

Kukutux tried to smile. Many Babies' stories of the men she had pleasured were like the stories old hunters told of long-ago hunts. The woman meant only to bring back memories of good times, but the stories filled Kukutux with sorrow as she longed for nights with her husband, his arms tight around her, his words of caring whispered into her ears.

Many Babies squinted at the sky, pointed with her chin toward a ruffle of clouds that spread toward them from the west. "Storm," she said and bent over her hook.

It was a jointed hook, its two pieces carved from bone and bound together with twisted sinew line. The straight strong shaft ended in a small socket that held the bulb end of the barb. It was a wonderful hook. The sinew would snap before the hook broke, and even if the barb broke, replacing it would mean carving only part of the hook instead of the whole thing. Better than my clamshell hooks, Kukutux thought, but then wondered if the hook would be worth spending a night with a trader as Many Babies had. Who could tell what a trader would do? What did a trader care if he angered or offended a woman? There was no need to protect a friendship with the woman's husband or father. There was no need to keep peace with others in the village. What protection did a woman have against a trader except her own wits?

Kukutux watched as Many Babies threw her pebble-weighted fishing line into the water. If a trader was happy with Many Babies, he would be happy with me, Kukutux thought.

Many Babies was old. Her face was lined, and her hair had swaths of white at each temple. She was not ugly, no. And though she had given Hard Rock five babies, she was still strong and straight. Unlike most women in the village, her cheeks were not sunken nor her body too thin from a winter of starving.

The whales had not come to Whale Hunter waters last summer, and there were few seals, but Hard Rock had managed to bring in enough sea lions to share and still have meat and oil to keep his wives well fed. In most families, hunters had taken enough only for themselves. The women and children had to live on what could be gathered from the beaches, saving oil and rich meat for the men. Hunters had to eat first. What hope would the village have if the hunters grew weak and thin?

Kukutux felt a tug at her line. She waited a moment, then jerked her hands to set the hook. She felt the weight of the fish, pulling, then suddenly the line was slack.

"Gone?" Many Babies asked.

Kukutux nodded.

"Check your bait," Many Babies said.

Kukutux did not look at the woman. She wrapped the line around the thick driftwood stick she held in her left hand. It was always that way when she fished with Many Babies. The woman told her what to do, as though Kukutux were a child just learning women's ways.

Kukutux told herself to be patient, to remember the joy she had felt when Many Babies invited her to fish in the ik. She asked only because I have no ik, Kukutux reminded herself. It is not because Hard Rock told her to ask me.

"It got your bait?" Many Babies asked.

"Yes."

"Wrap your hook better. You do not do it right. You are like your mother. She always lost her bait."

Kukutux pressed her lips together and wrapped another strip of gut tightly around the hook, then began to unwind her line, but Many Babies reached over, grabbed her line, inspected the hook. Kukutux looked away as the woman removed the bait, spit on it, then wrapped it over the hook once more.

"I wonder that you catch anything," Many Babies said. "I see why you are so thin. It is a good thing you do not have a husband to feed. It is a good thing you are not nursing a baby. You can eat all your fish. Me, I must share with my husband and my children, even with my sister wives' children. If you knew how to do a few things, you would eat well and be fat. Then you would have no trouble finding a husband."

Many Babies released Kukutux's line and let it fall into the water. She watched as Kukutux unwound the line, then said, "Yes, in these two years we have all mourned. The spirits favored me. I lost no one except a sister wife, but when life is lived as the spirits would have us live it—with respect to all things—then we are favored."

Kukutux took a long breath, let it out in a sigh. How many nights had she lain awake in her sleeping robes trying to recall something she had done, some impoliteness, some disrespect, that might have brought a curse to those she loved. How many times had she asked herself why she of all the people in the village had lost everyone—husband, child, parents, brother, sister—everyone but her brother's wife, and her brother's wife was a selfish woman.

"You are sure you did not eat puffin meat?" Many Babies asked. "It is taboo for women at the age of bearing children."

"I did not," Kukutux answered. Each time she was with Many Babies, the woman asked questions, as though in proving Kukutux at fault, she could restore the village to what it once had been.

"You did not step across your husband's weapons? You did not touch his food during your bleeding times?"

"No," Kukutux said softly. There was a strong jerk on her line. She waited a moment, then set the hook, felt the satisfying weight of a fish on the line.

"You are sure you did not . . ."

"I have a fish," Kukutux said.

"Another?"

Kukutux let herself smile at the frown on Many Babies' face. "Another," Kukutux said. "It is big."

She struggled with the fish, winding the line in slowly, letting it out again as the fish made a quick, hard run toward the shore and then turned back out to sea. It was a halibut. She was sure of it, but she was afraid if she said the words out loud, some spirit would think her too proud and turn the fish into something smaller. So she sat as though she fought against pogy or cod, and for a long time let the fish tire itself against the line.

Kukutux's arms began to ache, and she flexed her shoulders. Her breathing was jagged and short. The catcher's share of a halibut—if the fish was as big as it felt on her line—would give her meat for several days. Kukutux made herself take a long breath, but the hope in her chest seemed to take up so much space that she did not have room for air.

I want the fish too much, she thought. But what was better than rich thick slabs of halibut, boiled with lovage and dipped in oil? You are foolish, she told herself. What better way to lose a fish than to see it in your boiling bag before it is in your ik?

Many Babies coiled in her line and set it aside. From the corner of her eyes, Kukutux could see the woman twisting her hands, moving as though she fought a spirit fish on a line made of wind. Then Many Babies reached over, clasped Kukutux's hands.

"It is a halibut. It must be a halibut," Many Babies said.

Kukutux, arms and chest muscles aching, only nodded. Why waste strength on words?

"Let me take it. I will take it," Many Babies said. "I am stronger than you."

"No," Kukutux said. "No," she repeated, though it was difficult to find breath enough for words.

"Lean forward," Many Babies said, then after watching for a moment shouted out, "Lean back."

Kukutux did not listen. She knew she must think only of the fish and of the line that brought the fish's movements to her hands.

"I was catching halibut when you were only a baby," Many Babies said. "I was catching halibut when you knew nothing more than to make messes in your own bed."

"The fish is tiring," Kukutux answered. "Paddle us closer to shore. Perhaps we can pull him up with us on the beach."

Many Babies snorted, but she picked up the paddle and, nodding toward Kukutux's line, said, "Tell me the next time it heads toward shore."

Many Babies held the paddle just above the water until Kukutux called out, "Now!" Then she plunged the paddle into the water, moving the ik with quick, powerful strokes toward shore.

Kukutux wound the slack line, working as quickly as she could. The fish pulled back, slipped under the ik and again out to sea. Kukutux let out a little more line, then allowed the fish to fight. She called again when it headed toward shore.

Many Babies paddled, and finally Kukutux heard her cry out, "We have a halibut!"

Then there were men—Tall Hands and Fish Eater and two of the traders—in the water with gaffs and leisters, and Kukutux watched Fish Eater, that old man, as he plunged his leister into the fish. Tall Hands and Fish Eater brought the thrashing halibut to shore, and Tall Hands clubbed it until it was still.

Kukutux, the line still in her hand, climbed out of the ik. The halibut was as big as a large man. With the catcher's portion, Kukutux would have enough to dry and save.

But then Many Babies was beside Kukutux, pushing Kukutux away. "I caught it," Many Babies said. She ran to Fish Eater. "Fresh meat today!" she said to him. "You will have a double share for your help."

Kukutux opened her mouth to protest, but for a moment she had no words. She looked at Many Babies, raised the driftwood stick wound with fishline that ran to the halibut's mouth.

"I caught it," Kukutux said, her words soft. Fish Eater turned and looked at her.

"Many Babies . . ." he said, then narrowed his one seeing eye and looked away from Kukutux.

"I caught the fish!" Kukutux said, her words louder. "It is my fish."

Tall Hands and the traders turned and stared at her.

"You lie!" Many Babies said. "I caught it."

Again Kukutux held up her hand. The driftwood stick was painted with her mark, two circles side by side. She pointed to the circles. "See? My line."

Tall Hands shook his head, and the traders looked away, shuffling their feet against the beach gravel.

And Kukutux thought, How can they stand against Many Babies when she is wife to the chief whale hunter? But Many Babies had a hunter to bring her food, and Kukutux had only what she herself could find. If she stood against Many Babies, what would the woman tell Hard Rock? What if she asked Hard Rock not to take Kukutux as wife? Then what would happen?

Can I hunt seals myself and so have enough oil for the next winter? Kukutux thought. She had almost starved through the last winter, even with sea lion bellies of oil from her husband's hunting.

"We fished together," Kukutux said. "The fish took my line, but Many Babies helped me." She looked at Many Babies, hoped the woman would agree, but Many Babies threw back her head and stared hard at Kukutux.

"I caught the fish with my line," Many Babies said. "You think my husband will not believe me?"

"Look," Kukutux said. She coiled the kelp line around her stick until her hands were only an arm's length from the halibut's mouth. "My line," she said, and again she held the stick so the men could see the marks.

"What is her mark?" one of the traders asked.

"Two circles," Kukutux said, holding the stick toward him.

"Her mark is two circles?" the trader asked and looked at the men around him. Tall Hands shrugged, coughed, and turned away, but Fish Eater nodded.

"Then it is her fish."

Kukutux looked up, boldly met the trader's eyes. "Many

Babies should have an equal share,'' she said, but Many Babies had turned her back on all of them and was walking toward the ulas. Kukutux looked after her, but then said, ''More for the rest of us.''

She took her woman's knife from its packet and squatted beside the fish, ready to give shares. ''Tell your wives and sisters to come,'' she said. ''Everyone will have fresh fish today.''

Fish Eater went up toward the ulas, and Kukutux began to slice the fish into sections. Tall Hands took a portion. But as he was carrying his share to his ulaq, Many Babies came back and stood beside Kukutux.

''I have come for my share,'' Many Babies said.

''The head and half of what is left after the dividing is yours,'' Kukutux said, giving Many Babies more than what she should expect.

Many Babies laughed, a snort that blew out from her nose. ''You think that will make me tell my husband to take you as fifth wife?''

And Kukutux knew that Many Babies' arguing was not about a fish, but about a husband. So Kukutux said, ''You know the fish is mine. You know that I have just offered you the catcher's share. What more do you want?''

''You think I care about a fish?'' Many Babies said. ''No. My husband is a good hunter. I have food enough to eat, for myself and my children and grandchildren.'' Her voice was loud, and Kukutux, looking up from her knife, saw that other women of the village had begun to gather, each with a carrying net to take a share of the halibut.

''I do not want this fish,'' Many Babies said. ''I only want you to know what it is like to have someone else take something that is yours. What is that fish compared to my husband?''

There was murmuring among the women, and Kukutux's face began to burn.

''You think I do not see the way you look at my husband? You think he needs another wife to feed? You think I want to share my children's food with a woman who cannot even use both arms?''

Kukutux bent her head over the fish. She held some hope in her heart that one of the other women would speak for

her—Night Woman, who had also lost a husband and was now
third wife to a man too old to hunt; or Long Wood, an old
woman known for her wisdom. But the women were silent,
so finally Kukutux lifted her head and stood up. Her woman's
knife, red with halibut blood, was still in her right hand, and
she moved it, only slightly, so that the sharp edge of the blade
was out, ready to slice any false words Many Babies might
say.

"Your husband is a strong hunter," Kukutux said. "He is
a leader among our people. If he asks me to be his wife, then
I will be his wife. If he does not, I will find some way to live
through this next winter without a husband. I do not try to
dishonor him or you by my actions." She moved her head
toward the halibut. "Though I caught the fish, I have offered
you the catcher's share, and you know that I need the meat
more than you do."

"I will take the catcher's share," Many Babies said and
pushed through the women to grab a large slab of meat and
the halibut's head. The women made loud sounds of disap-
proval, but Many Babies took the meat and did not look back.

"Make our shares smaller," Long Wood said.

Kukutux shook her head. "I do not carry a child; I do not
nurse. I need less meat. Who knows, perhaps Many Babies
carries a child in her belly, one so small we do not yet know
about it." And though Kukutux said the words with gentleness, all the women laughed. Who did not know that Many
Babies was past the years of bearing children? Who did not
know that Many Babies would eat the fish herself?

TWENTY-SEVEN

MANY BABIES SCRAMBLED DOWN THE CLIMBING log and threw a slab of halibut meat on the floor between Waxtal and Hard Rock.

Waxtal looked up at the woman. She was Hard Rock's first wife. Waxtal remembered her from long ago, when the Whale Hunters and the First Men were preparing to fight the Short Ones. She had been beautiful, though loud and sometimes rude. But what Whale Hunter woman was not rude?

Even now, though most of the men and women of the Whale Hunter village were thin, their eyes dull with need of meat, Many Babies' face was still sleek and round, her hair shining with oil. She squatted beside the fish, and Waxtal could see that it was the catcher's share, the head with meat and belly fat still attached.

"I caught it," she said and pointed at the fish with all the fingers of both hands. "I did," she said again, and her words were broken with hard breathing as though she had been running.

Hard Rock looked at her, his eyebrows raised. "Good," he finally said.

"Ha! You say 'good'!" said Many Babies and coughed out a harsh laugh. "You do not know how hard I had to fight for my share—my share of a fish that I caught!"

Hard Rock cut his eyes over to Waxtal, a look that Waxtal understood. Why did women argue over things not worth argument? Why did they cry for things not worth tears?

"Who tried to take it?" Hard Rock asked, his words coming slowly.

Many Babies pressed her lips into a small circle, and Waxtal could see what she must have looked like as a child, her smile hidden behind a pout. "Kukutux," she said in a tiny voice.

Waxtal cut off another chunk of the dried meat Hard Rock had given him, chewed it slowly, and tried to remember a

Whale Hunter woman named Kukutux, but he could bring no face to his mind.

She must be one of the younger women, he thought. One who was a baby or perhaps not yet born when the Short Ones came so many years ago.

"Perhaps Kukutux needs the food. She has no husband," Hard Rock said.

Many Babies set her mouth into a frown and drew back her lips to show her teeth. Waxtal looked away. It was not good to be here with Hard Rock when he and his wife were fighting. If a man's face always brought remembrance of embarrassment, why spend time with that man?

Waxtal stood. He picked up the harpoon head that lay on the floor mats between Hard Rock and himself. "Remember. Three more," Waxtal said. He did not want to leave without the other harpoon heads, but more than that, he wanted the trade completed before Hard Rock could talk to Owl or Spotted Egg. Who could expect those two, barely more than boys, to see the worth in Hard Rock's broken harpoon heads? And Waxtal did not need Hard Rock to think that he was trading out of pity.

Hard Rock raised one hand toward Waxtal. "Wait, do not go," he said, then turned to Many Babies. "I will see that Kukutux is punished. Even if she needs meat, she cannot take what belongs to someone else."

Many Babies nodded, and raising her chin she said, "She can have my share. What is one fish to the wife of the alananasika?"

"Yes," Waxtal said. He opened his mouth to praise Hard Rock's strength, his honor. But Many Babies, lowering her voice so her words were almost a whisper, leaned toward her husband and said, "Kukutux needs a husband. Perhaps one of these traders will give something for her."

The words were cold in Waxtal's chest. What trader wanted a woman in his ik? Someone to feed, someone who would want beads and feathers? Someone to complain in hard weather, to whine during long days of paddling? Then he saw the smile on Hard Rock's face, the sudden straightening of the man's shoulders.

"Kukutux is a good worker and a young woman," Hard Rock said. "She will give some husband happy nights and many sons." He laughed, and Waxtal joined his laughter.

"Ah, a Whale Hunter woman!" Waxtal said, but he remembered Samiq's woman Three Fish, who ate as much as any man and did less work than most of the women. Owl and Spotted Egg might leave him here if he took a Whale Hunter woman for wife. And how could he bear to live in this ruined and cursed village? Who did not know that a curse like that could enter a man's soul, could bring illness or death? As a trader, he had some protection. He did not belong to this village, to this island, but if he lived here, even though he was not a Whale Hunter, could he expect to remain untainted?

Waxtal closed his mouth on his laughter and smiled at Hard Rock. "What man does not hope for the blessing of a Whale Hunter wife?" Waxtal said, the words coming warm from his mouth. "But it is difficult for a trader to have a wife with him. Dangerous. This Kukutux, has she no father, no uncle, to worry about her safety?"

"Everyone in her family is dead," Many Babies said, and she moved to sit beside Hard Rock as though she were one of the men.

"Perhaps then her family is cursed," Waxtal said, his words careful, slow.

Hard Rock frowned. "She is one of the strongest women. She carries no curse."

"She does not even cough," Many Babies said.

Waxtal pulled at his long, thin chin whiskers, raised one eyebrow, and turned to Hard Rock. "This is true?" he asked.

"It is true," Hard Rock said.

Waxtal shrugged. He opened his hand and looked at the harpoon head. "I will show this to Owl and Spotted Egg," he said. "I will speak to them about Kukutux, and then we will decide whether or not to take a woman. She would have to ride in the ik with them, since I have only an ikyak. If they do not want her . . ." He shrugged.

"Two bellies of oil for the harpoon heads, you promised," Hard Rock said.

"Yes," said Waxtal, "for this and three more." But he felt a shrinking inside as he thought of telling Owl how much he had promised for a few broken harpoon heads.

Waxtal climbed from the ulaq, stood at the top for a moment, and looked down toward the beach. A young woman was carrying a slab of halibut meat in a net bag strung from her arm. She was tall and thin and moved with quick grace, her feet small and brown under the edge of her birdskin suk. As she passed the ulaq, she looked up at him, her dark eyes large in a too thin face. She looked away, and Waxtal felt the blood rush to his loins. How many nights since he had been with a woman?

He looked at the harpoon head in his hand, focused his eyes on the broken barb until his thoughts left his needs. He was glad he had asked Hard Rock for a woman. Another man would only have to see the bulge at his crotch to know that Waxtal could be easily bought with the promise of a woman.

He watched as the young woman climbed up a ulaq. Waxtal brushed his hand across his hardening man part, then heard Many Babies' voice rise in a wail of complaints from inside Hard Rock's ulaq. Waxtal shook his head. What woman was worth the misery?

TWENTY-EIGHT

THE WALRUS PEOPLE

Chagvan Bay, Alaska

KIIN STOOD ON THE SHORE UNTIL RAVEN'S TRADE ik and White Fox's ikyak were only small dark spots on the blue water of the bay. She looked away as White Fox's wife pulled her hair over her face to hide her tears. Kiin held prayers in her heart for the traders' success, but if she hid her eyes from other women, it was not because of tears. There had been too many days of packing and preparing food, of carving and listening to Lemming Tail's complaints, too many nights in the Raven's bed, for her to feel sorrow at this parting.

Soon the other women turned back to the lodges, but Kiin

walked out on the tide flats, using her walking stick to find
sea urchins between rocks and in tide pools.

When she had filled her net gathering bag, she cracked open
a sea urchin and used her thumbnail to scoop out the orange
eggs. She popped her thumb in her mouth and smiled. The
winter had been long; it was good to have fresh food again.
But now it was time to return to the lodge. Her breasts, full
of milk, ached with the need to nurse Shuku.

"You should have brought Shuku with you," her inside
voice told her. "He would have been no trouble strapped under your suk. Then you could have stayed away from the lodge
and Lemming Tail even longer."

"Shuku was asleep in his cradle," Kiin answered.

Besides, now that he was a year old, he was more difficult
to carry, bouncing against Kiin's back, struggling to free his
arms from Kiin's suk, crying for more than his share of sea
urchin eggs. But Kiin smiled. No mother had a better son, she
thought, and ignored a sudden and painful remembrance of
Takha.

As she walked back through the village, she began to hum
a song, a lullaby sung by First Men mothers. In one moon the
people would leave this winter village to make a salmon camp
on the Walrus People's river. Salmon camp was a good time
of year, with songs and dancing, beach fires and much to eat.
This year she and Lemming Tail might be there alone without
the Raven, but that would not be terrible. They would have
less work to do without his demands.

When she ducked into the lodge's entrance tunnel, she heard
Shuku crying, and she shook her head at Lemming Tail's laziness. How many times in the two moons since Mouse had
been born had Kiin cared for him while Lemming Tail visited
other lodges? How many times had Kiin nursed both babies?
Lemming Tail should do the same, especially since Kiin was
gathering food.

She pulled aside the curtain that divided the lodge, and said,
"You could not feed my son while I was gathering food for
you?"

Lemming Tail sat on the sleeping platform, her legs thrust
out flat before her, her back against the lodge wall. Standing
beside the bed were three of Lemming Tail's brothers. The
men wore furred parkas and leggings. An ivory labret pierced

the skin beneath the eldest brother's lower lip, and its weight drew his face into a grimace. He held a feathered hunting lance, point up, as though it were a walking stick, but the other brothers carried no weapons and stood with their arms folded across their chests.

Lemming Tail smiled at Kiin and reached for the bag of sea urchins, but Kiin slung the bag over her arm and went to Shuku's cradle. He hiccoughed and held his hands out to her, tears like clear beads on his cheeks. Kiin tucked him close, and he laid his head against her neck. "You could not feed him?" Kiin asked again, anger making her words rise into impoliteness. She pulled up her suk and cradled Shuku in both arms so he could suckle.

"I am first wife," Lemming Tail said. "What more should I do than take care of my own son, my husband's son?"

"I was gathering food for us, for you," Kiin answered.

One of Lemming Tail's brothers stepped toward Kiin, but Lemming Tail rose to her knees and reached out to grab his wrist.

"Let me tell her," she said. She turned to Kiin and said, "I have decided you will not stay in this lodge. When my husband returns, you may come back. If he wants you. But remember, my baby is Raven's son. Your baby belongs to a man Raven killed."

Kiin ground her teeth to hold in her anger. "Who told you this?"

Lemming Tail shrugged. "Who does not know that Raven killed your first husband? And you told me yourself that Shuku was your husband's son." Lemming Tail licked her lips and laughed. "You think Raven will raise a son who might someday decide to kill him to avenge his own father's death?"

Kiin looked at the baby in her arms. "My son would not kill the Raven," she said, but even as she said the words, she heard her spirit voice whisper, "How can you answer for your son? You do not know what he will be when he is a man."

Lemming Tail's brothers laughed, and the eldest said, "We will let Raven decide what he wants when he comes back, but now we are here to see that our sister has no problems with you. Take your son and leave."

Kiin shook her head. Lemming Tail must know that a woman alone, without ik or lodge, and with a baby to care for, would soon die. But then Kiin's spirit whispered, "No, Kiin, you know you can go to the Grandmother and the Aunt."

I cannot, Kiin thought, and fear grew hard and brittle in her chest. How could she go to the Grandmother and the Aunt? If she lived in their lodge, her thoughts would soon enter the Aunt's dreams, and then she would know Takha was alive. How could Kiin take that chance?

"The Aunt already knows Takha is alive, Kiin," her spirit said, "and she has done nothing."

"She does not know," Kiin said, and realized she had spoken aloud, that Lemming Tail and her brothers were staring at her. Kiin's embarrassment and her fear suddenly changed to anger. She turned her eyes toward each brother.

They looked away, blinking.

"The Raven will punish you," Kiin said.

The youngest of Lemming Tail's brothers shuffled his feet and looked down, but Lemming Tail said, "What? My husband will punish me because I try to protect him? What more can a wife do than to protect her husband?"

"And if I do not go?" Kiin asked.

"That is why my brothers are here," Lemming Tail said.

Two of the men moved toward Kiin, but she said, "Do not touch me or my son. I will go, but I will take what is mine." She went to the basket corner and took the largest basket, one she had woven herself from split willow root.

"Nothing here is yours except your son," Lemming Tail said.

But the oldest brother looked at his sister and said, "Let her take what is fair. Some of the food, the oil, sleeping furs. What if you are wrong and Raven is angry? Do you want him to know you made her leave with nothing?"

Lemming Tail spat out angry words at her brother, but Kiin turned her back on them. She found a strip of dried seal meat for Shuku to chew on and set him on her sleeping platform, then she filled her basket, taking furs and sealskins, dried fish and meat, needles and awls, carving tools and carvings, and a parka and leggings she had made for herself in the manner of the Walrus People. As she packed, she planned.

For a day or two, she could stay with Shale Thrower or perhaps Ice Hunter and his new wife, but it would not be comfortable. The women would be afraid Kiin was asking for a place in their husband's lodge as second wife.

Then Kiin's inside voice said: "It is time to return to the First Men, to your own people." The thought pushed away all Kiin's anger and even her fear. Return to her own people! The words danced like a song in her mind. But what if the Raven decided to follow her? She must not lead him back to Samiq or to Takha.

Kiin put a large roll of twisted sinew into the basket, closed her ears to Lemming Tail's protests as she took a second roll. Then suddenly her thoughts cleared and she knew what she would do, something so simple that she almost smiled.

Yes, she thought, it is a good time of year for it, when low tide uncovers sea urchins and chitons, when birds will soon lay their eggs. Again joy came to her in a song, but she held back the words and instead strapped the basket to her back, bundled Shuku into his hooded parka and leggings, and adjusted his carrying strap so that he straddled her left hip.

"Our husband will be angry," Kiin told Lemming Tail. Kiin stopped beside the food cache, reached inside to pull out a seal belly of oil and one of dried seal meat. Turning to Lemming Tail's brothers, she said, "It is not a good thing to have a shaman angry with you." Then she picked up her walking stick and left the ulaq.

It was not difficult to find Shale Thrower. Wherever a crowd of women gathered, Shale Thrower would be there, as loud as an auklet on its nest. Kiin did not even have to interrupt, only to walk by, pack on her back, tumpline across her forehead, bag of sea urchins hanging from her arm. Shale Thrower called out to her, asked where she was going.

"My sister wife says I am not welcome in our husband's lodge," Kiin answered, allowing anger to edge her words.

"Where will you stay?" Shale Thrower asked.

"Perhaps Aunt and Grandmother would have a place for you," another woman said.

"I am second wife," said Kiin, "but even a second wife has a place in her husband's lodge. I will go to the River People and find my husband there. When he hears what Lemming Tail has done, she will be the one looking for a place to live, and I will be first wife."

Kiin walked on, hiding a smile as she heard the women's murmurings. "Tell Lemming Tail I take the ik," she called back to them.

She took the ik from the boat racks and tied her oil, basket, and sea urchins inside, then she pushed the ik out into the Walrus People's bay. She tucked Shuku under her suk, secure against her back so he could see out over her shoulder as she paddled. She would not take the ik far, but far enough.

She swung her paddle over the side of the ik, and her spirit whispered, "It will be a long walk."

"It will seem like nothing," Kiin said.

TWENTY-NINE

THE WHALE HUNTERS

Yunaska Island, the Aleutian Chain

KUKUTUX HELD A THIN SLICE OF HALIBUT MEAT over the flame of the oil lamp. Her stomach rolled, and she cut a sliver from the end of the meat, sucked it into her mouth. She closed her eyes as she chewed. What was better than raw fish?

She had saved this slice of halibut meat to eat fresh, but had prepared the rest of the halibut for drying, cutting the meat in a slant against the grain and leaving each piece attached to the skin at one end. She had hung the skin on a rack made of driftwood and sat beside it all day, tending a small smoky fire. Usually she just let the fish dry in the air, without fire or smoke to flavor it, but what else did she have to do now with no husband or son to sew for, no basket grass to cut, no berries yet ripe? Besides, she had to be sure no one took her fish. There were too many hungry children in this village.

She tried not to remember when all the drying racks were full of fish or seal meat, when the children were fat and the women had enough oil, not only for food and fuel, but also to smooth over skin and hair.

Kukutux cut off another piece of fish and popped it into her mouth. Now only Many Babies had oiled hair, and even most of Hard Rock's oil was from hunts long ago. Kukutux had not needed to sit close to Many Babies in her ik to smell the stink of old oil, moldy and rancid, stored too long. But at least they had oil. And Hard Rock had taken a seal only two days ago. Fresh oil, fresh meat.

But why think about Hard Rock? Kukutux asked herself. After today, what chance did she have of becoming his wife? Many Babies would tell Hard Rock about the halibut, and who could hope that there would be any truth in her words? Still, Kukutux told herself, there were other men besides Hard Rock. What about Dying Seal? He was a good man and, some people said, as good a hunter as Hard Rock.

But Dying Seal was in mourning for the woman he had taken as wife soon after the ash had fallen. What greater proof that their village was cursed than the death of White Feet, a young woman, large with Dying Seal's unborn child? Who could explain why one moment she had been laughing, the next clutching hands to her chest? And before night came, she was dead.

Many Babies had cut open the woman's belly, hoping to save the child within, but the baby, too, was dead. Dying Seal had a second wife, an older woman, one who could no longer give him sons, and they had taken all the village children who had been left without father and mother. So although Dying Seal now had only one wife, he had many to feed.

Dying Seal was a big man, with hands twice as large as most men's hands and shoulders twice as wide, though he was not much taller than Kukutux. Yet there was a gentleness in his eyes that made Kukutux smile when she saw him with children. Still, Dying Seal was not a man to have many wives, and more than once she had heard him arguing with other men as they discussed who should take care of the too many women in the village.

Kukutux had heard the crying in Dying Seal's voice as he asked, ''How can a man bear to see his wives without good clothing, without oil to warm the hands and protect the face? How can he come back from hunting with enough only for one and see the wanting in his women's eyes? How can a hunter eat his own share when he has three or four wives, all starving? But if a hunter does not eat, how can he hunt?''

Perhaps, Kukutux thought, when his mourning is over, he will look at me and see that I am thin and will not eat much. Perhaps he will again decide to take a second wife, someone to help with all the children. She took another bite of meat and heard the steps of someone at the top of her ulaq. She looked up at the strip of smoked halibut now hanging from a ulaq rafter and felt a shameful longing to hide the meat. Who in the village had less than she had? Was it right that she should have to share this small amount? But then she remembered the stories her grandmother had told her, of women selfish with food, of hunters who did not give shares of what they took, and how the spirits turned against them, allowing the strongest hunter to grow weak, the sleekest woman to become sickly. So she left the fish where it was and stood, waiting to see who would call down from her smokehole.

But though Kukutux waited, no voice came, until finally she herself called up, inviting the one at the top of the ulaq to come in. When she saw feet and legs, she knew it was Hard Rock. As the man climbed down into her ulaq, Kukutux pushed away frightened thoughts that spun themselves into her mind: that Many Babies had forced Hard Rock to come and ask Kukutux to leave the village, that Hard Rock would take away the portion of halibut she had kept.

Hard Rock stood before her, held hands palm up, so that Kukutux said, "I have meat." She offered the strip of raw halibut she had been eating, but a sinking came into her stomach as she realized that a hunter like Hard Rock would eat that meat and still expect more, perhaps all the halibut she had taken as her share, something she hoped would last her for five, six days of eating.

"Water," Hard Rock said, "only water."

Kukutux, her relief like a song bubbling in her chest, reached up for a seal bladder water container and handed it to him. Hard Rock squatted down, lifted the water container to his lips and drank, then wiped the back of his hand across his mouth and gave the seal bladder back to Kukutux.

He motioned for Kukutux to sit beside him, and she did so. He wore his birdskin suk, the black puffin skins joined with strips of sealskin. Beads cut from the insides of clamshells hung from the high stiff collar edge. Bits of seal esophagus, white from being frozen as it dried, were sewn as decoration in a long line down the front of the suk.

For a moment Kukutux let herself imagine being wife to such a man—a man whose name was known in villages on all the islands of the earth. But then she remembered Many Babies, the anger in the woman's eyes, the lies that floated so easily from her tongue. Better to be alone, Kukutux told herself. Better to live in quietness.

Hard Rock cleared his throat. Kukutux, head bent, eyes on the woven floor mats, waited, and finally, when Hard Rock did not speak, she looked up at him. She did not allow herself to look into his eyes, to show the familiarity that should belong only to wives, but instead watched his mouth, waited for his words.

Finally he said, "You need a husband." His voice was harsh.

"I understand that there are too many women for the men," she said. "I understand that I have neither uncle nor father to speak for me. Even my brother is dead."

Hard Rock stared straight ahead, as though he spoke to the oil lamp rather than Kukutux. "I had once thought to take you for myself as third wife," he said. "But Speaks-like-fire asked me to take his sister and then Fish Eater begged me to take his niece."

Kukutux nodded, but the fact that he had considered her for third or fourth wife made a warmth come into her chest, something that let her forget the stiffness of her left arm, that let her know men still saw her as desirable, not ugly, not lazy.

"All the men have too many wives now," Hard Rock said. "No hunter can feed the women and children he has."

Kukutux looked away, into the corner where she kept her baskets. Why had Hard Rock come to her? To tell her why she was alone, without a husband? Who did not know that? He did not seem angry, and he had not mentioned the halibut, but who could say what Many Babies had told him?

"I caught the halibut today," she said, her face still turned away from Hard Rock, her eyes still on the baskets she had woven before the ash had killed their basket grass.

When Hard Rock said nothing, Kukutux turned back and

looked at him. "I caught the fish," she said again. "I caught it, not Many Babies."

Hard Rock shrugged.

"She claimed the fish," Kukutux said. "She told the men on the beach that she caught it, that I was lying."

"You used her ik?" Hard Rock finally asked.

"Yes. I have no ik. Not since . . . not since . . ."

"You are saving wood to build a frame?"

Kukutux dropped her head. "I was."

"Now you do not?"

"No."

"You are too lazy to do this?"

"Who will build it?" Kukutux asked, suddenly angry. "I have no husband. If I save wood for an ik frame, who will build it? Who will give me sea lion skins for the cover?" The anger of her loss, of Many Babies' lies, and the ache of her belly, empty too long, pushed hard against her words until she spoke as loudly as a man arguing.

"It was Many Babies' ik," Hard Rock said. "She had right to the catcher's share."

Kukutux looked into the man's face. "This is something new?" she asked. "The people of this village have decided that the owner of the ik gets the largest share? Perhaps they made this decision while Many Babies and I were out in the ik. Perhaps they forgot to tell me this when I came ashore with the halibut still on my hook."

She waited, and when Hard Rock gave no answer, Kukutux said, "And does this decision say that the owner of the ik also lies about who caught the fish?"

Then she had no more words, nothing else to say, and she looked into Hard Rock's eyes, braced herself for the anger she thought she would see there. But his eyes were flat, and Kukutux saw nothing in them, not even the image of her own face.

Finally he spoke. His voice was quiet, the words spaced and clipped as though he spoke to one who was only beginning to understand. "There is a man who might take you as wife," he said. "There is a man who thinks you are beautiful. He has no woman of his own and will give a good trade for you. But first he asks only to spend the night, to see what kind of woman you are."

Kukutux's heart squeezed itself so tightly that for a moment she could not speak. Then she said softly, "All our men have wives."

"He is one of the traders," Hard Rock answered.

Kukutux stood, walked away from the man. In rudeness she turned her back on him, in rudeness she crossed her arms over her breasts, stood close to the door of her dead husband's sleeping place. "I am in mourning," she said, throwing her words back over her shoulder as though she threw fish innards to a gull.

"Your husband is dead these many months," Hard Rock said.

Kukutux shrugged. "Can a person put a limit on mourning?" she asked. "Does a wife say, 'One moon, two moons, sorrow will gnaw my heart, then I will dance, then I will sing'? Is that the way of our people? Perhaps that is the way of this trader. What is he? Caribou People?"

She turned and saw that Hard Rock was standing. "He has asked for you. Tonight," he said to Kukutux.

"No man in this village is husband, uncle, or father to me. No man has the right to say what I will do with my nights— who will come into my sleeping place or who will not."

"He has given oil for you."

Kukutux smiled and bent to pull out the one seal belly of oil left in her food cache. "No," she said. "This is my oil. I rendered it from seals taken by my husband. It is all I have, and it is mine. No one has given oil for me."

Hard Rock's face darkened, and Kukutux said, "Tell him I am in the time of my moon blood. Tell him if he comes to me tonight he will curse his man part. Then perhaps he will let you keep the oil."

Hard Rock curled his lips to show his strong white teeth, but though Kukutux's breath quivered in her throat, she did not let herself look away. He stretched his arm out to reach for the fish hanging from the rafters of her ulaq, and Kukutux had to press her lips together to keep from begging him to leave her this small amount of meat. Instead, she took a long breath and said, "If you do not have enough to eat, then take it. I know the pain of an empty belly."

Hard Rock pulled his hand away without taking the fish and climbed up out of the ulaq.

Then Kukutux squatted beside the oil lamp, took the small bit of raw fish left on the mat, and ate it.

THIRTY

THE SEA WAS EMPTY, NO SIGN OF SEALS OR whales, no ruffled water that told of cod swimming. Waxtal lifted his head toward the voice that called him and saw Hard Rock. The man came from one of the smaller ulas in the village. The wind blew against Hard Rock's suk, raising the feathers of its puffin-skin sleeves.

Waxtal felt his own eyes reach toward that suk in wanting. How much could he get for such a suk? Three, four caribou hides if he traded it to the Caribou People. Their women did not know the secrets of sewing birdskins.

Waxtal slid down the side of the ulaq where he, Owl, and Spotted Egg stayed. The ulaq was small but clean, with good oil lamps and fresh crowberry heather on the floors.

Hard Rock motioned for Waxtal to follow him to the lee side of the ulaq. Both men squatted on their heels. Waxtal glanced at Hard Rock, saw that the man's face was flushed, his knuckles white.

"I promised you a woman," Hard Rock said. "She is a young woman, beautiful, without a husband. Perhaps she would come and live in your ulaq to cook and sew, if she got enough pleasure from her night with you."

Waxtal smiled, felt the longing rise again in his loins. A woman without burden of husband, someone who would serve without asking the rights of a wife, what could be better?

But then Hard Rock said, "These next few days she is in moon-blood time." He shrugged.

Waxtal's disappointment was like a rock settling into his belly, but he made himself smile and reached out to clap a hand against Hard Rock's shoulder. "Who can change that?" he asked and laughed. "Women are women."

For a moment Hard Rock's face darkened, but then he, too, smiled, laughed.

"A trade is a trade," Hard Rock said. "I will get her for you when she can come."

"Good," Waxtal said and started to turn away, to climb again to the top of the ulaq so he could watch the sea.

"A trade is a trade," Hard Rock said again. "I will bring you someone else for tonight. You have my harpoon head?" he asked.

"Yes," said Waxtal. He drew the ivory point from a packet at his waist and laid it on the palm of his hand.

"Where is my oil?" Hard Rock asked.

"You have the other harpoon heads?"

Hard Rock reached inside the neck of his suk, drew out a pouch, and handed it to Waxtal.

Waxtal opened the pouch, shook out the harpoon heads. He nodded.

"Three bellies of oil," Hard Rock said.

"Three bellies?" The voice made Hard Rock turn. Owl and Spotted Egg stood behind him. "For that?" Spotted Egg asked.

Waxtal's face burned. "Two bellies," he said to the traders, and then said to Hard Rock, "I have not told them about our trade."

Hard Rock frowned, narrowed his eyes.

"Tomorrow morning," Waxtal said. "I will bring your oil then."

He waited until Hard Rock nodded, until the man turned back toward his own ulaq, then Waxtal strode down toward the beach.

Hard Rock pulled off his suk and threw it down beside Many Babies. She looked up. The end of a sinew thread was softening in her mouth, and she held a birdbone needle in her left hand.

"I talked to Kukutux," Hard Rock said.

"She lies," mumbled Many Babies, the sinew thread clamped between her front teeth. She pulled the thread from her mouth, twisted the wet end, and tied it around her needle. She guided the needle and thread through several awl holes in the sealskin she was sewing. "She lies," Many Babies said again.

"Kukutux caught the fish," Hard Rock said. "Why did you claim it? You have enough to eat. She is starving."

Many Babies set down her sewing and stood up. "I will not have enough to eat if you take her as fifth wife," Many Babies said. "You think you bring in enough with your hunting to feed five women and our children? Your hunting is cursed. It has been cursed since you allowed that Seal Hunter boy to live in this village and learn our secrets."

"What could I do?" Hard Rock said. "I was not chief then, and he was the old man's grandson. Who would believe he had the power to curse us, even in his death?"

"What is done is done," Many Babies said. "But do not make it worse for us by taking another wife."

"If I want her I will take her," Hard Rock said. "Do not tell me who I can or cannot have as wife."

"If you had listened to me before, you would have stood up to the old man. You would have made him send his grandson away." She sat down again and picked up her sewing.

"I have traded you for the night," Hard Rock said. "To the chief trader. He needs a good woman."

Many Babies looked up at Hard Rock, opened her mouth to speak. Slowly Hard Rock pulled his hunter's knife from its arm sheath, slowly he tapped it against his fingers. "Do not tell me no," he said.

Many Babies tilted her head, lowered her eyelids, and stared at him from slitted eyes. "Good," she said. "I will be glad to go. It has been a long time since I had a man between my legs."

Waxtal scooped up a handful of stones from the beach and threw them at the gulls fighting over a rotting fish at the high-tide line. They skittered away, screeching, then circled and settled again on the beach.

"Where are the harpoon heads?" Owl asked.

Waxtal turned and handed him the pouch.

"Two of them are broken!" Spotted Egg said. He looked down his long nose at Owl and said, "He traded three seal bellies of oil for broken harpoon heads. He ate our food all winter and now he does this to repay us."

''Two bellies of oil,'' Waxtal said and stooped to pick up more stones. He looked from the corners of his eyes at Owl. Owl seldom spoke, but sometimes during the winter when food was scarce, Owl had been the one who stood up for Waxtal, the one who pointed out Waxtal's strengths when Spotted Egg could only criticize. But Owl only shook his head.

''Who will want them?'' said Spotted Egg and threw the harpoon heads to the ground.

''Hard Rock probably promised him a woman,'' said Owl.

Waxtal's face burned. ''I did not ask for a woman,'' he said. He turned toward the water, then, looking back over his shoulder, said to Owl, ''You and your brother, you have had women each night since we came. I have been carving— speaking to spirits and carving—while you have been playing. How much of our trade goods have you given for those women? How many necklaces? How much oil? And for something you will not get back, something that you cannot trade to someone else.''

Waxtal held up the largest harpoon heads. ''Look, think about this,'' he said. ''It is a Whale Hunter harpoon head.'' He pressed his thumb against a broken barb. ''It has been used to hunt whales. What men have more power than those who hunt whales? You think I am foolish enough to believe that men will want this for a weapon? What is a weapon worth? An otter skin for a crooked knife. Two bellies of oil for a hunter's knife.'' He turned and held the harpoon head toward the sea, looked out toward the east where night had begun to gray the edge of the horizon. ''It is not a weapon; it is an amulet. It is power. What will a man give for power? His very soul.''

Waxtal lowered his head, but remained standing with his back to Owl and Spotted Egg. For a long time there was no noise but birds and waves, the occasional rise of a woman's voice coming from the outside cooking hearths near the ulas.

Finally Spotted Egg said, ''These people have no power. They are cursed.''

''You do not know what they were,'' Waxtal said. He turned and looked at Spotted Egg, at Owl, who was squatting on his heels. ''You do not know what they were, and those people we trade with this summer, those people out there in villages far from here''—he smiled and shook his head—

"they do not know what the Whale Hunters have become."
He moved to stand beside Spotted Egg, leaned so his face was
close to Spotted Egg's face. "Do they?" Waxtal said, his
words nearly a whisper.

"You want us to offer curses?" Spotted Egg asked, his
voice also a whisper, but edged with anger, so that Waxtal
could feel a spray of spit coming from the man's mouth.

"The oil Waxtal traded was his," said Owl. "He killed the
seals; he rendered the oil."

Spotted Egg looked at his brother, snorted. "Everything
Waxtal has is ours. He would be dead if we had not found
him."

"Perhaps I would be dead," Waxtal said. "Perhaps the oil
is yours, but you have no claim on my carvings. I have traded
for them in the world of spirits, and you have never been
there."

"Do not tell me about your spirit powers," said Spotted
Egg. "If you have such great powers, why did you bring us
here to this cursed village?"

Waxtal opened his mouth to speak, but Owl stood up, put
one hand on Waxtal's arm. "Be still, say nothing," he said,
moving his head to point toward the ulas.

Waxtal looked and saw Hard Rock walking toward them.
Spotted Egg nodded and raised his hands in greeting.

"I have a woman for you," Hard Rock said.

Slowly Owl looked at Waxtal; slowly he turned away.
"You did not ask for a woman," he whispered, and he
laughed, a soft laugh, but cold, like wind over ice.

Spotted Egg also laughed, anger in the laughter, and Hard
Rock raised his eyebrows at Waxtal.

Waxtal's hands were suddenly too cold, his face too hot.
"I did not ask for a woman," he said, saying the words loud
enough so that Owl and Spotted Egg would hear as they
walked away.

For a moment, Hard Rock turned to watch the brothers.
"They are angry," he said.

Waxtal snorted.

"They have had women every night," Hard Rock said, his
voice rising with the words as though he asked a question.

"They are boys," Waxtal said. "They cannot see beyond
the curse of this village to the power that lies within."

Hard Rock's lips closed over his teeth, and the muscles of his jaw tightened.

"But I know what is true," Waxtal continued. "I will be glad to have your woman for the night. It will be the last time I have a woman for many nights. I must go up into the hills, speak to the spirits. I have carving to do."

"Yes, I had forgotten," Hard Rock said. "You carve."

"Bring the woman to my ulaq and I will show you my work," Waxtal said.

Hard Rock nodded, then turned and walked back toward the ulas.

THIRTY-ONE

Goodnews Bay, Alaska

KIIN PADDLED NORTH TO THE LARGE BAY LESS than a day's travel from the Walrus People's village. There the water was calm, and she skirted the shore to the river that flowed into the back of the bay. She positioned Lemming Tail's ik parallel to the shore and climbed out, then pulled the boat up on the dark silty sand of the tide flats. Each summer the Walrus People made their salmon camp above the mouth of the river. Circles, dug a handlength into the ground and edged with stones, marked where they pitched their walrus skin tents.

The ground was still wet from recently melted winter snow, but she could cut grass and make a thick pad to protect their bedding skins, then haul the ik up from the tide flats and tie it in place so she and Shuku could sleep under it that night.

She took her supply basket from the ik and carried it to the high slanting beach that stretched up from the tide flats, then pulled Shuku from his carrying sling, took off his leggings and the sealskin wastecloth, and set him down on his short, strong legs. He stood for a moment, then sat down hard. Kiin watched as he pushed himself up to his hands and feet, then slowly stood erect, took three steps, and fell again. His mouth curled down in a quivering frown, but Kiin clapped her hands and praised him, then pointed up at a gull that was circling them. Shuku smiled, the slow half-smile of his father Amgigh. Kiin's chest tightened with a sudden stab of pain, but she closed her mind to her sorrow, picked up Shuku, and went back to the ik. She set Shuku inside, then grabbed the bow of the ik and pulled, thrusting her weight against it until it was high up in the ryegrass beyond the beach.

Using the woman's knife she wore in a packet at her waist, Kiin cut a handful of grass and carried it back to where she had left Shuku's clothes. She used the grass to wipe Shuku's bottom and legs, then cleaned the sealskin wastecloth. She rinsed the sealskin in the river and wrapped it around her suk sleeve to dry, tying it in place with a length of kelp twine. She pulled a dry sealskin strip from her carrying basket, rolled it between her palms to soften it, padded it with fireweed fluff from her storage basket, and wrapped it around Shuku, then put his footed leggings back on. He fussed and kicked against the leggings, but stopped when Kiin slipped him under her suk. He pushed himself up to her left breast and sucked the nipple into his mouth.

Kiin squatted down and looked out at the sea. She had been fortunate. The winds had been gentle as she paddled, but the day in Lemming Tail's ik had made her realize how difficult it would be to return to the First Men.

The earth, her people said, was mother, the sky father, but both were so immense, and she and Shuku were so small.

She thought back to the many evenings during the past winter when the Raven had spoken to White Fox and Bird Sings about their journey to the River People village.

Sometimes, the Raven burned a willow stick into a charred point and used it to draw an outline of the land—beaches, bays, and rivers—from the Walrus People's bay to the River People's village. Always, he included the salmon camp bay— a good place to stop, coming and going, between the Walrus and River villages. Each time he had done this, Kiin found some reason to come from her corner and offer water or food, so she had opportunity to see what the Raven drew.

Now, holding Shuku in one arm, she stood and walked to-

ward the beach. She stopped at the edge of the sand, pulled
up a stem of grass, and, crouching down, used the hard stalk
to draw the point of land that extended from the River People's
village out into the North Sea. She drew in the land that separated the Walrus People's small bay from the River People's
village, and then drew the bay where she was now.

From this beach, she would turn south. Mountains pushed
down close to the bay, but she could follow river valleys and
cut behind the Walrus People's village. Then she would follow
the seashore south and west to the Traders' Beach. She hoped
the day's travel in the ik—going north, away from the Traders'
Beach—would be worth the time spent, making the Raven and
the Walrus People truly believe she was traveling to the River
People's village.

Kiin sighed and stood up. The drawing helped. For some
reason, now the sky and sea seemed smaller, her journey not
so frightening. She gathered the few bits of driftwood that
were scattered above the high-tide mark, then carried the wood
to the salmon camp and piled it into a circle of blackened
stones, the hearth where the women prepared food for everyone in the camp. She went back for her storage basket and the
seal stomach of oil, brought them both to the camp. She dug
into her storage basket, found the bundle of fireweed fluff she
used for Shuku, and pulled out a handful. She wiped the fluff
over the sides of the seal-stomach oil container, then took her
firestones from their pouch at her waist. She wedged the oily
fluff between two of the driest pieces of wood and snapped
the stones together until a spark caught in the fluff. She blew
gently on the fire, coaxing it into the wood, sighing her relief
when the wood caught.

The heat of the flames tightened the skin on her face, and
she lifted her suk so Shuku could feel the warmth. She was
tired and wanted to rest, but she must first think about food.

She did not want to waste a day fishing, so decided to make
traps for pogy and cod by carrying rocks from the river and
stacking them into piles curved to hold small pools of water
that would trap fish as the tide went out. At the next low tide,
she would spear the fish with her walking-stick spear, cut two
flat strips of meat from each fish, and tie the meat to the outside of her carrying basket where the fish would dry as she
walked.

Shuku wiggled one hand from Kiin's suk and reached toward the fire. "No, Shuku," Kiin said and caught his fingers in hers. "Hot. It is hot." She stood and turned her back to the fire, pointed out toward the water. "See, Shuku," she said. "High tide will come tonight, but now we must build fish traps. In the morning, we will gather and clean fish, then begin our journey. It will be a long walk, but we are strong, Shuku."

Shuku babbled—his words in the language of babies, something understood only by spirits—and Kiin smiled. Almost she let herself think of Takha, wonder about the sound of his voice. But a darkness on the water suddenly drew her thoughts back to the salmon camp bay. An ikyak? Someone— perhaps Ice Hunter—looking for her? She sucked in her breath, then realized it was only a harbor seal.

She scanned the bay, studying each break in the ruffled surface of the water. If someone were following, she told herself, he would have caught her by now. A hunter's ikyak was much quicker than a woman's fishing ik, and almost any man in the village was a stronger paddler than she was. Even so, this journey would be much easier if she used the ik. With the ik, in less than a moon she would be at the Traders' Beach. But the Raven would look for her there first, and what would happen to Samiq, to Shuku and Takha, if he found her with her people?

"We must leave the ik," she said to Shuku, and squatted down on her haunches, her back warming in the heat of the hearth fire. "It is the only way we can be safe. By the time we get back to our people, the trading season will be over, and we will have the long winter together with your father to decide what to do about the Raven.

"If we are lucky, the Raven will find our ik here and think we have drowned."

She stood and used the butt end of her walking-stick spear to stir the fire, but a strong gust of wind blew in from the bay, and the flames pulled back into themselves, flattening against the char of the wood. Kiin slipped her suk down over Shuku and shielded the fire with her body. When the wind calmed, she went back to drag the ik to the camp. Staked beside the fire, it would keep her and Shuku dry and warm, and protect the flames against the wind.

By the time Kiin returned with the ik, the fire had burned

some of the driftwood into coals, and she banked sand over them, smothering the flames until only a few sparks remained. It would be best to save the wood until night. Now she must find rocks and make fish traps while the tide was out. She took Shuku from her suk where he had nursed himself into sleep. She laid him in the curl of the ik's hull, bundling a warm fur seal pelt around him, then wrapped him with a kelp line, arms to his sides, as though he were bound into a cradle.

She walked the beach, gathering as many stones as she could carry, then clustered them around boulders sunk deep in the sand. As she worked, Kiin lifted her voice to any spirits, asking that the pull of waves and tide would not take the stones, at least until the next storm. She made three traps, curved enclosures that would hold the fish long enough for her to spear them during the next ebb tide. Then she went back to Shuku. He was still asleep. She squatted beside him, picked up the bag of sea urchins she had gathered early that morning on the Walrus beach, and cracked one open.

The urchin eggs were good, filling her mouth with a rich fishy taste. She closed her eyes as she sucked her thumbnail clean. Yes, she thought, I did the right thing for Shuku and for me. It will not be an easy walk, but we will get back to our own people.

This time she promised herself she would not be afraid to tell Samiq what she wanted—to be his wife, second to Three Fish, but still his wife. What would be better than to spend days preparing food for Samiq, evenings sewing his parkas and chigadax? What would be better than nights spent with his arms close around her? What would be better than to carry his sons under her heart?

Kiin awoke to the scolding of gulls on the beach, the chattering of teal on the river. She glanced at the sky and saw that the sun was already above the horizon. She had slept longer than she had meant to, and she bit her lips as she looked out over the tide flats. The water had risen to ankle depth, and she knew some of the fish might have escaped from her traps.

"Less food for the journey," she said, the words a sigh that blended with the wind.

She stood and untied the ik, then flipped it upright. She reached for Shuku in the warmth under her suk, felt the sudden pop of his mouth as she pulled him from her breast. She ignored his cries as she set him into the ik. The sides were high enough to keep him from crawling out. She would change his sealskin wastecloth later. Now it was more important to catch fish. She picked up her walking-stick spear and a large carrying net from her supply basket and ran out onto the tide flats. A cod flipped in the shallow water behind the closest stone weir. She speared it and slipped it into her carrying net, then went on to the next trap. Four fish there. All pogy. There was one large cod in the third trap. The fish was too long to fit into her carrying net, so she left it on her spear and walked back to Shuku. He had stopped crying and sat with his thumb in his mouth watching her as she walked. When she came close, he began to cry again.

Kiin crouched beside him and slipped her hand over his mouth, using her thumb to pinch his nose shut. He stopped crying and she removed her hand. "Shuku, do not cry," she said. "If you cry, someone will hear. Maybe wolves. Maybe some spirit. Be quiet, Shuku, be quiet."

Shuku listened, but when Kiin was finished talking, he pulled his face down into a frown and began to cry again. Once more Kiin clamped her hand over his mouth and Shuku stopped. Kiin pulled her hand away and picked him up. "Ah, you are a brave boy, Shuku," she murmured as she held the baby close. "You are brave. No wolves will hear us."

She set Shuku back inside the ik and split open one of the pogies. With the curved blade of her woman's knife, she removed the innards, leaving the firm green flesh under its tent of bones. She slipped the innards into a clean clamshell, tied the shell halves together with a sinew line, then slipped the shell back into her basket. She would use the innards for bait tomorrow or the next day. She looked down at Shuku, at the clean trails his tears had left across his face. His breath came in shuddering jerks, but he did not cry.

"Ah, Shuku," she said. "You are a good boy, already learning to be a man." She picked up the pogy and used her thumbnail to pop out its eyes, then pressed them into Shuku's mouth. Shuku's lips quivered into a smile, and Kiin let herself laugh. What child did not like fish eyes? A bubbling of joy began to grow next to her heart. It was good to be able to give

Shuku treats without having Lemming Tail demand a portion for herself.

Kiin wrapped the fish in grass and laid it over the warm coals of her night fire. While the fish cooked, she repacked her supplies in the large basket, filleted all but one of the other fish, then tied the strips of meat to the outside of the basket.

For a moment she allowed herself to sit beside the coals, to smell the fish cooking, then she stood, took her spear and woman's knife, and went over to Lemming Tail's ik. She let her eyes follow the ik's smooth cedar ribs, the kelp lashings that bound each joint, the oiled split walrus hide covering. It was a good ik, watertight and easily balanced, light enough for two women to lift.

She picked up Shuku and slung him in his carrying strap, his legs straddling her left hip. She looked up into the sky, at the clouds moving in a gray line to cover the sun, as the tide moves to cover a beach.

Perhaps clouds are like the tide, Kiin thought, and perhaps the spirits who live at the Dancing Lights understand the clouds, use them in their fishing as easily as people on the earth use the tides.

She looked down again at Lemming Tail's ik and felt its spirit hovering.

She raised her spear to slash the hide cover, but stopped when her inner voice said, "Leave it, Kiin. It has a spirit, as all iks do. Who can say what that spirit will do to you if you destroy the ik?"

"Qakan destroyed our mother's ik," Kiin answered.

Her spirit moaned, its voice like the voice of someone afraid. "And remember what happened to Qakan," her spirit said. "Even now his bones lie on the Traders' Beach protected only by the rocks you heaped over him. The Raven cursed him, and his spirit cannot fly to the Dancing Lights. What will he do when your mother dies and there is no one to remember him?"

"I cannot leave the ik here," Kiin said aloud, speaking to her spirit as she would speak to another person. "What would the Raven think if he comes to the salmon camp and finds the ik, whole, without damage?"

Would he suspect she had gone back to her own people?

Would he go to the Traders' Beach, find her and Shuku and Takha, kill Samiq?

She raised her spear again, then remembered that if the ik were destroyed on rocks, the rock would break through from the bottom. She turned the ik over and, closing her mind to her spirit voice, thrust her spear through the walrus hide, then used her woman's knife to enlarge the tear. "I release your spirit," she said to the ik. "I release your spirit. Stay here until the Raven comes. Stay here and call him to this beach. Make him believe that I and my son Shuku are dead. Then go with the wind to my people the First Men. Tell them I am coming. Go there and wait for me. When I come I will build you another ik. I will decorate it with sacred things—shells and puffin feathers, seal teeth and all things beautiful. I will honor you, and you and I will be together as long as my body lives. And when I die, I will ask that you be buried with me so I can take you to the Dancing Lights."

Then Kiin dragged the ik down to the edge of the high-tide mark, settled it into the beach grass. She walked the beach until she found a rock, something heavy, but not too heavy to carry. She brought it back to the ik, lifted it above the ik's center thwart, and dropped it again and again until the thwart splintered. She took one of the necklaces the Raven had given her and used her knife to cut the sinew thread that held the beads together. She rubbed the necklace in the sand, slipping most of the beads from the cord, scattering them over the tide flats, then wrapped what was left of the necklace around the broken thwart. She stood over the boat, trying to put herself into the Raven's mind, trying to decide what he would think when he saw the ik.

She carried the stone back to its place on the beach and went to her supply basket. She pulled her amulet from her neck, ignoring the shiver that moved down her arms when its familiar weight was no longer against her chest. Working quickly, she used the pouch as a pattern and cut another from a piece of sealskin, punched awl holes along both sides, and sewed up one side with sinew thread, leaving the other open. She put a black stone and several shells she found on the beach into the pouch, then took it to the ik, wedged it under some of the bow lashings. She pulled long strands of hair from her head, twisted them into the splintered ends of the broken thwart, then took out her woman's knife, raised her left hand, and made a cut on the inside of her left arm. She bent over the ik, letting her blood drip against the walrus hide, over the amulet pouch, over the shell beads of her necklace. Then, kneeling in the sand, she prayed to any spirit listening, "Protect me, protect Shuku. Do not let the Raven know what I have done."

THIRTY-TWO

THE WHALE HUNTERS

Yunaska Island, the Aleutian Chain

WAXTAL STROKED THE WALRUS TUSK. HE HAD never done better work. He ran his fingers over the incised people and animals, moving his hands lightly, as though he were touching a woman. Even with that gentle touch, he felt the power of the ivory reach through his hands, and it burned as though he held his fingers near smoldering coals. He sighed and closed his eyes, felt a surge of blood strengthen his man part. He lay one hand on the walrus tusk, rubbed it as though it were a part of himself.

"Those fools," he said aloud, thinking of Owl and Spotted Egg. "They do not begin to understand the power of my carvings. And they do not begin to understand the power the Whale Hunters still have."

A voice seemed to answer him. Waxtal shook his head. He was alone in the ulaq, but perhaps it was some spirit brought by the power of the walrus tusk carvings. Waxtal's heart quickened, and he stood, straightening his grass aprons. He stroked his hands through his hair and over his long chin whiskers. The voice called again, and Waxtal realized that it came from the ulaq roof. Waxtal looked up.

It was Hard Rock.

Disappointment brought anger, and Waxtal squatted down again beside the walrus tusk, his back toward the climbing log. Then he remembered the woman Hard Rock had promised him. Good, he thought. There are times for spirits and there are times for women. "I am here," he called out.

As Hard Rock climbed down the log into the ulaq, Waxtal pulled his carving knife from a pouch at his waist, leaned over to make a line on the tusk.

Let him know he has interrupted my work, Waxtal thought. Let him know I have more to think about than a woman coming to my bed.

Waxtal looked back over his shoulder and frowned. The woman with Hard Rock was Many Babies. She was old and she was loud, but Waxtal did not let his displeasure show in his eyes. It was an honor to be offered Hard Rock's first wife.

Many Babies made slow eyes at him, then opened her mouth to touch her tongue to her top lip. Waxtal could see that she had once been a beautiful woman. Even under the loose lines of her suk he could see the wide curves of her hips, the bulge of her breasts.

Hard Rock stood beside his wife. The man kept his eyes on Waxtal, his head turned as though he did not even see the woman at his side. "This is your carving," he said. He walked over to Waxtal, squatted on his haunches.

"Yes."

Hard Rock reached to touch the tusk, but drew his hand back when Waxtal hissed. The man looked at Waxtal, brows drawn together, lips pressed into a firm line.

"It has a spirit," Waxtal said. "It is . . . it is alive."

"How do you know what to carve?" Hard Rock asked and crossed his arms over his chest.

Waxtal narrowed his eyes, thought for a moment. There was always danger in telling too much.

"It is a story," Waxtal finally said. "It tells what has happened to my people." With the tip of his carving knife, he pointed at a series of crosshatchings on the base of the tusk. "This is a far beach, east and south of here, close to the ice walls that mark the edge of the earth. Next you see the waves that destroyed our village." He pointed to a series of wide slashing lines rising up over circles that were a group of ulas.

''Here is where we take our ikyan and travel to the beach of the old man, the shaman carver.''

Hard Rock nodded.

''Here we trade with our brothers the Whale Hunters, and this is the battle with the Short Ones. This man is you.'' Waxtal laid the blade of his knife against one of the man figures, larger than the others, a man gripping a lance in each hand.

Hard Rock leaned close to study the carving, and Waxtal raised his hand to cover his smile. Why tell Hard Rock the truth, that the man carved was Waxtal, that the story told was Waxtal's story?

Many Babies leaned over her husband to look at the tusk. She smacked her lips together and asked, ''Do you pleasure women as well as you carve?''

She reached out to stroke Waxtal's hair, laughed, and curled her fingers around his ear. Hard Rock rose to his feet and pulled her arm away from Waxtal.

''I am sorry to make such a poor trade for your oil,'' he said to Waxtal. ''Perhaps you will find pleasure in the fact that she is my first wife. If not, choose any woman you want in the village. I will bring her to you.'' Without looking back at either Waxtal or Many Babies, Hard Rock climbed from the ulaq.

Waxtal leaned over the walrus tusk, used his knife to shave out a line on the yellow ivory. Many Babies knelt beside him. She moved her hands slowly up under his suk, stroking the insides of his legs. Waxtal's man part hardened, but still he kept his eyes and hands on the ivory. Let the woman wait.

A woman must understand that there are things more important to a man than she is. Tonight he must carve.

Soon Many Babies' hands were squeezing, rubbing. Waxtal's fingers grew cold, and he knew his spirit had left his hands to find joy between his legs. He sighed and set down his knife. Sometimes he had to think of others before he thought of himself. What woman, seeing this tusk, would not want him, even for one short night? What woman would not want the chance to carry his child?

He turned and pulled off Many Babies' suk, then laid her back on the floor mats. She opened her legs, and again he sighed. Why refuse the woman? There would be time again to carve. Besides, he did not want to insult Hard Rock.

THIRTY-THREE

THE WOMAN'S SNORES WOKE WAXTAL. HE groaned and shifted on the sleeping robes. If she had been his wife, he would have kicked her awake and made her move to her own sleeping place, but a trader cannot kick the alanana-sika's wife. He nudged her and pushed her slowly to her side. She snorted and for a moment was silent, then started snoring again.

Waxtal moved as far from her as he could, close to the curtained door that led into the ulaq's main room. Through the grass curtain's rough weave he could see the glow of an oil lamp. He squeezed his eyes closed, then heard the voices—Owl and Spotted Egg, their words nearly whispered.

Waxtal shook his head. Let them spend half the night talking. They passed their days in bed with one woman or another. He had better things to do. How could a man greet the sun with the Whale Hunters if he was awake all night talking? Besides, tomorrow he must seek a place in the hills to meditate and fast and speak to the spirits. What did Owl and Spotted Egg know about things of the spirit? They thought only of their bellies and their loins.

He yawned, then heard Spotted Egg say, "Leave him!"

Owl answered, but Waxtal could not make out his words. Waxtal sat up, leaned closer to the sleeping curtain. The men were still talking, speaking in the low quick speech of the Caribou People, but Waxtal had learned the language well during the winter he had spent with Owl and Spotted Egg.

Owl was usually easier to understand, because he talked more slowly than his brother. But though Owl spoke now, Many Babies' snores were too loud for Waxtal to hear what the man said. Waxtal scooted across the sleeping place to Many Babies' side and covered her mouth and nose with his hand. She jerked her head and pushed his hand away.

151

"Many Babies," Waxtal whispered. "Many Babies, sh-h-h-h. Be quiet."

The woman rose up on both elbows. "What?" she asked.

Waxtal pressed his fingertips against her lips. "Sh-h-h-h," he said. "You were crying in your sleep. It was a dream. Be quiet. Be still. You are safe."

She snuggled against Waxtal and reached between his legs, but Waxtal pushed her hands away. "Go back to sleep," he said, but hoped she would not sleep—at least until he heard what Owl and Spotted Egg were saying about him. Many Babies lay down, and Waxtal went back to his place beside the curtain.

He held his breath and waited. There was nothing, silence. He sighed. The men had probably gone into their sleeping places. Waxtal settled against the earthen ulaq wall. There was a chance Owl and Spotted Egg were eating and would talk more later. Best to wait. He had all night to sleep.

After a time Owl cleared his throat, and Waxtal smiled. He had been right.

"So we leave him," Owl said. "What then? The Whale Hunters will not want him. He is lazy and cannot hunt. Hard Rock will be angry with us, and we will not be able to come back here to trade again."

"You want to trade with these Whale Hunters?" Spotted Egg asked. "Already the curse of this place has sunk into my bones. We have stayed too long. I do not want to come back. What do we have to show for our time here? A few seal bellies of old whale oil. We have given more than that for their women."

"Waxtal has harpoon heads."

"Four, for three bellies of oil."

Again there was silence.

"So when?" Owl finally asked.

"Tomorrow. Waxtal has said he will go into the hills to fast. What better time to leave?"

"And if the Whale Hunters try to stop us?"

"Why should they? They do not need our mouths to feed."

"What about Waxtal's ikyak? Should we take it?"

"We would need more than the two of us to handle both ik and ikyak over a long journey. It is many days' travel to the next village."

''What about the tusks?''

Again silence, then Waxtal heard laughter, low, quiet.

''He has eaten several tusks' worth of food since he came to us.''

''I will take those harpoon heads, too. In many ways the old man is a fool, but he knows something about trading.''

''He says the River People will give two women for one harpoon head.''

''I would be content with one woman.''

Waxtal lay back against the soft furs that covered the floor of the sleeping place. So Owl and Spotted Egg thought they would take his things and leave him. Laughter moved silently under his ribs.

Waxtal waited until he heard Owl and Spotted Egg go into their sleeping places. He waited until he heard their breathing turn into the long softness of sleep. Then he crept to the packs the men kept hidden in the back of the food cache. Most of their trade goods were there. Only their weapons, their necklaces, several bellies of whale oil, and a few baskets of dried berries were in their sleeping places. The rest—oil, hides, furs, dried meat—was bundled in their caribou skin trader's packs in the cache.

Waxtal pulled out Spotted Egg's packs, then Owl's. He took almost everything from the cache and four of the water bladders that hung from the rafters. He brought his own weapons and his pack of carving tools from his sleeping place, then picked up a sealskin mat from the floor and laid it over the oil lamp until the flame drowned itself in the oil. In the darkness he hauled everything to the top of the ulaq. As he worked, he whispered prayers and promises to spirits, begging them to keep Owl and Spotted Egg asleep, to block their ears.

Finally he had only his tusks, one carved, one plain. He carried them up, then took everything to his ikyak. He packed bow and stern with the supplies and trade goods, pausing once to pull a string of shell beads from one of Owl's packs and drape the beads around his neck. He tied everything in so it would not shift, and balanced the load, side to side, fore and aft. He finally had to leave six seal bellies of oil on the beach—those and the traders' now empty packs.

It was dark, the black center of night. The tide was high,

so it would be easier, Waxtal hoped, to launch his ikyak and avoid the rocks that reached up from the seafloor. He carried two of the bellies of oil to Hard Rock's ulaq, called down softly from the roof hole. One of Hard Rock's wives came into the central ulaq room. An oil lamp burned, throwing the woman's shadow, long and dark, against the ulaq walls.

Waxtal could not remember her name. She had spent several nights with Spotted Egg; he remembered that, but nothing else. "I must speak with Hard Rock," Waxtal said.

"Who are you?" the woman asked. She moved to stand near the waist-high boulder, flattened and hollowed out on top, that was the ulaq's main oil lamp.

"Waxtal, the trader."

She hesitated. "Hard Rock is asleep," she finally said.

"I have oil for him, to pay for a trade we made. I have given promises to spirits and must go now, and fast. I want Hard Rock to have the oil before I leave."

The lamp lit the woman's head from the chin up and threw shadows across her eyes so that her face looked like a mask made to call spirits.

"Wait," she said. "I will get him."

Waxtal waited until the woman went to Hard Rock's sleeping place, then sat on the edge of the roof hole so that his feet hung down into the ulaq. He wrapped his arms around one of the seal bellies and began to descend the climbing log.

He set the belly of oil on the floor and went up for the other. He was still at the top of the climbing log when he felt a hand clasp his ankle.

"Waxtal?" Hard Rock's voice.

"Yes."

"Good. You have brought my oil?"

"Yes. I want you to have it before I go speak to the spirits."

"Good," Hard Rock said again. He reached up and took the belly of oil from Waxtal's arms.

"Can you eat before you go?"

Waxtal looked up toward the sky. It was still dark. "Yes," he said.

Hard Rock went to the food cache and pulled out dried meat and oil. He handed a fistful of the meat to Waxtal. "Where do you plan to go?"

Waxtal bit into the meat, chewed. "That is something the spirits will decide."

"You will come back?"

Waxtal shrugged. "I have had enough of Owl and Spotted Egg. Tell them to go on without me."

"They do not know you are going?"

"They know, but they had planned to wait for me. Tell them not to wait."

"I will tell them."

Waxtal folded a strip of dried meat and stuck it between jaw and gum where it would soften in the damp of his mouth. He spoke over the bulge of his cheek. "I have been glad to trade with you. I hope to come back, but perhaps it will be another year. Watch for me in the summers."

Hard Rock reached out, slapped a hand to Waxtal's shoulder. "I will watch for you."

Waxtal walked to the climbing log, then turned. He reached down into his suk and pulled out Owl's shell bead necklace. "You trained your woman well," Waxtal said. "Give this to her for me."

Hard Rock took the necklace. "She trained me," he said, and began to laugh. His laughter followed Waxtal up out of the ulaq, into the dark of the short night.

THIRTY-FOUR

OWL STRETCHED AND SCRATCHED HIS BELLY. "For a man who has not had a woman all winter, he did not make much noise last night," he said to Spotted Egg and nodded toward Waxtal's sleeping place.

"They are both old," Spotted Egg said. He laughed, a thin wheeze that came from the bridge of his nose. "Perhaps all he wanted was to sleep. Either way, he does not deserve a woman after the trade he made with Hard Rock. Three seal bellies of oil for four broken harpoon heads."

"Two seal bellies."

"So he says. He lied about the woman, why not the oil?"

"We should never have brought him with us. Then we would not have come to this cursed island. We would be at a Seal Hunter village, enjoying fat women and fresh meat."

Spotted Egg dipped his finger into the oil lamp, licked the seal oil from his hand. Owl made a face. "It is rancid," he said. "I can smell it from here."

Spotted Egg shrugged. He went to the food cache and pulled aside its curtain, rubbing the coarsely woven grass as he did so. "These Whale Hunter women cannot weave," he said.

"What is that to us?" asked Owl. He had taken his parka from a peg on the wall and was running his thumb along the stitches, smashing the gray-bodied fleas that had pushed their way into the valley of each seam. "We get mats from the Seal Hunter women. We get fleas from the Whale Hunters."

Spotted Egg, squatting on his haunches, reached into the cache, made a mumbled exclamation, and sat down hard on the floor.

"What?" Owl asked, looking up from the parka.

"It is almost empty," Spotted Egg said in a small voice.

"What?"

"Look." Spotted Egg held aside the curtain.

Owl strode across the ulaq floor, bunched the curtain into one hand, and ripped it from its pegs. He reached into the cache and pulled out a partially full sea lion belly of oil, a flattened water bladder, and one sealskin of dried fish.

"Everything is gone except what was here when we came," Spotted Egg said.

Owl went to Waxtal's sleeping place and also ripped that curtain from its pegs. Many Babies screamed and sat up, clutching at mats and sleeping furs.

"Where is Waxtal?" Owl asked her.

The woman's words came out in a rush, tumbling over one another. Owl finally crawled into the sleeping place, grabbed her arms, and pulled her to her feet.

"Speak slowly, woman. How do you expect me to understand your foolish language if you do not speak slowly?"

Many Babies jerked away from him and scrambled across the sleeping place. She picked up her otter suk, then, gathering in a long breath, rushed past Owl and out into the center of the ulaq. She looked around, then said to Spotted Egg, "Where is Waxtal?"

"That is what my brother asked you," Spotted Egg said. He kicked at the sealskin of dried fish. "Everything that was in the cache is gone—our trade packs, our food, our oil. There is nothing left but what your husband gave us when we came to this ulaq."

"Why should I know where Waxtal is?" Many Babies asked. "I was his for the night—as my husband the alananasika asked. That is all." She pulled on her suk. It bunched in thick folds over her breasts, and she jerked it down.

"You did not see him leave?"

"I was asleep."

Owl grabbed her shoulders, but Many Babies jammed her knee into his groin. Owl doubled over and sank slowly to the floor. Many Babies ran to the climbing log. "My husband will kill you if you touch me!" she screamed back at him.

Spotted Egg raised a fist. "Tell your husband this is what I think of Whale Hunters." Then he went to Owl, crouched beside him.

"I am not hurt," Owl said through gritted teeth.

Spotted Egg shook his head, picked up his parka, put it on, and climbed the log to the top of the ulaq. "I go to the beach to see if Waxtal left us our ik," he called back to Owl. "Come when you can."

Waxtal settled himself on the fur seal pelt and held his hands over the small flame of his hunter's lamp. The walrus tusk incised with his carvings lay on his right side, the plain tusk on his left. He was on a small island east of the Whale Hunters' island, and had found a ledge on the side of the mountain that rose above the beach where he had left his ikyak. He made a camp there, choosing a site where he could watch the sea as he sat on his fur seal pelt. The wind blew in from the water, cold and wet, biting deep into his bones.

He had worn his First Men feather suk, and so stood up, stepped forward to stand with the lamp between his legs, then hunched down so the bottom edges of the suk touched the ground. Heat from the lamp enveloped his legs. His skin prickled up into bumps, and he closed his eyes as the warmth spread to his belly and chest.

When he moved back to sit on the fur seal pelt, he began a chant, praise words that he hoped would please any nearby spirits. In the cold, his lips were stiff, and his voice sounded thin, almost like a woman's.

Why did the spirits make things so difficult? Why send rain and cold on the day he began his fast? How could a man live without eating in a wind that pulled all the heat from his body? It was difficult enough to rise above the hunger of an empty belly. How could a man stay in his prayers when his body shook from the cold?

Waxtal cupped his hands around the oil lamp and continued his chant. His song was a song of thankfulness for the sea, for the animals in the sea. The chant rose from his chest, poured from his mouth, and circled back to him in the wind. The words came into his ears, drew pictures in his mind—of otters, sleek and swift; seals, dark and fat; sea lions, large and without fear. He saw walruses and whales, sea birds and fish. Finally he saw the gifts these animals brought: hides and furred pelts, meat and fat, oil, teeth for necklaces, bones for fuel, ivory for carving.

He laid his hands on the tusks at his sides. The tusks were warm, as though they remembered the heat of the Whale Hunter ulaq where they had last lain. Under the fingers of his right hand, Waxtal could feel the lines he had carved. Their power moved up his hand to his wrist, then to his forearm—a trail of warmth that spread to shoulders and heart.

Again he saw the sea animals, this time as traders see them: three sea lion teeth for a bear claw, a seal belly of oil for a caribou bone scraper, a fur seal pelt for thirty puffin skins; a sealskin of dried whale meat for a caribou skin parka and leggings; six sea lion bellies of oil for a cormorant feather cape. He saw himself wearing the caribou parka and leggings, necklaces, and a birdskin cape, saw himself with a new woman each night. He saw himself with a new ik, one large enough to hold everything he would buy in trade, more things than most people knew were in the world. He heard the women's voices as they praised what he brought; he saw the fear in men's eyes as they began to understand the power of his trading; he tasted the food the women set before him; he felt their hands at his loins, caressing.

His chants still came to his ears, but they were lost in the visions of what he hoped to have, so Waxtal spoke but did not hear what he said. And his thanksgiving became thanksgiving to a bear-claw necklace; his prayers became prayers to a traders' ik; his praises became praises to fine parkas.

"Do something a wife is supposed to do. Sew. Weave a basket," Hard Rock said and shook his head, rubbed both hands over his face. "I will be back." He left Many Babies, still crying, in the ulaq.

He went first to the traders' ulaq. When he found no one there, he went to the beach. Owl and Spotted Egg were beside their ik, running their hands over the walrus hide covering.

For a moment Hard Rock stood watching the men, saying nothing, then he called out, "I shared my wives with the traders. I gave food and water and oil. They stayed in a good ulaq. My wife is in my ulaq now and she will not stop crying. What did you do to her?"

"We did nothing," Spotted Egg said, his voice loud, his words hard.

"Ask Waxtal. He is the one who had her," said Owl. "We each slept alone."

"Where is he?"

"He is gone," said Owl. "He took our meat and our oil and what was in our packs." Owl kicked at a caribou skin pack lying empty beside the ikyak rack.

"Look what he did to our ik," Spotted Egg said. Pulling a knife from his sleeve, he used the blade to lift one edge of a slit that ran the length of the ik's belly.

"You will go after him?" Hard Rock asked.

"With what? Will one of your hunters let us use his ikyak?"

"How can a hunter give his brother to someone else?" Hard Rock asked.

"You have no one who would trade ik for ikyak?" Owl asked.

"You want a hunter to give his ikyak for a woman's boat? A man cannot hunt whales from an ik."

"A traders' ik," Spotted Egg said.

"What is the difference?" Hard Rock asked. "Woman's boat, traders' ik. Both would dishonor the whale. But I will ask. Perhaps one of my hunters has become a fool."

Spotted Egg's face darkened, but he said nothing.

Finally Owl asked, "None of your women has an ikyak that belonged to husband or brother now dead?"

"Whale Hunter men take their ikyan with them when they go to the Dancing Lights," Hard Rock said.

"Would one of your women trade her ik?"

"For what?" Hard Rock asked and, bending over, lifted one of the empty trader packs. "What do you have to trade?"

Owl lifted the many strands of beads that hung around his neck.

"A woman needs her ik to fish," Hard Rock said. "You think a woman can eat necklaces? Besides, you cannot catch Waxtal's ikyak in a woman's boat."

In two quick steps, Spotted Egg was face to face with Hard Rock. He grabbed Hard Rock's suk in both hands. "We came to this cursed island, bringing our amulets and charms so you would gain favor with the spirits. Now we have lost everything. It is your fault. Your curse has come to us."

Hard Rock jerked his sleeve knife from its sheath, held it so the blade lay close along the side of Spotted Egg's neck. "I am responsible for you?" Hard Rock asked through clenched teeth. "You came to this island without invitation. You ate my food, lived in my village, used my women, and now you blame me for your loss?"

Then Owl was between them, pulling Spotted Egg's hands from Hard Rock's suk and circling the wrist of Hard Rock's right hand, forcing the knife away from Spotted Egg's neck.

Hard Rock stepped back, twisted his wrist from Owl's grip. "You brought Waxtal," he said. "He is one of you."

"He claims to be your brother."

"Only in the way that all Seal Hunters are brothers to all Whale Hunters. Only that."

Spotted Egg snorted and turned back to the ik.

"I will have my women help you repair your ik," Hard Rock said.

"We have four seal bellies of oil here," Owl said and pointed at the oil Waxtal had left on the beach. "I will give two for a woman—one who has no babies to care for—to help us with the ik. And to warm our beds at night. Be sure she can cook and sew." When Hard Rock said nothing, Owl patted the strands of beads at his neck. "She will have some of these necklaces, too," he said.

Hard Rock looked up toward the sky, then down at his feet. He scraped at the beach gravel with one heel.

"She can be old. We do not care," Owl said.

"Not too old," Spotted Egg added.

Hard Rock nodded. "I will try to help you," he finally said. "One thing we have in this village is women."

He went back to his ulaq. The length of shell beads that Waxtal had given him in the night was cold and prickly under his suk. He went into his sleeping place, to a back corner where the sod was soft between wall rocks and rafters. He pulled off the necklace, coiled it into a ball, and stuffed it into a crevice. He covered it with sod and a handful of thatching grass. Better to wait until the traders had left the island, then bring out the necklace, give it to one wife or another, perhaps to honor the birth of his next son.

The words of his chants had warmed him, and Waxtal, his mind full of the pictures of what he would be, reached for the carving knife he kept in a packet at his waist. It was a beautiful knife, made for him three years ago by Amgigh.

"A gift from my daughter's husband," Waxtal said aloud, bending the words so they became part of his chant. Then he included a song to himself for the bravery he had shown in saving Amgigh when a whale almost took his life. But what good had it done, saving the man? The spirits had marked him for death.

Probably because of Kiin. Kiin was Waxtal's daughter, yes, but what man would wish such a daughter for himself? She had been cursed from the day of her birth. The first time Waxtal had looked into the girl's eyes, he had seen that there was nothing there, no spirit, no soul, nothing but the emptiness of greed.

Waxtal ran his fingers carefully over the carving knife's obsidian blade. The blade was half as long as his smallest finger, and pointed at the end, on one side flaked to sharpness. He had retouched the blade often, and now it was very thin, side to side. Someday he would have to find another blade knapper, someone as gifted as Amgigh, and have another blade made. He would not replace the handle. It was ivory, made from whale jawbone, and during the years Waxtal had used it, the handle had seemed to mold itself into curves and hollows until it fitted his hand as well as his fingers fit together, side by side, long bone to knuckle.

Waxtal held the knife until it warmed to his touch, and then he pulled the carved walrus tusk across his lap. He let his fingers follow the lines of his carving until he came to the place where he had stopped, the place of Kiin's birth. He had carved the wedge shape of Blue Shell's woman part, and a circle above it that was the bulge of her belly.

At first, he had intended this portion of the carving to show his son Qakan's birth. He had meant to forget Kiin, but if he forgot Kiin, he must also forget Amgigh and Raven, two powerful sons that were his because of one cursed daughter. Perhaps the spirits did repay in some ways for the suffering in a man's life. And who had caused him more suffering than Kiin? Even Samiq's anger was because of Kiin.

When Waxtal had finished the circle and wedge that were Blue Shell, he had not been able to decide how to carve Kiin, so he put away his carving knife, hoping some idea would come to him from dream or spirit. This day, in his chanting, he suddenly knew what he would do. He bent over the tusk, leaning close into his work. He moved his knife so the point made another wedge, sign of woman, but he drew it with pointed side up. Then he drew a line that came from Blue Shell's wedge to this new one. He drew lines crossing the new wedge to show the disfavor of the spirits. When he had finished, he rubbed his hand over the ivory and smiled. It was good.

He closed his eyes and lost himself again in the chant. As he sang, he let himself see what joys would be his as chief of the First Men. He would have wives and ikyan, the softest furs for his bed, many parkas and a fine feather suk, warm leggings of caribou skin and a feather cape like Raven's. He would have a new woman whenever he wanted one, and the food cache would overflow with seal bellies of meat and fish and oil.

He lived in his dreams for much of that day, but then his belly began to ache with hunger, rolling and twisting until it pulled him from his chants. He opened his eyes and looked out toward the sea. It had darkened as it always did when the sun began its fall down the western side of the sky.

Waxtal looked at the tusk still cradled in his lap. In surprise, he opened his eyes wide, then opened his mouth in a wail of harsh words. There beside Kiin's wedge were other lines, circles and slashes, scored deeply into the ivory, as though someone had done them in anger. His breath caught in his chest, pressed against his heart until it ached more than his belly. The fingernails of his right hand bit into his palm, and he realized that he still held his carving knife tight in his fist. He opened his hand, dropped the knife. He had not made those lines. They were bold and deep, different from what he had done before.

He pushed the tusk from his lap and stood up, looking to see if there were signs of other men—grass crushed by feet, an ikyak on the beach far below. But there was nothing.

He sat down slowly and reached for the tusk, but could not make his hands close over it. Again he stood. His breath came too quickly, as though he had been running. He wrapped his suk closely around himself, then left the tusks and his hunter's lamp, his thick fur seal pelt. He climbed farther up the side of the mountain. He kept looking back until he could no longer see the tusks, then he settled into the wet grass, crouching so he could tuck his feet into the warmth of his suk. He bent forward and wrapped his arms up over his head.

He wanted to chant, but was afraid the spirits that had carved his tusk would hear and come to him, so instead he held a chant in his throat, like an amulet, to protect the path to his heart. He let its words fill his mind until they pushed the fear down into his belly, where it burned like fire on bone.

Hard Rock paused at the top of the ulaq and called. She Cries answered him, then came to the climbing log and looked up.

"Come in. I have food," she said, and as Hard Rock climbed down, She Cries pressed close to him and whispered, "My husband is not here."

Hard Rock nodded. She Cries picked up her baby and handed him to her husband's daughter. "Go outside," she said and pushed the girl toward the climbing log. Hard Rock stepped aside, making room for the scowling girl, the whimpering baby.

She Cries pointed to a floor mat near the largest oil lamp

and went to the food cache, brought out a section of smoked fish, and laid it on the floor mat in front of Hard Rock.

Hard Rock grunted and broke off a piece of the fish, ate slowly, without speaking. He pointed to a water bladder that hung from the ulaq rafters, and the woman pulled it down for him, waited while he drank, then hung the bladder again.

"You said when I arranged for you to be wife to Wind Chaser that you would help me when I asked."

She Cries smiled slowly and combed her fingers through the hair at the sides of her head. "Do you want my husband to know?" she asked.

"Why should I care if your husband knows?" Hard Rock asked and broke off another piece of fish.

"He does not share well," She Cries said. She lowered her eyelids to look at him through her lashes.

Suddenly Hard Rock laughed, spraying fish from his mouth. "I have four wives, woman," he said. "Do you think I need someone else in my bed?"

She Cries clamped her mouth shut. She drew in a long breath that flared her nostrils and puffed out her chest.

Hard Rock wiped fish from his chin and said, "I need you to talk to Kukutux."

She Cries turned her head away, and Hard Rock sighed. He took another bite of fish. "It is not an easy thing I ask. That is why I come to you." He paused, and when She Cries said nothing he continued. "We need oil. Even if we bring in several whales this summer, we need oil now. I do not have to tell you this. The traders have oil. They ask that they be given a woman while they are here. Someone to take care of their ulaq."

She Cries drew in her breath. "And you will give them Kukutux? Why Kukutux? Why not Long Wood? Why not Blue Hair? They have no husbands."

"They are old."

"Why not Round Eyes?"

"She has children to care for."

"Do they know about Kukutux's arm?"

"No," Hard Rock said, "but why worry? She paddles, sews, fishes. What difference does her arm make?"

"There are scars."

"So, she will keep her suk on."

"When she shares their beds?"

"Who sees scars in the darkness of a sleeping place? Besides, I have been in her ulaq when she was not wearing a suk. The scars are not terrible."

She Cries shrugged. "If they do not want her, I will go to them," she said.

"You will not miss your husband?"

"How different is one husband from another? I can sew, prepare food, and weave baskets. I am careful not to offend the spirits. I am strong and make strong babies. What more does a man need?"

"You already said your husband does not share well," Hard Rock answered. "And you have children. Kukutux does not."

"My children can care for themselves, and my husband will share—if he knows he will get oil."

"Then help me," Hard Rock said. "The traders have offered two seal bellies of oil for Kukutux. I will give you one."

For a time She Cries said nothing, then she smiled slowly, slowly nodded her head. "I will help," she said. "What do you want me to do?"

THIRTY-FIVE

The Alaska Mainland

FOR TWO DAYS, KIIN WALKED BACK TOWARD THE Walrus People's village. The tumpline of her storage basket had rubbed the skin of her forehead raw, and the pain made her head ache, but as she looked out over the lowlands, she knew that she had walked farther than she had dared hope. She crouched down, removed the tumpline and shoulder straps that held the basket to her back, and set it on the ground. It did not seem so heavy when she started walking in the morning, but by evening her back and shoulders ached as though she had been carrying a basket of rocks.

She pulled Shuku from his carrying sling and set him down. Feeling the firmness of the ground against his feet, he clapped his hands and took two quick steps before falling to hands and knees. He looked up, saw the basket and chortled, then crawled toward it.

"No, Shuku," Kiin said and swung him up in her arms, laughing as he kicked his feet in protest. She set him down again and then sat on her haunches, draped her arms over her knees, and closed her eyes for a quick moment of rest. She thought of the Traders' Beach, lifted those thoughts up toward the sky. Perhaps some spirit would see what she wanted and guide her feet. She knew from listening to the Raven and various traders who stopped at their village that she could walk to the Traders' Beach from the Walrus People's village without having to cross any part of the sea in ik or ikyak.

It was strange how much more the Walrus People—even women like Lemming Tail—knew about the earth than the First Men did. What had her mother told her when she was a child? That around everything was the circle of the sky; within that circle was the ice, then the sea, and finally the land. A man could take his ikyak and paddle days, even months, and not come to the ice, but if he went far enough, following signs of stars and sun, he would come to the end of the world, the great ice walls that were the barrier between the earth and the Dancing Lights. The First Men's island was one of many that stretched in a long line from ice to ice, and the islands' mountains were like the giant spine of some animal sleeping beneath the sea. But Lemming Tail laughed when Kiin said such things.

"Who does not know that your island is only a small stone in a river, like a rock that a man steps on to get to the other side?" Lemming Tail had said. "Who does not know that the earth stretches far beyond what a man can walk in his lifetime and that there are people, so traders say, who live beyond the ice walls?"

Perhaps Lemming Tail was right. The First Men traded only with the Walrus People and the Whale Hunters, but the Walrus People traded with the River People and the Caribou People and with people who, Lemming Tail said, lived in a land of standing wood, a place where giant logs—like those that sometimes came ashore after a storm—grew straight up from the ground like huge ugyuun plants.

But who cared whether First Men or Walrus People were right? Perhaps the spirits, knowing the inside thoughts of each trader, each hunter, allowed every man to see what he wanted to see. Who could say where thoughts ended and land or sea began? But if that was true, then it was good that Kiin believed she could walk back to her own people. What else mattered except living with her own people? What else mattered but having her sons safe, growing up with Samiq as their father?

Kiin's thoughts slowed, and she allowed herself to remember Samiq, the sound of his voice, of his laughter. She saw him with Takha in his arms, the boy strong and sturdy. She wished Samiq could see Shuku, could know that he was strong and well. She reached for Shuku, but her carrying strap was empty, hanging slack at her side. Her heart trembled within her chest, and she suddenly understood that she had allowed herself to be taken by the spirits into dreams.

"Shuku," she whispered, and opened her eyes, jumping to her feet. She scanned the tall grass that made everything on the hillside seem the same, one flowing sea of green. He was not there, not anywhere.

"Shuku!" she screamed. She listened, but the wind had grown stronger, and she could hear nothing but its voice and the rustle and sway of the grass sea.

She searched until the sun was only a half circle on the horizon, called until her throat burned, but still she found nothing. The fear that had started as a small catch at the bottom of her throat spread to encircle her chest, and with each breath it seemed as though a giant hand were squeezing against her ribs.

At first, she had run back toward the bay. She knew, even running, that it would take her until long into the night to reach the shore, but thoughts of Shuku drowning filled her mind. What mother did not fear the water spirits that called to young children, luring them to rocky places where waves could knock them down and draw them into the sea? As she ran, she found nothing, no marks from hands and knees. She heard no sounds of a baby crying. But who could hear anything over the wind?

She lifted her voice to call out to the wind spirits, in anger to cry against the loudness of their voices, but the wind continued to blow, and Kiin remembered how often she had told people that she had given Takha to the wind. Had the spirits, angry at her lies, angry with broken promises, taken Shuku instead?

She ran farther toward the bay, through long grass and into the heather of crowberries, then into a tangled growth of willows, but still saw nothing, heard nothing. She dropped to her knees, wrapped her arms up over her head, and began the slow ululations of a mourning song.

But then a voice came to her, her own spirit speaking, though it had been silent during her search: "Kiin, get up. Get up, Kiin. In all your years living with your father, through all the beatings, through the pain, is this what you learned? To quit? To cry and live without hope?"

Kiin raised her head. "I have lost my son!" she said, screaming the words, suddenly angry with a spirit voice that held no sympathy.

"Kiin," the spirit voice said, stern, like the voice of grandmother teaching granddaughter. "You ran toward what you most feared and did not think. How far can a baby go, one who can barely walk? Could he have come all this way? Go back to the supply basket, back to where you started, and begin there. Circle the basket and then circle it again. Make a wider circle with each pass. The grass is too high for you to see Shuku even if he is only a little way from you."

"I would hear him cry!"

"What if he is asleep?"

"There are sinkholes. . . ."

"Yes, and if he fell into one, he is dead. But what if he did not? Will you leave him while you cry? Will you let wolves find him before you do? It is the Moon of Birds Coming Back. The sun is long in the sky. You have light enough to see. Go look for him."

Kiin wiped her hands over her cheeks and stood up, then walked over the hills to the place where she had left her supply basket. When she reached the basket, she began walking in circles, wider and wider, calling and walking, sending prayers up to the mountains and to the wind, begging for her child to be given back to her. The circles stretched until she was at the

crest of the hill. She stopped, looked up to the mountains far
beyond and then down the other side of the hill.

The sun was settling into its bed in the sea, and the light
was dimming, but it was not the black dark of a winter night.
She called, but heard nothing except the echo of her own
voice. The wind blew in a sudden gust, cold against her back,
and parted the grass, as though the wind spirits were men,
walking. She watched, following the wind paths with her eyes,
then caught her breath as the grass split over a dark bundle
huddled on the ground at the bottom of the hill.

"Shuku! Shuku!" Kiin screamed. She ran, not feeling the
sharp edges of the grass as it caught at her feet, cutting the
skin between her toes.

She dropped to her knees beside her son. His eyes were
closed, his face smeared with dirt. Dried blood marked the
line of a grass cut across one cheek. She picked him up, and
his eyes opened; his mouth widened into a slow smile. He
drew a long shuddering breath. Kiin pressed him to her chest,
and he wrapped his arms around her neck, then drew back to
pat her cheeks with both hands. She stood up and carried him
to the supply basket, where she pulled out sealskins, laid him
down, and undressed him, proving to herself that his legs and
arms were strong, no bones broken.

Then she tucked him under her suk to nurse as she gutted
a fish she had caught the day before and ate it raw for her
evening meal.

At the end of the third day, Kiin found a good place on the
back of a hill, sheltered from the wind and hidden by long
grass. She flattened the grass so that Shuku could play while
she sewed sealskins into boots to protect her feet from the
sharp-edged grass.

She knew if she went straight west, following the path of
the sun, she would come to the Walrus People's bay. The day
before, she had seen the bay glistening like blue ice as she
topped each hill, so this morning, fearing women who might
come into the hills to gather roots or heather, she had walked
straight east, farther into the hills, almost to the base of the
mountains that guarded the Walrus People's village. She had
decided to spend the next day sewing and finding roots. There
were only two pieces of fish left from the salmon camp bay,

and who could say how many more days she would have to walk until she reached another beach? But once she got to a beach, she could find sea urchins and chitons, catch pogies and dig for clams.

"I will not starve," she said, speaking aloud to any spirits who watched. "I have lived before without a hunter."

She did not make a fire. The warmth would be good, but why take a chance that the smoke, white against a gray sky, would be seen? She held Shuku tightly against herself, wrapping sealskins and her fur seal pelt around them.

That night wolves awakened her, the sounds of their wolf songs, but their voices were distant, so she was not afraid. She had often heard wolves singing when she lived with the Walrus People. She drifted back into sleep, to be awakened again by skies nearly clear, and sun warm enough to remind her of summer.

She sat and sewed, fitting the boots as she worked and using scraps to make another pair of leggings for Shuku. In the Raven's lodge, Shuku had gone bare-legged and often naked, as most children did, but here in the wind, he needed something to keep him warm, especially when he was strapped outside his mother's suk. Yesterday he had wet through his leggings, and at the end of the day his legs were red and chapped. Now Kiin could dry one pair as he wore the other. When they came to a stream she could wash one pair out, and if she softened them with chewing and with oil, they would not rub sores into his legs.

When the sun finally set, Kiin put on her new boots, repacked her storage basket, and started walking. After sunset, the Walrus People would be in their lodges or on the beach, and there would be less danger of anyone seeing her as she passed high in the hills beyond their village. Still she was careful to stay below the hilltops so no one outside would see movement and come hoping to find something worth hunting.

The rhythm of Kiin's walking seemed to soothe Shuku into dreams, and he slept until sunrise. When he awoke, Kiin stopped and rested, peeling and eating some of the roots she had gathered the day before. After Shuku nursed, she stooped to take him by both hands and let him walk a short way himself, Kiin hoping to tire him so he would take a long sleep later. But as the day went on, it seemed he would never sleep.

He bounced against her hip when he was in his carrying strap and cried in protest when she tried to sling him under her suk to nurse.

At midday, Kiin allowed herself some of the dried seal meat she had packed, but even that rich meat was not enough to keep her feet moving, and finally she had to stop. She unstrapped the storage basket from her back and squatted beside it. Her thoughts seemed controlled by some troublesome spirit, so that dreams set themselves between her eyes and lids, catching her like a storyteller's voice and pulling her away from the world of wind and grass. Once her eyes closed long enough to allow Shuku to crawl so far away that Kiin had to stand to see him.

"How will I sleep?" she asked, speaking aloud, as though there were others nearby to answer her question.

Then she heard the soft whisper of her spirit voice: "You have had worse problems than this."

And Kiin remembered the kelp line she had brought from Lemming Tail's ik. Measuring off a length of it, she tied one end to her wrist, the other to Shuku's ankle. He tugged at the line and screwed up his face to cry, but Kiin handed him a small piece of dried seal meat to chew on and he forgot the rope.

Then Kiin squatted on her haunches, lowered her head to her knees, and slept.

THIRTY-SIX

KIIN PASSED THE WALRUS PEOPLE'S VILLAGE AT night, her steps guided by the full moon. Her spirit had warned her to go in darkness, before moonrise. Even now as she walked, she heard her inner voice, loud, like the voice of a mother scolding her child: "Hunters will see you! Hunters will see you! You know they watch for caribou on nights of full moon."

But Kiin answered: "What would be worse—being found by a Walrus hunter and brought back to the village or falling into a sinkhole? The Walrus hunters know why I left. I will tell them I lost the ik in the rocks of the salmon camp bay and decided to walk back to the village."

Her spirit did not answer, and Kiin continued to walk. She followed a path familiar to her feet, something made over the years by women hunting berries and roots.

She was almost past the village when the wind seemed to bring voices, of women and children, of grandmothers, of hunters, their songs holding the words of both mourning and celebration, as though the sounds of many days had been bound together and brought to her by the night. She was suddenly cold, even with the warmth of her suk against her skin, and she wrapped her arms around herself, around Shuku, and then crouched down in the grass.

"It is no one," Kiin whispered. "You hear only the wind, only your own heart beating." But she felt a chill, as though someone were beside her.

"Spirits," her inner voice said. "The Walrus People have been here a long time. They have given many children to the wind, many old ones to the Dancing Lights, men to the sea, women to childbirth. Is it so strange that spirits live here in the hills above the village?"

Kiin stood up, felt those spirits beside her like curious children, waiting to see what she would do. She wondered what politeness was required. Was it best to pretend you felt nothing? That their hands, cool against your face, were only the wind? That their voices were only the whispers of grass to grass?

Kiin took a long breath and once more began to walk. She looked up at the moon, high now in the east. It had drawn its light back to itself, into a bright haze that circled its face. A storm moon, hunters called it, and kept their ikyan ashore, tightly lashed to ikyak racks. Kiin tightened her arms around Shuku in his carrying strap. She would have to find shelter for them both. A place where they could wait out the rain and wind.

"The storm will not come for two or three days," Kiin's spirit whispered.

"Yes," Kiin said and again looked up at the moon. The

wind curled around her face, pressed cold fingers against her eyelids.

These spirits, Kiin thought. They are like the moon's light, circling.

In all her berry picking, in her root digging, she had never felt their presence. Why were they here tonight?

"Perhaps they, too, circle for a storm," Kiin's spirit said. "Perhaps they have come to protect the village."

"Against what?" Kiin asked.

Her spirit voice did not answer, and Kiin remembered the times the Raven had talked about the safety of the Walrus People's village site. How the bay protected against waves and wind. Kiin thought of Aka and Okmok, those sacred mountains. Had their anger spread like reaching fingers until it found this village?

Kiin walked more quickly, but still she felt the spirits press against her.

"You think I am afraid," Kiin said. "I am not."

Her own spirit answered, "Perhaps you are not afraid, but remember, these spirits see what you cannot. Their world is not your world."

Kiin's heart beat hard in her chest, like a voice that said: "Walk fast, walk fast, walk fast, walk fast." Kiin made herself stand still, made herself listen. Perhaps one of the spirits needed to speak to her.

Then her own spirit said, "Go. There is nothing you can do. You cannot change paths already taken."

"There is always something that can be done," Kiin said. "Some small thing."

She began to walk, and as she walked, she lifted prayers for the people in the Walrus village, for each man, each woman. Her steps were firm against the earth, as though her feet drew strength from rock, soil, grass. In her praying, Kiin began to sing, her own songs, celebrations of all things—the heat of the sun, the gray of beach gravel, the voices of birds. And as her songs continued, Kiin felt the spirits move, as though the words from her mouth pushed them back to their places around the village, as though the words she sang were what they had needed.

THIRTY-SEVEN

THE WHALE HUNTERS

Yunaska Island, the Aleutian Chain

KUKUTUX GESTURED TOWARD A PAD OF FUR SEAL skin near the oil lamp, and She Cries sat down. The woman cleared her throat, but said nothing.

She Cries was tiny, so when she was bundled against the wind or rain in her suk, someone might think she was a child. But her eyes did not hold the clear honesty of a child's eyes, and since Kukutux's brother had died, She Cries had aged. Lines scored her forehead and made a pinched place between her eyes.

Kukutux squatted on her haunches, tucked her hands around her knees, and said to She Cries, "Would you like water? It is fresh this morning."

For a moment She Cries said nothing, and Kukutux was sure the woman would ask for food, but She Cries only said, "Yes, water would be good."

Kukutux brought a water bladder and waited as the woman drank, then she hung the bladder on its peg above their heads.

"I have something important to ask you," She Cries said.

Kukutux squatted beside her and waited, but the woman was silent, staring into the lamp flame. Kukutux was patient. It would be rude to deny the woman time to order her thoughts. But Kukutux knew She Cries well enough to understand that her silence was a way of gathering importance to herself. So finally she stood and went to her basket corner, upturned an old basket, set it on her basket pole, and began to repair the bottom.

"I told you I have something important to ask you," She Cries said, her voice rising into a whine.

Kukutux shrugged. "I listen," she said. "Ask me."

She Cries clicked her tongue against the roof of her mouth, like a mother angry with a child. "Hard Rock wants to know what you think about the traders. He wants to know if you think they are good men."

Kukutux laughed. "Hard Rock wants me to give hospitality. I will have the honor of working for the traders, and they will give him oil. Hard Rock is not my father. What right does he have to take oil that I earn? He has food enough. His wives do not starve. But perhaps he needs oil for Many Babies. The oil she uses on her hair is so old it smells. Perhaps Hard Rock is tired of the stink of it in his sleeping place."

She Cries made small sputtering noises in her mouth.

Kukutux raised her eyes from her basket and looked across the ulaq into She Cries' face. "And you," Kukutux asked, "will you get some of the oil if you persuade me to go to the traders?"

She Cries opened her mouth, and Kukutux waited, but no words came out. The woman's face reddened, and for a moment Kukutux thought of saying some politeness that would take the edge from her words, but then Kukutux saw the roundness of She Cries' arms, the fullness of her cheeks. It had not been easy for She Cries—for anyone in the Whale Hunter village—but the woman was not starving, nor were her children.

"What right do you have to take oil for something I do?" Kukutux asked. "I did not offer you food today. This was not in rudeness, but because I have nothing to offer. Yet, you ask me to give myself to a man I do not know, with no husband or brother to protect me. You ask me so that you can have more."

She Cries raised her eyes, looked hard into Kukutux's face. "You think you are the only one in this village who has suffered?" She Cries asked. "You think you are the only one to lose husband or son? I know that you do not have enough to eat, that you need oil, but what can I do? Should I let my second husband's child starve so I can feed my first husband's sister? What wife could do such a thing?"

"You cannot share a bit of oil, welcome me to your ulaq, offer a small amount of food—in politeness?" Kukutux asked.

She Cries went on as though Kukutux had not spoken. "You think I do this for myself? No. I see that your mourning is eating away your life. You need someone to care for. You might think men do not want you because of your arm, but that is not true. You can paddle; you can sew; you can fish. Men see the pain on your face, the sorrow for a man now dead. They are not stupid. They know what will happen if they look at you too long. Your pain will come in through their eyes, push down into their chests. What man is a good hunter when pain presses against his heart?

"These traders are not bad men. The younger ones are strong and their faces are good to look at. The oldest one, Waxtal, he is small and weak, but Hard Rock says he has spirit powers, and also he is a carver. Think what will be yours if you live with the traders—oil, food, necklaces, all things that traders have in abundance. Perhaps they will decide to keep you as wife, or take you to a village that has many hunters and let you choose a husband there. Is it selfishness that I want these things for you?"

She Cries took a long breath and stood. She walked over to Kukutux, laid one hand on her head. "You want what you cannot have," she said. "Your husband, your son, they cannot come back to you. Do not forget, my sister, someday you will go to them. Will you go proudly, knowing you have left sons for the Whale Hunter people? Or will you have to tell them that you gave no help to those still living?"

When she finished speaking, She Cries left the ulaq. For a long time, Kukutux sat, hands on her basket, doing nothing.

THIRTY-EIGHT

WAXTAL CRADLED THE CARVED TUSK IN HIS LAP. It was cold against his legs. All things were cold—wind, ground, grass. He held his hands over his hunter's lamp, but even when he lowered his fingers into the tongues of flame, he could feel no heat.

I am like some spirit, he thought. I long for heat, but am unable to enjoy it. Then as though the thought had given him new eyes, he asked: What if I am dead? Could this cold, this hunger, have pulled away my life?

He began to shake. Again, he held his hands over the oil-lamp flame. Again, he felt no heat. Perhaps those spirits who in his first day of fasting had added their carving to his tusk had taken his life in trade for their work. Waxtal's throat tightened, and his chest shuddered with the full hard beating of his heart.

But then he thought, What man, dead, feels his heart beat? And suddenly he knew he was not caught in the world of the dead, but in some vision.

Why fear what I have been praying for? he asked himself. The spirits have granted what I asked.

He had planned to fast for four days and nights—four, the sacred number of the earth, of the four winds. He had brought four water bladders—one for each day. Two were empty. He picked up the third and drank, and as he drank, he asked himself, What spirit drinks?

He pulled his carving knife from its packet and held the blade over the tusk.

What better time to carve than during a vision?

He closed his eyes and let his thoughts go free. He carved as his mind filled with pictures of many things—a fine, large traders' ik, a cormorant feather cape, a necklace of bear claws, a mask carved from wood and painted in bright colors, a large ulaq with food caches full of meat and oil.

"So," Hard Rock told her, "say what you came to say." He did not look at Kukutux, but used his sleeve knife to chop up a piece of dried seal meat and crumble it into a bowl half filled with oil.

For a moment Kukutux could not take her eyes from the meat. Her stomach twisted, knotting so close to her throat that she was afraid she would not be able to speak. She had gone out for sea urchins this morning, but there were none, and she had heard the men speaking about several families of otters living in the kelp beds near shore. She had felt the rise of despair. What woman had any chance of finding sea urchins when too many otters lived near?

I will dig roots, Kukutux said to herself, ignoring a voice within that told her she would starve. What would taste better with the pogy she was sure to catch that afternoon? And at low tide, she would dig clams.

But she had caught nothing, and had found only a few clams. Even roots were hard to find, since the ash had killed so many plants. No wonder the Seal Hunters had moved to another beach. How much better for the Whale Hunters if they had done the same.

But Seal Hunters could find seals on almost any island. How could Whale Hunters leave this island and still catch whales? This island was the place where the whales passed as they moved spring and fall between the North and South seas.

Hard Rock belched, and Kukutux said, "I have decided to do as you ask."

Hard Rock looked up at her, his eyebrows raised. He patted the floor beside him. "Sit, have food," he said. He handed her the bowl of oil and seal meat. Kukutux lifted the edge of the bowl to her lips and pushed meat into her mouth. She gave the bowl back to him and wiped her chin with her fingers.

"More?" Hard Rock asked.

Kukutux reached for the bowl and took another mouthful.

"So you have decided you like the traders," Hard Rock said.

"No," Kukutux said and licked her hand and the oil that had coated her lips. "But I have no choice. If I do not go to the traders, I will starve."

"You did not realize this when I spoke to you before?"

Kukutux shrugged. "Sea otters have come and eaten most of the sea urchins," she said. "The berries and bitterroot bulbs are not yet ready. I have no ik for fishing or to take to the bird cliffs."

"So you will go to the traders. Good!" Hard Rock said and stood up. "I will tell them."

Kukutux held up one hand. "Wait," she said. Hard Rock crouched down. His woven grass apron touched the floor as it hung between his legs. He leaned his elbows on his thighs and looked at her.

"How much oil will you give to She Cries if I go?" Kukutux asked.

"Why should She Cries get oil?" said Hard Rock, with a short laugh.

"You think I am a fool?" Kukutux said. "You think I do not understand the woman who for three summers was my own brother's wife? You think she is wise enough to keep me from finding out, one way or another?" Kukutux echoed Hard Rock's laugh, short, rude. "They offered you oil if you got them a woman to care for their ulaq and warm their beds. You went to She Cries and offered her a share of the oil if she would help you."

"How do you know this?" Hard Rock asked.

"She Cries is a boaster. It is not difficult to find out what she is doing. There is always someone who will tell."

"So you want her share?"

"Yes," Kukutux said. "Her share. Two bellies."

"She lies!" Hard Rock said. "Her share is one belly."

Kukutux shrugged. "One then," she said.

"You want it now?"

"No. Save it for me. It will be the beginning of my winter cache. It will be safer here than in my empty ulaq, where anyone can come in and take it."

"I remember when the only thieves were gulls stealing from drying racks," Hard Rock said, and his voice was soft. Kukutux, looking at him, wondered if he expected her to answer, but his eyes were those of one seeing far off, and so Kukutux said nothing, only sat and waited until the man finally stood.

Then Kukutux said, "I, too, would steal—for my children. Perhaps what I do now is for my children, those I will have someday."

Hard Rock walked to the climbing log as though he did not hear what she had said. Kukutux followed him.

At the top of the log, he stopped and looked back at her. "Who told you about the oil?" he asked.

Kukutux smiled at him. "People talk," she said.

THIRTY-NINE

"SO THIS IS WHAT YOU BRING US!" SPOTTED EGG said, his voice too loud in the small ulaq.

Kukutux lifted her head, looked boldly at both of the traders. They were young—Caribou People, Many Babies had told her. Spotted Egg was wide of shoulder and tall. Though the storytellers always said Caribou men were tall, Owl was not. Still, he seemed to be a gentle person, someone who listened before he spoke, who saw beyond a man's words. Kukutux thought she might like Owl the best, though who could say? Both had cheekbones that rose to make ledges on the sides of their faces, and Owl had tattoos across his cheeks, like the lines Whale Hunter boys put on their chins when they become old enough to hunt.

The traders' eyes were round, and their chests were the thick, heavy chests of men who spend much time paddling an ikyak, who need to hold the wind near their hearts as a buffer against the sea.

"She is a strong one, a good worker," Hard Rock said and pointed at Kukutux with his chin.

Owl bent his head over his work, using an awl and a stiff piece of sinew to bind two lengths of sea lion hide into a storage packet. Spotted Egg stood and walked around her, reaching out to run his hands down the back of her otter skin suk, to lift the ends of her short hair.

"Your hair is cut," he said.

"I mourn," Kukutux answered.

She moved away, but Spotted Egg reached out and clasped her arms. "Take off your suk," he said.

The tone of the man's voice made Kukutux angry. Harsh words rose to her tongue, and she looked back at Hard Rock. He mouthed the word "oil." Kukutux clamped her teeth together to hold in her words. She pulled her suk up over her head and stood before the two men in her aprons and the necklaces her husband had given her before she became his wife.

Again Spotted Egg circled, this time nodding. When he came to her left arm, he stopped, gently circled her wrist, and pulled the arm away from her body. He looked carefully at her elbow, ran his fingers over the three jagged scars that went from forearm to upper arm. "This happened when the mountains . . . ?"

Kukutux nodded.

"Does it hurt?"

Kukutux almost smiled. "Why should you care?" she asked. "You cannot feel my pain."

Owl blew out a quick snorting laugh, and Spotted Egg's face darkened.

"She uses the arm," Hard Rock said quickly. "She fishes and paddles and sews as well as any woman."

"And in bed?" Spotted Egg asked.

"Whether or not I come to your bed will be my choice," Kukutux said. "I have agreed to cook and sew, bring in fish and eggs, dig clams. I promise nothing more."

"So this is what you bring us," Spotted Egg said again.

Kukutux pulled her suk on over her head—a good way to hide her face when the man's insults came to her ears. She pulled down the suk, smoothed it over her breasts and belly. Then she moved her eyes up to Spotted Egg's face, stared hard, and circled him as he had circled her. She made a small clucking noise under her tongue and shook her head, then she walked around the ulaq, peeking into the sleeping rooms. "Perhaps you do not need a woman," she finally said. "Better to bring in terns and gulls. What woman would want to clean up this mess?"

Again Owl snorted out his laughter, but Spotted Egg said, "You expect us to clean? We are traders. Waxtal used to do the women's work, but now that he is gone . . ." Spotted Egg shrugged.

Ah, the old one is not with them, Kukutux thought. Many Babies had said he was one of the Seal Hunters who fought against the Short Ones. But that had been long ago, before Kukutux had reached the age of knowing, and though Waxtal might have once been a great warrior, he was now like a with-

ered root, dark and full of wrinkles. His eyes seemed to hold
no wisdom, and without wisdom where did an old man get
his strength? He carved, Many Babies said, though no one had
seen his work. Perhaps, Kukutux thought, he carried his wisdom in his hands. Perhaps, in judging him by his eyes, she
was too harsh. Still, it was good there were only two traders
in the ulaq. What woman would complain? Fewer traders
meant less work.

Kukutux went to the food cache, pulled back the curtains.
She was surprised to see it was almost empty, but who knew
where traders kept their supplies? She pulled out a storage
container half filled with dried fish. With her woman's knife,
she began to chop the chunks of fish. At the back of the cache,
she found a tightly woven basket of dried berries and another
of hardened fat. Using her fingers as a scoop, she took out a
handful of berries, then broke off a chunk of the fat. She
chopped the fat into fine slices and said, "So you have your
father do women's work?"

She did not look at Spotted Egg, but could sense his anger.
"Waxtal is not, he is not . . ." he said, his words stumbling
over one another.

"I understand why he left," Kukutux went on, holding a
smile tightly between cheek and teeth, speaking quickly so
Spotted Egg would not have space to tell her what she already
knew—that Waxtal was not their father. "We of the Whale
Hunters treat our fathers with respect," she said and looked
up at Hard Rock as if expecting him to confirm her words.
She set down her knife and again went to the cache. "You do
not have much food," she said, and felt the laughter leave her
mouth. Were the traders nearly as hungry as the Whale Hunters? Perhaps that was why they had stopped on this island.
Perhaps that was why they stayed.

"Waxtal is not our father," Spotted Egg said. "We are
Caribou. Who can say what he is? No one wants him."

Kukutux looked at Hard Rock. The man's mouth was open
as though to speak, but he said nothing.

Kukutux crumbled the dried berries between her fingers,
then used the flat of her blade to mix the berries with fat and
fish. She found four wooden bowls in the cache and divided
the food among them, then handed each man a bowl and kept

one for herself. She squatted down and, holding the bowl close to her lips, pushed the food into her mouth.

When the men had finished eating, Owl turned his head to nod at Kukutux. "She is good enough," he said to Hard Rock. Then he said to Kukutux, "We know what is here in this ulaq, and we expect you to guard it while we are gone. Eat what you must eat and keep oil in the lamps, but everything else must be here when we return."

Almost she asked the man where they were going, but then told herself there was a time for politeness, a time to respect others, and this man had not treated her rudely. So she nodded, finally asking, "When do you think you will return?"

Owl shrugged. "Who can say?" he answered, speaking those Whale Hunter words with a Caribou tongue, the rhythm so different that Kukutux could hardly keep a smile from her lips.

"You go now?" Hard Rock asked.

"Long Wood and Old Goose Woman repaired our ik," said Owl.

"We have a better chance to catch Waxtal if we go now," Spotted Egg said. He turned to Kukutux. "Make more of that," he said, lifting his bowl. "It is good."

Kukutux worked as the men gathered their things, and when they were ready she gave them a seal bladder she had filled with the mix of fish, fat, and berries. Spotted Egg and Hard Rock left the ulaq, Owl close behind them. At the top of the climbing log, Owl stopped and looked back at Kukutux.

"There is basket grass from the Walrus beaches in my sleeping place. I have heard you have little on this island. Use it if you want." Then he, too, left the ulaq.

For a time Kukutux waited. When the men did not return, she began looking into sleeping places, counting and stacking furs and mats, making sure she knew what the traders had. She found the basket grass, fine and strong—all of it the white inner mother grass that is best for weaving. Then she went to her own ulaq, gathered basket and sewing supplies, sleeping furs, fishhooks and line, and brought them back.

She put her things in the one empty sleeping place. In the food cache, she found a good piece of dried seal meat. She stuck it into her mouth to soften and sat down with the basket grass and a bowl of tepid water.

She would worry about the traders when they returned. For now, all was good. What more could a woman want than food and oil, a quiet ulaq, and a lapful of basket grass?

FORTY

IT CAME BEFORE SUNRISE, AND IT WAS A NEW voice, something Waxtal had never heard before. It seemed to come not through his ears but through his fingers, carried not by the wind but by his blood.

At first he could not make out the words—as though he were listening to men speaking at a distance. Then the words became clear, a chant, a song he did not know. It spoke of the sea, of sand and mud and fish. It spoke of walrus pups, newborn, and of cold water, of warm sun on old rocks. Until finally Waxtal understood that the song was a walrus song and it came from the carved tusk.

The song flowed up through his arms and gathered in his chest. It seemed to cradle his heart in gentle hands, to lift it in joy so that he opened his mouth and sang word for word whatever the tusk sang. "This is why I have come," Waxtal whispered, interrupting the song. "This is why I am here, in rain and cold."

He settled more deeply into his suk, lifting his shoulders so the collar rim slipped up over his ears. He flattened his palms against the carved tusk, again felt the song. He closed his eyes and listened. He rubbed the tusk, thought of the power it would bring him, of the trades he would make. Every man, every woman on all the beaches of the world would know his name, would honor him, would wish they had his power.

Yes, as soon as it was morning, he would leave. He would not go back to Hard Rock, but to Tugix's island, to the old village there. He would see what was left. Perhaps the old man Shuganan, many years dead, would have something to tell him. Perhaps the old man's spirit, seeing Waxtal's carved tusk, would give him another portion of power. Then Waxtal would go on to other villages, until he had gathered enough power to go to Raven. They would meet—shaman to shaman, trader to trader—and as father of Raven's wife, Waxtal would ask for help in killing Samiq. Then all things would be his.

Waxtal laughed, then listened for the tusk's song, but the song had faded so that Waxtal was not sure if what he heard was song or wind, so he slept.

Words woke him, and first, still caught in his dreams, he thought the tusk was speaking again. He opened his eyes.

Owl and Spotted Egg stood over him, each man with a knife clutched in his right hand. Almost, Waxtal reached for his sleeve knife, almost. But age had slowed him. Perhaps in his youth, he would have had a chance, but now, against two, it was better to fight in a different way.

He turned his eyes toward the sea. It was calm, and fog lay heavy against the water. Waxtal's gaze was drawn to the brightest part of the sky, that place where the morning sun struggles to pull itself up out of the waves. That brightness gave him the strength to raise his voice in the chant the tusk had taught him, the walrus song that had come from his carving.

From the edges of his eyes, he watched Owl and Spotted Egg, watched and waited as the two men slowly lowered their knives, stood listening. Then finally, Waxtal said, "I was given a vision."

For a time neither man spoke, then finally Spotted Egg said, "Come with us to the beach."

"This is a sacred place," Waxtal said. "I cannot leave without many prayers."

"Pray then," Spotted Egg said, his voice low and hard. "We will wait for you beside your ikyak."

"I have many things here," Waxtal said, spreading his hands palm up over his hunter's lamp and tusks.

Owl made a rude noise at the back of his throat and picked up the carved tusk. Spotted Egg reached down and jerked the fur seal pelt from under Waxtal, then picked up the other tusk. "Come soon," Owl said, and the two men turned their backs and walked away in long easy strides.

Waxtal closed his fingers over the emptiness where his tusks had been. He stood, adjusted his suk, then squatted down again. He tried to remember some song or prayer, a blessing for the sacredness of the earth, but he could think of nothing except the cold that seeped up from the ground. Then he remembered a song of thanksgiving, something First Men hunters sang to animals they had taken. He opened his mouth, but instead of thanksgiving, his words came as a request for protection, something sung in a wavering voice. As he sang, pictures came into his mind, and he saw Owl and Spotted Egg with his tusks, taking his ikyak to leave him here on this beach with no food, no oil. He saw his tusks given in trade, to someone who would steal the power meant for him.

So Waxtal ended his song, scooped up his hunter's lamp, and ran until he caught up with Owl and Spotted Egg. He followed them to the ikyak.

Kukutux stood and stepped back, flexed her shoulders. She tilted her head to see her basket from all directions, to check for the smoothness of the stitches, the slope of the sides. "It is good," she said aloud, then pressed her fingers to her lips. "It is good you are alone," she said. "It is good that no one else heard you praise your own work."

After eating her fill from the cache, she had stayed up late to work on the basket. It was a large basket, and now, nearing the second night, she had almost finished it. She had eaten twice this day, and again she was hungry. She smiled, thinking of how many days she had been happy to eat one poor meal. But what would Owl and Spotted Egg think when they returned if they found an empty cache? She must bring in some food, if not sea urchins, then clams and ugyuun stalks.

She pulled on her suk and, snuffing out all but one of the oil lamps, left the ulaq. She went back to her own ulaq, now dark except for the small square of light coming in through the roof hole. But she knew the ulaq well and found the large slice of gray slate set in its place against one wall.

Kukutux rummaged through the storage cache and brought out a gathering net. She strung it on her arm, picked up the slate clam scoop, and left the ulaq. She hefted the slate to the top of her head, held it there with one hand, and walked to the clam flats. The morning had started out with much fog, but the day had warmed until now it was good to be outside, a day for gathering and fishing. Several women were at the clam flats, each of them bent over their shale diggers, scooping out sand to uncover small, fat clams. Many Babies was there, and She Cries. Many Babies came over to Kukutux and pointed to a section of beach near the high-tide line.

"Dig there," she said. "No one has tried there yet."

Kukutux merely smiled and shook her head. "Save it for another," she said, knowing well that whoever dug there would find little. She walked near the edge of the water, ignoring Many Babies' protests, and heard She Cries say to Many Babies, "Why should she dig at the high-tide line? She wants clams, not stones." Then Many Babies was quiet.

As though the spirits favored her, Kukutux found many clams, even when most of the other women had few. Kukutux had nearly filled her carrying net when she heard Speckled Basket cry out, "Traders. I see their ik."

The words were like rocks in Kukutux's chest, and she looked up, shading her eyes. Yes, Speckled Basket was right. It was the traders' ik. "An ikyak, too," Kukutux said.

"The same traders or different ones?" Speckled Basket asked.

"The same," Kukutux said.

"You should go back," Many Babies said to Kukutux. "You are their woman now."

Kukutux turned away from Many Babies' words and continued to dig. Why should Many Babies tell her what to do?

But She Cries said, "You should go. They will wonder where you are."

Without looking at the women, Kukutux went to the edge of the water. She lowered her gathering bag to rinse the clams, then washed her scoop, sluiced off the water with the edge of her hand, and settled the scoop back on top of her head.

As she walked toward the village beach, small spirits wove worries into her thoughts. What if the traders did not like the food she prepared? What if she did not have enough clams to satisfy them? Then she thought of sleeping places and the needs that seemed to rule every man's life.

"What will I do if one of them wants me for his bed?"

Kukutux asked aloud. She waited, as though the wind would answer, as though the bothering spirits would carry wisdom as well as worry. When no answer came, she spoke for herself, and in a strong voice said, "Hope for a son."

FORTY-ONE

THE RIVER PEOPLE

The Kuskokwim River, Alaska

RAVEN TOOK THE FOOD OFFERED HIM AND NODded his thanks to Dyenen's wife. She was an old woman, her back humped, her vision dimmed by the white caul that covers the eyes of the very old.

"My traders call you Saghani," Dyenen said, speaking in the River People language.

Though the words were polite, Raven could feel the old man's uneasiness. Dyenen sat with his back rigid, his right hand caressing the bulge of his sleeve knife.

What child did not know the stories of times long ago when River and Walrus People were one? What child had not heard the stories of the anger, the killing that had driven them apart, one tribe following the rivers, the other finding a place on the shores of the North Sea? But why let the anger of men long dead destroy the living? So Raven pretended not to notice the old man's nervousness.

Even with the anger that divided them, River and Walrus had always been traders, setting aside their battles to visit one another's villages and exchange goods. Raven himself had made trading trips to the River People, so he understood most of Dyenen's words, but he turned toward White Fox and waited for the man's translation. It was best if Dyenen did not know that Raven understood.

What did the storytellers say? Knowledge hidden is a strong man's power.

White Fox repeated Dyenen's words, and Raven nodded his head slowly, and slowly said, "Saghani s'uze' dilaen." Saghani—Raven. Yes, it was his name, yet he would not limit its power only to a name. Long ago, in his vision quest, he had become raven. He had flown; he had looked down on the earth, had seen the smallness of the men beneath him. What man, after seeing such a thing, could be the same?

The shaman laughed, shook his head, and looked at the other River hunters gathered in the lodge. They, too, laughed, raised hands with fingers spread to show their approval that Raven would attempt to speak their language.

The shaman's wife, reaching out to ladle more food into bowls, turned her head to laugh with foul-smelling breath into Raven's face. Raven forced himself to smile at her. Then to push her away, he thrust his still-full bowl toward her and said, "Good!"

White Fox repeated his word in the River People's language: "Ugheli."

"Ugheli!" Raven shouted out, which again brought a roar of approval from the River hunters. But the shaman narrowed his eyes, and Raven saw that quick moment of doubt, so reached over and slapped the back of his hand against White Fox's arm, pointed with his chin toward a River hunter who was speaking, then leaned close to get White Fox's translation of the man's words. They were nothing important, those words, only an inquiry as to which hunter had provided the meat the shaman's wife served, but Raven nodded his head, lowered his eyes as he listened to White Fox's words, as though there was some importance in what the man said.

The old shaman moved his eyes quickly toward the River man and back again with some satisfaction toward Raven.

Enough, then, Raven told himself. No other River words will come out of my mouth until I decide Dyenen must know I speak his language. The old man has used his years well. Wisdom guides his eyes. Raven pulled a necklace of wolf teeth from around his neck and handed it to the shaman.

"Dyenen, in honor of your wisdom," Raven said. He did not wait for White Fox to translate, but instead stood and removed a string of shell beads from his neck. He left the circle of men who sat around the fire coals at the center of the lodge, and, careful to walk behind each man so as not to give insult, went to Dyenen's wife. The old woman was standing at the back of the caribou skin lodge, near the door, so that she could go quickly to the outside cooking hearth for more food. Raven draped the necklace over the old woman's head. She showed no surprise, only reached up to stroke the necklace with one crooked finger. Raven tried to look into her face, to see something that would give him an idea of her place in this village. Was her advice eagerly sought or taken lightly? Did the hunters treat her with honor or with tolerance? But the cauls of her eyes did not let him see into her soul, and so he earned nothing with his gift, except perhaps an extra bowl of meat.

He turned and went back to his place beside the River People shaman. He picked up his bowl and began to eat, catching snatches of conversations between the hunters. Though he understood much of their language, they spoke too quickly for him to understand everything. Besides, the thin walls of the caribou skin lodge seemed to let words escape outside into the wind, where they tumbled like willow leaves in a storm. As though hearing his thoughts, the wind suddenly increased, pushing in one side of the lodge wall and forcing the fire's smoke from the roof hole at the top of the lodge back into the faces of the hunters.

The River People men did not seem to notice, but Raven's eyes met those of White Fox and Bird Sings, each man pulling himself more tightly into the warmth of his fur seal parka. How could the River People live in such flimsy lodges? Raven wondered. They were nothing more than a double thickness of caribou skin stretched up into a dome over bent willow and held to the ground with sharpened sticks and a circle of river rocks. Raven longed for the sturdy earthen walls of his own lodge, the sweet thin smoke that rose from his oil lamps, so much better than the thick, throat-clogging smoke from the wood burned in every River People lodge.

One of the River People hunters waved the smoke away from his eyes and laughed, saying loudly, "Spring wind. It is good to get away from the dark winter lodges, no?"

Other hunters laughed their agreement, and though Raven almost joined their laughter, he remembered to look at White Fox for a translation. When White Fox had finished, Raven, too, laughed and tried to think of some compliment to give the River People's spring lodges. He thought of one good thing, something he enjoyed in spite of smoke and cold—the brightness of the skin walls. So he raised his voice above the din of the River hunters and said, "What Walrus hunter does not appreciate the brightness of a River man's spring tent?"

White Fox leaned against him and said in a quiet voice, "The tents belong to the women."

"Tell them what I said," Raven answered.

"It is an insult," White Fox whispered. "You are asking me to call these hunters women."

"Tell them what I said," Raven told White Fox.

"Insult them?"

"No, explain. Tell them what I want to say, and what I said instead."

White Fox spoke to Dyenen, his words slow, deliberate. As White Fox spoke, Dyenen's face first darkened, then he began to laugh. He nodded his head and laughed again as White Fox finished his explanation.

"Good," Raven said quietly to White Fox, then widened his eyes and shrugged his shoulders, allowing himself to smile as Dyenen, in turn, explained to all the men what Raven had said. The men, too, laughed, then laughed again when White Fox explained that the Walrus men owned their lodges.

Raven watched Dyenen from the corners of his eyes. There was no trace of caution, no shadow of worry in the old man's face. Good, Raven thought. Let him think his power puts him beyond my reach. Let him laugh. Let him think I am a fool. What man hesitates to trade with a fool?

FORTY-TWO

RAVEN WALKED THE LENGTH OF THE TRADE goods White Fox and Bird Sings had laid out. The skies were clear, promising no rain, so they had displayed their goods outside on a ridge of ground that rose at the back of the village. Raven reached into one of the grass bags and took out a strip of dried meat. The rich heavy taste filled his mouth and nose, but he was no fool; walrus meat was too strong for the River People. Even their hunters were raised on the soft flesh of fish, the fine-grained meat of caribou. White Fox had protested at the bags of walrus meat Raven insisted they bring, the man saying, "They will not eat it. You know most River men do not like the taste."

Raven had laughed. "All the better for us," he had said. "If they wanted it for food, we would have to sell it bag by bag, traded in equal measure for fish or caribou meat. Now we can sell it piece by piece as medicine for power, something to be ground up and taken with water or eaten in small amounts before a vision fast."

White Fox had smiled and Raven had laughed, but now that assurance seemed to have left him, and Raven felt as he did before every trading session. He held his body taut against the doubt that churned his belly and made the edges of his head throb. He reminded himself that each trading began this way, with Raven's eyes newly open to flaws, as though he were seeing the trade goods for the first time, the seal fur pelts that could be thicker, the baskets that could be more evenly woven, the wooden bowls too thick or too thin, the edges of the dried meat—were they beginning to show the white powder of mold? So he looked away, told himself all things were good, better than what these River People had to offer, these men whose breath and clothes and skin stank of fish.

He saw the first group of men coming, and suddenly the uneasiness was gone, and he was again Raven, shaman, able to read men's thoughts through their eyes, to know their hearts by the sets of their mouths, to understand their wants by the tightening of their fingers.

He stood up and stretched his arms out toward them, smiled, and stepped up on a small rise of ground he had found before Ice Hunter's sons had spread out the trade goods, a hillock so small that few people would notice it, but something that gave him more height. Though it seemed a foolish thing, Raven had found that the man whose eyes were highest often had the advantage in trading.

Most of the River men brought dried fish to trade. Fools, Raven thought, though he was careful to keep a smile on his face. What did he need with fish? He already had enough for the journey home. While here they would eat from Dyenen's caches. Why worry about providing food for themselves?

The last of the River men had a girl with him, his hand tight around her upper arm. She was young, but with the curves of a woman. This time Raven turned away, sure his face would show his displeasure. A daughter traded for a night of favors by a father wanting furs or spearpoints was often worth less than nothing. In a man's bed, the girl would either be like someone dead, or she would fight, kick, gouge. Either way, the brief moment of release was not worth the struggle.

Then Raven asked himself why he should care. He was not here to trade the goods laid out before the River People. That was for White Fox and Bird Sings to do. His trading would be with Dyenen, and for something far more precious than those things brought in by a hunter or made by the hands of a woman. What Raven wanted in trade, he would give anything to get—anything except his life. But that was something Dyenen could never know.

Until Dyenen came, Raven would watch, would see what the River People seemed to favor. Already, White Fox had approached the father and daughter. The father pointed toward a pile of obsidian, then picked up a small piece, no larger than a man's thumb. He pulled the girl toward White Fox, spoke to him, but White Fox shook his head. Again the father spoke, moving close to look into White Fox's eyes, but White Fox backed away, again shook his head. Raven held his smile in his cheek as the father reached beneath his caribou skin parka and pulled out a fistful of bear claws. White Fox held up both hands, and the man, still gripping his daughter's arm, again reached into his parka and this time brought out a medicine bag, made from the skin of a flicker.

Raven drew in his breath. What man did not know the powers of the flicker, a small bird never seen on the Walrus beaches? White Fox smiled and began bargaining. His words, spoken in the River People's language, were just loud enough for Raven to hear as he dickered for more nights with the daughter.

Finally the deal was made. Three nights, the first tomorrow. The daughter stood with head down, lips pursed, but as the two turned to leave, White Fox called out to them, stopped the girl with a hand on her shoulder, and as she stood, face averted, White Fox slipped a shell bead necklace over her head. The girl looked at him, made a quick murmur of surprise.

With a gesture of impatience, the father reached for the necklace, shaking his head at White Fox, but the girl clutched the beads with both hands. White Fox said a few words so that soon both father and daughter were smiling, both laughing. And Raven, too, laughed his admiration for White Fox's trade. For a necklace of shells White Fox had bought himself three nights' pleasure, and who could say? Perhaps more would come after that, for nothing more than a few words of praise for the girl's comely face and young body.

Near evening, as White Fox and Bird Sings were gathering trade goods into bundles, Dyenen came. Raven called to the men, told them to roll out the skins, display the trade goods again, but when Dyenen saw the traders begin to unroll their packs, he gestured for them to stop.

"I will come tomorrow," he said in the River language, and White Fox called up to Raven: "He says he will return tomorrow."

"Good!" Raven called. He patted the basket of Kiin's carvings he kept hidden under his birdskin cloak.

Dyenen walked slowly up to stand beside Raven, the two saying nothing as Bird Sings and White Fox worked. When all was packed away, Dyenen left, and Raven, Bird Sings, and White Fox returned to the lodge given them for their stay with the River People.

Three River People women were there waiting with Bird Sings' wife, with food and bedding laid out. Dyenen left them alone, and the women brought bowl after bowl of fish, meat, and roots, until they could eat no more. Bird Sings' wife then settled herself close beside her husband, looking up at the River women with hardness in her eyes. The River women went to stand between White Fox and Raven, their lips curled in smiles, eyes boldly darting to the faces of both men.

"Do we choose?" White Fox asked.

"Ask them if they can stay," said Raven.

White Fox asked, and the women giggled, nodded their heads. One met Raven's eyes. He smiled and, remembering White Fox's lesson, reached beneath his parka, took out a

necklace of long birdbone beads. As the woman clasped the
necklace, Raven grabbed her wrists and pulled her over to
the mound of furs that was his bed. Then, turning his back on
the others in the lodge, he pulled off her leggings and rolled
her over to lie beneath him.

FORTY-THREE

DYENEN CAME THE NEXT MORNING—EARLY, EVEN
before White Fox and Bird Sings had unrolled the sealskin
packs, even before the women had gathered at the outside
cooking hearths.

In the early sunlight, the man looked older, weaker than he
had the evening before. The long edge of his nose was sharp,
almost as if some stone knapper had honed it. His eyes were
set deep into his face, with lids that looked as thick and heavy
as the curtains that hang over sleeping place doors. He was a
tall man, though not as tall as Raven, and wore a stiff robe of
long brown fur, something musty with age.

In bold familiarity, Raven reached out and touched the fur.
He was surprised by its softness.

"Musk ox," the old man said, and at his words White Fox
called out the same words, the animal carrying the same name
in both languages, a name that did not sound like either a River
People or a Walrus word but something spoken by others,
perhaps those hairy men with tails that storytellers said lived
at the edge of the world.

White Fox came to stand beside Raven and Dyenen. Directing his words to White Fox, Dyenen said, "Tell your shaman that I have come to trade. Tell him that I have furs,
caribou parkas, and the best fish spears, even a few flint spearheads made by the men who live along river flats far to the
south."

Raven pretended to listen to White Fox as the man translated, then held his hand out toward the bundles of trade goods

Bird Sings was unrolling. "Much was traded yesterday," Raven said, "but we have some things left. Pelts, seal oil, dried walrus meat. We have necklaces and feathers from sea-birds, shells and obsidian. All these things we will trade for your pelts and spearpoints."

White Fox repeated Raven's words, and Dyenen grunted back an answer, then waited until Bird Sings had finished arranging the trade goods. The old man spent a long time looking at everything. Now and again he would turn to Bird Sings and ask a question, and Bird Sings would answer. Raven did not watch, but instead squatted down on his haunches. He drew a handful of dried fish from inside his parka sleeve and began to eat.

When Dyenen had finished looking, he came back to Raven, squatted beside the man. Raven handed him a piece of fish, and both men, saying nothing, ate. Finally, Raven stood. Dyenen, licking his fingers, slowly straightened to stand beside him.

"Your women make good meat," Raven said, and waited while White Fox translated his words.

Dyenen nodded. "It is better when warmed over a flame."

Yes, Raven thought as White Fox repeated Dyenen's words. He had seen the River People hold the skin side of a dried fish over the fire, waiting until the skin wrinkled and writhed in the heat. He had tried it himself and found it to be good. The flame seemed to bring out the oil in the fish and to soften the flesh. But who had time to build a fire or wait for the women to bring the cooking hearth coals to life? When a man was hungry, he should eat. That was the way of the Walrus People.

"So," began Dyenen, "a man might see things that would be useful. A man might have something to trade for those things."

Raven sighed as the old man continued. Perhaps he had been foolish to pretend he understood nothing of the River People language. The trading would be long and tedious, hearing everything said twice. The River People always spoke in careful circles. Their long speeches reminded Raven of a wolf following the trail of a caribou, looping back and away, back and away, and finally circling wide before the attack.

"Does he want to trade or not?" Raven asked, breaking

into the long tangle of words coming from the old man's mouth.

"Yes," said White Fox, his eyes telling Raven to be cautious, to honor politeness.

Yes, Raven admitted to himself, he must be careful. He took a long breath and forced the impatience out of his mouth, away from his tongue.

White Fox and Dyenen finally came to an offer of goods for goods. Then Dyenen said, "I also have a wolfskin."

White Fox looked quickly away, and Raven knew the man was shielding his eyes. White Fox had hoped to get a wolf pelt. Walrus women would give much to have wolf fur for parka ruffs. White Fox shrugged. "I have fur seal pelts," he said to the man.

"Three," Dyenen said and held up three fingers.

White Fox laughed. "One," he said.

"Three."

White Fox shook his head and stood up, walked away.

"Two," Dyenen called after him.

"One and two grass mats, woven by the Seal Hunter women," White Fox offered, turning back to the shaman.

Dyenen lifted his head to look at the sky and noisily sucked his teeth. "Yes," he said, "if I can choose the pelt."

"Bring the wolfskin. We will see," White Fox answered.

Dyenen stood, extended a hand, palm out, toward Raven. Raven nodded and watched the man walk back to his lodge.

"You did not show him the carvings?" White Fox asked Raven.

"I will," Raven answered. "He is a good trader, but you are better."

White Fox did not acknowledge the compliment, but as the man returned to the trade goods, he walked with shoulders back, head high.

You are a good trader, yes, Raven thought. And I am better. Tonight I will have the secrets of this shaman's power, how he holds his place over these River People, and I will have it for a basketful of wood and ivory.

The chanting came from within the lodge, Dyenen's voice and yet another voice, high and like a woman's. For a moment Raven stopped outside and listened. Two people inside, maybe three, he thought. He waited. The sky had begun to darken, but still there was light enough to see the village, the white-gray smoke rising from each of the many lodges—three tens at least. And ten, twelve people in each lodge.

He had never seen a bigger village, nor a village that had so much food, especially at this time of year, before the birds had laid spring eggs. The winter caches, platforms raised on poles higher than a man's head, were still packed with meat and fish, dried berries and fat, and it had not been an easy winter. How did one man hold so many people together in peace? How did he empower his hunters to feed them? Was he a caller, a shaman who could bring in caribou, bear, or moose so his people always had meat?

Raven had come alone. It had not been an easy decision. What was more important, to have the freedom of speaking to Dyenen, one on one, of trading, shaman to shaman; to have the freedom of making his trades without White Fox's knowledge of what he was doing, or to have the advantage of hearing without the old man knowing that he understood? In some ways the decision had been made for him. White Fox was enjoying his evening with the River girl, the woman he had traded for. Why interrupt? Why have the man's resentment like a dark cloud over this trading session with Dyenen?

Again Raven heard the voices, the high singing words of a woman. Speaking in what language? Not that of the River People, not even Caribou. Then another voice, a man's voice, a young man, someone strong—a hunter?—speaking also in that unknown tongue. Then Dyenen's voice, the voice of a man growing old, but not yet feeble. For a long time Raven stood outside the lodge. When the voices stopped, he waited for the man and woman to come out, but no one came, and from inside the lodge, there was only silence.

So, Raven thought, these people are like the First Men, sitting together sometimes a whole day without speaking. It was a custom that always made Raven feel as though his muscles would soon jump through his skin. He laid his left hand against the lodge and raised his right hand to scratch at the caribou hide door covering, a custom of politeness among the River People. The voices began again, and this time, Raven, one hand still pressed against the lodge cover, felt the lodge tremble as though the old shaman spoke not to people but to the lodge itself.

Then Raven had had enough of waiting, enough of wondering. He scraped his nails against the caribou skin, once, twice, and Dyenen called for him to come in. Raven lifted the door flap and crawled in through the narrow entrance tunnel. There was a fire in the center of the lodge, wood smoldering, the smoke making an uncertain path to the smokehole overhead. The smoke burned Raven's eyes, and he blinked away the irritation, waited until the tears cleared, then settled himself on his haunches beside the fire. Suddenly he realized that he and Dyenen were the only ones in the lodge. There were no others, no people to own the voices Raven had heard.

"You are alone?" Raven asked, without the politeness of a greeting, without the raising of hands or the offering of food.

"You speak the River language?" the old shaman said.

"Some, not well."

"Better than you led me to believe."

Raven smiled. "Three days I have been in this village. Quickly I learn." He shrugged and then remembered that the River People did not shrug shoulders but instead held hands out, fingers pointing up. "In ways of politeness I have ignorance," he said.

"So I see," said Dyenen.

"White Fox has discovered the ... the joys of your women," Raven said.

Dyenen did not reply, did not act as though he had heard. Raven pulled his smile into his mouth. The River People were not ones to discuss women, even in jokes, though their women often seemed eager to join a man in his bed.

"There was ... I heard a woman, a man," Raven said and turned his head to look into the shadows of the lodge, to see if his eyes, clouded by smoke, had missed seeing them, or if there was some other door into the lodge. But there was no one and no door.

Again Dyenen ignored Raven's words, and instead passed him a dish with fish and the leaves of the plant the Walrus People called goose tongue. Raven took some of each and ate.

In silence they sat, watching the fire, Raven still blinking his eyes against the smoke. Finally he said, "I have come to trade."

For a long time Dyenen said nothing. He ate, leaned forward to put more sticks on the fire, and ate again. Finally, he said, "I did my trading today. I have what I need."

Raven pulled the basket of Kiin's carvings from under his robe. "You did not see everything. I have things to trade, shaman to shaman."

He looked up to be sure Dyenen was watching, then stood and swung his black feather cloak from his shoulders, laid it on the floor of the lodge between himself and the old man. What could be better to show the white of Kiin's ivory, the yellow and gray of her wood?

Squatting again, Raven cradled the lidded grass basket in both hands and slowly opened it. He brought out the largest carving first—a walrus, as long as a man's hand. Kiin had carved the body from a whale's tooth. The long sharp tusks were curves of walrus ivory. Raven did not look at the shaman, but heard the man's indrawn breath. Beside the walrus, Raven laid three seabirds, the smallest no larger than the last joint of his little finger, each carved with wings spread as though to catch the wind. He set out ivory seals, some with glittering obsidian eyes, and a sea otter lying on its back, a baby on its belly. There was a man in an ikyak, a puffin almost as large as the walrus, lemmings, and, most beautiful of all, a wolf, an animal Kiin had never seen until she came to the Walrus People's village. The wolf was sitting with its head thrown back, and Raven set it so it looked up, as though the lodge's smokehole were the moon.

"Almost I hear its song," the old man finally said, one crooked finger pointing at the wolf. They sat for a long time, Dyenen with his eyes on the carvings. This time the silence did not bother Raven. It was a silence of praise, better somehow than words. Finally, Raven picked up the smallest seabird, a gull, wings out, head to one side. Without speaking, he handed it to the shaman. The old man's hands trembled as the bird fell into them, but he leaned close to study it, lifting the carving to the tips of his fingers, moving it in the varying light of the fire.

Finally Dyenen asked, "Did you carve these?"

"No."

"Why do you show them to me?"

"For trade."

The man's eyes widened. He sucked in the sides of his cheeks until his face seemed more bone than flesh. "I have nothing to give," he said. "You will not take pelts or dried fish."

"No, I will not."

Dyenen handed the carving back to Raven. "I have seven daughters," he said. "One is yet a child and another a new baby. The other five have husbands. I have no one to offer in marriage."

"Wives I have."

"What then?"

"We are shamans," Raven said, choosing his words carefully, letting them run through his head first in his own Walrus tongue, then bending them into the clicks and throat sounds of the River People language. "Power I have. Power I offer in these." He swept a hand out over Kiin's carvings. "The same I ask in trade."

Slowly the River shaman raised his head; slowly he pulled his eyes away from the carvings.

"You do not feel their power?" Raven asked, lifting his chin toward the carvings.

"They pull at a man's eyes," the shaman said.

"At his soul," answered Raven.

The shaman shifted on his pad of furs. He looked into the fire, taking long breaths, then he cupped his hands in the fire's smoke, as though it had the power of water to cleanse.

"Power is not something to be traded. It must be earned," the shaman said.

"You do not wish for more power to . . ." Raven paused as he searched for the word he needed. ". . . to help your people?"

"I do not want what I should not have."

Raven picked up the walrus carving, let his hands caress the whale tooth ivory, let himself wonder again how Kiin could get such smoothness from the sharp edge of a knife.

"You have a large village," Raven said. "You need this power. Your people need it. To stay strong."

"You came then for me?" Dyenen asked with a sly smile. "Not for yourself?"

"What trader comes for another, whether that trader be shaman or not?'' Raven said. ''I come for myself. For my own power.''

''Ah,'' said Dyenen.

''Your power I know,'' Raven said. ''Your power is here. This village.'' Raven spread his arms as though he could see the River People's village through the lodge's caribou skin walls. ''So many people with food for all, with peace for all.''

''Why should I share that power?'' Dyenen asked.

Raven held one hand over the carvings as a man holds hands over a fire. ''If you do not feel it, you do not need it,'' he said.

''And if you trade me these,'' Dyenen asked, ''what about your own power?''

''Carvings I have of my own, carvings I cannot trade.''

''If you do not need these, then why do I?''

Raven held his hands out, fingers up, made himself smile, but the man's words grated in his chest. ''If you do not feel it, you do not need it,'' Raven said again, and handed the shaman the walrus carving. From the edges of his eyes he watched as the old man cupped the carving in his hands and began a slow chant, eyes closed.

Raven waited, impatience battering from within.

Finally Dyenen said, ''Yes, I will trade.''

Raven pressed his lips in a line to keep the laughter that suddenly came to him from escaping his mouth. ''Power for power,'' he said.

''Power for power,'' Dyenen agreed.

The old man stood up, took a step forward to balance himself, and went to a curtain of caribou skin at the side of the lodge. He thrust the curtain aside and reached into the darkness under it. He came back to Raven with a pelt in his hands, laid it reverently at Raven's feet. ''This for the carvings,'' he said.

The skin was of an animal Raven did not know. It was large—as long as a man's arm—and was whole, with head, legs, and short black tail attached. The skull had been removed, so the head skin folded forward from the neck like a closing flap.

Raven reached out to touch it, let his fingers hover above it, and when Dyenen made no objection, allowed his hand to settle into the soft, dense fur. The animal was the gray-yellow color of old grass, and the ears were tufted with black.

Dyenen reached over and lifted the animal's head, and Raven saw that the skin had been left open at the neck so the whole animal was a pouch. Dyenen pushed his hand inside and pulled out packs of folded caribou skin, each knotted with colored strings.

"You asked how one shaman kept so many people together in peace, with game enough to hunt, with fish enough to catch," Dyenen said. "You asked about my power." He spread the packs beside the carvings. "These are my power," he said. "I had thought to give them to a son, but my wives give only daughters. When a man is old, he must pass on his knowledge before the spirits take him. Otherwise what he has learned loses its worth. Better to share knowledge with a man who honors the spirits than with someone who has no understanding of powers beyond his own."

Raven looked at the packs. Two tens, three tens in all, each no larger than his hand.

"May I open them?" he asked, his fingers above the knots of the pack nearest him.

"A man would lose power if he opened the packs without knowing their secrets," Dyenen said.

For a moment, Raven felt the weight of disappointment, but he drew his hands away. Why take the chance of destroying the power that was so close to being his?

"You will trade these for the carvings?"

The old man nodded. "For all," he said.

"For all," Raven repeated, "but you must tell me the secrets hidden in the packs."

"Yes, if you do the same for me." Dyenen pointed to the carvings.

Raven raised his head and thought for a moment. Kiin seemed to give her carvings no special treatment, nor had she told him of any taboos that must be kept. But yes, he did remember her anger when Lemming Tail put one in water. Kiin had told the woman they must be cleaned with oil, so he said, "If a man honors each carving in his heart and sometimes rubs them with oil—oil of sea animal, not tallow from land animal—then the powers stay strong."

Dyenen nodded and, placing the walrus on the feather cloak, picked up each of the carvings, studied each, turning it in his hands, holding it to the firelight.

Raven waited for a long time, watched the old man fondle the carvings, but gradually Raven's eyes grew heavy with the need to sleep, so he finally said, "And now . . . you will tell me what I need to know?"

Dyenen looked up at him in surprise. "There is too much power in these packets for the knowing to come in a few words," he said. "You must study with me for many days—one moon and half of the next."

The old man placed the packets back into the fur skin and handed it to Raven. "Take it with you. Treat it with respect. This animal, the lynx, has power. It is a medicine animal that holds good things in its belly. Take this with you, but do not open the packets until I have told you what you need to know."

Dyenen stood and, taking the carvings one by one, set them in different places on the lashings of the lodge's willow frame. Then he went to the entrance tunnel and waited until Raven picked up his cloak and left.

Raven came out into the night and looked up to see the wide band of stars that lightened the skies. The stars were fires, the Walrus People said, of those who had died. He wondered if the Walrus People's dead knew the dead of the First Men, those people, Kiin had told him, who danced in the lights. And he wondered where his own light would be when he died. He clutched the lynx skin to his chest.

Why think of death? he asked himself. Better to think of the power that would soon be his, of the village he would someday have, as large and strong as the River People village.

FORTY-FOUR

THE WHALE HUNTERS

Yunaska Island, the Aleutian Chain

KUKUTUX HEARD THE ANGRY VOICES EVEN through the ulaq walls. She ran to the climbing log, then backed away as the whalebone rafters trembled with the weight of the men who were yelling. The old trader—Waxtal—was first into the ulaq, then Owl and Spotted Egg, the two men still yelling at Waxtal in words of the Caribou language, words Kukutux could not understand.

Spotted Egg carried a short blunt throwing spear. He raised it over his head, gestured with the pointed end toward Waxtal. Waxtal, eyes darting toward the climbing log, dropped to his knees and wrapped both arms over his head. "No," he cried out in the language of the First Men, then began to speak in the traders' tongue. When he finished talking, he lowered his arms to look up at Spotted Egg, but Spotted Egg again threatened the old man with the spear.

Kukutux stood, her back against an earthen wall, watching. The old man's body was smeared with dirt, his face drawn and gray, and Kukutux remembered that Hard Rock had said Waxtal had spirit powers.

Yes, Kukutux thought. He has the look of someone who has been fasting.

Waxtal sidled toward the climbing log, but Spotted Egg took two quick steps toward the old man, his spear raised. Kukutux pressed herself more tightly against the wall. She looked away from the men, but then heard a thin pleading cry, and could not make herself stay still. With a thrust of her heel, she pushed away from the wall. She caught Spotted Egg's left side with her shoulder and shoved him hard, then ran to stand

205

between him and Waxtal. The hit was quick enough to make Spotted Egg lose his balance, and he lowered his spear to catch himself with the fingertips of both hands.

Kukutux felt Waxtal clasp her shoulders. His hands were trembling.

Spotted Egg, scowling, straightened and let out a mouthful of words, loud, harsh.

"She cannot understand you," Owl said, speaking slowly in the First Men's tongue.

"Move, woman!" Spotted Egg bellowed.

"He is an old man," Kukutux cried. "How can he fight? He does not even have a weapon."

"Do not interfere in what you do not understand," Spotted Egg said, his voice slower but still hard. He moved forward, pushed Kukutux, but Kukutux braced herself, bending her knees, pressing her feet hard against the floor, so that under his hand only her shoulders moved. "Leave us!" Spotted Egg said.

Kukutux let herself look into his eyes. I have withstood worse than this, she thought. What is a man's anger compared to losing son and husband?

"Go, now!" Spotted Egg said.

"Why?" Kukutux asked. "So you can kill him? Then who will clean up the mess? I did not come to this ulaq to wipe a man's blood from the floors. I did not come to this ulaq to have a dead man's curse on me. Hard Rock says this man has spirit powers. You think a man killed here would not use whatever spirit powers he has to curse this ulaq and everyone in it?"

"Woman, you do not understand," Owl said, and his voice was gentle. "For what he has done, this old man should be dead. He does not deserve your pity."

"Hard Rock told me the old man went to fast, to pray. You would kill him for this?"

"He stole our supplies, everything we had. Did you not see this when you came to our ulaq? He left us only what we had stored in our own sleeping places. Everything else he took."

"Where did you find him?" Kukutux asked.

"Why should we tell you?" said Spotted Egg. "You are only a woman. What do you understand of men's ways? By what right do you question us?"

"By the right of one who is about to be cursed by your spear."

Spotted Egg rolled his eyes, spat out angry words in the Caribou tongue at the ulaq rafters, then said, "We found him on an island near here. One east and north."

"The Island of Beautiful Mountain," Waxtal said quietly.

"It is an island where many go to pray," said Kukutux. "Was he praying when you found him?"

"I was praying," Waxtal said, and Kukutux turned to look at him. "I was praying," the old man said again. "I had fasted for almost four days and the spirits gave me a vision."

"You took our trade goods. You took things that did not belong to you," Spotted Egg said.

"I did no more than what you planned to do to me," Waxtal said.

Kukutux looked at Owl, then at Spotted Egg. Both men's mouths were open to speak, but they pressed their lips together, looked away, eyes studying the grass that padded the ulaq walls.

Kukutux took a long breath and walked to the peg where she had hung the bag of clams she had gathered earlier that morning. She took the bag and said to Owl, "I have food to prepare. If you must kill him, do it outside."

Speckled Basket and Old Goose Woman had built a fire in the rock-lined steaming pit, and all the women brought their grass bags of clams. When the fire died down, Old Goose Woman brushed the ashes from the rocks and the women set their bags in the pit. Speckled Basket covered the clams with layers of wet seaweed, then the women squatted on their haunches, taking time to talk and laugh as they waited for the clams to cook.

Kukutux had set her clams in with the others, but though she sat with the women, she did not join their conversation. Her thoughts were on Waxtal and the traders. All the anger, all the threats, were about an ikyak of trade goods. What did it matter, all those necklaces, all those bear claws and caribou skin leggings? The oil, yes. Oil was food, heat, but how could a necklace compare to a man's life? Should a man honor things more than people? What foolishness.

When the clams were ready, Kukutux used a forked stick

to pull out her bag and carry it, hot and steaming, back to the ulaq. Owl and Spotted Egg stood beside the climbing log, speaking to one another in low voices, but Kukutux walked past them as though they were not there.

The center of the main room was piled with trader's packs, bellies of dried meat and oil. Two long walrus tusks lay against one wall. Kukutux sighed and wove her way among the trade goods to the food cache. She pulled out bowls and a skin of oil. She poured a small amount of oil in each bowl, then brought one to Owl, another to Spotted Egg.

She dumped a pile of the steaming clams at their feet. "Where is Waxtal?" she asked.

Spotted Egg shrugged, but Owl pointed at one of the sleeping places. Kukutux felt his eyes follow her as she took clams and a bowl of oil to the sleeping place. "I have food," she called in. The old man did not answer. A chill tightened her stomach.

"You did not kill him," she said, looking back over her shoulder at Spotted Egg.

Spotted Egg laughed. "If I had killed him, he would be outside," he said. "Food for birds."

"Do not worry, Kukutux," Owl said, speaking politely. "We did not kill him."

Kukutux pushed open the curtain with her elbow and saw the old man sitting with eyes closed, hands folded in his lap. "I have food," Kukutux said softly.

Slowly the old man opened his eyes; slowly he said, "I cannot eat. In return for my life, I promised the spirits I would fast one more day."

Kukutux let the curtain swing closed. She took the clams and the bowl of oil and sat on the far side of the ulaq, away from Owl, away from Spotted Egg. And as she ate, she thought about the old man.

FORTY-FIVE

THE RIVER PEOPLE

The Kuskokwim River, Alaska

THE NEXT MORNING, DYENEN WAS WAITING FOR Raven. The old man wore a fine caribou skin parka with gray-and-white wolf fur at the edges of sleeves and hood. Red-dyed moose hair was sewn in long raised lines at the parka's shoulders. Raven, afraid his eyes would show too much admiration for the parka, looked up toward the sky.

"Sun today," he said and lifted his walking stick to the fog that lay heavy over the river.

Dyenen grunted and said, "I told you to bring the lynx skin, Saghani."

Raven closed his mouth over the quick words that had risen to his tongue. Dyenen had not told him to bring the lynx skin. But the man was old. Why expect him to remember everything he said or did not say? Raven nodded and walked back to the lodge that he and Ice Hunter's sons shared. Both men were still in their sleeping robes. Bird Sings was bundled close to his wife.

She is a lazy one, Raven thought. She should have food ready for me. Instead, she stays in her husband's bed.

White Fox slept on the other side of the lodge, arms and legs flung out over the place where the River girl had slept the night before. The girl was gone, but if White Fox had treated her well she would be back. Raven smiled. Though a man could give his body easily to a woman, enjoying her for a night and forgetting her by the end of the next day, a woman seemed bound by that same giving, and would almost always return.

Raven had hidden the medicine bag under the bundle of his

sleeping robes. He reached in and pulled it out, slung it over his shoulder, and went back to Dyenen.

The sun was high enough to catch the frosted edges of the grass and river willows, and bird songs wove themselves between the village lodges.

"A good day for learning," Raven called out to Dyenen.

Dyenen only turned and began to walk toward the river. Testing his path with the end of his walking stick, he altered his course to follow the river's bank, his eyes turned down to the earth. Raven adjusted his steps to Dyenen's slower pace, and he, too, watched the ground, wondering what Dyenen hoped to see. They walked until the sun had melted the frost from the moss that padded the ground between willow thickets and the thin, dark spruce.

Dyenen laid his hands on the trunks of trees he passed, curling his fingers around the yellow-and-gray willows, none thicker than a man's wrist. Raven, too, laid his hands against the cold, hard trunks—smooth willow and scaly black spruce, sticky with pitch. The spruce thrust up from the earth, their dark uneven branches like the barbs of a Whale Hunter's harpoon.

Dyenen cleared his throat, and Raven waited for the man to speak, but Dyenen said nothing.

Raven felt the tightness of impatience stretch into his chest. Finally he asked, "You have no chants, old man? Walrus People shamans use prayers and chants."

"What shaman can share his chants?" Dyenen answered, still walking.

"Do not forget what I gave you in trade," Raven said. He strode with his eyes down, watching the ground, hoping to see something worth seeing.

"What man can trade prayers?" asked Dyenen. "They are the gifts of spirits, honoring a man who has prepared himself with long hours of fasting, with pleadings and praises, with a good mind that sees beauty in the earth."

"So all you give is a lynx skin?" Raven asked, his words louder than he meant them to be.

Dyenen stopped, slowly turned his head to look at Raven.

"I offer what is in your medicine bag," Dyenen said. "Power is something each man must seek for himself. If he is worthy, he will receive it. In that bag is the power to help your people, to have your village grow, to keep men together in peace. That is what you want, no?''

"That is what I want," Raven said, "but do I forever walk to find it?''

"What, you are a boy? You tire more quickly than an old man?''

Raven ground his teeth against Dyenen's insults, but he said nothing. He raised his eyes to the trees, then looked beyond the trees to the river, its shadowed edges skimmed with a thin crust of ice, the water still carrying brown swirls of silt from the breakup. A river otter, the animal a dark patch of fur, surfaced, then was gone. Raven lengthened his stride until he was several steps ahead of Dyenen.

Let the old man see who is man and who is boy, he thought.

Dyenen's breathing grew heavy. Raven smiled and again quickened his pace. Finally he came to a place where the bank rose into a hill. Spruce and willow gave way to bushes with a fragile bark that danced in tatters with the wind. Raven stopped, turned. Dyenen was no longer behind him. Squatting down on his haunches, Raven waited.

He sang a Walrus hunter's song, something the soft-muscled River men, those eaters of fish, would not know. Even when he had finished his song, Dyenen had not come. In disgust, Raven went back, wending his way through the trees until he found where Dyenen's trail turned off, away from the river.

Raven followed the trail until he came to the old man.

Dyenen sat on his heels, his back against three closely grouped willows. He looked up at Raven and said, "In the Long Ago, there was a raven. Very fast. He scorned the porcupine, that slow one, and each day challenged him in laughter to a race. Each day, the porcupine refused. But one day, tired of the raven's taunts, the porcupine agreed. The race would be the length of a certain river.

"The porcupine knew it would take him a morning of steady walking to go that far, but he told himself that after the race, the raven would leave him alone, and so it would be worth the walk. Besides, there was some good bark at the end of that river, the porcupine's favorite kind. When the call was given to begin the race, the porcupine started to walk. But the raven flew up and away, making loops and spirals in the sky, flying first one way and then the other until he was far out of sight. The porcupine did not look up at the raven but just kept walking, and he did not stop for anything.

"Finally just ahead, he saw the end of the river, where it widened out to become a lake. The porcupine put his head down as porcupines do and kept walking until finally he was there. He looked all around, but the raven was nowhere to be seen. The porcupine did not worry about that for long. He climbed up a tree and began to eat bark, but finally up in the sky he saw a tiny black speck. It got larger and larger until the porcupine could tell that it was the raven. The raven landed and called out that he had finished the race. Then overhead the porcupine began to laugh, and the raven knew he had been beaten. The raven flew away and never bothered the porcupine again.''

Dyenen looked up at Raven and smiled. From a packet at his waist he took out two pieces of dried meat and handed one to him. Raven took it, then said, "Am I a child that you must tell me stories?"

Dyenen used his sleeve knife to cut a thin sliver from the stick of meat in his hand. He pressed the slice to the flat of his knife blade with a thumb and raised it to his mouth.

"Evidently," Dyenen said and began to eat.

FORTY-SIX

THE FIRST MEN

Herendeen Bay, the Alaska Peninsula

SAMIQ LIFTED HIS IKYAK FROM THE RACK.

"You should not go alone."

Samiq turned. It was his father, Kayugh.

"I do not plan to hunt."

Kayugh reached out to stroke one of the harpoons Samiq was fastening to his ikyak.

"What man goes without harpoons?" Samiq asked. "I may see seal or sea lion." He looked into his father's eyes. "For many years you were the leader of this village. The people came to you with their problems. You understand my need to pray."

Kayugh turned, lifted his chin toward the hills behind the First Men's ulas. "Is there no place in the mountains for a man to be alone, to speak with the spirits?"

Samiq stroked his ikyak. "This is best for me," he said.

Kayugh nodded. "I understand that there are times when a man must be alone, but you should not hunt alone. You must choose a hunting partner."

"Yes, I will choose," said Samiq, and carried his ikyak to the edge of the water, stepped into the craft, and used his hands to slide it into the waves. He paddled out toward the mouth of the bay, until he could no longer hear the voices of the people, could no longer see the smoke rising thin and gray from the ulas, or his father standing on the shore.

Yes, now that it was spring, he needed a hunting partner. The past summer, after Amgigh had died, Samiq had done little hunting. Why hunt with a hand that could not throw a harpoon? But he had practiced enough now to hunt again. He would never be what he had been, but he could bring in meat. And he could fish. He could pray. In those ways he would add strength to his village.

As he paddled, he considered hunting partners. His father and Big Teeth were already partners, and First Snow usually went with them. That left Small Knife. Sometimes Kayugh took the boy, sometimes First Snow took him, but it was best for a man to have the same partner, someone who understood your strengths and also the ways you were not so strong.

You should take Small Knife, Samiq told himself, and was suddenly ashamed that he had not shared with the boy before this.

Today, this afternoon, Samiq thought, if the sky stays good, I will take him out. It was usually not wise for father and son to be hunting partners. Their skills were seldom matched, the father at first much ahead of the son, and later behind. But in a small village, what choice did a man have?

Samiq dipped his paddle into the water. It was always good

to feel the cold of the sea through the sides of the ikyak. It was good to feel the pull of waves against his paddle. A song came to his mind, something Kayugh had taught him, and he began to sing. Gradually his singing changed to prayers, and his thoughts lifted not to mountains or whales, but to the creating spirit, the one that in his mind he called "Mystery." Was it not that great spirit who had brought the whales to their bay last fall? Those whales had given the oil and flesh that had kept his people alive and strong through the winter.

So Samiq prayed, grateful for sky and earth, for meat and oil. He asked for babies that would someday become hunters. He prayed for each man and woman and child in their village, and for Kiin and Shuku in the Walrus village. Last of all he prayed for himself—for wisdom, only that. And when his prayers were finished he saw, as he often saw, the greatness of the earth, how strong, how beautiful, all things are. In comparison, Samiq's problems seemed so small that a man could face them without fear.

"I need a hunting partner," Samiq said to Small Knife.

The boy looked up from the bit of wood he was whittling and held himself very still.

"I know it is difficult for a son to be a partner with his father, but we can help one another," said Samiq. "My hand is weak, but my knowledge is strong, and I can teach you to hunt the whale. You are a Whale Hunter and should know what your people learned in their many years of following the whale."

"I am Whale Hunter, but also First Men, and proud to be both," Small Knife said. "I would be honored to be your hunting partner."

It was the answer of a man. Samiq saw the glow in Small Knife's eyes, and was proud that the boy kept his excitement from bursting forth in the jumps and shrieks of a child.

Samiq gave him an obsidian blade to mark their partnership, a blade made by Amgigh. Then the two went together, circling the bay, watching for sea lions and harbor seals. They saw nothing, and when the sun was near setting, Samiq motioned toward land, to the beach on the other side of the bay.

They set up a camp, using sealskins and their ikyan as a shelter, and small flames from their hunter's lamps for warmth.

They ate dried meat, and Samiq told stories of First Men hunters: Kayugh and Big Teeth, and Kayugh's father, a man Samiq had never known except through stories. Samiq told of their hunts—successes and failures—and what they had learned from the animals they hunted.

When Samiq's string of stories ended, he was quiet, and in the silence, Small Knife said, "I have heard the women talking. They say you are wise. Will you answer a question for me?"

Samiq smiled. "I do not know if I will answer until I hear the question. So ask."

"What is the best a son can do for his father?"

For a long time Samiq did not have an answer, then finally he remembered his own prayers. "Find wisdom," he said.

"Wisdom?"

"Many good things come from wisdom: respect, honor, knowledge, love."

Small Knife looked down, nodded his head. "So how does a son find wisdom?" he asked.

"Pray, study the earth, learn the ways of the animals."

"So the best thing a father can do for his children is give them wisdom?"

"A father cannot give wisdom to anyone. Each person must find wisdom for himself."

"So what is the best thing a father can do for his children?" Small Knife asked. "Feed them?"

Again Samiq thought carefully about his answer, then he said, "Once there was a village whose chief was a great hunter. The people did not have to do anything but cook what he brought for them. They grew fat on the meat and oil he supplied. But finally the hunter grew old and died, and there was no one to hunt for the people. One by one they starved until the village was too small even to be a village.

"The best thing a father can do for his children is teach them what they need to know to take care of themselves. The best thing a father can do for his children is to allow them to grow strong."

Small Knife said nothing, and in the silence, Samiq rummaged in his hunter's pack for a water bladder. He took out the ivory stopper, drank, handed the bladder to Small Knife.

Small Knife took it in both hands and tipped it up, sucked

out a mouthful of water. He swallowed and said, "Our village is too small. We do not have enough hunters."

Small Knife's words surprised Samiq. Why should a boy worry about such a thing? Then Samiq reminded himself that Small Knife was no longer a boy, but a man, a hunter. So Samiq gave Small Knife a true answer and did not try to make things seem better than they were.

"Yes, it is too small," he said.

"If another tribe comes to us," Small Knife said, "as when the Short Ones came to the Whale Hunters before I was born, if that happened . . ."

"We would fight for our women and children," Samiq said quietly.

"But we would die."

"We might," Samiq answered, "but remember, sometimes the strongest fighting is done with words, not weapons."

"Words cannot kill."

"Sometimes they kill the spirit."

"My Whale Hunter grandfather said a spirit cannot be killed."

"If a man does not care about anything, about himself, or others, about the earth or animals," Samiq said, "then do you see that his spirit is dead?"

"Yes," said Small Knife. "So you are learning to fight with words?" the boy asked.

Samiq nodded. "But I must also be able to fight with the knife."

Small Knife lifted his right hand. "Even with your hand?"

"Yes."

"It will not be enough to fight with words?"

"Some men are not strong enough to fight with words. In their weakness, they use weapons. So I must also be able to use weapons."

Small Knife nodded, then asked, "How will you learn?" He slipped his sleeve knife from its sheath and held it up. "With the knife, I mean?"

"I have been thinking about that," said Samiq. He looked long into Small Knife's eyes. "Would you help me?"

Small Knife slipped his blade back into its sheath and cupped his hands above the flame of his hunter's lamp. "Yes," he said.

Then they sat in silence. When the chill of the air began to stiffen Samiq's body, he turned and pulled two furred robes from his ikyak. He wrapped himself up in one, threw the other to Small Knife. "Go to sleep," Samiq said. "There is much to do tomorrow."

FORTY-SEVEN

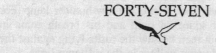

THE WHALE HUNTERS

Yunaska Island, the Aleutian Chain

WAXTAL OPENED HIS EYES. THE VOICES, A DULL hum that wove in and out of his dreams, had changed. He listened. Hard Rock. Waxtal's heart quickened. He braced his hands against the floor and tried to stand, but the days of fasting and the journey back to the Whale Hunters' island had taken his strength.

He sank down on the floor of his sleeping place and heard Hard Rock, questioning. He heard Spotted Egg's quick answers, Owl's slow, strong voice, and he knew he must get up, speak to Hard Rock for himself. Besides, it was morning. His days of fasting were over, and he was hungry. He pushed forward to his hands and knees, then slowly to his feet. He lifted his arms to the water skin hung above his head and let himself drink. The water gave him strength. He drained the skin and threw it aside.

Let the woman fill it. He had had enough of filling water skins. Sudden joy flooded his chest. Let the traders say what they would. He had fulfilled his promise to the spirits. Who could say what powers that would give him? Perhaps enough to pull Hard Rock his way. He pushed aside the curtain and walked out into the main room of the ulaq.

He ignored the three men, but let his eyes rest on the woman. Her face was round, her lips full. She had the long narrow eyes so often seen on Whale Hunter women. She was tall and strong, though it seemed to Waxtal that she held her left arm too close to her body, standing with one hip outthrust, elbow leaning against her hipbone.

She would be welcome in his bed, but probably Owl or Spotted Egg had already claimed her. Or perhaps, being brothers, they had shared her. Since she had come, the ulaq was clean—no bones or food scraps on the floor—but his tusks were not in their usual place beside the low boulder lamp. For a moment, his heart squeezed tight and his breath came in short, quick gasps, but then he saw the tusks lying against the far wall, the ivory glowing yellow in the oil lamp light.

"Waxtal," Spotted Egg said. His voice was a low growl that prickled the hair on the back of Waxtal's head.

"I have completed my fast," Waxtal said. The words seemed to use up the strength the water had given him. He glanced around the ulaq, looking for his walking stick, and remembered he had left it in his sleeping place. He slumped down, suddenly afraid he would fall, here in front of Hard Rock and the traders, in front of the woman who now lived with them. The woman came to him, helped him to sit as though he were an old man, and before he could protest, she put a bowl of broth in his hands.

He raised the bowl to his lips, drank the broth. It was good, rich with fat and sharp with the taste of bitterroot bulbs. It was warm, but not hot enough to burn, and the warmth seeped out through the wooden sides of the bowl to pull the morning stiffness from his fingers.

Hard Rock squatted on his haunches beside Waxtal, looked at him, but Waxtal said nothing, only raised the bowl once more to his lips. "You took their trade goods," Hard Rock said.

"Only because they were going to take what was mine and leave me here."

"This is true?" Hard Rock asked. He looked up at Owl and Spotted Egg.

Owl shrugged.

"He is too old to keep up with us," Spotted Egg said.

"He took everything?" Hard Rock asked. "Everything that was in this ulaq?"

"No," Owl said. "Not the things that were here when we came, not the whale oil or the dried fish."

Hard Rock lowered his head, but Waxtal, looking over at the man, saw the beginning of a smile on his face. "You think he should be killed for taking what was yours," Hard Rock said.

Again Owl shrugged. "It does not matter to us. We do not want him with us, that is all."

"That is not what Spotted Egg told me," Hard Rock said. Owl looked at Spotted Egg, narrowed his eyes.

"We did not have to bring him back here with us," Spotted Egg said. "We could have killed him where he was. We could have taken everything and been gone."

"But you did not," Hard Rock said. "Why not?"

"He was fasting, praying," Spotted Egg said. "Why take the chance that some spirit in that place would be angry?"

"So you thought it was better to bring him here, let the Whale Hunters' island carry the curse?" asked Hard Rock. "Better to let me decide whether he lives or dies? I have enough problems with curses."

"It is your choice," Owl said. "We will kill him or let him live. But if he lives, we will not take him with us."

Hard Rock stood, walked the length of the ulaq. "Why should I want him dead?" he asked. "He took nothing that belonged to the Whale Hunters."

"Good," said Spotted Egg. "You feed him. I am sure the Whale Hunters need another old man to care for. As for us, we will leave. There is nothing for us here. We have tasted your whale oil. It is old. We have tasted your women. They are—"

Owl interrupted, said something in Caribou to Spotted Egg, his words too rapid for Waxtal to follow.

"Tomorrow, then, we go," Owl said to Hard Rock. "We thank you for your hospitality and leave you the skins of oil you see here in this ulaq as our thanks." He pulled back the grass curtain that hung over the entrance to the food cache. Waxtal, squinting, counted four seal bellies. "We also leave you the old man. Do what you want with him."

Waxtal drew in a long breath and looked at Hard Rock, but Hard Rock was already at the climbing log, and, saying nothing, he left the ulaq.

"Tell me what you need done," the woman said and stood up from her basket pole.

Spotted Egg pulled his parka from a pile of skins heaped near the entrance of his sleeping place. "There is a hole under one sleeve," he said, then also threw out leggings and boots, tossing them into a pile at the woman's feet. "Owl, you have clothes for mending?" he asked.

Waxtal turned his back on the traders, raised his bowl, and licked it clean. He went to his tusks, picked up the carved one and took it into his sleeping place, then carried in the plain one.

He laid his hands on the tusks, felt the clamoring of voices at his fingertips. Yes, he thought. He would wait here, out of the way. He would wait here and guard his tusks. But once Owl and Spotted Egg had left, he would go to Hard Rock and make his offer. Owl and Spotted Egg might think they were taking all the trade goods, but they did not know what he had to trade—knowledge that Hard Rock would give all he had to possess.

FORTY-EIGHT

THE RIVER PEOPLE

The Kuskokwim River, Alaska

"EACH PACKET HOLDS A DIFFERENT MEDICINE," Dyenen said. "Each string that ties the packet is a different color with different knots." He pulled several packets from his lynx skin medicine bag, then nodded toward the medicine bag that Raven carried. "See, Saghani, you have the same."

Raven reached into his bag, found packets that were tied in the same manner as Dyenen's packets.

"That is how you know what is in each," Dyenen said. "Now listen and remember." He spread his packets on a flat dry growth of moss and motioned for Raven to do the same.

Raven reached into his own medicine bag, spread the packets out, then squatted on his heels beside the old man.

Dyenen held up a packet and waited until Raven found his tied with the same color string and in the same series of knots.

"Lovage," Dyenen said. "It is found in sand near the sea. The plants are tall with leafstalks red near the bottom. The leaves are shiny and divided so three are one. Leaves and stems should be picked before the flowers come. Eat them green for sores in the mouth or dry them for tea that will take away that pain which comes low and deep in the back. Red string, three single knots."

He picked up the second packet, opened it, and spilled out nettle roots. "Dried nettle," he said. "The roots are good for toothache. Pound them and hold them on the jaw wrapped in grass heated over coals. Pick it in spring. It grows in shaded places where old villages once stood. It grows like a man, tall and with one stalk. The leaves are good for stopping the flow of blood. Red string, two double knots."

He went on, his eyes on the packets, his fingertips gathering stains from the herbs.

But as Dyenen spoke, a coldness crept into Raven's chest. There was nothing here, no stones carrying the glitter of spirit powers, no fur from sacred animals, no amulets consecrated by fasts or visions. Just herbs, plants that anyone could gather, that any wife could boil, that any old woman could use for backache or fever or leg cramps.

He had traded away Kiin's carvings for something a child could do.

Dyenen's words continued, a long line of foolishness about pain and plants, about teas and powders. The chill in Raven's chest turned into the heat of anger, anger so large that Raven could not even fit words around it. And so he sat in silence, Dyenen's voice no more important than the noise of the river that flowed beside them, no better than the whisper of spruce branches in the wind. Then above those noises, he heard the loud, strong call of a raven, and looking up, he saw the bird above them, the tips of its wings bent in the wind, the sun turning the black of its feathers into blue and green and red. The bird rose on the wind currents, and Raven felt his heart lift also. The old man had power. There was some way to get that power.

When Dyenen had talked about every packet, he put them all back into his lynx skin bag. Raven replaced his own packets, though not with the same care Dyenen used. Both men stood, and Dyenen said, "So the trade is done. Medicine for medicine. Each day I will teach you more, other ways to use the packets. I will show you the plants, where they grow, what they look like. Soon you will know as much as I do."

Raven looked down at the old man and slowly shook his head. "You think old women's medicine, herbs and plants, are a worthy trade for my carvings?" he asked. Without giving Dyenen a chance to answer, he continued, "I know you have power. I have seen it. I came to your lodge. I heard voices. Yet you were alone inside. The lodge was trembling with your power. The hunters say you call animals. The hunters say your power brings fish, caribou, beaver. None of that have you shared with me."

Raven turned away from the old man and began following the river back to the village. The old man said nothing, and Raven did not look back to see whether he followed.

When they came to the first lodge, Raven turned and was surprised to see the old man close behind him. Raven had not slowed his pace, had not worried whether Dyenen could keep up with him.

"I will give back the carvings," Dyenen said and held his hands out for the lynx skin bag.

"A trade is a trade," Raven answered. "I said I would give you the carvings, and I will, but I expect something more for what I have given."

"I have nothing more."

"You are shaman of this whole village. Do not tell me you have no power."

"What is more powerful than the earth?" Dyenen asked. "What is more powerful than the plants that grow from the earth?"

Raven bent over, picked a brown shoot of joint grass just pushing up from the spongy soil. "You would tell me that this is more powerful than the wolverine, than the bear or wolf?"

"I would tell you that each power is different," Dyenen said.

"I am not a fool," Raven said. "I know there is power in the medicine bag. I will stay and learn the secrets of this power from you. But I also know you have the power of animal calling. I know you have the power of spirit voices. Maybe I was a fool to think you would understand the power of my carvings and accept them in trade for all your knowledge."

"I have given you the most powerful knowledge I have," Dyenen said.

Raven clenched his teeth, felt them move in their sockets. "The voices, the animal calling, those things I want. What do you want? What in trade can I bring for those powers?"

"I have all things I need. There is nothing you can give me."

"Some men have everything they need," Raven said, "but no man has everything he wants." He fixed his eyes on Dyenen's eyes.

Dyenen turned away. "I am content," he said.

Then Raven remembered something. Dyenen had no son.

"And you do not wish for a son," Raven said slowly.

The old man stopped, turned his head to look at Raven. "You think I could not trade for a boy?" Dyenen asked. "You think there are no River families who would give me their sons?"

"A son of your loins," Raven said. "A son by your own seed."

Dyenen laughed. "You cannot give me that."

"You are right," Raven said. "No man can offer such a thing, but a woman can be traded—a woman with spirit powers, a woman who has the gift of sons."

The old man stood still, his chest moving in slow, long breaths. "You know such a woman?" he asked.

"Yes," Raven said.

The old man raised his eyes to Raven's eyes. And as though he saw truth there he said, "Tell me about her."

FORTY-NINE

DYENEN STROKED THE WALRUS CARVING, FELT ITS spirit spread into his hands. At first he had not believed Saghani. Who would? These carvings made by a woman? But there had been only truth in the man's eyes as he spoke of Kiin, of the twins she had birthed: two sons, healthy and strong. A woman like that, could she not give him sons? He was old, but not too old to have put a daughter into Far Sky's womb, not too old to enjoy a woman in his bed almost every night.

"If this woman is honored among her own people, she might not want to come to this village," Dyenen had said.

Raven lifted his hands, spread his fingers. "Her father gave her to a man who is worth little, lazy and a poor hunter."

"If she has such power, why does she stay with him?"

"He gave much, in furs and weapons, to her father as bride price."

"And the husband would be willing to trade her? Does he not know the value of her carvings?"

"He fears her carvings. He does not understand them. He has offered her to me before in exchange for trade goods."

For a long time Dyenen sat and thought. He had much in skins and pelts, land animal furs that would have much value among the Walrus People. Perhaps the woman would be happy at this River village. It was a good village; the women would be kind to her.

"Does she like to carve?" Dyenen asked.

Raven raised his eyebrows and let out a short laugh. "Why would she not like to carve? But she must hide her carvings from her husband. She brings them to me, trades them for food for her sons and herself—food that her husband cannot provide."

"I would let her carve. I have wives enough to do the work of cooking and sewing, gathering wood for the fire and tending the dogs. You think she might come? Her sons, being born together, must have great powers. I will send furs to trade for her and for her sons.''

"If I bring them, I will expect something for myself,'' Raven said.

"The secrets of the spirit voices, the animal callings?'' Dyenen asked.

Raven smiled. He stood. "Yes.''

Dyenen stood also. "It is agreed,'' he said. "When will you bring her? This summer? Next year? I am an old man.''

"I will leave tomorrow,'' Raven said. "I will bring the woman and her sons to you within this moon.''

"No,'' Dyenen said. "I told you it would be a moon and another half moon to learn the secrets of the medicine packs. I must do as I promised.''

"I release you from your promise,'' Raven said.

"How can one man cut the ties of another's promise?'' Dyenen asked. "If I cannot keep promises to you, why should the spirits believe my promises to them?''

Finally, Raven lifted his hands in a gesture of goodwill and, shaking his head, left the lodge. Dyenen followed him outside, and with the walrus carving in his hands, watched as the man walked between the clustered River lodges back to the traders' lodge.

Dyenen smiled. Unlike Saghani, he had not had to divulge his secret—he understood the Walrus language just as Saghani understood the River People's tongue. There was an advantage to age—the years of experience that provide wisdom in dealing with the young, those who believe age gives nothing but brittle bones and stiff joints.

Yes, Dyenen thought, at worst I will lose the furs I send as bride price. At best, I will get a woman who understands things of the spirit. A woman who might, with the power of her born-together children, give a son. And all for a little knowledge, knowledge that was not even something of the spirits. How foolish of Saghani to think that the voices he heard and the shaking lodge skin were something of great power. They were tricks, taught to all River People shamans, passed from shaman to shaman. And the calling of animals— yes, that required prayers, chants, but were these more important than a man's knowledge of animal trails, of the cycle of years that all animals follow? Lynx live best during abundance

of hares; bears' numbers increase after years of many salmon;
caribou follow ancient paths in cycled years of tens and twen-
ties, waiting for the slow-growing plants they eat.

So Dyenen would give this knowledge to Saghani, and
Saghani would think he had all power, but what power was
greater than the power Dyenen had offered Saghani that morning—the knowledge of medicine? What man, when he was
sick, would not trade all the spirit voices on earth for medicine
that would push the sickness from his body? What kept a
village of people honoring their shaman? The knowledge that
he could help them conquer the powers of sickness.

Raven crawled into the traders' lodge. Yes, he would trade
Kiin. He would be sure she made him many carvings before
he returned to the River village, carvings enough to last him
through years of trading.

Each time he came to the River village, he would see her
and trade for more carvings. Besides, the old man would not
live for many more years. Dyenen would give Raven the secrets of his power, and then Raven would build his own village
into something large and strong, ready for the time when the
old man died. Then Raven would return to the River People
and claim Kiin again as wife.

All he had to do was find another child, a boy the same age
as Shuku, trade something for the child, and bring him to Kiin.
Who, of the River People, would know it was not Kiin's son?

But where to find the child? He would have to be a First
Men child, a child that carried the smooth skin and round head,
the long eyes of the First Men, but what mother would give
a son to a trader?

When the answer finally came, Raven laughed aloud. It was
so simple. An Ugyuun mother, of course! They always had
more children than they could feed. A few seal bellies of oil,
a walrus belly of meat. Any Ugyuun woman would give her
soul for food. Why not give a son?

FIFTY

THE WHALE HUNTERS

Yunaska Island, the Aleutian Chain

KUKUTUX CARRIED ANOTHER SEAL BELLY OF OIL
to the top of the ulaq and handed it to Spotted Egg. She shook
her head. The foolishness of traders. Why haul all their trade
goods into the ulaq two days ago only to carry them all back
out again today? She went down the climbing log and picked
up a bundle of baskets, sized so that each one slipped inside
the next. She tossed them up to Spotted Egg.

Perhaps the traders were worried that the Whale Hunter people would steal their trade goods. How could two men stand
against a village? But if they worried about that, why leave
the trade goods in the trading ik this night? Kukutux shook
her head. Who could understand traders?

The carrying and lifting were not easy. Kukutux's left elbow
had begun to ache, and she wondered if Old Goose Woman
had any ugyuun root Kukutux could make into a poultice,
something that would draw the sharp spirits of pain from her
arm.

Ah, well, she told herself, be thankful the traders have not
taken their anger out on you. But then a quiet thought came
to her: there was still one night. One night before they left.
Kukutux lifted a seal belly of dried fish, shifted it up to her
left shoulder, and climbed to the top of the ulaq.

You have been through worse things, she told herself.

When all the trade goods were out of the ulaq, Kukutux took
her gathering bag and walked the beach. It was not yet low
tide, but the water had begun to ebb. Perhaps she would find
something fresh to add to a meal of dried fish. She used a

walking stick to turn over small rocks and poke into crevices between the boulders that guarded the shallows of the Whale Hunter's wide beach. She found a few sea urchins—not enough to satisfy even a child—but she went back to the ulaq, and when she saw that Owl and Spotted Egg were not inside, she took the urchins to the old man, called to him through the curtain of his sleeping place.

"Do you pray?"

The old man cleared his throat. "My praying is done," he said, and peeked out from the side of the curtain.

"I have these," Kukutux said and handed him the gathering bag. "They are not much."

The man's eyes opened wide, and his mouth split into a smile. "The others, Owl and Spotted Egg, they are leaving?" he asked.

"Tomorrow, if the sky is good," Kukutux said. "Do you need water?"

The old man let the curtain close, but returned quickly with an empty water bladder. She took the bladder and gave him a full one. He nodded and said, "Tell me when they have left." Then he let the curtain fall between them.

Kukutux stood and sighed her relief at the empty ulaq. She hated the stacks of trader's packs that had cluttered the room. Soon the traders, too, would be gone, but first she must feed them. She went to the cache and pulled out all the food packs that Owl and Spotted Egg had left.

She set out dried berries mixed with seal oil, dried seal meat, smoked fish flavored with crumbled ugyuun leaves.

When she was finished, the traders had still not returned, so she went into the sleeping places, checked to be sure she had emptied the ulaq of what belonged to Owl and Spotted Egg. Of all the things the traders had brought into the ulaq, only a few packs of food and the old man's walking stick remained. Then she remembered the tusks. They, too, were gone. She felt a sudden sadness close down over her heart. Did the old man know? Should he know? What if the tusks were the source of his powers? Was it right that the traders take them? She walked to the old man's curtain.

"Your tusks are not here," she called. "Have the traders taken them?"

"They are in this sleeping place with me," the old man

answered, his words muffled as though his mouth was full.

He is eating the sea urchins, Kukutux thought. "Good," she said. She turned away from the curtain, but the old man called to her.

"Thank you for the sea urchins. I was hungry." He paused, then said, "You have seen my tusks?"

"You said you had them," Kukutux answered.

"I mean, have you looked at the carvings?"

"I saw that there were lines made on one," Kukutux answered.

"Come in, look."

Kukutux glanced at the roof hole, then told herself it did not matter if the traders found her in the old man's sleeping place. She would tell them she wanted to be sure the old man had nothing that belonged to them. She pulled aside the curtain, rolled it up, and tucked it into the grass thatching that covered the ulaq walls. Then she crawled in beside him.

The old man held the carved tusk across his lap, his hands stroking it as a mother smooths her baby's skin. Kukutux looked around the sleeping place, checking for packs, trade goods, but the sleeping place was bare except for a few furs and grass mats.

"See? The tusk," the old man said, using words to pull her eyes back to him. Kukutux moved close, bent low over the tusk. Lines, cut deeply into the ivory, spread from the large end of the tusk halfway to the point. Taken together, they flowed like grass under the wind, and drew the eye like the flame of an oil lamp.

"It is beautiful," Kukutux said.

"If all my life I have only these tusks," the old man said, "it is enough."

Kukutux sat back on her heels, remembered thinking much the same thing as she held her son, new in her arms, his hair still damp from birth. Almost, she could feel the warmth of him against her breast, but then she heard the voices of Owl and Spotted Egg.

"I will try to bring you food later," she whispered as she left the old man's sleeping place.

Hard Rock had come with Owl and Spotted Egg, so Kukutux served all three men, then took food for herself and went to her basket corner to eat.

The men ate without talking, but when they had finished, Hard Rock began to speak of whale hunting. He spoke of hunters still living and some long dead whose names he could not say for fear of calling their spirits back to the village. Kukutux listened to his stories as she sat, hands empty, enjoying a rare time of doing nothing.

When the hunting stories had ended, Hard Rock said, "There was a time when other men came here, to this island. We named them the Short Ones. They came to the Seal Hunters first, destroyed their village, so that everyone died except one woman. She was granddaughter to that one who was then our chief and is now dead. She came to our island to warn us, she and other Seal Hunters."

Kukutux smiled. She had heard the story before, a story of fighting and bravery by both men and woman. Now as Hard Rock spoke, he mentioned Waxtal's name, and Kukutux knew he spoke of the old man huddled in his sleeping place.

"He killed a Short One and was wounded himself during the battle. He gave us the idea that let us defeat the Short Ones. He told us to put two climbing logs in each ulaq so our hunters could go up back to back, protecting each other as they fought. So you see," Hard Rock said, "it is difficult for me to say, 'Yes, kill the old man,' for he saved Whale Hunter lives long ago."

Owl nodded, though Spotted Egg stood and paced quickly from one side of the ulaq to the other. "It is your decision," Spotted Egg said. "The man is not a good man. For some reason he was thrown out of his own village by the chief of his tribe. Who knows why? It seems as if he would do no harm, but who can say?"

Hard Rock stood and stretched. He had taken off his suk and used it as a cushion on the floor. Now he picked it up and pulled it on.

"Do not kill him," Hard Rock said. "Leave him here. The woman will take care of him." He pointed to Kukutux, and a spark of anger burned in her heart, but she said nothing. Why complain? She had no husband. This Waxtal, even though he was old, should be able to hunt.

Hard Rock left the ulaq, and for a time Owl and Spotted Egg bent their heads together, speaking in soft words as though afraid to let Kukutux hear what they said. Kukutux smiled and stood, purposely going near to pick up leftover food and the men's bowls. Their words became whispers, until Kukutux, laughing, said to them, "Why whisper? I do not speak the Caribou tongue. Talk as loudly as you wish. Unless you are afraid the old man will hear you."

Spotted Egg scowled, but Owl stood up, a smile on his face. "Spotted Egg says that it will be many days until he has a woman again in his sleeping place. He wonders if you will come."

Spotted Egg, eyes staring straight ahead at the ulaq wall, said nothing, so Owl bent down, lifted the many necklaces that lay against Spotted Egg's chest. "Choose one, and if you will have us both, choose two."

Kukutux felt the skin over her cheeks burn. "If I choose to sleep alone?" she asked.

Owl shrugged. "It is your choice," he said, but his eyes were gentle as they lingered on her face.

Kukutux looked away, and in her mind, she saw the food left in the cache. She had a sealskin from her own ulaq half full of oil, a seal belly of oil coming from Hard Rock, two sealskins of dried fish, a handful of dried seal meat, a basket of berries. Enough to get her and the old man through to the seal hunting season, but if the old man was a poor hunter, what then? A winter of starving.

She leaned close to Spotted Egg, watched his face as she fingered each necklace. "Not this one," he said, laying his hand flat against the bear claw necklace that curled in a wide circle around his neck. "Any of the others."

"Two?" Kukutux asked.

Spotted Egg's nostrils flared, but he nodded.

"This and this," she said, choosing one necklace of seal teeth and another of shining circles cut from the white inner layer of clam shells.

Spotted Egg took off one necklace and then the other. He handed them to Kukutux. She held them up to the lamplight, let herself believe for a moment that the necklaces were hers, that she could wear such things, have something so beautiful for herself. Then she looked back at Owl and Spotted Egg and laughed. "They are mine?" she asked.

"If you come to our sleeping places," Spotted Egg said.

Kukutux nodded. This was the time to trade. If she waited

until after, when their needs were satisfied, it would be too late. "They are beautiful," she said, "but I cannot eat necklaces. If they are mine, they are mine to keep or to trade, yes?"

She waited, but the men gave her no answer.

"How much oil will you give me for this?" she asked and held out the seal tooth necklace.

Spotted Egg turned to Owl, and the men looked at each other but said nothing, as though their eyes in looking spoke for them. "None," Spotted Egg finally said.

The muscles in Kukutux's neck tightened and the back of her head began to ache, but she kept her face still, neither smiling nor frowning. "How much dried meat then?" she asked.

Spotted Egg ground his teeth and shook his head.

"None?" Kukutux said. Again she laughed; again she said, "I cannot eat necklaces." She leaned toward Spotted Egg, let the necklaces slip from the ends of her fingers into his lap. "Then these are yours," she said. She turned away from the traders and sat down, her back toward them.

She felt their eyes, watching, waiting, and the skin on her arms pulled up into bumps, so that she clasped her elbows to keep from shivering. She did not let herself turn to face them. What am I against two young men? she asked herself. How can I fight if they decide to take me? Still, she did not let herself move. The ulaq was so quiet she could hear her own breathing.

"One," Spotted Egg said, and the loudness of his voice made Kukutux jump.

She looked at him over her shoulder.

"One seal belly of oil," he said.

"For both of you?" Kukutux asked.

"You are worth more?" asked Owl.

Kukutux stood up and faced the men. "I was worth two necklaces not long ago," she said. "You are the traders. You know what your necklaces are worth. Why ask me?"

"Two bellies of dried meat," Owl said.

"Two seal bellies of oil," said Kukutux. "Or three of dried meat."

"One meat, one oil," Owl said, and did not look at Spotted Egg when the man's breath hissed out over his teeth.

"Who is first?" Kukutux asked.

FIFTY-ONE

KUKUTUX RAN HER HAND OVER THE SOFT FURS
that lined the floor of Owl's sleeping place.

"I will give you the oil and the meat, even if you do not
choose to come to my bed," Owl said. "But I cannot speak
for my brother."

"I will do what I promised," Kukutux answered. She
glanced at Owl, then looked away. His eyes were intense, and
she could feel the power of him, as though he reached across
his sleeping place and touched her. She began to untie the
strings that held her aprons, but he shook his head and said,
"Lie down on your stomach."

Kukutux looked at him, questions in her eyes, but he was
patting and straightening the sleeping robes as though he were
a woman. Kukutux lowered herself, her muscles tense. Then
his fingers were against her back, rubbing in close circles
across her shoulders. She felt herself relax.

"You work very hard," he said to her, and his words so
surprised Kukutux that she nearly laughed.

"Who does not work hard—man, woman, or child?" Kukutux asked.

"Waxtal does not work hard, Kukutux," Owl answered.
"Remember that. You are a woman whose heart is soft. Remember—not everyone deserves your sympathy. Do you not
have enough sorrow in your life?"

"What do you know about my sorrow?" Kukutux asked.

Owl's hands stopped. "You think I cannot see that you are
sad?" he asked. "But you are a strong woman. A man would
be fortunate to have you as wife."

Kukutux rolled over to look into Owl's eyes.

"It has been long enough," he said to her. "You may go
to my brother now if you wish."

"No," Kukutux said. "I will do as I promised."

Owl took a long breath and leaned over to untie her aprons.

233

When his fingers touched her, his hands trembled. Then he was stroking her belly, her breasts, the soft skin of her inner thighs. He parted her legs and moved over her, his hands still caressing.

His fingers were tight on her shoulders as he moved in rhythm over her.

Kukutux had not had a man since her husband died, and there was a part of her body that wanted to rise into Owl's arms, find pleasure in the feel of him moving within her. But there was also that part of her, something within her chest, that seemed to wail out her grief, that let her think only of the hunter who had shared so many of her nights.

Her skin remembered White Stone's touch—his large, gentle hands. So she held herself still and pushed away any pleasure brought by need. And though she wrapped her arms and legs around Owl's strong body, she felt stiff and cold, as though she kept herself apart, only watching what some other woman did.

Owl tensed, gathered her tight against the hardness of his chest, and then relaxed, his weight settling on her like a sleeping robe. The sweat between their bodies prickled Kukutux's skin, but she did not move until his breathing deepened, and she knew he was asleep. Then she gently pushed him to one side. She wiped her breasts and between her legs with one of the sleeping skins and crawled from the sleeping place.

She was naked, without her apron, which she had left near the curtain. She reached back, grabbed the apron, and fastened it at her waist. Who could say what spirits would be waiting at the top of the ulaq, ready to come in with sickness or strife through those three openings between her legs? She moved to the oil lamp she had left burning and warmed her fingers in its flame.

"One more," she whispered. She gave herself the luxury of looking into the food cache, seeing the oil and meat Owl had put there for her. "One more," she said again, then squared her shoulders and turned toward Spotted Egg's sleeping place. She wished he had claimed her first. It would be over now with him, and only Owl would be left. Owl was the quiet one, the gentle one. He had treated her well. But who could say about Spotted Egg?

She walked to Spotted Egg's curtain and had reached to

pull it aside when a voice, soft, whispering, came to her from the other side of the ulaq. "Why do you go to him?"

Kukutux turned, saw Waxtal sitting outside his sleeping place. "Are you hungry?" she asked, the politeness coming without thought.

"Why do you go to him?" Waxtal asked again, and Kukutux pulled her hand away from the curtain, turned and went to the old man, squatted down beside him.

"He has given me oil and meat, enough for me to live a few more moons."

"You have no husband?" the old man asked.

"No."

"I need a wife," he said.

Kukutux's breath seemed to catch at the base of her throat. "There are other women here on this island who need husbands," she said.

"You would not take me as husband?" he asked. "I am a strong hunter."

At first Kukutux shook her head, but then the old man said, "I have the power to lift the curse on this island. If you do not believe me, remember my carvings. Remember the stories about the old Seal Hunter shaman whose power helped defeat the Short Ones. He is the one who taught me to carve. He is the one who blessed me with his powers. Ask Hard Rock. I was the one who was at the old shaman's side when he died. I was the one who received his blessings."

For a long time, Kukutux said nothing. Finally she answered, "Talk to me about this tomorrow. Now I have to go to Spotted Egg."

She walked to Spotted Egg's sleeping place, did not let herself look back at the old man, but instead pulled aside the curtain, sighed as Spotted Egg reached for her, as he untied her apron and ran quick, rough fingers up the insides of her thighs. Then she lost herself in thoughts, the good and bad of being wife to a trader, until Spotted Egg was finished, the man lying over her, his mouth open in sleep, wet against her shoulder.

FIFTY-TWO

WOULD IT BE SO TERRIBLE TO LIVE WITH THE Whale Hunters? Would it be so terrible to have a young, beautiful wife? Waxtal leaned back against the wall of his sleeping place and sighed. Owl and Spotted Egg had left the ulaq early that morning. Their loud voices had awakened him, and he had lain hidden under bedding furs, with knives in both fists, waiting to see if they would come for him or his tusks.

But they had not. He had not heard them even mention his name. Good. Someday he would face them, but it was better if that time came when he was chief of a village, with all the powers of a shaman, and with young men, perhaps his own sons, to defend him.

Now, he had only to wait. Wait until the woman came back to the ulaq, wait for the meal she would prepare for him, wait to speak to Hard Rock and see what the man would give him in return for Samiq's life.

Kukutux watched as Owl and Spotted Egg held one last trading session on the beach. Spotted Egg held up a pair of caribou skin leggings. They were decorated on the sides with a fringe made of stiff hair dyed dark red. Men were holding up packets of birdbone needles, jointed hooks carved from whale jawbone, obsidian knives, bird nets. Spotted Egg walked among them, finally made his choice, and handed Crooked Bird the leggings. In exchange, Crooked Bird gave Spotted Egg two fishhooks, a whale tongue skin chigadax decorated with white bits of seal esophagus at shoulder seams and chest, and one obsidian bird dart blade.

Kukutux shook her head and looked away. Crooked Bird did not need caribou skin leggings. With the chigadax he could hunt whales; with the bird dart he could kill birds; with the hooks he could fish. What would the leggings bring in? One time wearing them in an ikyak or on the beach and they would

236

be wet, soft, easily torn on rocks. If one of his wives did not
get the salt out of them, they would stiffen and crack. And for
all the care they would require, what food would they help
him bring in? Nothing. A woman might be glad to wear them
in the hills when she was berry picking. The long grass was
sharp. But what man would allow a woman to wear something
that he had bought for a whale tongue skin chigadax?

Kukutux squatted at the edge of the beach, no longer inter-
ested in what one person or another might receive in trade. It
would be good when the two men left. Then perhaps the
Whale Hunter people could go back to living as they had always lived, hunting whales, picking berries, gathering food
from the beaches.

She was tired. The night before, after Spotted Egg had finished with her, she had not been able to sleep. Her mind had
been full of the old man's offer. Had it been something true,
something from his heart? Did he mean her to be his wife for
as long as he stayed with the Whale Hunters or for always?
If he left, would she want to go with him? What would it be
like to visit many villages, to learn the ways of traders? Would
she want to face the seas, she and one old man, alone in ik or
ikyak? Then her thoughts had turned to fear, and she had considered the many things Owl and Spotted Egg might do to
harm the old man before they left.

Finally, she had slept, but it was a sleep of many dreams,
and when she awoke in the morning, she felt as though she
still lived in those dreams. She went outside to the cooking
hearth, prepared a broth of fish, and thickened it with bitterroot
bulbs. She lifted the cooking skin from its place over the fire
and carried it inside, hung it from the rafters, and dipped out
a bowl for the old man. She slipped it into his sleeping place
with only a whisper for fear Spotted Egg or Owl might see
her. But as the morning lightened, sending a brightness into
the ulaq from the roof hole, Kukutux's fears also lightened,
and she looked back on her night of dreams and worries as a
woman looks back to the problems of her childhood, with a
smile for silliness.

She had fed Owl and Spotted Egg, packed food and water,
and carried it out to their ik. And finally they had left the ulaq,
left without a word to the old man, without even a glance at
his sleeping place. Kukutux had followed them to the beach,

and here she was now, fighting against the sleep that reached out from the night to claim her.

She stood, shook her head, and stretched her eyes open wide. There will be time to sleep once they leave, she told herself.

Suddenly the women around her parted, made way for Owl, who was coming toward her. "One last trade," Owl was saying, speaking the words in the strange singing voice of the Caribou People. He stopped beside Kukutux, looked down at her. He held out a necklace, not one of the small ones Kukutux had chosen for herself the night before, necklaces she had traded for oil and meat with little regret, but a necklace of light blue stones, each stone separated from the next by a tiny bead, so bright and yellow it seemed as though each were a bit of the sun, rolled and pierced and strung on sinew.

"I have nothing to trade," Kukutux said and held out empty hands, but Owl draped the necklace over her fingers, brushed his hands against hers.

"You will not come with me, will you?" he asked and looked so hard into her eyes that Kukutux had to look away. "I do not always travel," he said. "I have a good lodge. I need a wife."

Remembrance of the pleasure Owl's hands had given her crowded into Kukutux's mind, but then she looked back at the Whale Hunter island, at the rise of hills beyond the beach; at the mountains, standing in their robes of cloud; at the people she had lived with all her life. A great and choking sorrow rose up in her throat. How could she leave her home? What did she know about this man?

She thought of Waxtal. If she left, perhaps he would not share his powers with the Whale Hunters. Perhaps in anger he would not lift the curse that had come to destroy her people.

"I cannot," Kukutux finally said. She pulled her hands away from Owl's hands, but he lifted the necklace, held wide the circle of blue beads, and dropped it slowly over her head, reaching with gentle fingers to stroke the otter fur of her suk. "It is yours," he said quietly and turned away.

When they pushed their ik out into the sea, Kukutux left the beach, went back to her ulaq, stood at the top, and watched until the dark line of the trader's ik became a part of the waves.

FIFTY-THREE

WAXTAL MOVED CLOSE TO THE SLEEPING PLACE
curtain and looked out through the narrow space between curtain and wall. The woman had returned to the ulaq. He
watched as she dragged the grass mats and crowberry heath
from Owl's and Spotted Egg's sleeping places.

He crawled from his sleeping place, stood, and stretched,
pulling up his shoulders, then curling his arms over his head.
The woman looked back at him and smiled, a tight smile that
did not show her teeth.

"They are gone?" he asked.

"Yes," the woman said softly. She laid one hand against
her chest, and Waxtal noticed that she wore a new string of
beads, a necklace he had long admired, with tiny gold beads
barely larger than the corner of an eye, and stones the unusual
blue-green color of the sea. Owl had told him that the necklace
had belonged to many different traders and had passed from
hand to hand on a journey from some land to the south and
so carried a blessing from the sun.

"From Owl?" Waxtal asked.

"Yes," the woman said, and though her eyes were looking
at Waxtal, it seemed that she saw beyond the ulaq, to other
things, perhaps other times.

Waxtal laughed. "You must have given him a good night!"
he said.

Waxtal thought the woman would smile, but she only
shrugged her shoulders, so that Waxtal felt a sudden rise of
anger, something that pushed his words together into a tight,
hard line as he said, "You have considered what I asked?"

"You said you have powers," the woman answered, and
stared at him as though she could see through skin and flesh
into his soul.

"You have seen my carving," Waxtal said.

"Yes." The woman waited.

239

Did she think she needed to know more than what his carving revealed? "There is much power in that carving," Waxtal said. What else could he say? He was trader and carver, perhaps already a shaman. What man, given the vision Waxtal had been given, would not consider himself a shaman?

"The carving is good," the woman said, "but what does it do for my people? Will it lift our curse? Still we see no whales, and now the otters have come in to take our sea urchins. Already some of the old ones speak of giving themselves to the wind spirits this next winter so the hunters and children might have more food."

Waxtal shrugged. What did the woman expect him to do about that? Why worry about a few old people?

He stretched out his arm and pointed at the cache, but in pointing, he saw that since his fast, his hands had changed, the veins high and bulging under the skin, the knuckles thick, the fingers bent. "I need food," he said. He squatted on his haunches and crossed his arms.

From behind the curtains of his sleeping place, he heard a whisper, the tusk speaking: "Your hands are the hands of an old man," it said.

But Waxtal thought, My hands are the hands of a carver. You would not be able to speak if it were not for these hands. And he turned his head so the thoughts would go out from his eyes into the sleeping place.

"These Whale Hunters, what do they know of carving?" the tusk asked. "They think you are old. They will tell you to give yourself to the wind spirits. You must leave this place."

The woman handed Waxtal a bowl of broth. He cupped the bowl in his hands, raised it to his lips, and turned his mind away from the tusk.

The woman said, "What will you do to help us? You are not a young man. Can you still hunt?"

The woman's words came to Waxtal's ears, but almost he did not believe she had said them. What woman insults a man, any man, let alone a carver, a trader, a shaman?

"Woman!" he roared out, but the word was so large that it blocked his throat and he began to choke.

Though he choked, the woman said, "I am Kukutux. Per-

haps among your people it is polite to call someone 'woman.'
I will be honored to call you 'old man.' ''

Waxtal coughed until he was finally able to draw in a
breath, then, wiping tears from his eyes, he said, "Call me
Waxtal.'' He reminded himself of what he had learned from
being husband to Blue Shell—though a woman needed to be
afraid of her husband, there were times for gentle words.

He set down his food bowl and said quietly, "How was I
to know your name? You did not tell me, and the traders,
angry at the success of my vision fast, would not speak to me
these past few days. Why do you think they left so quickly?
They know they cannot help the Whale Hunters. They know
their powers are weak. They know their weakness would leave
them open to the curse that I will soon drive from the Whale
Hunters' island.

"Do you think spirits that carry a curse are content to fly
away, up into wind or sky or sea? How much better to go to
some other man, to enjoy the warmth of that man's body, the
joy of his woman, the taste of his food.

"They told you I took their trade goods? Only what was
mine. Do you think those two young men had anything of
their own to trade? I have been trading for years. Do you think
I have nothing to show for those years? I brought most of my
trade goods on this journey. Some I traded for the tusks. But
what was left I brought here. Now Owl and Spotted Egg have
it, all but the few skins of oil and meat they left. Those things,
they are mine. Why do you think they were so generous with
you?'' Waxtal stopped, took a long breath, and pointed at the
blue stone necklace Kukutux wore. "You think one night in
a sleeping place is worthy of that?''

Kukutux curled her fingers around the necklace.

"Owl gave it to you, but it was not his to give. It is mine.''

Kukutux's eyes widened, and then her shoulders slumped.
She looked up at the ulaq rafters and shook her head, then
took off the necklace and handed it to Waxtal. Waxtal smiled
and placed the necklace carefully over his head. He reached
inside his suk, pulled out a necklace of shell beads, something
good but not as beautiful.

"Here,'' Waxtal said, but Kukutux did not take it. "It holds
special powers,'' Waxtal said. "I wore it during my fast.''

Kukutux reached out, let the shell beads brush against her

fingers, then shook her head. "No," she said. "Keep anything that will add to your power. I ask only that you help my people."

Waxtal tilted his head, smiled as though he teased some small child, then he put the necklace on again. "I am sorry I cannot let you keep this," he said and lifted the blue stones. "Each stone carries much power." He tucked the necklace inside his suk and raised the bowl of broth to his lips. He took a sip. Some of the broth trickled from the corners of his mouth into the thin tangle of whiskers that hung from his chin. "Perhaps someday my wife will wear the necklace, if she gives me many sons," he said, but his last words seemed again to catch in his throat, and once more he began to choke.

Kukutux pulled down a water bladder, handed it to Waxtal. He took a careful sip, then wiped his chin with his hand.

He gave Kukutux the water bladder, finished the broth, and handed the bowl to Kukutux to fill again. She gave him more broth, then went to her basket corner, sat down, and began weaving. When Waxtal had finished the second bowlful, he turned toward Kukutux. Her fingers were busy, baskets spread in a circle around her.

"They let you keep the grass?" he asked.

Kukutux picked up a sheaf of fine split strands and held it out to Waxtal. "It is also yours?" she asked.

"No," he said. "It was Spotted Egg's. He traded for it. Oil for grass. Even Owl was angry with him."

Kukutux shrugged and bent her head over her work.

"You have not answered me," Waxtal said.

When Kukutux did not look up at him, his stomach twisted and he bit the insides of his cheeks. The salt taste of his own blood was hot against the back of his throat. What did he need with this woman? he asked himself. Did he want another Blue Shell, someone with a beautiful face, but deceitful spirit?

He opened his mouth to tell Kukutux to leave, but before he spoke, she said, "If you help my people, I will be your wife." And when she spoke, Waxtal saw her hope—like the flame of some lamp burning.

So, she was doing merely what he had always done, trading goods for goods. She would be his wife if he would use his powers to help the Whale Hunters. How could he be angry at that? How could he be angry when he already knew what he had to offer—something Hard Rock could not refuse?

"Bring Hard Rock," Waxtal said to Kukutux. "Bring him here. Tonight you will be my wife."

FIFTY-FOUR

HARD ROCK SAT DOWN OPPOSITE WAXTAL. KUKU-tux pretended to be busy beside the food cache, but from the corners of her eyes she watched.

For a long time neither man spoke, each looking down at the mat where Kukutux had set out food. Finally Hard Rock said, "So you want to take this woman as wife?"

Waxtal straightened and looked into Hard Rock's face. "Yes."

"You will stay here with us, be part of this village?"

Kukutux saw the quick widening of Waxtal's eyes, heard the hesitation in his words. "I am a trader," he said. "Sometimes I will travel. Sometimes I will be here."

Hard Rock nodded. "We need hunters," he said. He gestured toward the walrus tusks now beside the largest oil lamp in the ulaq. "It is good you carve," he said. "But when people are starving, it is more important that you hunt."

Waxtal jutted out his chin and did not answer. He picked up a strip of dried seal meat and folded it into his mouth. "When there are no animals," he said, the meat bulging in his cheek, "even the best hunters bring in nothing. What if there was a man in the village who had spirit powers to call animals? Then who would be most important?"

"If you stay here, you must be able to hunt," Hard Rock said, his words clipped and strong, as though he spoke to a child. He stood, walked over to Kukutux. "You want this old man as husband?" he asked her.

Waxtal rudely interrupted. "Since when do women pick their husbands?" he asked.

"Whale Hunter women always have that choice," Hard

Rock said. "What man is fool enough to live with a woman who does not want him? But perhaps Seal Hunters were not given the gift of wisdom.

"You want him?" Hard Rock asked again.

Kukutux looked at Waxtal, saw his gnarled hands, the gray in his hair. She looked at the walrus tusks, the beautiful design the man had carved. She turned her head toward the food cache, remembered what it was like to have a hunter in the ulaq. "If he can hunt," she said.

"Three of us go at high tide to hunt seals," Hard Rock said to Waxtal. "You will come too."

Waxtal frowned. "I have not prayed. I have not oiled my chigadax for many days."

"You have time to pray," Hard Rock said. "What hunter leaves his chigadax without oil?"

"What shaman caught in a vision fast thinks of his chigadax?"

"So you claim to be shaman?"

"Only since my fast."

"I have known few shamans. For most, the gift is revealed to them in childhood. Who are you to claim something as an old man?"

"You knew the shaman from Tugix's island," Waxtal said. "His powers have passed to me."

"If you are shaman," Hard Rock said, "you are welcome on this island. But a man's words have little worth if he does not have the power to prove their truth. Oil your chigadax, pray, and come with us. We will see if you can hunt."

The sea rose in a high swell under Waxtal's ikyak, and he looked out at the horizon. He followed the Whale Hunters, their ikyan outdistancing his soon after they left the beach. But they were young men with hard muscles.

Do not worry, he told himself. What are muscles compared to the powers of a man who speaks to spirits, who hears spirits speak to him?

The water was cold through the thin walls of the ikyak, and that cold seeped through the fur seal pelt Waxtal sat on. The chill reached the bones of his legs, and his knees began to tremble. But what hunter does not know that cold pondered is worse than cold ignored? So Waxtal began a song, a seal hunt-

ing chant he had learned while still a boy. The song had been
given to him by his grandfather—a man who was not a great
hunter, who more than once had used his walking stick to lay
welts across Waxtal's back. But even this song was better than
thinking only of his discomfort, so Waxtal blocked the remembrance of his grandfather from his mind and continued to
sing. He sang loudly with hopes that Hard Rock might hear
that he sang, might think, if seals were found, that Waxtal had
called them.

They paddled the rest of that day, seeking sea animals, but
they found none, until finally in darkness they returned to their
island.

Waxtal was lifting his ikyak to a place on the rack when
Hard Rock came to him. "So if you are shaman, why did you
not call us a seal? I heard you singing."

Waxtal made himself laugh. "Today I went as hunter. Was
that not what the woman wanted? The song I sang was a seal
hunting song given to me by my grandfather when I was yet
a boy. It is a good song, but has no shaman's power. I will
go now and oil my chigadax. What hunter leaves his chigadax
without oil? When you want to hunt again, tell me. I will go
with you." He walked toward his ulaq, then looked back at
Hard Rock. "When you are ready for me to be a shaman and
call animals for you, tell me. I will do that also."

Kukutux gathered fishing supplies and left the ulaq. Waxtal's
chants followed her, and even on the beach, over the noise of
waves and gulls calling, she thought she heard his voice, the
singing that seemed to lift itself up into his nose and come
out blunted and coarse, as though the song had pushed itself
through the hard bones of Waxtal's head.

What do you know of chants and shaman's powers? Kukutux chided herself. What powers do you own that allow you
to criticize what someone else does?

She squatted in the lee of a boulder, used a strand of hair
to tie fish guts to her gorge hook. The tide was ebbing, but
the water was still deep enough to fish from the top of a rock
that reached out into the sea from the south side of the beach.
She unrolled a length of line from her holding stick, knotted
on a small stone for weight, and threw her hook out into the

water. She used her stick to roll the line in, singing as she
fished, a song her mother had given her.

> *"Fish give yourself to my hook.*
> *Feed my children.*
> *I will honor you."*

Those simple words sung over and over.

Finally she felt a tug on the line, coiled it in, and brought
up a fine pogy. Again she baited her hook, threw out her line,
and sang her song. Before the tide was too low to fish from
the rocks, she had caught six pogies, the fish glistening in her
carrying bag.

Six pogies! Kukutux thought. She remembered winter days
without food, nights gnawing seal hide strips to fool her mouth
into believing it was being fed. As she neared her ulaq, again
she heard Waxtal's song. Perhaps he does have powers, she
thought. At least to call fish.

FIFTY-FIVE

The Alaska Peninsula

FOR A MOON OF WALKING, KIIN KEPT TO THE
shore, following the beaches and digging for clams, finding
sea urchins at low tide. Sometimes she passed small islands,
their stone cliffs filled with the noise of nesting auklets and
murres. But she could not reach the islands without an ik, and
so she turned her face away from the bird cliffs, and did not
let herself remember the taste of new eggs, boiled hard in
water or sucked raw from the shell.

This day, she had been walking against rain that blew in
from the North Sea. Her carrying basket kept the back of her
suk dry, and Shuku was a small warm bundle strapped against
her chest, but she knew she would probably spend the night

chilled and wet, huddled beneath sealskins that could not keep away the cold.

"Remember why you walk," she told herself. "What is a little rain if you will soon be with your people?"

She began a song, something that helped keep the rhythm of her feet, and when the sky darkened toward night, she looked for a place, protected by rock or cliff, that would shield her against rain and wind.

The gravel beach was dotted with stones, smooth and waterworn, the size of gull eggs. The stones made walking difficult, but she would rather walk on the beach than through the sodden grass above the high-tide line.

She had stopped to look in all directions, hoping to find some outcropping of rock, when she saw three boulders at the base of a nearby hill. They were far enough from the shore so the water at high tide could not reach them, and they would give some shelter from the rain. Perhaps she could make a tent from her sealskins to keep herself and Shuku dry.

She carried Shuku to the rocks, slipped the tumpline from her forehead, and set down her carrying basket. Shuku whimpered, and Kiin shushed him, then pulled the sealskins from her basket. She used her walking stick as a center pole and draped her sealskins over it to make a shelter within the semi-circle of the rocks. The ground was wet, but the sealskins would keep out the rain, and the rocks blocked the wind. There were worse places to spend the night.

Kiin pulled Shuku from her parka; he made smacking sounds with his lips. Kiin laughed. "So you are hungry," she said. Her dried meat was gone, but she had fish and roseroot. She gave Shuku a piece of fish, then put some of the roseroot in her mouth, chewed. She spat out the chewed root and pressed the paste between Shuku's lips. He made a face but ate what she gave him.

"We will have to stop soon and catch more fish," Kiin told Shuku. She thought of the bird islands they had passed and of eggs, and tried not to feel the ache of hunger in her stomach.

Shuku answered her in a burst of baby words, and Kiin gathered him into her lap and raised her suk so he could nurse. She allowed herself one small piece of fish and chewed it slowly, savoring the taste. "Tomorrow we will find more roseroot and perhaps some ugyuun," she told Shuku. "If we catch fish, we will have a feast. I must keep you fat so your father will be proud of you.'' Kiin closed her eyes and thought of Samiq, of Takha. Her need for them was so strong it made an ache against her heart, like something broken beneath her ribs.

She opened her mouth to begin a song, but over the sounds of wind and rain she heard a chattering, like the noise of many voices. She sat very still, listening, so that even Shuku stopped sucking and pulled away from her breast.

She pressed a finger to her son's lips. ''Sh-h-h-h, be still,'' she whispered, then pulled her suk over Shuku and crept from her sealskin shelter.

The rain had changed to mist, and though the sun had set, enough light still came from the western sky to reveal the outline of the shore. She walked up through wet grass to the top of the hill behind the boulders. She stopped, listened again, then laughed. ''Birds, Shuku!'' she said. ''Birds. Listen!''

She walked, not caring that her feet were being cut in the wet grass, not caring that the mist was soaking into her hair. At the top of the second hill, she saw it, a sheer gray cliff, rising up from the sea, a cliff thrusting toward the sky and alive with the nest murmurings of murres.

''Eggs, Shuku, eggs!'' she said and danced in a quick circle, her son giggling in his hidden place at the front of her suk.

The morning was bright, a rare day of sun and clear blue skies. Mist rose from low places between hills as though drying fires burned in all the valleys. Kiin left her sealskin shelter, Shuku slung at her side. Two mesh carrying baskets hung from each of her arms. She could not bury the eggs for storage in oil and sand, but she could boil them hard and they would last for many days.

It was not a difficult climb. Though the cliff rose sharply from the water, the hills behind the stone beach sloped gently up to the cliff top. When Kiin went with others to gather eggs, they used a harness, one person lowering another. By herself, Kiin had to lean over and reach down to the topmost bird ledge. She crouched at the edge and looked over, following the ledge with her eyes to the place where it came within an arm's length of the cliff top.

''There,'' she said to Shuku. ''You see, I can reach the eggs over there.''

She walked back from the edge and trampled down the grasses, then, using a rock she had brought from the beach, she pounded a driftwood stake into the ground and tied a kelp line around it. She set Shuku on the ground, gave him a piece of fish, and tied the kelp line around his chest, looping the line over his left shoulder and between his legs, then tying it again so it would not slip off.

"Now, Shuku," Kiin said, "you stay here and I will go get eggs."

She walked back to the cliff, not turning even when Shuku started to whimper. "You will be happy later when we have eggs to eat," Kiin called back to him. She went to the edge of the cliff and pounded in another driftwood stake, tied on another kelp line, and this time bound it around her own waist. Then she lay on her stomach and reached down to push the murres from the flat mat of feathers and grass fibers that was beneath each bird's egg.

When they scolded her and pecked her hand, Kiin told them, "Lay another egg. I will gather here only once. You will still have your bird child, but my son and I must eat."

She set each egg she gathered on the grass beside her, leaving a trail at the cliff edge as she worked. Shuku's sobs subsided into a whining little song, something sung to the rhythm of hiccoughs and soft shuddering sighs.

"Only three more, Shuku," Kiin called to him. She looked back over her shoulder as she leaned forward to reach another egg, then again felt the sharp edge of a bird's beak against the fragile bones of her fingers. She jerked her hand away from the bird's attack and at the same time slipped on the wet grass. She tried to fling herself back, but could not regain her balance.

It happened quickly, but as she slid over the edge, her eyes saw all things. She saw the bird that had attacked her hand, its wings extended, breast feathers fluffed, the dark centers of its eyes drawn in as small as the point of an awl. She saw its dark-spotted green egg. Then there was only the cliff, gray, dark. Kiin reached toward the stone, clawed with her fingers, scraping away skin, shredding fingernails to slow her fall. And then the kelp rope caught, jerking her in a backward arc until the bones of her spine ground into one another.

"Let the rope hold. Let it hold," Kiin prayed, and hoped that some spirit heard her.

Her heart was beating so quickly that it seemed as if a bird from the egg ledge had become trapped under her ribs. Slowly she raised her head, then reached up to clasp the rope. She tightened her hands around the kelp line, looked up, and saw that two nails from her right hand and one from her left had been torn off. Her right forearm was scraped raw, and shreds of skin hung from her fingers.

The cliff was sheer and smooth, with few cracks for handholds, and no ledges nearby except for the egg ledge five or six arm's lengths above her head. The birds began to come back to the ledge, but they were silent, so that the only sounds Kiin heard were the wind and the sea and the creak of the kelp fiber rope against the rock.

"Climb," Kiin's spirit voice said. "If you stay here, the edge of the cliff will cut your rope."

Kiin looked down at the waves of the North Sea crashing white against the cliff, and her breath seemed to stop and swell in her chest. She turned her head up, and with her eyes caught and held the egg ledge, as tightly as if she were holding it with her hands.

"Climb up. Climb up," her spirit voice said.

Kiin gripped the kelp line and pulled. The rope, narrow, taut, was like a knife blade against her skin. Tears seeped from her eyes, but she moved her left hand a short distance above her right. "I can do this," she told herself, told the wind spirits as they swung her against the rock. Slowly, right hand, left hand, she moved up the face of the cliff. Finally she drew her feet up, braced them against the rock, walking them up the cliff as she pulled, gripping small crevices and outcroppings with her toes.

Sweat prickled her groin and armpits, and her heart was like a drum beating hard in the hollow of her chest. Her hands burned, and she had to press her lips together to keep the pain from finding a voice. Again she raised her right hand, but this time her fingers would not grip. For a moment she was still, hanging there on the side of the cliff. She looked up at the ledge, hoping it would be close, but though a loop of line hanging below showed how far she had moved, the egg ledge seemed as distant as it had been when Kiin began her climb.

"It is nearer," Kiin's spirit whispered. "It is only your pain that makes it seem so far away. Do not look up. Do not look down, only climb. Only climb."

Hand above hand. Hand above hand. The pain in Kiin's shoulders seemed to match the burning in her arms. Hand above hand. Hand above hand. The wind was blowing harder, coming in from the sea, pressing Kiin against the cliff. The muscles of her right leg cramped, and she had to stop.

"I can't," she said.

But her spirit said, "Who are you to quit when you are so close to the egg ledge? Look up, see?"

Kiin looked up. The ledge was close. If she stretched, she could catch it with her fingertips.

"A few more steps. Only a few," her spirit said. "When you get to the ledge, you can rest, and then it will be nothing to reach the top of the cliff."

Kiin pulled her right leg up another step, moved the left hand, then the right. Her right leg cramped again, this time so tight that Kiin cried out with the pain. She doubled the leg up to her chest, then tried to straighten it, pulling against the tightening muscles. The cramp eased, and Kiin drew in a long breath. She slowly leaned her weight on the leg and moved her left leg ahead, moved her right hand on the rope, then gasped as another cramp hit.

Her right leg slipped against the rock, and her left leg, not yet secure in its next step, also slipped. She fell, the full force of her weight against her hands.

For a moment, she was able to hold herself up, but then the rope began to slip under her fingers. Blood from her climb had made the kelp line slick, as though it were oiled, but finally Kiin was able to tighten her hold and stop her slide. She looked up at the rope, saw how far she had dropped by the bloodstains left behind.

"I was at the top," she cried out, and the wind took her words, threw them into the cliff.

"Climb, climb again," Kiin's spirit told her.

"I can't," Kiin said and did not try to stop her tears.

"And if you do not, you will die," her spirit voice answered. "The wind moves your rope even now. The rocks at the edge of the cliff will cut through, and you will drop into the sea."

"And so I will be dead," Kiin said, screaming the words out against the wind, against the sea, against the gray rocks of the cliff. "I do not care."

"You, you who have lived through curses and slavery, you do not care? What about those you love—your mother, Chagak, Kayugh? What about Samiq and Takha?"

Kiin leaned her head into the crook of her elbow, gasped against the pain of her hands as she clung to the kelp line.

"Listen," her spirit voice said. "Listen and tell me what you hear."

At first, Kiin heard only the wind, bird voices and waves against rock, but then, rising like a song over the sounds of the earth, she heard Shuku, his voice lifted, as though he called for her.

"Shuku," Kiin whispered.

"Yes, Shuku," her spirit voice said.

Kiin swung out against the rope, braced her feet against the cliff, and once more began to climb.

When Kiin reached the egg ledge, she hooked her heels over the edge and was still, allowing the muscles in her legs to rest. The climb had worn the skin from her toes, and blood trickled down her soles to stain the feathers of the murre nests.

"The rope, the rope," her spirit voice called to her. "It could break. Pull yourself up. Pull yourself up!"

"Be still," Kiin said. "Leave me alone; let me rest." But she began to pull herself up. The sudden fear that her spirit voice was right, that the rope would break and send her into the sea, gave her strength, and she eased herself up until she was standing flatfooted on the ledge and could rest her upper body on top of the cliff.

She still held the rope, but reached to clasp it above the frayed part that rubbed the edge of the cliff. For a long time, she did not move, but finally Shuku's cries broke through the numbness of her mind and she pulled herself over the cliff edge and onto the grass and rocks. She lay there breathing hard, still clasping the rope, as though her hands could do nothing else but grip and pull.

Shuku's cries seemed louder now and the sounds of the sea gentler. "Shuku," Kiin called. "Shuku."

The baby's cries stopped and then started again. Kiin

pushed herself up to her hands and knees and crawled to him.

His face was red, his hands and cheeks smeared with dirt. When he saw her, he began to cry harder and held his hands out to her. She scooped him into her lap, then lay on her side in the grass and lifted the tatters of her suk so Shuku could nurse. She did not let herself look at her hands. The pain was not as strong as the softness of Shuku's skin against hers.

As she sighed and looked out over the cliff at the North Sea, she saw the speckled murre eggs, lined up at the edge of the cliff like some game of shells and pebbles played by a giant child. Suddenly in spite of her pain, in spite of her tiredness, she began to laugh.

"Oh, Shuku," she said. "We have eggs. So many eggs. Enough to last us all the way to the Traders' Beach."

FIFTY-SIX

THE WHALE HUNTERS

Yunaska Island, the Aleutian Chain

"WHICH ISLAND?" HARD ROCK ASKED AS HE crawled from his sleeping place.

"The Island of Four Waters," Red Feet answered. The man stood beside the climbing log, both hands wrapped around a walking stick. He lifted the stick to jab it again and again into the ulaq's woven grass floor mats.

"That small island," Hard Rock said slowly. "You are sure?" He frowned and pointed at Red Feet's walking stick. Red Feet set the stick against the climbing log and squatted on his haunches.

"I myself saw them. I myself heard them."

"You have seen walrus before?"

"In the ocean."

"That is not the same. Perhaps they are sea lion."

"No."

"How many?"

"Too many to count."

"Fish Eater was the first to see them?"

"Yes."

"Go ask him to come to me," Hard Rock said. But as Red Feet stood to leave, Hard Rock reached out a hand and said, "Wait. I will go to him. There is someone else I must also see." He pulled his suk from a peg and was up the climbing log before Red Feet could answer.

Kukutux heard the men coming and pulled back from the climbing log, pressed herself against a wall in one of the dark corners of the ulaq. Their voices were loud. Were they angry?

Then she heard laughter, and Hard Rock descended into the ulaq even without calling down. Three hunters followed him: Red Feet, Fish Eater and Dying Seal. The men ignored her except for Dying Seal, who, when he saw her in the corner, raised a hand in greeting. Kukutux raised her hand, then slid down to a squat, leaning against the wall.

"Waxtal is here?" Hard Rock asked after pacing the ulaq, one side to the other. He stopped to peer into Kukutux's shadowed corner. "Waxtal is here?" he asked again.

"In his sleeping place, but he prays," Kukutux said, wondering that the man did not hear the high singing chant spinning out of Waxtal's sleeping place.

Hard Rock stood still, his hands hanging loose at his sides, as though he did not know what to do next.

"When will he be finished?" Dying Seal asked.

Kukutux stood and walked out into the lamplight, lifted her shoulders in a shrug. "Who can say?"

"He is a shaman," the old man Fish Eater said. "I told you he is a shaman. I told everyone when he first came with the traders, but who listens to an old man, one who can barely hunt? Who listens?" He straightened his shoulders under his otter skin suk and clasped one hand with the other, rubbing swollen knuckles. Then he looked at Kukutux, spread his fingers, and said, "See what happens to an old man when he hunts? For each seal he takes, he trades two days of pain. I told them I saw walrus. They did not believe me. They made me go back, show them the island. Filled with walrus it was, so close together a man could not find ground to step on between them. 'Walrus,' I told them. Now they believe. At least those two,'' he said, pointing with curled fingers toward Dying Seal and Red Feet. ''But this one, this chief, he thinks he knows more than an old man. He says I should go with them. All of us together and again see the walrus. He wants to hunt them. With what? What man among us has hunted walrus? Should we use seal harpoons? What walrus would not push them aside, laugh at our small weapons? Should we defile our whale weapons with walrus blood?''

As Kukutux listened to the old man, Hard Rock continued to pace. He stopped several times before Waxtal's sleeping place curtain, and Kiin saw him incline his head to listen to Waxtal's chants.

Finally he turned to her and, interrupting Fish Eater's complaints, said, ''Has he told you not to bother him? Has he told you to be quiet when he prays?''

''He has told me nothing,'' Kukutux answered.

''Then I will talk to him now.'' Hard Rock said the words loudly, but then he stood and stared at the sleeping place curtain as though it would move aside without his touching it. Finally Kukutux leaned close to Hard Rock, pulled open the curtain. Hard Rock bent to look in, and before he spoke one word, Waxtal's voice, loud, clear, came from the sleeping place.

''You found the walrus I called for you?'' he asked.

Hard Rock jumped back as though the man had hit him.

''You think the spirits do not talk to me?'' Waxtal asked. He came out of the sleeping place, straightened, and stretched his arms up toward the ulaq rafters.

''You called the walrus?'' Dying Seal asked, and Kukutux saw the doubt on his face.

''Have you ever seen walrus near this island before? Your fathers or grandfathers told stories of long-ago times. Did they speak of walrus?''

''No,'' said Fish Eater. ''But I saw them first. I saw them and brought the others. They did not believe me.''

''You believe now?'' Waxtal asked.

''I have not seen them,'' Hard Rock said, ''but Dying Seal is a man known for his honesty.''

''So will you go with him to see for yourself?''

"We go together," Hard Rock said. "All of us."

Waxtal turned away from the men. "I call walrus. I do not hunt them," he said as he returned to his sleeping place.

Hard Rock reached out, clasped the man by both shoulders, and pulled him back into the ulaq's main room. "If you are shaman, we will honor you as shaman, but not until it is proven. You told me you wanted this woman as wife. Go with us now. It is not even a day's journey to the Island of Four Waters and back. Get your chigadax and spears. Get your water bladders and oil lamp."

He released Waxtal and looked at Kukutux. "You told me you would be his wife if he was a hunter. What if he is shaman?"

"If he can bring in enough meat to last through winter, what do I care if it is from a hunter's share or a shaman's share?" Kukutux answered. Then she helped Waxtal gather his things. She filled water skins and an oil bladder, found a hunter's lamp, and quickly mended a tear in his chigadax.

But when the hunters left, Kukutux did not climb to the top of the ulaq to follow them with her eyes. Instead she stood in the center of the main room, now still and empty after the frantic scurryings and loud voices of the hunters. She closed her eyes and sighed. Perhaps her time alone after the deaths of her husband and son had deformed her spirit. Otherwise why would she so enjoy the quiet of an empty ulaq? What woman would trade quiet for the blessing of children? The noise of aunts, uncles, parents, grandparents? Still, she reminded herself, most of life had some side of blessing. Why not enjoy what was hers?

She repacked a sealskin of dried meat and pushed it back into the food cache. As she worked she thought about what the hunters had said. She carefully wiped the stopper of the oil belly the traders had left. The oil was fresh. How tempting to take a small bowlful, eat it with the dried fish she had planned to have for her next meal. But the oil was the best oil. Better to save it for Waxtal. For the one who hunted.

Hard Rock had asked her if she would be wife to Waxtal; twice now he had asked. Both times she had given tests: if he could hunt, if he was a shaman. Why? Was it only a moon ago, those starving days, when she would have taken any man? Why now was it difficult for her to say yes?

Waxtal was not a beautiful man. His face would not give pleasure to a woman as Hard Rock's face did. His body was not strong like Dying Seal's body. His eyes were not the soft eyes of the trader Owl. But he did have powers. What was more important to those children she might bear—gentle eyes, a beautiful face, or the power to keep them fed, to protect them from curses?

"What woman does not make sacrifices for her children, even those not yet born?" Kukutux asked aloud. "Yes, I will take Waxtal as husband." Then she remembered something her mother had told her. Oil, fresh oil, made strong babies. She went back to the food cache, took out the belly of new oil, pulled the stopper.

"For my children," Kukutux said.

FIFTY-SEVEN

THE HARPOONS ARE NOT LONG ENOUGH; THE points are not large enough. What man ever killed a walrus with a seal harpoon? Waxtal shook his head, hoping to drive away the fear that seemed to weigh down his arms as he paddled. Already Hard Rock, Dying Seal, and Red Feet, even Fish Eater, were so far ahead that he could barely see their ikyan against the glare of the sea.

Waxtal centered his thoughts on his amulet. It lay against his chest, heavy and warm, as though its power were so great that it gave off heat. Before he left the ulaq, he had shaved a thin piece of ivory from the blunt end of his carved tusk. As soon as he put the ivory into the amulet's soft leather pouch, he had felt the difference. He slipped the string of his amulet over his head and knew he was stronger, more sure.

But now, doubt slapped up from the waves, and he heard the taunting voices of those spirits that so easily slid over the sea to find a man in his ikyak. They ridiculed, and their whispers were like needles piercing his body. "Ho! It was your power that brought the walrus. Your power! When have you called animals, any animals, even lemmings? Do you think one time of prayer and fasting can bestow power like that? Then every man should do the same. What hunter would ever come home without meat?"

"I called the walrus," Waxtal said aloud. "I called them. Perhaps with my knife against the tusk, perhaps within my dreams, perhaps with my chants. I was the one who called them. Would one of the Whale Hunters call walrus? They hunt whale. Would Owl or Spotted Egg call? They are Caribou. I am the one who carves a walrus tusk. I am the one whose daughter is wife to a Walrus People shaman. I called them."

Then the water spirits seemed to leave him, and suddenly Waxtal's arms were again strong. He paddled hard until he came close to Red Feet's ikyak and stayed there until the sounds came over the waves—the great echoing call of the bull walrus, the bleatings and growlings of lesser males. And turning their ikyan into the wind, the Whale Hunters came to the island. Hard Rock and Dying Seal stopped their ikyan, holding their paddles upright in the water until Red Feet and Fish Eater were beside them. They turned and waited for Waxtal to join them.

"The walrus are here," Hard Rock said, then asked Waxtal, "Is this the island where you came to fast?"

Almost, Waxtal said no, but he closed his mouth before the word could escape. He raised his head and looked into Hard Rock's eyes. "Yes," he said, and thought, Who will know the difference? Owl and Spotted Egg are gone. They will never be back. He had been the one to call the walrus; why not take all credit? Why not get what he could for these hard months spent on an island cursed by the man who had cursed him? "Yes, this island," he told Hard Rock and, lifting the blade of his paddle from the water, pointed toward the hills above the gray rock of the beach. "There in those hills."

"You called these animals while you were here?" Dying Seal asked.

"I called them," Waxtal answered, "but they did not come until I had left."

"What if we had not found them? What if Fish Eater had not come this way in his seal hunting?" Hard Rock said. "You should have told us you called them."

"Would you have believed me?" Waxtal asked. "Look at me. I am not a young man. I am not a strong man. Even all my trade goods, those many bundles of pelts, the bellies of oil, I gave all for the walrus tusks. So now, because I have so little, men in your village doubt that I am a shaman, that I have the powers of a shaman. Has any man ever seen walrus on this island? No. And someday when I have taken my powers up to the Dancing Lights, the walrus will leave here again." He turned and looked at Red Feet, then back again at Hard Rock and Dying Seal. "If I had said, 'Walrus have come to the Four Waters Island—go hunt,' would you have believed me?"

The men did not answer, and for a time, in that silence, they watched the beach, the skirmishes of the giant bull, his large body like a mound of red-brown rock, his bellows like something heard in the groanings and crackings of ice rivers.

Then Red Feet took his sea lion harpoon from its lashings on the ikyak deck, fitted his throwing board to his right hand, and slid the harpoon into the groove of the board, the butt of the shaft against the ivory hook that held the harpoon in place.

"No," Waxtal said. "We are not ready to hunt. We insult the walrus with our seal harpoons." He looked at Hard Rock, realized he had spoken words that should be said only by the alananasika. He braced himself for Hard Rock's anger, but to Waxtal's surprise, Hard Rock showed no anger, only fear.

He is afraid of my power, Waxtal thought, and a rill of laughter lifted itself into his mouth. Waxtal began a chant, a prayer for protection, praise for any walrus that would give itself to a hunter's harpoon. Who could say what good it would do? He had listened enough to the braggings and boastings of Walrus People hunters. Who did not know that the way to hunt walrus was on land, where they were slow and easily taken? In water they knew their full power. What chance did a hunter have against them?

Again Waxtal called out, "Wait!"

But Red Feet said, "That one, he is mine," as though Waxtal had said nothing. He pointed at a smaller walrus some distance from the bull.

Waxtal looked, saw the stain of yellow on the walrus's tusks. It was a seal killer, that walrus, tusks yellowed by the blubber of seals he had taken. Waxtal had heard stories of such walrus attacking a hunter's ikyak.

"Wait!" Waxtal said, but his words were too slow, and Red Feet threw the harpoon, cried out when it hit the walrus in the chest, when a gout of bright blood left a trail as the walrus moved awkwardly into the water, then disappeared beneath the waves.

"Look," Hard Rock said and pointed at the harpoon shaft, bobbing, butt up, in the waves. The shaft was attached by a line of braided sinew to the harpoon head, which was embedded in the walrus. Hard Rock, Fish Eater, Red Feet, and Dying Seal drew their ikyan in a circle around the harpoon shaft, waited for the walrus to surface as a man waits for seal or sea otter. But Waxtal did not move his ikyak into the circle, and when Hard Rock motioned to him, he shook his head.

Waxtal closed his eyes, put all his strength into the words of a chant. Then behind the darkness of his eyelids he saw the sudden brightness of light, and at the same time heard the screams of the hunters. As he opened his eyes, his ikyak was raised up on a swell of water, a giant wave, coming as though the sea itself fought the Whale Hunters. From the crest of that wave, he saw the walrus lift itself out of the water, and Waxtal knew that the walrus was pulling power from the wave, gathering strength to overcome the pain of the harpoon head. The animal flung itself against Red Feet's ikyak, splintering the bow and knocking Red Feet from the hatch.

Waxtal pushed against his paddle, moved into those small chopping waves that sometimes follow the wake of a large wave. Almost his ikyak flipped, but fear added strength, and he righted himself, turned, and paddled quickly away from the beach, away from the strong towing currents that defy a hunter's paddle. And when he had pulled himself far enough away, he looked back. Three ikyan still floated, a man in each. Waxtal watched, waited, and when he saw the sea was calm, he paddled back to the others, raising his voice in chants, so they would know he was praying for all of them, his strength not in hard arms or skillful paddling, but in prayers and chants and shaman's powers.

*   *   *

"He cannot live," Dying Seal said. Still he and Hard Rock tied their ikyan together. They pulled the man from the water and laid him across the ikyak decks.

Waxtal drew close, looked, then quickly turned his head aside. No, even with all his chants, with all his prayers, with the powers of the most powerful shaman, Red Feet would not live. What man could live with chest crushed, jaw pulled away, mouth gurgling blood at each breath?

Hard Rock looked up at Waxtal, moved his paddle in an angry slash. "Lead us!" he said.

Waxtal opened his mouth to remind Hard Rock that Red Feet had acted foolishly. He, Waxtal, had warned the men about using seal harpoons against walrus. But there would be time to speak when they were safe again on the Whale Hunters' island. Who could say whether spirits, watching, seeing their harpoons, might send another wave against them, leave them all in the sea to join the whispering voices that the wind carries to hunters in ikyan? And so he started out through the waves, the paddle heavy and hard in his hands.

FIFTY-EIGHT

KUKUTUX WAS ON THE BEACH WHEN THE MEN returned, Waxtal in the lead, Fish Eater trailing, Hard Rock and Dying Seal with ikyan lashed together, Red Feet lying across the bows.

Kukutux closed her eyes in sorrow when she heard Red Feet's two young wives begin the mourning chant, and she remembered her own agony when her husband was killed hunting whales.

Then over the mourning song, she heard Waxtal's voice. His yelling was a rudeness that drowned out the women. "I called the walrus, but told you Whale men not to hunt. Who does not know that walrus are dishonored by seal and sea lion harpoons? What man is so foolish as to dishonor the animal he needs for food?''

Dying Seal came from his ikyak, grasped Waxtal's shoulders, and squeezed his strong hands until Waxtal's words faded to a whisper, until the old man's mouth closed. ''Who is so foolish as to dishonor the dead?'' Dying Seal asked, then released Waxtal so quickly that the man staggered as though he had been hit.

Hard Rock, Dying Seal, and Fish Eater left the beach, Hard Rock without saying anything. But Waxtal stayed, removed ballast rocks and oil bladders from inside his ikyak, then began to rub oil into the seams as though there were no mourners, as though Red Feet had come back from the hunt alive and walked now on two strong legs like any other man.

Kukutux went back to the ulaq, took food outside to the cooking hearth. She hung a boiling bag over the fire, filled it with water and fresh and smoked fish, then waited for Waxtal.

He came, muttering angry words, but Kukutux pretended she did not hear. The man climbed down into the uluq and then out again, walking stick in his hand. He swung the stick against rocks and clumps of grass as he walked, but Kukutux ignored him until the stick swept close to her bare feet. Then she stood up and said in a loud voice, ''The food I prepare is food I brought in myself. If you want to eat, you will put down your stick.''

But Waxtal swung the stick again, this time slapping the end against Kukutux's shins, leaving a stinging welt.

In anger Kukutux picked up her woman's knife. In anger she slashed the blade across Waxtal's fingers. Waxtal cried out and dropped his walking stick, raised his hand to his mouth to suck at the blood dripping from the cut. Kukutux lunged for the stick, grabbed it just as Waxtal reached for it. Then she raised one knee and broke the stick over it, and poked the broken pieces into the hearth fire, keeping Waxtal away with the blade of her women's knife until the stick began to smolder and char.

''It was sacred, that stick!'' Waxtal screamed at her, but Kukutux only swung a wide arc with her woman's knife. Waxtal jumped back, and Kukutux stooped down to pick up one of the hearth stones with her left hand. She raised the stone as if to throw it.

Ignoring the pain in her left elbow, the protest of bone and muscle against the weight of the stone, she said, "You, Seal Hunter, do not think you can treat Whale Hunter women as you treat your own Seal women. Do you believe Whale Hunter men are the only ones who gather strength from years of eating whale meat? Do you think none of that power comes to the women? Be glad I broke only your stick."

Waxtal opened his mouth, snarled, but Kukutux, strong with stone and knife, was not afraid. Then she heard a voice calling and carefully moved her eyes from Waxtal to see Hard Rock coming toward them. Waxtal's voice changed to whining, and when Hard Rock drew close enough to hear, Waxtal pointed at Kukutux and at his walking stick now burning with bright yellow flames in the hearth fire.

"She used my walking stick to feed her cooking fire," Waxtal said, his voice quiet, like the voice of a man considered wise, sought for his good counsel.

Kukutux dropped the stone back into its place and wiped her hand on her suk. "He hit me with it," she said.

Hard Rock frowned. "With his stick?"

Kukutux nodded.

"You believe a woman?" Waxtal asked.

"Yes," Hard Rock said.

Waxtal's face pulled itself into a smile. "What man does not at times have to teach wisdom with a stick?"

Anger knotted tight in Kukutux's chest. She opened her mouth to speak, but Hard Rock waved her to silence. "It seems whatever happened," Hard Rock said, "Kukutux has been able to take care of herself. Now you must come with me to my ulaq. The hunters want to talk to you."

Waxtal walked with Hard Rock back to his ulaq. Kukutux watched them leave. Hard Rock's steps were heavy, his weight settling first on his heels, but Waxtal walked so lightly that even grass crushed under his feet sprang back quickly into place.

When the two men were inside Hard Rock's ulaq, Kukutux used a forked stick to carry a burning coal to her own ulaq, now empty and dark. Her feet felt their way down the climbing log and then to each oil lamp. Two of the four lamps had enough oil so the wicks remained burning, then Kukutux laid the coal in one of the empty lamps and went back to the hearth fire. She used two strong sticks to take the boiling skin from the driftwood tripod that held it over the fire. Carefully she carried it, not to the traders' ulaq, but back to her own ulaq, and hung it from the rafters over one of the burning lamps.

She made three trips to the traders' ulaq. She took all things that were hers: sleeping furs, mats, basket grass and baskets, bellies of oil and dried meat, water bladders. And she brought them back to her own ulaq. Then she went into her dead husband's sleeping place, found the few weapons he had not taken with him to the Dancing Lights. A broken harpoon head. A crooked bird spear shaft. A gaff to land fish. A boy's spear. She laid these things at her side, then ladled herself a bowl of broth and meat from the boiling skin. If Waxtal came for her, she was ready to fight.

"What more could I do?" Waxtal asked. "I called the walrus. I brought them to your hunters. I told you not to hunt them with seal harpoons. Do you think whales are the only animals hunters must honor with careful taboos?" He made a rude noise with his lips, and blew out air from between his buttocks.

Hard Rock wrinkled his nose at the stink, and Waxtal said, "The walrus, they still smell the stink of your foolishness." Waxtal stood and looked at the men. When he had come as a young man to help these Whale Hunters against the Short Ones, there had been so many hunters in this village that they could not all fit into one ulaq. Now, how many? He let his eyes move from one man to another, eight, ten, and many of them old. He pointed rudely at Hard Rock. "The curse that came to you from the man Samiq is still here."

Hard Rock pulled in a quick, harsh breath. "The man is dead. Do you wish to bring another curse on us by using his name?"

"There are things I know that you do not know, things the spirits reveal to one who honors them," Waxtal said. "I have brought you walrus—good for meat, hides, and oil. I have lived with the Walrus People. My daughter is wife to a Walrus People shaman. I know how they hunt; I know what honors a walrus. I have brought you meat and you accuse me of bringing a curse. The curse you have is Samiq's curse. You think his curse will leave you? You say his spirit will go the way of all spirits—to the Dancing Lights? You know nothing, and when one who can help comes to you, you turn him away.''

There was a rising murmur among the men. In one corner of the ulaq, Red Feet's brother and father raised their voices in anger. In another corner, Crooked Bird, husband to Speckled Basket, raised hands in a plea for understanding. But Waxtal ignored them all. He turned his back to them and climbed to the ulaq roof hole. At the top of the climbing log, he looked down at them. ''You do not need to live with the curse. I know how to lift it. I gave you the walrus and asked nothing in return. Yet when one of your hunters breaks taboos, you blame me for his death. I will give away nothing more.

''Decide what you have to trade. If it is a good trade, I will tell you how to lift the curse.'' He raised one hand and held it out toward Red Feet's father. ''Decide now,'' Waxtal said, ''before this becomes a village of women and children.''

That night, Kukutux saw it as she slept, saw it large and rolling in the surf, and woke with a start from her dream. The vision carried the fullness of life, but she was not sure what she had seen. Another man, dead?

She sat up and shook her head. ''It was not a man,'' she whispered and fought to remember the image that had filled her mind. No, what man had the shape of a fish? What man had skin the color of mountain cranberries?

She lay down again and turned her cheek into the soft fur seal pelt she had arranged under her head. She patted the spear lying beside her.

You are safe, she told herself. Go back to sleep.

FIFTY-NINE

AFTER HER DREAM, KUKUTUX COULD NOT STAY away from the sea. It was as though some voice called her, and the pain that had been with her since the deaths of her husband and son seemed to deepen.

''Why are you here?'' she asked herself, moving her head so the words would flow out with the wind and be carried above the hearing of the men who squatted in the lee of the ikyak racks, the women who waded out in the shallow ebb tide to pry chitons from rocks. ''Why are you here when there is much for you to do in your ulaq?''

She reminded herself of the crowberry heather, now, under the long days of summer, growing quickly on the hills. It was time to throw out the old heather that lay on the ulaq floors, replace it with new. She thought of fish she could catch, of the suk she was making. She should walk down the beach, gather chitons from rocks farther from the village, leave these close rocks for the old women and children. She might even find a few sea urchins left by the sea otters that now crowded the kelp beds just offshore.

But something kept her on the beach, watching, as though she could see beyond water and sky to understand the dream she had been given.

Finally she made herself turn, made herself walk back to her ulaq. It had been four days since Hard Rock and Dying Seal had brought the dead Red Feet to the village, four days of mourning. They had made the burial, piled the rocks over Red Feet and what remained of his ikyak, but hunters still spoke in soft voices, as though afraid to attract the attention of spirits. Who could say? One of them might be the next man killed during a hunt.

The women followed their husbands with fear-filled eyes, finding excuse to watch beach and sea from the tops of their ulas, even in cold, even in wind, as though by watching they could keep away those spirits that might bring death.

Perhaps it is only what I feel from those around me, Kukutux thought. Perhaps it is their fear, their worry, that brings me to this beach.

The images of her dream returned—something red in the sea. A man's body? Another Whale Hunter killed? Some worrying voice entered her mind, wailed out against fears too large to be contained by words.

At the top of the ulaq, Waxtal yawned and stretched. He had meant to get up and greet the sun with the Whale Hunters, but his bedding furs were warm, and for some reason his bladder had not pulled him early from his sleep as it often did. He blinked in the brightness of the day, in the white fog lifting from the beach. He scraped the grit from the corners of his eyes with a fingernail and flicked it into the wind, then shivered and ducked back into the ulaq to get his suk.

The wind was cold, too cold for a man to wash in the stream, but without a woman in the ulaq, he did not want to use a night basket for his urine, did not want the bother of emptying it every day or storing urine as the Walrus People did so it would ripen and could be used to wash oil from fur and grease from hair or set dye colors so they would not run or fade.

He scratched his belly, then slipped on his suk and went back outside. He scanned the beach, saw Kukutux walking toward the ulas. Then she stopped and looked toward the sea, her face like a mask, set, unmoving.

He followed her gaze and saw nothing. He remembered what Hard Rock had told him about her, that Kukutux's eyes were like the eyes of an eagle, seeing farther than most people could see, that even as a child she had always been first to see hunters returning, had always given first warning of storms on the far horizon, or schools of fish swimming towards the Whale Hunters' beach.

So he waited, his eyes on the sea as were Kukutux's, and then he, too, saw something in the surf, rolling and bumping, so at first he thought it was a log brought as driftwood to the beach. Then he saw the red color, felt the quick beating of his heart—a man? Owl or Spotted Egg, their ik overturned? The currents might bring them here to this beach.

But no, it was too large to be a man.

As Waxtal watched, he suddenly knew what it was, and as though he were again young, he ran to Hard Rock's ulaq, and up to the roof hole.

He took a long breath and called down.

"I am Waxtal. Is Hard Rock here?"

Hard Rock himself answered, his words mumbled as though he had something in his mouth. He came to the climbing log, looked up at Waxtal. One of Hard Rock's cheeks bulged with whatever he was eating, and for a moment the man chewed, then finally in rudeness asked, "What?"

Waxtal smiled and said, "The Whale Hunters have been

good to me. I have decided to give you a gift. In these last four days of mourning I have been calling something to this beach. It will be here soon. Use it as you wish.''

Then he went to stand beside Kukutux, who still stared out at the water, she and the other women who were on the beach.

''I called it,'' Waxtal said, his words soft as he moved his mouth close to Kukutux's ear. ''I called it.''

She took a step away from him, and then another. ''Why?'' she asked. ''What is it?''

''The walrus,'' Waxtal said.

''Red Feet's?'' Kukutux asked, then clamped her hand over her mouth.

''Do not worry,'' Waxtal said. ''I will not let his spirit harm you.''

''You called it?'' Kukutux said, her brows drawn together, her lips tight. ''Why?''

''A hunter should have his last kill—to give to his family,'' Waxtal said. He shrugged his shoulders. ''You think it will not lift his wives' sorrow to know that their hunter still cares enough about them to send meat?''

Two women left their gathering bags and called the men at the ikyak rack, then Hard Rock was beside Kukutux and Waxtal.

''It is the walrus,'' Waxtal said and watched as the men waded into the water. Three of them carried sharpened fish gaffs, another a walking stick, others ikyak paddles.

''They can touch it?'' Hard Rock asked.

''To bring it ashore,'' Waxtal answered, ''but someone must pray over it and say the proper Walrus chants before it is butchered and divided.''

''You know the chants?'' Hard Rock asked Waxtal.

''Yes.''

Waxtal watched the men drag the animal ashore, then turned to Kukutux. ''Go to that ulaq where the people mourn. Tell them to come here, to see what the spirits have given them.''

Kukutux climbed up the ulaq, called down into the smoky interior. There was no answer, so she called again, waited until she heard a soft voice, then looked down into the wrinkled face of Most Hands, mother of that one who had died. ''There is something on the beach you should see, Mother,'' Kukutux said gently, using words of politeness to show her concern.

But the old woman answered in a harsh voice. "How can I be mother," she asked, "with all my children at the Dancing Lights?" She turned from the climbing log and moved back into the shadows of the ulaq. "I will not go to the beach. Let me stay here. Perhaps the spirits will have pity and let me die."

Again Kukutux heard the soft murmur, no doubt the voice of Pogy, Red Feet's first wife, mother of his little son. Or perhaps that of Fish Catcher, Red Feet's second wife.

"Even if one of your children sent you a gift, even if now that gift is on the beach, you will not come?" Kukutux asked. She knelt so she could press her face down into the roof hole, so her words would carry to all the people there.

The old woman turned slowly, and in the dark Kukutux could see the red of the woman's eyes, the lines that tears had left on her cheeks.

"From Red Feet?" the old woman asked, and Kukutux heard a quick shushing, a plea against the use of the dead man's name. But the old woman looked away from the roof hole and said in loud, sharp-edged words, "What do I care if he comes back? What do I care if he takes all of us to the Dancing Lights?"

The soft voice answered, "My son is young. He needs years to hunt. He needs summers in an ikyak, winters to learn the stories of our people."

"What do you know?" the old woman said. "You were only his wife." She climbed to the roof hole. Kukutux offered both hands to help the woman from log to roof. Pogy also came, her son in a carrying strap slung at her side, and Fish Catcher, her belly big in pregnancy. They followed Kukutux to the beach, the old woman last, clinging with one hand to the back of Fish Catcher's suk.

When Pogy saw the walrus, she lifted her voice in mourning, cried out as though it were the first day of her loss, and when Kukutux moved to put an arm around her shoulders, she pushed Kukutux away.

"I do not want it. I do not want it," she said.

But Red Feet's mother tottered out onto the beach, walked up to the walrus, the red-and-brown animal larger than the largest man. She planted her feet solidly beside it and called out, "My son's last kill. It is mine, as was his first kill. The meat is mine and I will share it with no one."

Hard Rock left the gathering of men, went to the woman, bent down, hands on knees, to look into her wrinkled face. "Grandmother," he said, "you cannot eat a whole walrus. Share it with all the village so your son will be able to hold his eyes forward in pride among the hunters of the Dancing Lights."

The old woman sighed, then lifted her hands and dropped them to her sides. "I will share," she said, and she stepped back from the carcass.

Hard Rock turned to the women on the beach, many already holding butchering knives. "The shaman says there must be prayers."

"He is not shaman; he is trader," Most Hands said, squinting at Waxtal.

"He called the walrus to our beach," Hard Rock said.

"It is a gift!" the old woman screamed. "It is from my son. It is a gift." She lifted one curled hand toward Waxtal. "He did not do it!"

"He has great powers," Hard Rock said. "He talks to spirits. He . . ."

Then Waxtal was beside Most Hands. Lifting a necklace of birdbones from his neck, he draped it over the old woman's shoulders. "I spoke to your son," he said. "In the days of mourning, before he went to the Dancing Lights, I listened to what he told me. He wants you to have this necklace. He wants you to gather berries and sea urchins to help feed his son." Waxtal looked over his shoulder at Pogy standing with the baby on her hip. "He wants you to have this walrus, you and his wives and the people of this village. He asked me to call it here for him. I have done that." He cleared his throat. "My powers are only the powers of a shaman," he said, "so the calling took four days, but now the walrus is here and the meat is for all of us to use."

The old woman clasped the birdbone necklace with both hands, stepped away from Waxtal, and said in a quivering voice, "You take the hunter's share."

Waxtal smiled, and the smile made a shiver come to Kukutux's arms. Was the man as powerful as he claimed? Could he talk to dead men and yet not fall under their power to pull him into the Dancing Lights? How else would the walrus have come except by someone's power?

But in Waxtal's eyes, in the set of his teeth, the smoothness of his words, she saw only greed. Even now, as she stood under the curve of the sky, it seemed as though all things—the sea, the beach, the ulas, even the ikyan on their racks—were pulling toward Waxtal, as though he had the power to take them into his soul, as easily as a man drinks soup from a bowl.

Waxtal walked to the edge of the waves, reached down to cup water in his hands, then carried it back to the walrus and splashed it over the animal. Again and again, four times, he carried water. Then, calling to the women, he said, "I need something from the sea, mussel or clam."

One of the women held up a jointed chiton from her gathering bag, the dark shell curled almost into a circle.

"Good," Waxtal said. He took the chiton and put it into the walrus's mouth. Then he began a chant, something in a language Kukutux did not know, the words too harsh to be the Caribou tongue spoken by Owl and Spotted Egg.

When the chant was finished, Waxtal reached out to one of the women, who gave him her butchering knife. Waxtal bent over the walrus, made the first cut, working to get the knife through the thick hide, cutting a few strokes, then stopping to hold out his hand toward another woman and continuing with a fresh sharp blade, slashing from neck to anus, along the belly.

Waxtal spoke to the old woman as though he had just heard her words, as though he had not spent time in chants and rituals. "No," he said, "the hunter's share is yours. I do not want it. I do not need it. You and your son's wives should have that share."

"Then the chief's share," the old woman said.

Pogy's eyes widened, and she looked at Hard Rock. Both hands flew to cover her face.

Kukutux wondered what Hard Rock would say. An old woman could not give away the chief hunter's share. But Hard Rock said nothing.

Waxtal shook his head. "I will take no share, none of the meat," he said. "It is not for me but for the village." He walked several steps toward his ulaq before turning back, reaching out to stroke the walrus tusks, one, then the other. He smiled up at the old woman, who stood with a knife in her hand, hers the right of cutting and dividing. "The tusks are beautiful," he said. Then he walked back up the beach, looking at no one, speaking to no one. Kukutux turned her head to watch him until he climbed up the traders' ulaq and disappeared inside.

SIXTY

WAXTAL SAT DOWN BESIDE THE OIL LAMP. THE wick needed trimming. He took out his sleeve knife and pushed himself to his feet, looked at the braided moss wick, at the thin spire of black smoke that circled up from the sputtering flame, then sat down again, put his knife away. Who could say what would happen to that knife if he used it to do woman's work? Why risk a curse, especially on this island of curses?

He thought about getting something to eat, but the woman had left him only half a sealskin of dried fish and a handful of seal meat. What a fool she is, Waxtal thought. Women never had vision for things of the spirit. But what could he expect? Even most men did not.

He crawled over to his walrus tusks, sat down beside them, and laid his hands against the cool ivory. He closed his eyes and pictured the dead walrus on the beach. Perhaps he had called it. Who could say? Why else would it wash up here, an animal that did not float when dead? What could have brought it here except his own powers?

He thought back to his own poor village. Perhaps they were all dead, starved during their first winter away from Tugix's island, without food or oil. It would not bother him to return to a death ulaq filled with their bones, even those of his own wife Blue Shell. Let them all be dead.

But what about Samiq? Waxtal smiled. No, he did not want

Samiq dead. Samiq needed to see Waxtal as shaman, needed to see his power. Then let the man die, let Waxtal's own spear kill him. Of course, if all those people were dead, who would be left to live in his village? But why worry? He had called walrus to the Island of Four Waters and a dead walrus to his beach. Yes, he had called all of them. Who else could have done so? If Hard Rock was able to call an animal, it would be a whale.

I called them, Waxtal thought. I called the walrus. And if I can call walrus, I can call men, hunters and traders who will come to my village. And because I call them, I will be chief. Waxtal's stomach growled. He laid his hand over his belly and said, "Wait, soon you will have food. They will bring more than if I had taken the hunter's share." So he sat and waited until sleep reached out to claim him.

He awoke to a voice calling from the top of the ulaq. It was the widow Pogy and the old woman Most Hands. Each carried fresh meat, sliced and cooked, dripping with oil. Pogy also carried a bladder of cooked bitterroot bulbs, which she handed Waxtal as she came down the climbing log. The bladder was warm from the bitterroot, and also carried the rich smell of smoked fish. He opened it and saw that the woman had flaked the fish into the root and also sifted in dried ugyuun leaves. He reached to scoop out some of the bulbs, licked the food from his fingers.

"For you, for the meat you gave us," Pogy said, and though her eyes were swollen from her mourning, Waxtal saw that she was a beautiful woman, tall and strong, the bones of her face tight under her skin, her eyes large, her nose small.

Too bad, he thought, that Red Feet had not died sooner. If Pogy were not in mourning, Waxtal would ask for her as wife rather than the one they called Kukutux. Though Kukutux was not ugly, her bent arm would hinder her strength, and she was a woman of sharp mouth and bitter words. But who could say? If Waxtal decided to stay on this island for the winter, perhaps he would take Kukutux for a short time, then when Pogy had completed her mourning, he would throw Kukutux away. Who could blame him? Even Hard Rock complained about Kukutux's temper.

"Thank you," Waxtal said, dipping his fingers again into the bitterroot. "It is good."

"It is I who should thank you," said Pogy. "It is not easy for a woman alone to get meat."

The two women left, and Waxtal's eyes followed Pogy as she went up the climbing log. His eyes lingered on her feet and legs, and he wished he could see higher up into her suk, but the shadows let him see no farther than her knees. Still, even that made Waxtal forget for a moment about his empty belly. But when he could no longer hear the women at the top of his ulaq, he sat down beside the oil lamp and ate.

Three women came that night, all bringing cooked walrus meat, the meat strong in flavor, perhaps not as good as seal meat, but better, Waxtal told himself, than whale. One woman promised him a seal belly of walrus oil, and looking at his lamp, took her woman's knife and trimmed the wick. Another brought walrus meat cut very thin, between each piece a slice of raw fish, the walrus cooked in oil until a crisp crust formed to hold in the juice of the meat. Another brought a stew simmering in thick broth, and hung the container from a rafter.

When each woman left, Waxtal took the food she had brought and put it into one of the empty sleeping places. Why have extra? If some of the men stopped later—to talk about hunting walrus—why have food that they would eat, they who had wives and mothers to cook for them?

Waxtal ate until he was full, then laid what was left of the meat that Pogy had brought on a mat, rolled up the mat, and pushed it into the food cache. He sat down, cross-legged, and looked long into the flame of the oil lamp. And as though he were in a dream, he heard voices.

At first he thought it was someone else bringing food, but then he realized that the voices came from within the ulaq itself. Moving carefully toward the sound, he finally came to the carved tusk. He bent his head, listened to the voices that were little more than a whisper.

"What?" said one voice. "You leave nothing for those who might come?"

"Why should I?" Waxtal asked, also whispering. "I gave them a walrus and took nothing for myself. What more should I do?"

"You called the walrus?" the voice asked.

"Who else?"

"Selfishness earns nothing but regret," the voice said,

words that Waxtal had heard before, from grandmothers teaching grandchildren.

"Am I a child that you must tell me that?" he asked, but he went back to the food cache, pulled out the mat, and laid it on the floor beside the tallest oil lamp. "There," he said and said it loudly. "There is food."

The voice did not answer, and though Waxtal went back to the tusk, squatted beside it for a time, the voices did not speak again. Finally he went into his sleeping place, took out his packet of carving tools, and settled beside the brightest oil lamp. He reached for a bit of walrus meat and chewed it as he brought the carved tusk over to the lamp and set it on the floor beside him.

He closed his eyes to see if some picture would come to his mind, some idea of what he should carve next. Soon he was making lines, pictures of Samiq, the man with one hand short and drawn in against his chest, with marks like spears for the curses that were being thrown against him by spirits.

Waxtal heard Hard Rock call from the top of the ulaq. Waxtal set aside the tusk and laid his tools beside it.

"Come in; I am here!" he called up to the man.

Hard Rock came, pulled off his suk. The man was barely sitting before Waxtal offered him the remains of the walrus meat Pogy had brought.

Hard Rock took a piece, chewed it slowly, swallowed slowly. Finally he gestured with his chin toward Waxtal and said, "You called the walrus."

"Yes."

"It is good you are here. At least our village now has fresh meat."

Waxtal inclined his head, set his mouth into a smile.

"Our hunters," Hard Rock said, "they do not know how to hunt walrus. You can help them?"

"Some. I have hunted with the Walrus men, but I do not know all their secrets. I do know they do not hunt with seal or sea lion harpoons. I have told you that already."

Hard Rock nodded.

"You must have your men make weapons for walrus. Long shafts of the strongest wood. Bone foreshafts as long as a man's forearm. Spearheads should be as long as a man's hand, wrist to the end of his longest finger.

"Also tell your men that walrus are taken from land," Waxtal said. He looked away from Hard Rock and fixed his eyes on the oil lamp. "Do I need to tell you why?"

"I saw what happened," Hard Rock said. He picked up another piece of meat, and though Waxtal's belly was so full it pressed uncomfortably against his ribs, he too took a piece of meat. "If we do all these things, will you bless our weapons and make chants for our hunts?"

"Yes," Waxtal said. "The Whale Hunters have been good to me." He moved his hand in a wide sweep. "You allow me this ulaq." He smiled, knowing that Hard Rock would see the bareness of the room.

"The women brought you food?" he asked.

Waxtal pointed to the mat beside Hard Rock. Hard Rock looked at the few pieces of meat and raised his eyebrows.

"I ate some before you came," Waxtal said. "I would have saved more if I had known you were coming."

For a time there was silence, then Hard Rock asked, "If we do these things, we will be successful in the hunt?"

Waxtal opened his mouth to speak, then closed it again. He shrugged. "Who can say?"

"There is still a curse," Hard Rock said in a quiet voice, the voice of a man who has worked too long, too hard, without sleep.

"Yes," said Waxtal. "Why do you think your hunter was killed?"

"Because of his harpoon. Because we did not offer prayers."

"That is enough to curse a man's hunting," Waxtal said. "That is enough to make him return from days on the sea with nothing—perhaps for one summer, even two. But to kill him?" Waxtal shook his head.

"Is it the same curse that has plagued this island these two years?" Hard Rock asked.

Waxtal lowered his head, and for a long time did not speak. Finally he closed his eyes and began a long chant, something in the Walrus tongue, followed by words and phrases in the First Men language, then again in Walrus, the words blending like braided strands of twisted sinew. When he had finished the chant, he opened his eyes and said to Hard Rock, "You must leave this island."

Hard Rock's eyes widened. "I must leave this island?"

"You and your strongest hunters. It is the only way."

"If we leave, will the curse leave our people?"

"If you do what must be done."

"What must be done?

Waxtal bowed his head, waited a long time before answering. Finally, he said, "Sometimes the spirits do not tell everything that needs to be told."

"If we do not know what to do, what sense is there in leaving our island?" Hard Rock asked, anger hardening his words.

Waxtal held his hands out, palm up. "Go to each ulaq, to each hunter in this village. Ask each man to spend the night praying. I will do the same, and in the morning I will tell you what must be done."

Hard Rock stood, and Waxtal pushed himself to his feet. He waited as the man pulled on his suk, then walked with him to the climbing log. At the top of the log, Hard Rock turned back, looked down at Waxtal. "I came to tell you that the people want you to have the walrus tusks."

Waxtal raised one hand. "Tell them I said thank you. You go now to your men. You pray. Tell them to pray. Tell them that I, too, will spend the night in prayer."

Waxtal climbed the log, crouched at the top of the ulaq, outside in the cold wind without a suk, and watched as Hard Rock went from ulaq to ulaq.

Later, back inside his own lodge, Waxtal warmed his hands over an oil lamp flame and laughed. "Four tusks," he said. "Even the spirits will not be able to stand against my power." He went into his sleeping place, curled himself up into his robes, and slept. He was shaman. His dreams would be his prayers.

SIXTY-ONE

WAXTAL LOOKED AROUND THE CIRCLE OF MEN.
Their heavy eyes answered his question, but still he asked,
"You prayed?"

"Yes," Hard Rock said and paused to let each man answer
for himself. "Have the spirits spoken to you?" he asked Waxtal.

He nodded. "They spoke."

The men waited, their eyes fixed on Waxtal's face. He felt
their nervousness, the energy of their questions. It brought
strength to his hands and arms, to his back and legs, and so
for a moment he said nothing, only waited while their power
flowed to him. Finally he said, "I know why you are cursed."

A groan rose from the men in Hard Rock's ulaq. "Everyone
here knows why we are cursed," Hard Rock said. "If that is
what the spirits told you, then you have nothing important to
tell us."

The men around Waxtal suddenly seemed larger, stronger.
He flexed his hands into tight fists, but still he could feel his
power ebb. "Samiq," Waxtal said, and the word did what his
hands could not—pushed the Whale Hunters back to the size
of men.

Hard Rock hissed, as did several of the others. "You curse
us with his name," Hard Rock said.

"The spirits have told me what you do not know," said
Waxtal. He paused, looked into the face of each hunter. "I
am a trader as well as a shaman. What will you give me for
the power to end the curse?"

"Tell me first what I need to know," Hard Rock said, leaning forward and looking long into Waxtal's face.

Waxtal laughed. "If I tell you, then why give me anything?"

"And what if your knowledge does not lift the curse?"

"I will return what you have given."

Hard Rock waved his hand toward the North Sea. "How will I find you? I am not a trader. I do not know the sea paths that lead to the Caribou People and the Walrus Men."

"I will stay with you until the curse is lifted," Waxtal answered.

Hard Rock grunted, looked at the other men.

"What will you give me?" Waxtal pressed.

For a time, Hard Rock sat and said nothing. Waxtal's stomach rolled, and he wished he had eaten before coming. He had thought to save his own food for later. Hard Rock's wives always had meat ready, but this morning there had been nothing except a blessing asked by Hard Rock and the promise of continued fasting.

"What do you want?" Hard Rock finally asked. "An ikyak? Furs, sealskins? Food, oil?"

"All those," Waxtal said, "and a woman."

"You expect all those things?" Hard Rock asked.

"Not an ikyak," said Waxtal. "I have a fine ikyak. But something from each man—food, fur, oil, perhaps only a gathering bag of sea urchins." Waxtal slowed his voice, lowered his head, and looked up, moving his eyes around the circle of hunters. "Whatever each man feels his hunting is worth. That and a woman."

"I gave you a woman," Hard Rock said. "Where is she?"

Waxtal shrugged. "She returned to her own ulaq. I do not know why. I want her back. Or else another woman. Someone young who is good at fishing and sewing."

"I will get her back," Hard Rock finally said. "Tell us now what you have to tell us."

"Bring me first what you have to bring. Then if what I tell you to do does not lift the curse, you may take back what each man gives."

Waxtal's stomach growled. Why stay here in this ulaq without food, he thought, when my own ulaq has meat ready? I do not need to fast. I am not cursed. He stood and said to Hard Rock, "Bring what you have to bring—to my own ulaq. Then I will tell you."

Kukutux teased away two strands of sea lion sinew from a chunk she kept in her storage basket. She dipped her fingers in a wooden bowl of water and moistened the sinew, then began to roll it on her thigh.

"Kukutux!" It was Hard Rock.

Kukutux ignored the voice and pulled the sinew, checking length and twist, then rolled it again.

Hard Rock descended halfway down the climbing log and jumped to the floor. In two long strides he was at her side. "I called," he said, his words an accusation.

Kukutux shrugged. "I am working," she said, and raised her left hand, the long twist of sinew thread hanging from her fingers.

"Why did you leave the trader?" he asked.

"He is not a good man," said Kukutux.

Hard Rock's eyes widened, as if he could see, just by looking, the spirits that her words might offend.

"He is shaman!"

"He hit me!"

"Perhaps Seal Hunter men hit their wives."

"I am Whale Hunter!"

"You are what your husband is."

"I am what I choose to be! What Whale Hunter woman does not choose her own husband? Every Whale Hunter man knows that he shatters his own spirit when he hits his wife." Kukutux set down the sinew and stood to face Hard Rock. "He is not my husband."

"Lucky for him!" said Hard Rock. He paced the length of the ulaq and back. "He has promised to tell us how to break the curse if you return to him."

"That is all he wants?" Kukutux asked.

Hard Rock stammered over his words, finally saying, "That and a few trade goods. Something from each hunter."

Kukutux let a smile lift one corner of her mouth. "A few trade goods," she said, mimicking Hard Rock's voice.

Hard Rock sighed. "So, I should tell him you will not come?"

"Tell him."

"I should tell him you do not care if more hunters are cursed. If more young men like Pogy's husband—like your husband—die?"

Kukutux turned away. "And if he does not know how to lift the curse?" she asked.

"You can come back to your own ulaq, live without a husband or choose someone else."

Kukutux turned and looked into Hard Rock's eyes. "Do you believe he can lift the curse?"

"I do not know," he said slowly. "But what if he can? How can I refuse to let him try?"

Kukutux wrapped the sinew into a coil and set it into her sewing basket. "If the curse is not lifted, I can choose my own husband?"

"Yes."

"Anyone?"

"Yes. You will go?"

"I will go," Kukutux said, "but do not forget your promise." She began to gather her things.

From oldest to youngest, they came, beginning with Fish Eater. He brought a seal belly of oil, old judging by the stink of what had seeped from the stoppered end, but for Fish Eater it was probably much to bring. Oil to light lamps for many days. Big Ears was next with seal fur pelts, then Fish Swimming with a sea lion belly of dried fish, three bladders of rendered seal oil, and a sleeping robe of pieced otter pelts. Then Hard Rock came, with arms laden.

To honor the alananasika, Waxtal stood. Hard Rock laid at his feet a harbor seal parka with hood made in the manner of the Walrus People; two spear shafts, straight and strong; three ivory harpoon heads, each in a black basket of woven whale baleen; and two sea lion bellies of fresh seal oil. Waxtal kept the smile from his lips, but nodded and sat again to await the trades of younger men, each of whom tried to outdo the others.

Waxtal pressed his lips together in satisfaction. Who could put an adequate price on a man's hunting skills? So each trade was better than the last until only a few boys were left. They had little to offer except what they had begged from mothers and grandmothers—baskets, gathering bags, sinew, braided kelp lines. But what trader turned away such things?

When the goods were gathered in piles at the corners of the ulaq, Hard Rock brought Kukutux, the woman with sullen face, her arms loaded with all things a woman deems important—baskets and needles, furs and water bladders. Waxtal did not look at her, did not let her know he even knew she was in the ulaq, but from the corners of his eyes, he watched for her reaction when she saw the piles of goods. But she looked past them, as though everything the hunters had offered had always been there. She set down the things she had brought with her and went to the food cache, began to prepare food.

Waxtal realized the men were watching him. He realized that the ulaq was quiet, the silence broken only by the noise of Kukutux's knife, the woman doing whatever women do to prepare food. And in this she was like all women, thinking that there was nothing more important in the world than the small things a woman does.

Waxtal stood, held his hands out over the men, closed his eyes, and started a chant. It was a chant of blessing, and though he began in the words of the Walrus People, to give some sense of mystery, he soon changed to First Men words so the Whale Hunters could understand what he said, could know that he invoked blessings. He moved his hands and then his feet in slow rhythm with the words. Their gifts had earned them more than some quick statement. What hunter did not enjoy ceremony?

So Waxtal chanted, and finally when he saw through the slits of his eyes that some of the men were restless, he went to the trade goods. He laid his hands on each thing offered and mumbled words of blessing, then picked up a seal belly of oil that one of the younger hunters had given and held it out, the belly heavy enough to make his arms tremble under its weight. He held it and said to all the men, "The spirits say this seal belly goes to the new widows, the wives of the one taken by the walrus. The spirits say it is the first sign that the curse will be lifted from this island."

A murmur swept over the circle of men and He Swims, brother of Pogy, stepped forward and took the sea lion belly from Waxtal's arms. "For Pogy, I thank you," he said, his eyes lowered in respect.

Waxtal answered, "Do not thank me, thank the spirits." He waited until the young man had again taken his place in the circle of hunters, then said, "I have promised I would tell you what the spirits have said to me. Listen and do not speak. Listen and hear, for it will not be easy to lift this curse, and some may not want to do what must be done."

He looked around the circle at each man, tried to see each hunter with harpoon and spear in hand, tried to see which men could act against other men, tried to remember which of the older hunters had fought best against the Short Ones. Then he began: "Two, three summers ago, a young man of the Seal Hunters came to this beach. He was grandson of the Whale Hunters' alananasika, that old one now dead and honored among those in the Dancing Lights.

"That old one, he wanted the son of his granddaughter to learn the ways of the Whale Hunters. Who would not? Why let a grandson, skilled with harpoon and ikyak, live among the Seal Hunters? Who believes that a Seal Hunter is more skilled, more powerful than a Whale Hunter?"

There was a murmur of agreement before Waxtal continued.

"Even the boy's mother, the woman Chagak, though daughter of a Seal Hunter man, wanted her son raised by his grandfather, to know the strong ways of the Whale Hunters. But this woman Chagak—in her dreams of the power that would come to her son—lied to her grandfather, did not tell the truth to the old man. The boy Samiq . . ." A sudden hush of breathing made Waxtal hold up one hand and say again, "This boy Samiq was fathered by a Short One, one of the enemy who came to this island. And while the Whale Hunters rejoiced after the battle with the Short Ones, the Short Ones' spirits, defeated on this island, gathered their power into one man, then only an infant suckled by a Seal Hunter woman."

The hunters whispered, heads nodding, eyes flashing anger, so that Waxtal had to hold up both hands, wait until silence again settled before he could go on. He opened his mouth to speak, but one man interrupted.

"How do you know this?" a voice said from behind him. It was the hunter Dying Seal.

"Two ways," Waxtal answered. "First, because I was with the Seal Hunter shaman, Shuganan, when he died. At that time his powers became my powers." Waxtal drew a carving knife from a sheath at his waist and held the knife out flat on the palm of his right hand. "His gift to carve became my gift. He himself told me about Samiq. He himself feared what the child might become.

"And second, because Samiq told me."

"He knew when he came to this island? He knew he was enemy to us?" one of the younger men asked, the one called Crooked Bird.

Waxtal shook his head. "No, he did not know until he was

back with his own people, until he challenged his father for leadership of the Seal Hunters and took them east to the Traders' Beach.''

"No," said Hard Rock. "The young man you speak of, he is dead. He died here on this island, crushed under the rock of a ledge, he and his wife and a boy from this village."

Waxtal smiled. "He is alive. I have seen him, talked to him. He rules my village, and his power is an evil power. Why do you think that I, no longer a young man, left my own people to trade?"

"How do we know you are telling us the truth?" Dying Seal asked.

"If my words were not true," Waxtal said, turning to face Hard Rock, "would I so easily say Samiq's name?"

"You claim to be a shaman. Shamans have powers. You say the old one's name, the Seal Hunter shaman."

"Shuganan lives through me," Waxtal said. "We are one."

The men spoke among themselves, and watching, Waxtal saw the doubt in their eyes. He laughed and said, "You will not accept the knowledge of a shaman. Will you accept the knowledge of a Seal Hunter?" He paused and said, "The woman that he brought back with him is Three Fish. The boy is Small Knife."

As though they were women, the hunters lifted fingers to mouths, covered their surprise with cupped hands.

Hard Rock said, "Tell us what we must do to break the curse."

Waxtal felt his spirit lift, as though something bound too tightly had been released. The freedom made him laugh, and through his laughter he said, "Kill Samiq."

Kukutux offered food, but the men refused it, so she sat and listened and waited. They planned and talked, spending most of that day discussing a journey to the faraway Traders' Beach, a place where none of them except Waxtal had ever been. The men were like boys in their excitement, hands waving, eyes snapping. Only Dying Seal was quiet, the man so still that if his eyes had not gleamed from the dark corner where he sat, she would have thought he slept.

Finally the planning was finished, all words spoken, and the men, even Hard Rock, left. Kukutux sat with her hands in her lap. Yes, if it would lift the curse, she would be wife to the trader. There were worse things. It was worse to see the children in the village hungry, to hear their cries for food, to see sorrow in the eyes of young mothers, to hear the mourning songs of widows.

Finally Waxtal came to her, stood over her.

"You want food?" Kukutux asked.

Waxtal said, "You are my wife."

"Yes," Kukutux answered, but did not lower her eyes in respect, did not bow her head. The man's fists clenched.

"There is food in that sleeping place," he said and pointed with his chin toward the sleeping place nearest his own.

She got up and went there, sure that Waxtal had lied. Who kept food in a sleeping place? He only wanted her to go easily, willingly. Then he would come in, demand his rights as husband. But there was food—a boiling bag of stew, the meat and broth cold and covered with a hardened layer of fat. "Do you want some of this?" she called out to Waxtal.

"Yes, I am hungry."

"If you wait, I will take the stew outside and warm it," Kukutux said, carrying the bag suspended between her hands.

Waxtal shook his head and instead brought two bowls, dipped each into the meat, broke some of the fat into each bowl. "Hang it up over an oil lamp. It will gradually warm," he said.

She hung the cooking bag, then squatted beside him. He handed her a bowl. "Eat," he said.

She waited until he took the first bite and then ate. When her bowl was empty, he asked, "Your husband was killed hunting?"

"Yes."

"You are ready to be wife again?"

When Kukutux did not answer, he asked, "How long has he been dead?"

"More than a year now," Kukutux said.

"Long enough," said Waxtal.

He stood up and extended one hand to her. His fingers looked old, knuckles swollen, but in her mind she saw his hand wrapped around a walking stick, saw the fingers tighten as he raised the stick to strike her.

"You have another wife?" she asked as she stood, ignoring his outstretched hand.

"She is dead."

"We both mourn."

"You will not have a terrible life," said Waxtal and spread his arms as though he would embrace the stacks of trade goods.

"It is not mine."

"You are a woman. What woman expects to have all of this?" He laughed. "But I will give you something because you are my wife," he said. "Choose."

"Anything?" Kukutux asked.

"Anything."

Kukutux looked long at all the furs and skins, the meat and oil. Finally she pointed at Waxtal's chest, at the blue stone necklace that Owl had given her.

"That," she said.

Waxtal narrowed his eyes, hesitated, but finally took off the necklace and handed it to her. Then she went with him into his sleeping place.

SIXTY-TWO

The Alaska Peninsula

KIIN PEELED THE SHELL FROM AN EGG AND HELD the egg out to Shuku. He curled his lips and turned his head away. "It is better than nothing," Kiin told him. But she held it up to her nose and knew why he refused it. Too many days had passed since she had gathered and boiled the eggs. Mold discolored the white and had begun to eat into the yolk.

Kiin sighed and looked out over the North Sea. She should fish. The shore here dropped steeply from the beach. She could use a handline to catch pogies and perhaps even cod. She glanced up at the sky, at the position of the sun. Better to wait until low tide, she thought, then gather sea urchins or dig for clams. She lifted the carrying basket from her back and sat down. She did not let herself remember that she had said the same thing the day before, and yet during low tide had done nothing.

She had been walking steadily for two months and knew she must be more than halfway to Traders' Bay. If she could make herself keep walking, in less than two moons, she would come to the mouth of the Traders' Bay. Then she would be close enough to sit and wait for one of the First Men hunters to find her.

In the time since she had fallen, Kiin's hands had healed, leaving only small pink scars against her brown skin. Her fingers where the nails had been torn away were tender, but already she could see the thin ridges of new nails growing in. To protect her fingertips, she had carved wooden nails for herself, thin slices that she tied to her fingers each day to protect the soft skin of the nail beds.

But each day walking became more difficult. Angry red lines had crept up from the cuts on her feet, and now reached nearly to her knees.

Each morning, Kiin wrapped her feet in sealskin strips before she put on her boots. Each night she unwrapped her feet and washed them with seawater. But every day, she had to stop sooner, to allow herself more time to rest. Two days ago, she had walked only to the next hill, and then had stayed, moving once to the beach to gather a few pieces of driftwood that had floated in from the North Sea, and to dig clams. Yesterday, she had done nothing.

She reached into her carrying basket beside her in the beach grass and found the seal belly storage container. The container, once bulging with fish, was now flat, empty. Three pieces of fish hung drying on the outside of the basket.

"Three pieces," Kiin said, looking at the fish, and the words were like stones in her chest. She handed one piece to Shuku. I should eat, she thought, but she was not hungry. Her face was hot, even in the cold wind, and her eyes seemed to see too much too quickly, making her head throb and her stomach ache.

"I will fish," she told Shuku. She pulled a kelp fishing line from the basket and tied it to a hook she had carved from a clamshell. She knotted the line, then, feeling her stomach rise into her throat, she closed her eyes.

After a moment of rest, she broke a small section of fish from one of the two remaining pieces on the basket and tied it to the hook with strands of her hair, then picked up Shuku, put him in the sling, and adjusted it so that he was against her back, his head peeking out from the neck of her parka.

Kiin wrapped her left hand with a strip of sealskin, then slowly rose to her feet. Her suk had been ruined in the fall, so she wore the parka and leggings she had brought from the Walrus village. She took off her boots and walked slowly toward the water, across the gravel beach, and down the slope of sand left by the tide. She waded out until the sand dropped off into deep water, then uncoiled her line, twisting it around her padded left hand. The cold water numbed the pain in her feet, but Shuku's weight against Kiin's back made it difficult to keep her balance in the waves. She stood, feet apart, knees bent, bracing herself, and she prayed to the grandmother spirits of sun, moon, and earth to send her a fish.

When the bite came, Kiin thought it was only another wave, pulling against her as it drew itself back into the sea. Then she realized that the pull was from the line, and she knew it was a fish. She raised her eyes to thank the spirits, but the gray of the sky made her head ache, and so she looked instead at the line, played it out carefully as Crooked Nose had taught her long ago. If it was a cod, she needed to jerk the line hard to set the hook in the fish's mouth. If it was a pogy, she must be more careful and wait until she was sure the fish was not just nibbling the edges of the bait.

She felt the line move in a long, strong pull. Cod, she thought, and jerked hard, lifting her left hand up and back. She twisted the line once and then again around her hand, and, moving with the fish, she allowed it to tire in its fight against the line.

Almost, her feet stopped hurting, almost she forgot she was carrying Shuku. There was only Kiin and the fish. If the fish gave itself to her hook, then she would have enough for at least another day's walking, perhaps two. She looked up at the sun, squinted against the brightness of the gray clouds that covered it.

She coiled the fishline around her hand, once, twice. The cod was finally tiring, swimming in smaller circles. Kiin con-

tinued to wind the line until finally in the clear water she could
see the fish.

"Not cod, halibut," she gasped, "halibut," and laughed as
Shuku raised his voice in a crowing yell.

She began to walk backward, bringing the fish into shallow
water until at last it flopped on the sand. She had no club, so
she picked up a rock and slammed it into the halibut's head.
The fish quivered and was still. Nearly the size of a sea otter,
it lay flat and dark on the gravel. Food for six, seven days,
Kiin thought. She hooked her hands into the fish's gills and
pulled it higher up on the beach.

The effort seemed to force the pain back into her feet and
legs. She unwrapped the fishline from her left hand, then sat
down beside the fish and loosened the sealskin strips around
her feet. Above the wrappings her legs were swollen and red,
and the sudden release brought more pain.

"We have food, Shuku," Kiin told her son, but even as she
spoke, her eyes closed, shutting away the too-bright sky. "We
should rest, Shuku. It is nearly low tide. We should rest, and
then I will gather sea urchins. We will make our camp up in
the grass of the next hill, and for a day, we will stay, drying
our fish and eating our sea urchins. And then we will go on
to find your father."

She let herself lie down on the beach. She pulled Shuku
from her back to her chest so he could nurse, then curled on
her side around the halibut. She would lie here for a little
while; she would close her eyes just for a moment.

SIXTY-THREE

THE WHALE HUNTERS

Yunaska Island, the Aleutian Chain

KUKUTUX PUSHED HERSELF UP FROM HER KNEES, then reached down once more to lay her hands against the rocks that covered her husband's grave. "White Stone," she whispered, "I would be content to sit here forever beside you."

She wiped tears from her cheeks with the backs of her hands, then went to the small mound that was her son's grave. "At least your bones will be a part of this island," she said to him. She turned away, walked back through the hills to the beach where all the people of the village had gathered.

The men's ikyan and three longer, wider women's iks, filled with sealskin packs, lined the shore.

The people were gathered in families, and so Kukutux looked for her husband Waxtal. She saw that he was already in his ikyak, paddling away from the beach.

"Let him go; let him be gone," some perverse spirit whispered within her. "Then you can stay behind. He will not know until everyone stops for the night. Then it will be too late to come back for you."

The thought was like some sweetness in Kukutux's mouth, but she reminded herself that she was Waxtal's wife, and a wife went with her husband.

"If I stay here," she whispered into the wind, "then perhaps Waxtal will not lead our men to Samiq's beach, and Samiq will not die. What chance will there be for this village if Samiq lives and the curse remains?"

She realized that Hard Rock had moved to his ikyak and was speaking to the two old men and seven old women who

290

were to stay on the Whale Hunters' island. "Take care of the children we leave with you," he said. "We will be back next summer. Watch for us."

You will be back, Kukutux thought. I will not.

Waxtal did not plan to return. He had told her he would stay at the First Men's village after the battle at the Traders' Beach. He would stay and take his place as chief.

Kukutux looked up at the Whale Hunters' mountain Atal, then again toward the hills where her husband and son were buried. Now all she would have for a remembrance was the strip of fur from her son's wrapping blanket and the strand of hair and the bear claw from her husband's sleeping place. The ache in her chest was so great that each breath was like a knife, cutting.

She sighed to lift the weight of her sorrow, then asked herself, "Is my pain greater than Speckled Basket's? She must leave a child two summers old with her grandmother. Is my sorrow more than what Old Goose Woman feels, seeing both son and daughter leave?"

Kukutux waited as Hard Rock continued to speak, listing the number of seal bellies of oil, the skins of meat and fish he was giving to the old ones and the children—enough for them to live through the winter and beyond.

We who are going with Waxtal, Kukutux thought, we are the ones who will be hungry. But as Waxtal had explained during the many evenings spent planning the journey, the women who were not paddling would use handlines to catch fish. The men in their ikyan would be ever watching for seals and sea lions.

Besides, there would be birds to catch, sea urchins, chitons, and clams to gather. Waxtal and the traders had come this way just the year before. He knew the good beaches, the places to find food.

At last Hard Rock finished speaking, and the men got in their ikyan, seven hunters in all. Kukutux was in an ik with Hard Rock's second wife and her older children, and with Speckled Basket and She Cries and She Cries' stepdaughter, Snow-in-her-hair. Unlike most of the women, She Cries would not leave her baby on the island, though She Cries' mother could have cared for the child. Others chided the woman, but Kukutux would not. If Kukutux could hardly bear to leave her son's grave, why criticize She Cries for not leaving her baby?

Though she did not fault She Cries for her choice, Kukutux noticed that as the people gathered on the beach, She Cries hardly glanced at her mother and gave the woman no words of farewell. Seeing the sadness in the old woman's eyes, the tears on her cheeks, Kukutux went to her, put her arms around the thin, hard-boned shoulders, and wept her own tears of leaving into the old woman's tangled white hair. Then Kukutux went back to the ik and helped the women push it into the sea.

Because of her strong eyes and weak arm, Kukutux sat in the bow. One last time, she looked back at the Whale Hunters' island, then set her eyes ahead to the flat blue expanse of the sea.

She wondered about Owl—whether he and his brother were also on this sea, traveling far to the east in their traders' ik. Then her thoughts sped to the far shore of the Traders' Beach, to Samiq and the battle that was coming to the First Men's village.

SIXTY-FOUR

The Alaska Peninsula

KIIN FOUGHT HER WAY UP THROUGH DREAMS. SHE was a child in her father's ulaq. She felt the bedding mats against her cheek, smelled the heavy scent of meat cooking, heard a man's voice.

She shivered and tried to take herself back into sleep. But no, if her father was awake, she was sure to be beaten. She should have been up long before now. She should have taken out night wastes and brought water from the stream, trimmed the oil lamp wicks and been ready to help her mother with food for the new day. She cringed as she thought of her father's walking stick cracking hard across her back.

She reached one arm out from her sleeping robes to find her suk, something that would offer protection for her skin, but her hand found nothing, not even the cool hard earth-and-stone walls of the ulaq.

She opened her eyes and tried to sit up, but all the muscles of her arms and legs burned with pain, and she felt the familiar throb of too-full breasts. "Shuku," she whispered, and fear closed in around her throat.

No, she was not in her father's ulaq, nor even in any lodge made by the Walrus People, and her arms and legs ached as though her father had used his walking stick against her.

Where am I? Where is Shuku? Then she remembered the halibut, the beach. How could she have been so foolish as to fall asleep with Shuku helpless against the tide?

Was she now in some spirit world? If so, she must find Shuku so they could make their way together to the Dancing Lights. She sat up, clamped her teeth against the pain, and spoke to the fear that hampered her thoughts: If I am dead, then why do I hurt? If I am dead, why am I inside a lodge and not outside with wind and sea?

She thought of death ulas, of dead ones bound legs to chest and wrapped in grass mats. Her fear returned. Perhaps she was now in a death ulaq, some lodge used by another village, a strange people, with traditions unlike the First Men's.

She forced herself to hands and knees and crawled in darkness, reaching out to touch the walls as she moved, until her hands found a woven grass curtain. Pulling the curtain aside, she peered into a large room, saw thin flickering light in the far corner, and near the light a man and woman talking. The woman nursed a baby.

"Shuku?" Kiin said, but her throat was raw and the words were only a harsh whisper.

The woman looked up and stood, the baby still nursing. "Baby?" she said in the Walrus tongue and held the child toward Kiin.

Kiin pushed herself to her knees, then to her feet, and took several stumbling steps. The woman hurried to her side, holding the baby in one arm.

Kiin grabbed the woman's shoulder and, with breath held tightly behind her teeth, looked down at the baby. In one joyous cry she called out, "Shuku!"

Shuku, nursing with eyes closed, jerked and turned, then let loose of the woman's breast and held out his arms toward his mother. Kiin, her legs too weak to hold her, dropped down to the floor, sitting in the manner of the Walrus People, legs folded. The woman said something to the man and he left the ulaq, then she laid Shuku in Kiin's lap. Shuku reached up to wrap his arms around his mother's neck, pulled himself to his feet, and held tightly, humming a small tune of baby words between quick breaths.

Kiin looked up at the woman, pressed her lips together to hold in her tears. "Thank you," she said in the Walrus language.

The woman smiled and, pointing at Shuku, said, "He . . . he . . ." She paused and traced fingers down her cheeks, to show a line of tears. "I . . . mmm . . . I." Her face wrinkled in concentration, and she finally pointed to her breast, the nipple still pink and elongated from Shuku's sucking. "I, me did," she finished and smiled.

"Thank you," Kiin said again, then for the first time noticed the weave of the woman's grass apron. Kiin smiled and changed her words from Walrus to those of the First Men, asking, "You are First Men?"

The woman raised her eyebrows and began to laugh. "I am named Small Plant Woman. You are not Walrus?" she asked, speaking clearly in the First Men's language and pointing at Kiin's clothing—the Walrus People parka, the caribou skin leggings.

"No, First Men," Kiin said. "I am Kiin, from the Seal Hunter People."

The woman tried to answer but could not force her words out through her giggles, and Kiin, with Shuku warm and well in her arms, felt giggles rise in her own throat, so that for a time neither woman spoke, but let laughter weave its net between them, catching them together in joy.

They are Ugyuun, Kiin told herself as she sat with Small Plant Woman and the six other women who had come to the ulaq. Each woman had the snarled and dirty hair of the Ugyuun. Even the smell of their skin was like something sour and old.

With the knowledge came a heaviness in Kiin's chest, but then she rolled up her leggings, looked at the cuts and scrapes on her shins and feet. They were well healed, with no red lines running up from her wounds to spread their poison to her heart.

"So," her spirit voice whispered, "they are Ugyuun. You see the caring in their eyes; you hear their laughter as they speak to one another about the small things of life. Why should you care what village they call their own? They are good people."

And Kiin nodded. What mattered the most? The cleanliness of a woman's suk or what she carried in her heart?

"Six days you slept," an old woman said. "Six days my daughter here, she watched over you and fed your baby when she could not get you to feed him."

Kiin looked at Small Plant Woman. "I slept for six days?" she asked.

Small Plant Woman's soft smile told Kiin she held no resentment over the time Kiin had claimed from her.

"Six days," the old woman said again and nodded her head quickly many times, something all the Ugyuun women seemed to do when they wanted to impress Kiin with the truth of their words.

"Sometimes, though, you seemed awake," said Small Plant Woman. "You spoke in Walrus words and often called your son. He is named Shuku?"

"Yes," Kiin said.

"What happened to your legs and feet?" Small Plant Woman asked.

Kiin crossed her arms over Shuku, the baby sitting in the circle of her legs. He watched the Ugyuun women, sometimes looking back over his shoulder at Kiin, his dark eyes as serious as those of an old man. "I fell down a cliff," Kiin explained. "I was gathering eggs."

"Yes," Small Plant Woman said. "My husband Eagle found you on the bird beach. You and your son."

"You did not know to put salmonberry leaves on your legs?" an old woman asked. She shook her head at Kiin and clucked her tongue against the roof of her mouth. "There are salmonberries in the mountains."

"Yes," Kiin said, meeting the old woman's eyes. "But my thoughts were on other things."

"You were on that beach alone?" another woman asked, and then the other women, the four that sat on the floor with

Small Plant Woman, and the two that stood behind them with arms crossed, all began to speak, their words flowing together in many questions, their voices rising until finally one of the women standing in the back shouted out, "Be quiet! We are worse than murres on their eggs."

Kiin thought she recognized the woman—her sharp-edged nose—from long ago when Kiin and her brother Qakan had come to this Ugyuun village before Qakan sold Kiin to the Raven. A chill of uneasiness passed over her, but her spirit whispered, "She will not remember you. You are strong now, inside. Then you were only beginning to be strong. You do not look the same. You are not the same."

So Kiin lifted her head, let her eyes shine with the strength she had won through prayers and songs and living. She laughed as the Ugyuun women laughed, and waited for the next question.

Again the old woman spoke: "Small Plant Woman says you are named Kiin. Was the name something you chose yourself or was it given to you by another?"

"By my father," Kiin said.

"Why would a father call his daughter such a name?" another woman asked.

Kiin pressed her lips together, felt her face grow hot. Yes, what father would name his daughter Kiin—"Who," a denial of her existence?

Kiin looked at the woman. "He wanted a son," she said, explaining nothing more—not the beatings nor the years she had lived believing she had no soul, the years when she could not speak without stuttering.

Several of the women nodded their heads, then one asked, "Where is your husband?"

"Not far from here," Kiin said. "The Traders' Beach."

Several of the women nodded.

"Why do you wear Walrus clothing?" Small Plant Woman asked. Another woman, young and looking so much like Small Plant Woman, with thin face and round black eyes, that Kiin knew they must be sisters, nodded her agreement with Small Plant Woman's question. "Why do you call your baby by a Walrus name?"

Kiin looked into the Ugyuun women's faces. Each woman

was thin; each woman's skin too pale, each woman's lips dry and peeling. Kiin thought of what the Raven would give for her return, and she was afraid.

"My father is a trader," Kiin said slowly, beginning with words that were true, hoping the Ugyuun women would see that truth in her eyes, in the straightness of her words. "My brother also, until he died. These clothes were made by my own hands after the manner of the Walrus People. When other women see them, they want them for use in winter, and so my father can trade these things and bring in knives, oil, and meat to the Seal Hunters because of what I made."

Some of the Ugyuun women, including Small Plant Woman, smiled their understanding; but others, like the large woman with the loud voice, narrowed their eyes as though they wanted to see through Kiin's skin to the secrets she hid in her heart.

"And the baby?" the loud-voiced woman asked. "Why is he Shuku?"

"His name was given by a Walrus shaman," Kiin said. "It is a name of power."

The woman tilted her head, as though considering Kiin's answer. Her next question was about sewing leggings, so that Kiin knew the woman believed her. Then all the women were talking, and Kiin hugged Shuku to her chest, and smiled her happiness at being in the Ugyuun village, safe and so close to the Traders' Beach.

SIXTY-FIVE

LATER THAT DAY, SMALL PLANT WOMAN HELPED Kiin climb up out of the ulaq. They sat together on the ulaq roof, Small Plant Woman with Shuku in her arms. It was a warm day; the sun was high in the sky, shining against the top of Kiin's head.

Her joints ached at elbows and knees, but she stretched her arms up toward the sky, winced as the scabs on legs and feet pulled against her skin.

Small Plant Woman looked into her face and said in a quiet voice, "I have goose grease, new this spring. It will soften the scabs."

Kiin smiled at her, but shook her head. How could she take goose grease—which could be used for food—from a woman who had so little?

"I am fine," Kiin said. "Already the sun makes me feel strong." She held her arms out toward Shuku, and noticed that despite her sickness, despite the days of starving, her arms and hands looked fuller, stronger, than Small Plant Woman's. Who could not see, in the lines on their faces, the brittleness of their hair, that the Ugyuun women had starved during the winter, perhaps through many winters? Yet these six days, Small Plant Woman had fed her and watched over Shuku.

Shuku leaned toward his mother, but for a moment Small Plant Woman held the boy tightly, pressing him to her chest. "I had a son," she said softly, then released Shuku into Kiin's arms.

Kiin glanced into the woman's eyes. She saw pain there, but the pain was private, something that belonged to Small Plant Woman, so Kiin looked quickly away.

"Last winter was hard," Small Plant Woman murmured.

Kiin nodded, though she did not remember the winter being particularly hard. Who could say? Perhaps any winter was a hard winter for the Ugyuun People. Who did not know that the Ugyuun men were poor hunters? Why else would their children always have the lip sores of those who ate ugyuun raw, without carefully peeling away the outer stalk, something hungry children might do?

Small Plant Woman slid down the side of the ulaq and led the way into the lee of a larger ulaq. There she squatted down on her haunches, motioning Kiin to do the same. Kiin moved slowly, her knees and hips so stiff that she finally laughed and said, "I have become like some old woman."

Small Plant Woman smiled, then began to speak of the little things of living: slicing fish to dry, finding where the best berries grew, weaving mats. She told Kiin about the arguments that raged between a young woman named Crowberry and She

Calls Out, sister to Small Plant Woman's father. As Small Plant Woman spoke, Kiin came to realize that there was something more important Small Plant Woman had to say.

It always brought a smile to Kiin's face to hear hunters as they talked first of weather and hunting before any man spoke of what truly lay against his heart. Now she realized that women did the same. Their stories might be of berry picking and preparing food, of other women and their words, but still, it was the same. So Kiin clasped her hands together over Shuku and made herself listen in politeness until Small Plant Woman was ready to say what she needed to say.

Questions rose in Kiin's mind, made her legs jump in restlessness. Eagle, Small Plant Woman's husband, had found her. Would he expect something in exchange for saving her and Shuku? What did Kiin have to give? Small Plant Woman had said nothing about Kiin's carrying basket. Had it been lost? Kiin's carving tools were in it.

Small Plant Woman finished a story about two Ugyuun women, how a fight between their children had become a fight between them, then she said, "My husband Eagle found you. He is out now in his ikyak, hunting seals, but when he returns he will talk to you."

"You are good, you and your husband, to take me into your ulaq," Kiin said.

Small Plant Woman looked away, would not meet Kiin's eyes, and nervousness began to twist into a hard, tight knot in Kiin's belly.

Eagle came to Kiin that evening, after a second oil lamp had been lit in the ulaq, after Small Plant Woman and Kiin had put away food and moved the cooking skin from its place over the large oil lamp to a hook hanging from the rafters near the back ulaq wall.

The man was large and thick, with hands as big as seals' skulls. His face was flat, dipped in at the middle so the end of his nose was no higher than his eyebones, and his skin was black with soot. His suk was well made, of puffin skins and fur seal pelts, but it stank of mildew, so that Kiin took small breaths through her mouth to keep the smell from her nose.

"I found you," he said, without politeness of small words. "You and your son."

"Thank you," Kiin said.

"I have your pack."

Kiin nodded. She looked across the room, saw that Small Plant Woman was cradling Shuku on her lap. Shuku was fussing, whining sounds that told Kiin he was hungry. Small Plant Woman laid the baby on his back, moved him toward her left breast. Looking past Eagle, Kiin said to Small Plant Woman, "I will feed him."

But Small Plant Woman acted as though she had not heard, and Eagle said, "Milk is milk. Who cares which woman feeds him? He belongs to both."

His words were like a slap against Kiin's head. She opened her mouth to speak, but could say nothing.

"I found you; if you have no husband, you are mine," Eagle said.

Kiin sat, mouth open. She pulled her eyes away from Small Plant Woman and looked at Eagle.

Her spirit voice spoke. "Eagle!" it hissed. "Who would think to give the man such a name, slow and dirty as he is?" But Kiin shook her head until she heard not her spirit voice, but only the clear strong words of her own thoughts.

"I was traveling without my husband," she said.

"Alone?" Eagle asked, his eyes narrowing, his lips drawing into a wet circle.

"Yes," Kiin answered.

"How can a woman travel alone without a hunter? Without a man to protect her against spirits?"

"I am shaman," Kiin answered, and the words, like knives cutting, sent pain into the center of her chest, so that her spirit voice cried out against the lie, and Kiin had to clamp her teeth together to prevent the cry from escaping her mouth.

At Kiin's words, Shuku screeched, and Kiin jumped to her feet, fear so heavy in her chest that she could not breathe. The spirits might punish her for a lie, but would they also punish her child?

Without looking at Eagle, she went to Small Plant Woman, pulled Shuku from her arms, and settled the child, sobbing, tightly against her chest.

"He bit me, so I pinched him," Small Plant Woman said, her voice quiet and without anger.

Kiin's fear left her, and she smiled at the anxious look in the woman's eyes. Kiin held Shuku at arm's length and said to Small Plant Woman, "He is old enough to know better." Then she said to Shuku, "No! No! Do not bite!"

Shuku raised one eyebrow at her, and he looked so much like his father Amgigh that Kiin held him close again, his head hard and warm under the curve of her neck.

Then Eagle was at her side, pulling her down to squat next to Small Plant Woman. "You have a husband?" he said to Kiin as though there had been no interruption in their conversation.

"Yes," Kiin said. "Samiq of the First Men."

"You know them," Small Plant Woman said to her husband. "They live on the Traders' Beach."

Eagle cleared his throat, then cupped his hands in front of him and looked at his wife. Small Plant Woman stood up and went to the corner where she and Kiin had hung the cooking skin for the night. She picked up a wooden bowl and scooped out some of the seal meat stew, now cold, the tallow a soft yellow coating over meat and ugyuun stems. She gave it to Eagle. He scooped out some of the stew and pushed it into his mouth with his fingers.

"If you do not want to go back to him, I need a second wife," he said through the food. "This one is a good woman, but her babies are not strong. They do not live."

From the corners of her eyes, Kiin saw Small Plant Woman quickly lower her head, turn away as though to deny her husband's words.

"Many times," Kiin began, speaking slowly, "babies die in hard winters. A mother cannot make enough milk if she does not have enough to eat."

Eagle took another handful of meat and said nothing, so Kiin continued: "Hunters must bring enough seals, not only for the day they are living, but so their women can store oil and dry meat for those winter moons when ice keeps the ikyan ashore and winds keep hunters in their ulas."

"The women here, they fish," Eagle said. "They dry the fish for winter. We do not starve."

Kiin took a long breath and said, "Fish is not enough to give a woman good milk. She must have oil, and meat that is fat."

Eagle raised the bowl toward her, pointed at her with his chin. "And you know this because you are shaman?"

"I know this because I am a woman who has nursed babies.
A hunger comes to all mothers with babies, a need for oil, for
fat."

Again the man's eyes narrowed. "You have another child?"
he asked.

"A son who is at the Traders' Beach with his father."

Eagle nodded. He looked at Kiin, did not look away until
she met his eyes. "If you want to go back, I will take you
there," he said. "To your husband and the Traders' Beach. It
is only a few days from here." He scraped out the last bit of
meat, then licked his bowl and handed it to Small Plant
Woman. She set it back in the pile of bowls that crowded the
floor in front of the food cache. "He will probably give me
something for bringing you back," Eagle said, and let out a
long belch. He looked at his wife, the woman still beside the
food cache. "Good," he said to her, patting his stomach.

"If you are shaman, then you have powers and know how
to talk to the spirits," Eagle said.

Kiin, eyes lowered, only nodded.

"I have heard stories of the two old women, sisters, who
were once of the First Men and now live with the Walrus
People. They are shamans, it is said. You know them?"

"I have heard of them," Kiin said carefully.

"The Walrus People," Eagle said. "One of their villages
is not so far. Sometimes their traders come here after they
have been to the Traders' Beach." Eagle belched again, but
the belch turned into hiccoughs, hard and loud, until Small
Plant Woman reached up to the rafters for a bladder of water
and brought it to him. She stood at his side as he drank, then
patted him on the back until the hiccoughs stopped.

Eagle held the water bladder out toward Kiin, but she shook
her head. Eagle shrugged and handed the water back to his
wife, then reached out and caught her wrist, circling it with
his fingers. "This woman, she needs a child," Eagle said. "I
found your pack. I know what is in it—not what a woman
carries. There are knives, such as men use, and animals made
of wood and ivory."

He stopped, and Kiin said, "I carve."

Eagle nodded, and a glow came into his eyes. Kiin shuddered. Would this man, like the Raven, try to keep her for her
carvings?

"If you are shaman and you carve," Eagle said, "can you make something to bring strength to my wife's child?"

Small Plant Woman, standing beside her husband, laid one hand over her belly.

"You are with child?" Kiin asked.

"Not yet," Small Plant Woman answered, "but children come easily to my womb. They do not live through any winter."

Kiin looked at Eagle. "I am not shaman in the way that most people are shaman," she said. "My strength is in my carving and in my songs. My powers are not great powers, but you saved my life and my son's life. I will try to help your wife with her babies. You must bring in enough seals so that Small Plant Woman can have oil to last through two winters."

"I am a good hunter."

"Then do this. For a son."

Small Plant Woman knelt beside Kiin, wrapped her arms around Kiin's shoulders, whispered her gratitude in Kiin's ear.

"I will try, I will try," Kiin whispered back, suddenly afraid that in claiming to be more than what she was, all power would leave her.

Eagle bellowed out a laugh and stood, picked up his wife, the water bladder still in her hands, and carried her into a sleeping place.

Kiin settled Shuku in her lap, raised her parka so her son could nurse. Shuku's quiet swallows were drowned out by Eagle's noisy lovemaking. Kiin smiled. Eagle had said the Traders' Beach was only a few days away by ikyak. Perhaps by the next full moon, she would see Samiq, would be back with her own people. Joy leaped in her heart, until she remembered her promise to Eagle, and she lifted prayers to the spirits, prayed they would not be angry. And her spirit voice whispered, "You claimed no more than what you are, a woman who sings, a woman who carves. Are not those powers as great as any the Raven claims?"

So Kiin turned her thoughts to songs, and as though hope and joy lent power to her voice, words came easily from her mouth, a song for strength, a song of hope, a powerful song for Small Plant Woman.

SIXTY-SIX

THE WALRUS PEOPLE

Goodnews Bay, Alaska

"A SHORT CAMP. JUST FOR TONIGHT," RAVEN SAID.

White Fox and Bird Sings pulled the trading ik up onto the salmon camp beach, but Raven turned away, pulled his feather cloak tightly around his shoulders, and walked down the beach, studying tide marks and debris left by the waves. He strode quickly until he was too far for the men to call him and ask for his help with ik or supplies. They had brought Bird Sings' wife with them. She was strong. Raven needed time to plan, to decide what he must do next.

First, a quick stop at their village to drop off trade goods and pick up Kiin. Bird Sings' wife was not nursing, and if Raven went to the Ugyuun village to trade for a baby, he needed someone to feed it. A baby was not like a stack of trade goods, something to be bargained for and then stowed in ik or ikyak until needed. He wanted a healthy baby, too, not some starved infant that would die before he could get it back to Dyenen. Kiin was a wise woman. She would be able to tell him which baby was well, which was not. And it was an advantage that she did not speak the River tongue. By the time she learned the language and told Dyenen that the Ugyuun baby was not truly her son, Raven would already know the old man's shaman secrets, and once given, the secrets could not be taken back. But first Raven had to think of a way to get Kiin to agree to come with him.

If Kiin were like Lemming Tail, he could tell her that they were going to the Traders' Beach, that he was returning her to the man Samiq, but Kiin was not like Lemming Tail. Kiin would know, by sun and stars, which direction they traveled.

Perhaps he could promise her spirit powers or honor for her carvings. But each of those ideas left an uneasiness in his chest. Kiin had come with him to the Walrus village only to save Samiq's life. What did he have that she valued as much as that? Perhaps a promise to return her to her own people after a year. But would she believe him?

Then suddenly he knew—Shuku. Raven had promised Shuku to Dyenen, had he not? It would be Kiin's choice if she wanted to go with her son or stay with the Walrus People. . . .

Bird Sings' wife, her shrill voice lifted in a strange cry, brought Raven from his thoughts, and he turned to see the woman waving her hands over her head, motioning toward a pile of driftwood high on the beach.

Bird Sings and White Fox left the ik and joined the woman. White Fox raised a hand toward Raven, motioned for him to come.

Raven walked slowly. Why hurry for something discovered by a woman? But he squinted his eyes to see better, curious about what would excite Ice Hunter's sons, who usually hid all thoughts behind slow-closing eyes and stern faces.

Then Bird Sings lifted something from the pile of wood, and as Raven drew close he saw that it was a necklace, the strand broken. Bird Sings lifted it, and beads spilled from the sinew cord.

Bird Sings' wife looked up at Raven with fear in her eyes. "It is Kiin's," she whispered.

Raven frowned, squatted on his haunches between Bird Sings and White Fox. He used his walking stick to pry into the pile of wood and heavy, wet sand.

"It is an ik," he said slowly.

"The necklace is Kiin's," Bird Sings' wife said again. She began to dig in the sand, uncovering pieces of wood that had been the ik's skeleton.

"We can save most of this," White Fox said. "The wood is still good, even the walrus skin—a woman might use it for boots or floor mats."

"Do what you want with it," Raven said, speaking as though to a small, pestering child.

White Fox pulled on a leather thong, jerked it out of the sand. A pouch was attached, and when White Fox saw it he dropped it quickly. ''An amulet,'' he said and leaned forward to fix his eyes on Raven's. ''This is Lemming Tail's ik. The necklace and the amulet are Kiin's.''

Raven stood up and walked away as though White Fox had said nothing. White Fox moved to follow him, but Bird Sings reached out, caught his brother's arm, held him back. ''Let him go,'' he said. ''It is a hard thing to lose a wife.''

Raven turned back. ''It is not Lemming Tail's ik,'' he said. ''It is not Kiin's necklace.''

White Fox and Bird Sings looked at each other from the corners of their eyes, then Bird Sings said to his wife, ''I will gather driftwood and start the fire. You save what we might be able to use,'' and he pointed at the remains of the ik.

That evening and the next morning, Raven spoke little. When White Fox tied the torn walrus hide and broken pieces of framing wood into the traders' ik, Raven stared for a moment at the load, but still said nothing.

Paddling toward the Walrus village, Raven seemed to have the strength of two men, so that White Fox in his ikyak paddled hard to keep up with him. And as though spirits sent tide and winds to help in the paddling, they made the journey from the salmon beach to their village in only half a day.

When they arrived, Raven, with one hard push of his paddle, grounded the ik and stepped ashore, then walked in long, quick steps through the village, saying nothing to anyone who greeted him, his eyes fixed on the lodge that he and his wives shared with Grass Ears.

He called out even as he entered the low tunnel that led into Grass Ears' section of the lodge, shouted for Lemming Tail and Kiin, and did not greet Grass Ears' wives, the two sisters with eyes as round as their faces. They whispered something, heads bent close, but Raven did not stop to talk to them. He pushed aside the woven curtain that divided the lodge.

Lemming Tail, her son beside her, sat on the sleeping platform. She smiled slowly at him, cocked her head to one side. ''You brought me gifts?'' she asked.

Raven frowned, wrinkling his brow as if the question puzzled him. ''I have gifts,'' he said. ''Where is Kiin?''

''You do not need Kiin,'' Lemming Tail said. ''She does

not know how to please a man in the sleeping robes.'' She stretched out both arms to him. "Come to me," she said. "I will earn my gifts."

"Go get Kiin," said Raven. "I have gifts for both of you."

Lemming Tail licked her top lip and looked around the ulaq, as if searching for Kiin. She shrugged her shoulders. "You should not have left her," she finally said. "You know she did not want to live with the Walrus People."

"What do you mean?"

Again Lemming Tail shrugged. "She is not here. She left only a few days after you did." Lemming Tail thrust out her lower lip. "She left and took my ik."

In two steps Raven was across the lodge. He reached for Lemming Tail, but the woman scooted up against the wall. Mouse began to cry.

"You let her go?" Raven asked.

"How could I stop her?"

"You have brothers, and Grass Ears would have helped."

Lemming Tail covered her face with her hands, but Raven had already turned his back on her, was already pushing his way through the dividing curtain.

He paused long enough to say to her, "I am hungry. Prepare something. I will return."

The curtain fell into place, and Lemming Tail, ignoring her son's sobs, scrambled from the sleeping platform to the food cache and began pulling out seal bellies of dried meat.

•

"Is she dead?" Raven asked.

"Possibly," Woman of the Sun answered. She did not look up at Raven, but continued to weave the death mat that was stretched across her lap.

"You found her ik?" asked Woman of the Sky.

"White Fox told you?" Raven asked.

"No one told me," she said.

"We found an ik. It might be Lemming Tail's." The ceiling of the old women's lodge was low, and Raven could not stand to his full height, but he paced with head bent, shoulders hunched. Finally he squatted on his haunches in front of the old women. "Lemming Tail said Kiin stole the ik and left. Lemming Tail said Kiin planned to return to her own people."

Woman of the Sun shook her head and answered, "Lemming Tail's brothers forced Kiin from the lodge. They said she must live somewhere else until you returned. Kiin told the women she would go to the River People village to find you. She took Shuku with her.''

"Kiin is not dead?" Raven asked again.

"Kiin?"

"Yes, Kiin!" Raven shouted, his words holding no politeness.

"I have had no dreams," said Woman of the Sun.

Raven stood, strode from the lodge.

Woman of the Sky turned to her sister. "She is not dead?" she asked.

Woman of the Sun only shook her head slowly. "I have had no dreams," she said again.

Lemming Tail's brothers were not hunting. They could have been. Other hunters had seen sea lions that morning at the mouth of the bay, but the oldest brother's ikyak needed repair, and he and his two younger brothers had stayed ashore, all resewing seams and rubbing the ikyak cover with walrus grease until the skin was nearly translucent.

When Raven had landed the trading ik, the two younger brothers, working near the ikyak racks, had turned questioning eyes toward each other. "My wife needs me," the youngest said, but the oldest brother said, "Stay here. He is nothing. He pretends to be shaman, but he is nothing. Have you ever hunted with him?" He laughed. "A woman could bring in more meat."

So they stayed, oiling the ikyak skin and waiting.

When Raven came to them, they were not surprised, but the youngest whispered, "What did she tell him?"

"Our sister? She told him nothing."

"I have spoken to my wife Lemming Tail," Raven said. "She told me that you, the three of you, drove Kiin from my lodge, that you used Kiin like a wife to shame me, the three of you, and in her shame Kiin left the village. My wife Lemming Tail says that in her kindness, she gave Kiin her ik. My wife Lemming Tail says she is no longer your sister."

"We did not," said the youngest, but the oldest brother, walking up to Raven until there was only a handbreadth between them, said, "I would not soil myself with your woman.

She is Seal Hunter. What Walrus man risks a curse by joining with a Seal Hunter woman? But you are not enough even for the Seal Hunters. As soon as you left, Kiin went back to her own people. I did not stop her. Our village is better without her."

"You say your sister lied to me?"

"I say you lie."

"You owe me the price of a wife," Raven said. He ran his hands over the ikyak the brothers were repairing. "I will take this instead."

"It is not yours to take," the oldest brother answered.

"Then will you consider this?" Raven said and pulled a walrus harpoon, the harpoon head attached, from its ties on the ikyak deck.

The man reached for the harpoon, but Raven stepped back and turned the point toward him. Raven held up the remains of Kiin's necklace. "If Kiin had decided to return to her own people," he said, "why did I find this on the salmon camp beach? It is hers. I gave it to her myself."

"Many women have necklaces like that," the oldest brother said. "My own wife . . ."

"Life for life," Raven said and suddenly threw the harpoon. The throw was awkward. The harpoon was made for a throwing board. But the point was sharp, and the weapon pierced the oldest brother's chest.

The man clasped his hands around the shaft, his face twisted in a gurgling scream, and he fell, then lay still.

And as though he had done nothing more than offer a man a fish, Raven said to the other two brothers, "Lemming Tail says he was the one who took Kiin. She says that you two tried to stop him. Is that so?"

The youngest brother drew out his sleeve knife, stepped forward, but the other man clasped his brother's wrist, held tightly. "That is so," he said. "We tried to stop him."

"Then I give you the right to leave this village," Raven said. "Gather your things, take your wives and children, and go. I do not want to see you again." Raven prodded their brother's body with one foot. "If you want, you may take him. If not, the hunters here will bury him." Without waiting for their answer, Raven turned and went to his lodge.

SIXTY-SEVEN

THE WALRUS PEOPLE

Chagvan Bay, Alaska

RAVEN STUCK THE DRIFTWOOD IN LEMMING TAIL'S face and held out a crooked knife, its thin andesite blade set into the side of a caribou rib bone. "Carve!" he demanded.

Slowly she reached for the wood. Raven slapped the rib bone into her hand. Lemming Tail wiped her forearm over her eyes and began a slow, quiet weeping. "What do I carve?" she asked.

"How should I know?" Raven said. "I did not tell Kiin what to carve."

"I am not Kiin!"

"Woman of the Sun and Woman of the Sky told me what happened. Kiin is gone because of you and your brothers. I promised her and her sons to a shaman of the River People. I will not break my promise to him. So you will be Kiin. Her powers will be your powers. Your children will be her children."

"You will take me to the River people?" Lemming Tail asked in a small voice.

"Yes."

"When?"

"Carve!"

Lemming Tail, her teeth gritted, held up wood and knife and, staring into Raven's eyes, gouged the wood again and again.

"Do what you will," Raven said. "You will be the one who suffers when the River People shaman discovers you cannot carve."

Lemming Tail threw knife and wood to the ground. "What

310

do I care? If he kills me, he kills me. But before I die, I will tell him what you have done."

"How will you tell him?" Raven asked. "He does not speak your language. You will have to wait until you learn the River People tongue, and by then I will be far away—too far for an old man to follow."

Lemming Tail raised her head, took a long breath. "When do we leave?" she asked.

"You need time to pack and to mourn," Raven said. "Six, seven days."

"Kiin is dead?" Lemming Tail asked.

Raven shrugged. "Who can say? Woman of the Sun has had no dreams."

"Then why should we mourn?"

"I did not say I would mourn. You should mourn. Your oldest brother is dead," Raven said, and stopped to watch Lemming Tail's eyes. "For what he did to Kiin, I killed him. In your mourning do not forget to pray that your younger brothers will spare you."

"Why should they do anything to me?" Lemming Tail asked in a small voice.

"Because of what you told me," Raven answered. "Because of what you said your brothers did to Kiin."

"I told you nothing! I told you nothing!" Lemming Tail said, her words rising into a scream. She scooped the crooked knife from the floor and lunged toward Raven. He caught her, grasping her arms, his long fingers circling her wrists.

"You think after killing your brother, I could not kill you?" he asked, whispering as though with words of love. He released her left hand and twisted her right arm behind her back until she dropped the knife. He clamped his forearm across her neck. "Mourn," he said, "then we will leave. It is good you are going to the River village. There you will be far enough away from the Walrus People so you will not have to fear your younger brothers. They have sworn revenge."

SIXTY-EIGHT

FINALLY THE MOURNING WAS FINISHED. THE PACK-
ing was done, and Raven and Lemming Tail had made a
plan—so Dyenen would believe Lemming Tail was Kiin.

They left the village in early morning, telling no one. For
a long time Lemming Tail paddled hard and said nothing, a
thin, tuneless song coming from her mouth. Finally she began
to speak, jabbering about the water and the ik, about the River
People, until Raven closed his ears to her voice. But he heard
her when she said, "This is not the way to the River People."

"You are a trader? You know the trade routes?" Raven
asked.

"I am not stupid. I see the sun. I know its path in the sky."

Raven laughed. "You may please the River shaman more
than I thought," he said. "First we will go to the Ugyuun
village. The people there are First Men. We will trade with
them, then we will go to the River People."

For a time Lemming Tail said nothing, then finally Raven
heard her voice, something almost under her breath. "I have
baskets." Louder she said to Raven, "Do the women make
fine parkas? Do they have necklaces?"

"They are First Men," Raven said, "so the women make
birdskin suks, not parkas, and they are poor. Their hunters are
lazy, so in winter the women often starve, but they will have
many necklaces, also baskets and mats, things you might trade
for. Do not trade the carvings you have made. Let me trade
those. I will get more for them than you will."

He looked at Lemming Tail as she dipped her paddle into
the water, at the shining black hair that was gathered into a
loop of wolverine fur at the back of her head.

"I want to trade my own carvings," she said in a high,
pouting voice.

"You will do what I say," Raven answered. "You should
be dead, you know, your life in trade for Kiin's."

The woman seemed to pull herself into a small bundle under the fur of her parka. Why tell her that the carvings were worthless, the wood gouged and splintery? He would not trade them with anyone. He would throw them away, where no one would find them.

Once I have Dyenen's secrets, he thought, it will be Lemming Tail's problem to carve what the old man wants. I do not have to go back to the River village. There are other places to trade. Let Lemming Tail suffer for her deceit.

She had not been a good wife. It would be a relief to be rid of her complaints and sloppy ways. Before Kiin came to him, during those days when Yellow-hair and Lemming Tail were his wives, he had been accustomed to the stink of dirty floors and moldy clothing. But with Kiin, the lodge was always full of the good smells of food cooking; the floors were clean, the fleas picked from the seams of his clothing, the oil lamp wicks trimmed and without smoke. It was a good way to live, and he did not want to go back to what had been before.

Once he had given Lemming Tail to Dyenen, he must find another wife for himself. Not a young woman. Young women expected a man to give too much of himself. He did not have time to think about gifts or worry about a woman's foolish tears.

When he learned Dyenen's secrets, he must make them a part of his life, must decide the best ways to use them among the Walrus People. He could not do that without long days of careful planning. He could not do that with a young woman who would expect all his thoughts to be of her. He would find a widow, old but not too old. She could cook and clean and sew. When he had all power as shaman, then he would worry about young women for his bed.

When they came to the Ugyuun village, even before they had finished pulling the ik ashore, Raven saw Lemming Tail wrinkle her nose in disgust.

"There is not one good ikyak on the rack," she said, and pointed with all the fingers of her left hand. "Where are the lodges?"

"There, see?" Raven said. "Those mounds. Did no one ever tell you about First Men lodges?"

"Kiin," Lemming Tail said. "But who would believe Kiin? You are a fool to come here. They will have nothing to trade."

Anger rose hot in Raven's chest. What right did a wife have to question him? But he only said, "You are not afraid to use that dead one's name?"

"Kiin is not dead. She only hates you and did what she could to get away."

Then Raven was at Lemming Tail's side, one hand clamped tightly around her jaw, his fingers biting into the soft hollows of her cheeks. "I am your husband," he said, his words whispered yet loud. "You will do as I say. You will treat me with respect or I will leave you here with the Ugyuun people and take another woman to trade to Dyenen."

Ugyuun men were coming to greet them, and both Lemming Tail and Raven faced them with smiles, Raven with hands held out in greeting. "I have come to trade," he said in the First Men language, and pretended not to see the surprise on the faces of the Ugyuun People. Few traders came to their village. Why go where men have little to trade? Why go to a village so poor that there was little food to share with visitors?

Raven held one hand toward the ik. "My wife and I have food enough to share with any man who will shelter us in his ulaq," he said, and hid his smile as three hunters stepped forward to offer their ulas, then turned to argue among one another over who would keep the trader and his wife.

We are fortunate, Raven thought when he saw the ulaq that was finally chosen. It was not clean and seemed dark, with only two smoky oil lamps to give light, but it was large. A log with notches cut into it for climbing slanted down from roof hole to floor. Raven heard Lemming Tail mutter angry words under her breath as she groped her way down the climbing log.

"Be polite," he hissed.

"I will not stay here tonight."

"If I decide we stay, then we stay."

"They are filthy. Their lodges are not fit to store rocks."

"Be quiet. They will hear you."

"They are too stupid to speak Walrus," she said.

"You do not know," Raven answered. "Be quiet and offer to help when you can. It will get you better trades."

Lemming Tail pursed her lips and nodded, then followed

him quietly, stood behind him as he squatted on his haunches in the manner of the First Men and began to talk to them.

They spoke of fish, then of seals, finally of a hard rain that had come to the Ugyuun beach the day before. As the men spoke, Raven, his eyes finally adjusted to the dark, sought the corners and niches in the thick earth walls. There were baskets, most old and broken. There were several long straight spear shafts leaning in one niche, something tradeworthy, especially to the people of the islands, those few Whale Hunters who came to trade.

A woven grass mat hung against one wall, perhaps a cover for a storage space. The weaving was in stripes of light and dark grass, and its beauty captured the eyes. River People women would give much for such a thing, Raven thought, though there was little else of value. He doubted that the food cache overflowed with seal bellies of oil. Even the village's hunters had the pale, unhealthy skin of those who do not get enough to eat.

Finally, when there was a lull in the conversation, Raven pointed with his chin toward the grass mat. "Your wife weaves?" he asked the oldest of the Ugyuun men.

"Yes," he said.

"She is gifted. Perhaps she would make a trade."

The man lifted his hands. "You will have to ask her. I cannot give away what she makes."

Raven nodded, glad that Lemming Tail did not understand what the man had said. The First Men always treated their wives too gently, always gave more than wives should be given.

"She is here?" Raven asked, turning to look around the ulaq.

"No, she is with her sister. She will be back to prepare food."

As though called by her husband's words, the woman descended the climbing log, her long thin legs white under the edges of her suk.

"Smoke," her husband called. "A trader has come. He has brought food, but needs you to prepare it."

"Only oil and dried fish," Raven said.

"This is the trader's woman," the Ugyuun man said, and leaned forward to ask Lemming Tail's name.

For a moment Raven had to stop and think what the name was in translation, then he said, "She is Lemming Tail. The baby under her parka is Mouse, my son."

The Ugyuun woman began chattering to Lemming Tail, peeking inside the parka and making soft sounds in her throat at the baby.

"My wife does not understand the First Men tongue," Raven said, but the Ugyuun man laughed and, jerking his head toward the two women, said, "There are some things all women understand."

Raven, too, laughed, then leaned back to listen as the Ugyuun men began telling stories of hunts they had made, seals and sea lions they had taken. They were men who did not know the power of hunting walrus, but Raven was careful to keep his disdain hidden under words of praise.

They began their trades for small things—baskets, necklaces—then for whalebone and soft brown sea otter pelts. Raven gave oil, dried meat, parkas, leggings. When Lemming Tail was busy with the women, Raven went to the ik. In pulling out their trade goods, he took her carvings, dug out a space in the beach gravel, and buried them. Later, in trade for a small section of walrus hide, he got four necklaces—two of shell, one of whalebone, and another of stone. He came to Lemming Tail as she worked, and gave her the necklaces.

"For your carvings," he said.

Lemming Tail, smiling at the women around her, leaned back to whisper into her husband's ear, "When do we leave? It is too dark here, and the women stay in this ulaq all day. I am ready to go. Why did you come here? For a few necklaces and otter pelts?"

Raven also smiled at the women, smiled as he pulled his wife to her feet, smiled as he helped her up the climbing log to the clear outside air. They sat down on the roof. Lemming Tail breathed in, then coughed, clearing her lungs of the oil lamp smoke. She reached inside her parka for Mouse, the baby squalling his protest as she took him from her breast. Then he blinked his eyes in the sunlight and reached up to grab his mother's hair.

"No," Lemming Tail said, and pulled the hair from his fist. Raven took the boy, set him on the grass and thatch of the ulaq roof. "He needs to be in the sun," Raven said. He had once thought the boy was his, but seeing so clearly the features of Shale Thrower's husband on the boy's face, he could not even pretend to believe what Lemming Tail still insisted was true.

"I spent too much time with Shale Thrower," Lemming Tail had told Raven. "Why else would my child look like her husband? But that is your own fault. You were the one who brought Kiin into our lodge. Who can stay long in a place with that woman? Her tongue is as sharp as a harpoon head."

Taking Lemming Tail to Dyenen was a good thing, Raven thought. Why have Mouse around to grow up looking like another hunter? It was not as if the man was Raven's brother or hunting partner, not as though everyone would think Raven had shared her willingly. Surely he would find a better wife than Lemming Tail. Someone who knew how to keep a lodge clean, and would not stray from his bed.

"So," Lemming Tail said, "when do we leave here?"

"When we get what we came for."

"Which is what? I have my necklaces. You have furs and the spear shafts you wanted."

"I came here to get you a son."

Lemming Tail narrowed her eyes. "You will trade me for a night's pleasure to these dirty Ugyuun men?"

Raven laughed. "You have never refused a night with any man before, woman," he said.

"I have been a good wife to you. Have I ever refused your bed? Was I like Kiin, stiff and still as though your hands were not even touching me?"

Raven frowned. Finally he said, "We are here to get you a son. A baby, one already born."

Lemming Tail's mouth opened, and she moved her lips as though to speak, but no words came out.

"Dyenen wants Kiin not only because of her carvings but because she had two sons, born at the same time. He is an old man, but his wives have given him only daughters. He wants a son."

Lemming Tail curled her lips into a scowl. "So I must take some other woman's son, raise him as though he were my own. I must work twice as hard to raise two babies!"

Raven shrugged. "I could have killed you," he said. "You

cost me a wife, someone whose carvings are so valuable that a man could live on the trades he gets for them.'' Raven turned and stared at Lemming Tail, allowed his anger to burn in his eyes.

''Kill me then,'' she said. ''At least in the spirit world I will have time to spend in joy, in laughing, not always caring for babies, one not even my own!''

Raven ground his teeth in anger, but calmed himself with thoughts of the power that would be his if Lemming Tail went to Dyenen without trouble.

''You would give up being a shaman's wife?'' Raven asked softly. ''A shaman whose power is known to all the traders of the world? You would give up the parkas and leggings, embroidered with dyed hair and hung with shells? You would give up being his woman of the sleeping robes, while his other wives do the sewing and cooking?''

Raven was still, letting his words work in Lemming Tail's mind.

Finally she turned to him. ''He is old?'' she asked.

''Old but strong, with good years left to him.''

''He is ugly.''

''No.''

For a long time, she said nothing, then, straightening her shoulders and brushing her hands over the front of her fur parka, she said, ''Tell me about his lodge. Tell me what he has in it. Tell me how a woman of the River People should act—to please her husband.''

SIXTY-NINE

THE UGYUUN PEOPLE

The Alaska Peninsula

IT IS A DREAM, KIIN TOLD HERSELF. HOW MANY times since she left the Walrus village had she dreamed that the Raven had found her? More than she could remember. This was just another of those dreams. The Raven would never come to the Ugyuun village to trade. What did the Ugyuun people have that anyone would want?

Kiin had spent the day walking the beach looking for driftwood and bone, to carve and as fuel for cooking hearths. She had filled two baskets—one that hung on her back, a tumpline across her forehead, and one that she carried atop her head. For all that the Ugyuun people had done for her, at least she could gather fuel for them.

She had left Shuku with Small Plant Woman and so had been able to work that much faster. But now, even with the weight of wood on her back and the pressure of the full basket against the top of her head, she was sure she had done nothing more than dream her gathering.

Her steps seemed slow as she approached the ik, but how else did a person walk in a dream? Inside the ik were the Raven's paddles, banded with yellow. Red ocher colored the ik's thwarts. Tied to the ik's ribs were Raven's walking stick, trade packs, and storage bags of food. Kiin's heart clenched inside her chest, but she reached out to touch the ik's walrus skin covering. The oiled hide was smooth against her fingers.

"It is not a dream," the inner voice of her spirit whispered.

"He could not know I am here," Kiin said. "But he would not come here to trade."

She reached down and stroked the hardened caribou hide of a trade pack, then moved her hand to a thwart. She touched the wood, and a splinter caught one finger, pricked into her skin. She pulled her hand back, sucked at the drop of blood that welled from the wound.

"It is not a dream," her spirit said again.

"It is not a dream," Kiin repeated. She backed away from the ik, set both baskets of wood near the path that led to the village, and ran up into the hills. She did not stop running until she had found a thick growth of willow where she could hide. She crouched down, clasping her knees to her chest, and panted until she had caught her breath.

If he has come to bring me back, I cannot escape, Kiin thought. If he has come to trade, and no one tells him about me, he will never know I am here.

Her spirit voice whispered, "Shuku. Small Plant Woman has Shuku. What if the Raven sees him? Then he will know."

Kiin lowered her head to the tops of her knees. Her heart was a stone in her chest as she remembered Eagle's promise to her that morning: "The next good day, I will take you with me to the Traders' Beach. You and Small Plant Woman can go in her fishing ik. I will take my ikyak. Perhaps my brother also will go. We will make a trading trip."

The man had laughed, and Kiin had joined his laughter. A few days to the Traders' Beach, then she would be with Samiq, with Takha.With all her people.

Tears stung her eyes, and she pressed her lips against her knees to hold her sobs inside her mouth.

Her spirit voice chided her: "So you will sit here like a child until he finds you? You will let him have Shuku again? After all you have done to return to your people?"

"What can I do?" Kiin whispered.

"Go back to the village, find out which ulaq the Raven is in. Find Small Plant Woman and Shuku. Go now. You do not have time to cry."

Kiin stood up, wiped her hands over her face. There was a path that led from the village into the hills where berries grew. She pushed her way through the willow thicket until she found the path, then followed it back to the village. For a time, she crouched beside the refuse heap at the mountain side of the ulakidaq. She waited until one of the village women came by, an old woman with empty berry baskets hanging from each arm. Kiin had seen her before, but could not remember her name.

"Grandmother," Kiin called out, "I need your help."

The old woman looked at Kiin, frowned. "You are the Walrus woman that Eagle found during his long hunt," the woman said. She was a large-eared woman, and she spoke loudly, as though to fill those ears with her own voice.

"I am Kiin of the First Men," Kiin answered. Then, choosing her words carefully, she said, "I need to see Small Plant Woman. Could you bring her to me?"

The woman snorted. "I am old. You are young. You cannot walk to her ulaq yourself and see her there?"

Kiin gestured toward the woman's berry baskets. "If I promise to fill your baskets, will you get her for me?"

The woman raised her eyebrows, and her face creased with a slow smile. "You will fill all four?" she asked.

"All four."

"Today?"

"Yes."

She handed Kiin the baskets and started back toward the village. Her walk reminded Kiin of Shuku's wide-legged waddle. When the woman had gone a short way, Kiin called to her.

The old woman stopped and looked back over her shoulder at Kiin.

"When you tell Small Plant Woman to come to me, do not say my name."

The old woman snorted. "I do not remember your name, Walrus woman," she said.

"Whatever you say to her, whisper so others do not hear," Kiin said.

The old woman wrinkled her nose, and Kiin held up the berry baskets. The old woman shrugged and toddled on toward the village. Kiin stepped back into the trees that fringed the refuse heap and waited.

The chief hunter was a young man. His face was dark, his eyes sunken beneath a jutting forehead. He wore his hair in a strange way, pulled back and up, then tied at the top of his head. The man's suk, though decorated with shell trim and fringe, was in poor repair, and his ulaq stank of old urine and rotted meat.

Lemming Tail raised one hand to cover her nose, but Raven, aware of the insult, grasped her wrist and pulled her hand down to her side. "It is no worse than my lodge before Kiin," he whispered to her.

Lemming Tail drew back her lips and hissed at him, then smiled at the chief hunter. The hunter's wife gestured to Lemming Tail, and she went with the woman and helped serve food to the men.

Both men ate, neither speaking until the meat was gone. The Ugyuun woman offered water from a seal bladder, and after he and the chief hunter had drunk, Raven asked, "Do many traders stop here?"

"Many come," the chief said. "Many trade."

"Ah-h-h-h," Raven said. "I am glad." He smiled. "But now I understand why your men are such good traders. A man like me must be careful of a village like this: full of men who understand trading and make hard bargains."

The chief laughed. "So," he said, "you will stay with us?"

"Not long," said Raven. "I came to you to make one trade. I need something for a man much like you—the chief hunter of our village."

"My weapons are not for trade," the chief said.

Raven held up his hands. "This is nothing for hunting. Our chief is a strong hunter. Three summers ago he found a good wife, a woman of the First Men. Their first summer together, she gave birth to a son, but the baby died. Since then, she has lost three babies who came too soon from her womb. The shaman tells us that she grieves so much for her first son that she cannot give the chief a living son. Now she does not eat, does not sleep, and talks only of going to the Dancing Lights with her children."

"He is better to let her die. Then she will be happy and he can get another wife."

"He does not want another wife. He thinks she will be happy if she has a son. So I was sent to find a son, a child of a First Men village. My wife came with me," Raven said and pointed with his chin to Lemming Tail. "She nurses our own son, Mouse, and has enough milk for another."

The chief looked at Lemming Tail and nodded.

"Do you have a child here, a baby boy of perhaps six, eight moons, that we could take back to be raised as the son of a chief?"

For a time the Ugyuun man said nothing, then he asked, "You would give a good trade, much oil, much meat?"

"All the oil I have with me, all the meat, except enough for the journey my wife and I must make to take us back to our own village."

Again the chief nodded. "I will talk to my hunters," he said. "I will see if one will give his son to be raised by a chief."

Small Plant Woman came out calling Kiin's name. Kiin hurried to meet the woman, shushing her, then pulled her into the willow trees.

"Kiin . . ." Small Plant Woman said. "Why do you hide?"

"Where is Shuku?"

"In the ulaq, asleep in your sleeping place. Where is the wood?"

"Beside the path that leads up from the beach," Kiin said.

"Good," said Small Plant Woman, then asked again, "Why are you here?"

"I saw a trader's ik on the beach."

"Yes, a trader and his wife came this morning after you left to gather wood."

"Why do they come?" Kiin asked.

"To trade, why else?"

"I know him," Kiin said. "He killed my husband's brother."

"So you are afraid of this trader? He seems like a good man. He laughs often, and his wife is a hard worker, though she does not speak our language."

"Is his wife called Lemming Tail?" Kiin asked.

Small Plant Woman laughed. "Do you think my husband would bother to find out such a thing?"

Kiin tried to smile, but her face was stiff, as though her tears had dried into a mask. "This trader—he has threatened to kill my husband and take me as his wife."

"Then you are right to hide," Small Plant Woman said. "I will find out how long he plans to stay. Will you wait here?"

"I must go get berries for . . . for . . ." She held up the old woman's berry baskets.

"Blackfish."

"Blackfish," Kiin said. "Bring Shuku. I will take him with me."

"You do not need him. I will keep him safe."

"The trader," Kiin said, "he will know him."

"What man recognizes a baby, especially one who is not his own?"

"If he brought Lemming Tail with him, she will know whose baby it is."

Small Plant Woman shrugged. "Then stay here and wait. I will bring Shuku."

SEVENTY

LEMMING TAIL WAITED UNTIL THE CHIEF HAD LEFT the ulaq, then she came to Raven's side, leaned up against him, and whined, "When can we leave? Already I am itching with their lice. Already I am sick from their food."

Raven blew a sigh of disgust from his mouth and pushed the woman away. "When they bring us the baby. Then we will leave."

"When will that be?"

"I do not know." He made a slashing motion with his hand and said, "Leave! Go do things a woman should do!"

The chief's wife turned and looked at them, a smirk on her face, and Raven's cheeks grew hot in embarrassment—laughed at by an Ugyuun woman. But why be angry with an Ugyuun woman when the one at fault was Lemming Tail? What would be better than to give Lemming Tail to Dyenen and be rid of her?

There was the sifting of dirt from the ulaq rafters, and the sound of voices at the roof hole.

"I have a baby for you," the chief called. He came carrying

a bundle in one arm, stepped down three notches of the climbing log, and jumped to the floor. "His mother is dead, and the father says it will be too much trouble to raise him to the age of hunting. But the man wants much oil."

"I have much oil," Raven said. He stood and waited as the chief brought the baby to him.

He unwrapped the child.

"How many moons?"

"Ten," the chief said. The baby lay quietly in the chief's arms, his eyes fixed on something in the rafters. He was about the same size as Mouse and had the round face, the long eyes of the First Men.

Raven nodded. "Good," he said, then called to Lemming Tail. "Take him. I will go get the oil."

Lemming Tail sat in the chief's ulaq as Raven and several of the Ugyuun men carried in ten seal stomachs of oil and three of dried fish, another two of seal meat.

Mouse jabbered, poking at the Ugyuun child with his pudgy fingers, but the Ugyuun baby gave no response. Lemming Tail laughed at her son. "You will both be good hunters," she said, and looked up to see the chief's wife watching, the woman with a smile on her face.

Lemming Tail offered the Ugyuun baby her breast. For a time the baby did nothing, only let his lips rest against her nipple, but then he began to suck, not with hard, strong sucking like Mouse, but gently, as though he were a new baby.

Lemming Tail stroked back his hair. He was not an ugly baby, this child of the Ugyuun village. She clasped his hand and waited for him to wrap his fingers around hers, to hold tightly as Mouse did, but the child's fingers did not move. Lemming Tail frowned and glanced up at the chief's wife. The woman looked quickly away.

Lemming Tail used a finger to break the baby's suction on her nipple, then sat him up on her leg. His head bobbled, and he tipped to the side. Again she sat him up, then tried to stand him on his legs. He sank down as though he had no strength.

"This baby is ... is sick," she said to the chief's wife, but the woman remained with her back to Lemming Tail. "She is too stupid to know the Walrus language," Lemming Tail said to Mouse, and still the Ugyuun woman acted as though Lemming Tail had not spoken.

When all the oil was in the ulaq, Lemming Tail stood, went to her husband's side, and pushed the Ugyuun baby into his arms. Raven jumped up, thrust the baby back at her, and shouted out a string of angry words.

"Be quiet and listen to me," Lemming Tail said. "Look at the child. He is not strong. He is older than Mouse, but cannot even hold up his head. No wonder the father was willing to trade. The child will never be a hunter."

"Be quiet," Raven told her. "He is a boy. I do not care if he hunts."

"Of course you do not care," Lemming Tail said, so angry that spit flew from her mouth as she spoke. "You do not have to live with the River shaman. You do not have to please him, day by day. He believes he will have two strong sons. What do I say when he discovers that one—"

"Tell him that the child was strong when he lived in the Walrus village. Tell him the child caught the weakness of the River People."

"You told me that the River People were strong. You said—"

Raven clamped a hand over Lemming Tail's mouth, but Lemming Tail caught the edge of Raven's hand with her teeth and bit down hard.

Raven jerked his hand away and slapped her across the face. The Ugyuun men looked aside as though they saw nothing, and Lemming Tail covered her face with her hands.

"This is your choice," Raven said. "You can be Lemming Tail and stay here with the Ugyuun, or you can be Kiin and go with me and Mouse and the Ugyuun child to the River People. So I ask: are you Kiin or Lemming Tail?"

"I am Lemming Tail!"

Raven turned to the Ugyuun chief. "What will you give for this woman?" he asked, speaking in the First Men tongue.

The man raised his eyebrows in surprise and looked over at his wife.

"What did you say to him?" Lemming Tail asked.

"She sews well and makes healthy sons," Raven said.

The man pointed to three seal bellies of oil.

"He says he will give me three seal bellies of oil for you," Raven told Lemming Tail.

"You gave ten for this sick baby."

"Five," Raven said to the Ugyuun man and held up five fingers.

"You trade for your own oil!" Lemming Tail said. "What about Mouse and the Ugyuun child? Who will feed them?"

"They will not starve before I get to the next village. I will get a woman there."

"You think you can get a woman so easily? You think any woman will come with you?"

"You are Kiin?"

"I am Lemming Tail!"

The Ugyuun man pointed at the oil and held up four fingers.

"You should be happy I keep the babies," Raven said. "With the oil I leave here, you will not starve for the first months of winter. If you fish, you will have enough food to stay alive until next summer. But it is sad to see a beautiful woman hungry. The River People women are fat even at the end of winter." Raven sighed. "Your shaman husband would have been glad to see your beautiful legs in caribou skin leggings. Have you seen the embroidery the River women do? Their clothing brings much in trade. Each woman has more necklaces than she can wear."

Raven looked up at the Ugyuun chief, then said to Lemming Tail, "You could have a dog," Raven said to Lemming Tail. "Most River People wives have their own dog to carry packs and guard their children."

"I do not want a dog."

"Four," Raven said to the Ugyuun man and held up four fingers over the oil-filled seal bellies.

Lemming Tail screeched, "Wait!"

"You will accept the Ugyuun child?"

"Yes," she said.

"You are Kiin?"

For a long time Lemming Tail stood with head lowered, eyes down. Finally she whispered, "I am Kiin."

SEVENTY-ONE

KIIN WAITED, HER FINGERS MOVING IN SMALL, quick patterns over her hands. How long should it take a woman to get a baby? The tiny stinging insects the Walrus People called long noses hummed in her ears, and she slapped at her neck, wondering why these small ones plagued the land of the Walrus and Ugyuun yet did not live on the islands of the First Men.

"Come, Small Plant Woman, come," Kiin whispered, then, angry with herself for her own impatience, she took her woman's knife from the packet at her waist and cut several branches from a willow tree. She murmured her gratitude to the tree, then sat on her haunches and used her knife to peel off the bark. The soft spongy inner bark—soaked in water and taken as a bitter tea—made good medicine, something to ease small pains. Besides, who did not know that waiting went more quickly when hands and eyes were busy?

"We are ready, then," Raven said and motioned for Lemming Tail to follow him up the climbing log.

"Good," she muttered under her breath. "I am ready to leave the dark houses of the Ugyuun."

She waited beside Raven at the top of the ulaq as he used eyes and ears to test wind and sea.

"We will return first to our own village?" Lemming Tail asked.

Raven frowned at her and kept his eyes toward the sea. "If the sea is calm, we will stop only for water. We will not stay even a night."

"I must say goodbye to Shale Thrower," Lemming Tail said.

Raven looked down at Mouse. With one long-fingered hand he tugged at the baby's hair. "To Shale Thrower or her husband?'' he asked. He slid down from the top of the ulaq before Lemming Tail could reply.

Lemming Tail had bound Mouse in a sling at her left hip and carried the Ugyuun baby strapped under her parka as though he were a new infant. She bit at her lip and, tucking an arm around each baby, slid down after Raven. She did not intend to hurry to the beach. Let Raven do the work of launching the ik. So when she heard a man call, she stopped. She looked back over her shoulder, saw that he was speaking to an Ugyuun woman standing atop the next ulaq. A baby was slung against her hip. The man spoke in the First Men tongue, gesturing for the woman to come to him. She set the baby down on the ulaq roof and left him there as she followed the man into another ulaq. The child was only a little larger than Mouse, plump and wearing a parka of soft sea otter skin, only its eyes peering out from the drawstring hood.

Lemming Tail whispered to Mouse, ''He wears a Walrus parka. I did not know Raven had brought one to trade.'' She went closer, standing on her toes to see the child.

Lemming Tail laid one hand against the baby under her parka, raised her shoulders in a long breath, then quickly scrambled up the side of the ulaq. She grabbed the baby sitting there.

''A boy,'' she whispered to the spirits. ''Let it be a boy.''

She tipped him over. His buttocks above his leggings were bare. She saw the small pink penis, let out a quick breath of joy, pulled up her parka, and took the Ugyuun baby from the carrying strap. She laid him on the ulaq and slipped the other baby under her parka.

Then she ran to the beach, hugging both children to her, two healthy boys. She waited while Raven made adjustments to the loaded ik, tested knots.

''We should go,'' Lemming Tail said. ''Now.''

Raven raised his eyebrows at her. ''You are so ready to leave?'' he asked.

Lemming Tail set her mouth into a frown. ''I itch with their lice,'' she said. ''My nose is full of the stink of their lodges.''

He laughed. ''So you would rather live with the River People.''

''Yes.''

Raven motioned for her to get into the ik, then pushed it

from the beach, stepped in, and began the long, strong paddling that would take the ik beyond the pull of shore waves.

Lemming Tail, too, paddled—deep, powerful pulls. Raven laughed and called to her, "So on this trip you have learned something. I can tell the River shaman you are a good paddler."

But Lemming Tail, looking back over her shoulder, did not answer. She plunged her paddle in hard strokes until the village was only a smudge of smoke in the gray and green of the Ugyuun's hills.

Finally, Kiin heard someone coming. She stood, her legs stiff from squatting for so long. Her heart beat hard under her ribs. It had been too long. Something was wrong. The Raven knew she was here. Why else would Small Plant Woman take most of the morning to bring her Shuku?

"I am here," Small Plant Woman called, but her voice was small and thin.

"You have Shuku?" Kiin asked. She stepped out of the willows, around the refuse heap, and onto the path where Small Plant Woman stood.

"The trader is gone, he and his wife," Small Plant Woman answered.

A quiver in her voice made Kiin's heart flutter. "You have Shuku?" she asked again.

"Kiin . . ." Small Plant Woman said, and her voice broke on the name.

The woman's arms were empty, and Kiin rushed forward, clasped her shoulders. "Where is Shuku?"

"Kiin . . ." The woman's eyes were suddenly wet, her shoulders shaking. "The trader, he . . . he took him."

The screams began, and first Kiin thought they were Small Plant Woman's screams, but finally she knew they came from her own throat.

Then there were others—Small Plant Woman's husband, the chief, and old Blackfish. Their hands were on her, pushing her toward the ulas, and Small Plant Woman was talking, her words coming through her tears. "I left him only a moment on the ulaq, only a moment while I went to help my husband find something. I came out and Shuku was gone."

Then other voices were speaking, words jumbled together,

coming so fast that Kiin could understand little of what was being said. Finally they took her to the chief's ulaq, guided her with careful hands down the climbing log, and there Broken Tooth told her how he had traded his son, a child of ten moons who still held to the ways of a new baby. The Raven had given ten seal bellies of oil and five of dried meat, but then Broken Tooth showed Kiin that he still had the baby, the boy staring at the ulaq roof as he was held out toward Kiin.

"They must have come back and taken Shuku instead of my son," the man said. "I did not mean for that to happen."

"Here," he said. "You choose. My son or the oil."

But at his words the screams began again and would not stop.

SEVENTY-TWO

THE WALRUS PEOPLE

The Bering Sea

LEMMING TAIL KEPT THE UGYUUN BABY UNDER her parka all that long day of paddling, but the child's wriggling almost made her wish she had chosen to keep the first baby.

"Think of your place as shaman's wife," she said into the wind. "It is worth a few days with a struggling baby."

Finally Raven called out to her, pointed at a long sloping shore, and paddled the ik toward land, where they would spend the night.

Lemming Tail helped Raven beach the ik, then turned her back on him and walked to a sheltered place of thick boulders. At Raven's protest she called out, "You want me to have two sons. I must feed them both. Are you not man enough to unpack a belly of oil and some dried fish? Are you a little boy who needs a mother?"

Raven spat out several insults, but dragged the ik farther ashore and untied a seal belly of oil, another of dried seal meat. He took what he needed for himself, then squatted beside the ik and ate.

"You can bring me nothing?" Lemming Tail called.

"Are you a little girl who needs a father?" Raven answered.

Lemming Tail leaned back against the boulder and checked both boys. Each suckled, hands cupped around a breast. The Ugyuun baby glanced up at her, his eyes wet with tears. He shuddered and looked away, but did not release his hold on her breast.

"Greedy," Lemming Tail said. "You will get used to me. Remember, you drink my son's milk. Do not take more than your share."

Suddenly she jumped up, jerked the baby away from herself while urine dripped from inside her parka onto her leggings.

"You stupid child!" Lemming Tail screamed. "Did your mother teach you nothing? I told Raven he was foolish to take an Ugyuun boy. You are older than Mouse, yet you still wet your mother's parka!"

She pulled the baby roughly from his carrying strap and set him on the ground. She ignored his cries as she carried Mouse, still nestled at her breast, back to the trading ik, found a bundle of sealskins, and pulled one out of the kelp twine that bound the pack. She peeled off the parka, set Mouse beside the ik on the beach, and went to the edge of the water. She waited until a wave washed close, then dipped in the sealskin. She used it to wipe off her breasts and leggings, then to wipe the urine from the inside of her parka.

Shivering, she slipped the parka back on over her head, picked up Mouse, and went back to the Ugyuun baby. He had curled up on the sand, bare rump up, his legs, clad in sealskin leggings, tucked under his chest. He had soiled himself. Lemming Tail snorted, then bent over him, used the wet sealskin to wipe his buttocks, and left him there again as she walked down the beach to a tide pool, where she rinsed the sealskin.

She looked for Raven but did not see him, so she shrugged her shoulders, took a food pack from the ik, and brought it back to where she had left the Ugyuun baby. She pulled out smoked fish, a strip of dried seal meat, and a container of berries mixed in fat. She gave Mouse a piece of dried fish, took one for herself, then reached over to shake the Ugyuun baby.

The baby moaned, hiccoughed a sob. Sighing, Lemming Tail picked him up. She turned the baby to face her, loosened his parka hood, and gasped.

"Shuku!" she exclaimed. She shook her head, closed her eyes, and opened them again. "No," she said, laughing. "My eyes play tricks. You are bigger than Shuku." With the tips of her fingers, she felt at the baby's neck. There was a braided sinew cord, and she pulled it out from beneath his parka. An ivory carving—half an ikyak—dangled from the cord.

For a moment, Lemming Tail sat very still, forehead furrowed, then she said to the baby, "How did you get to the Ugyuun village? Is your mother there?" Her eyes narrowed. "If your mother is there, what do you think Raven will give for that knowledge?"

The baby hiccoughed again, reached for the chunk of dried fish in Lemming Tail's left hand.

Lemming Tail gave him the fish. Mouse dropped his piece of fish and tried to pull himself into his mother's lap, pushing against Shuku with one hand and one wide little foot.

"Mouse, no," Lemming Tail said. "You can both sit here." She picked up the dried fish Mouse had dropped, brushed the sand from it, and settled the babies, back to back, each with fish.

Leaning her chin against Mouse's head, she said, "If I tell him I have Shuku, we will go back. The Ugyuun People will hate me for stealing this child, and Raven will take no part of the blame. If Kiin is not there, Raven will be angry with me, maybe even angry enough to leave me with the Ugyuun.

"And if Kiin is there, if the Raven can make her come with us, he will trade her instead of me to the River shaman. Then Kiin will have the honor of being a shaman's wife, and Raven might yet decide to leave me with the Ugyuun."

With an arm around each baby, Lemming Tail stood, again looked up and down the beach for Raven, then set the babies on the ground and used sealskins to make a windbreak for them. She tucked them inside, then set out food on a mat for Raven.

When Raven returned from walking the beach, Lemming Tail met him with a smile. She gave him dried fish softened in seawater, and seal meat chopped fine and mixed with berries and fat. As he ate, she rubbed his shoulders, until finally he set aside his food and took her there on the sand, and did not ask about the babies until they had finished.

She said, "The one you brought from the Ugyuun People, he is better than I thought. He is not as good as Mouse, but then he is not your son as Mouse is."

"I know well whose son Mouse is," Raven said. "I do not need any more of your lies."

Lemming Tail turned her back to the man, took the babies from their shelter, and tucked them under her parka to nurse. She lay down on her side, moved the babies so that one supported the other, and did not reply to Raven's accusation.

SEVENTY-THREE

THE FIRST MEN

Herendeen Bay, the Alaska Peninsula

"I AM STRONG ENOUGH NOW," SAMIQ SAID TO HIS father. He squatted on the beach sand and stroked the fingers of his right hand, the index finger tied to a birdbone, the other fingers curled into his palm.

Kayugh shook his head. "Remember how quickly Raven moved, even after fighting long and hard with your brother."

"I had never fought with knives. Now I have. Each day Small Knife and I, we fight."

"With knives?" Kayugh asked.

Samiq laughed. "With wood, shaped to the size of a knife, but blunt."

"You tell me this so I will say you should go to the Walrus People, so I will agree you should fight Raven for Kiin?"

"I tell you this so you know that I am going."

"You think the boy Small Knife can prepare you to fight

the shaman Raven? He has powers beyond the strength of his arms. Have you prayed? Have you fasted?''

''Yes, always I pray,'' Samiq said. ''And I will fast.'' He looked beyond his father, called out.

Kayugh glanced over his shoulder to see Small Knife.

''Watch,'' Samiq said to Kayugh, then asked Small Knife, ''Did you bring your weapon?''

Small Knife's eyes slid quickly to Kayugh, then back to Samiq. ''I have it,'' he said quietly.

''I told your grandfather about our fighting,'' Samiq said.

Small Knife looked into Kayugh's eyes.

''Show me,'' Kayugh said, and backed away to give the men room to fight.

Samiq untied the bone that straightened his forefinger, then took a short, knife-shaped stick from his waist packet. He pried up the fingers of his right hand and let them spring back to hold the knife tightly, then he crouched, facing Small Knife, both men with arms out, legs bent, circling.

Small Knife made the first move, springing in to slash his wooden knife in a wide arc toward Samiq's stomach, but Samiq jumped back, avoiding the blade. Before Small Knife could regain his stance, Samiq lunged in. He caught Small Knife's right forearm. The boy lifted his knife toward Samiq's face, slid the blade across Samiq's cheek, leaving a red welt.

Kayugh crossed his arms over his chest and watched. He was surprised at how quickly Samiq moved, perhaps more quickly than Raven, but who could say for sure? Once the knife was secure in Samiq's hand, no one watching would have known the man was crippled. If Samiq could keep Raven from knowing, perhaps he had a chance. Samiq was strong, and it was not difficult to see that the fight with wooden blades was lasting longer than a fight with real knives, but still Samiq had allowed Small Knife's blade to touch him on cheek, arm, and knee. A welt from a wooden blade was nothing, but what if each wound were laid open, bleeding?

Finally, the two backed away, both men drawing in long breaths, and Kayugh held up his hands. ''You are right,'' he said to Samiq.''You are good. There is a chance you can take Raven, especially if he does not know about your hand, and so work to knock the knife from your fingers. But you must spend more time in prayer before you go. A man's inner strength must be as great as his outer strength if he is to succeed.''

"I will pray," Samiq said.

Kayugh nodded.

"And if he knocks the knife from your hand?"

"Try," Samiq said and held his hand out to his father. Kayugh reached out and pulled against the fingers, but each was locked in place. He shrugged and turned away from Samiq, then turned back quickly, before Samiq could react. Kayugh kicked up, his bare foot meeting Samiq fingers with a solid hit. The wooden blade remained in Samiq's hand.

Kayugh smiled.

"I heard your mother talking today with your father," Three Fish said. She and Samiq were in the ulaq, and Three Fish was nursing their son.

Samiq bent over her, rubbed a finger along their son's cheek. They had named him Many Whales so that the name could be spoken once again in hope and respect. Samiq sat down beside his wife, and Many Whales, his mouth still on his mother's breast, pointed at his father. Samiq reached over and cupped the boy's hand in his own.

"She asked if you will fight Raven," Three Fish said.

"What did my father tell her?"

"He said yes."

"Do you think I should?"

Three Fish looked at him, eyes meeting eyes. "It will make no difference if I say no."

Samiq looked down.

Three Fish stroked one hand over their son's dark hair. "You already have a wife and a son."

"Yes, a good wife, a fine son," Samiq said, "but Kiin is also my wife. And I made promises to my brother. I told him I would take care of Kiin and her sons."

"We have Takha," Three Fish said and looked over at the boy sitting in the basket corner, playing with three baskets and a heap of smooth beach stones. He piled the stones in one basket, then dumped them into another.

"You are a good mother and a good wife. You are my first

wife. Whether Kiin is here or not, you will have the same place in my heart.''

''I want Kiin back with us,'' Three Fish said. ''My father had two wives. When his first wife died, I mourned for her as for a mother. I know it will be good for Takha to have Shuku. Their power is not complete without each other. I just do not want you to fight.''

''I will pray. I will plan. If I do not succeed, at least you and Takha and Many Whales will be safe here. Small Knife will hunt for you.''

''He is a man. Soon he will take a wife, live with her, hunt for her father.''

''I will ask my father to go to other First Men villages, to bring you back a husband to live here and train our sons. Three Fish,'' Samiq said and reached out to turn her head toward him, ''I must fight. How can I say I am a man if I do not?''

For a moment Three Fish's eyes flicked down to Samiq's right hand, then up again to his face. ''You are a man,'' she said. ''Let it be enough that I tell you so.''

Samiq smiled, a smile he might give a child. ''Three Fish,'' he said, ''I will fight.''

''When?''

''Soon, after fasting, after prayer.''

Three Fish lowered her head. Finally she said, ''Will a woman's prayers help?''

''Yes,'' Samiq said. ''Pray.''

SEVENTY-FOUR

THE UGYUUN PEOPLE

The Alaska Peninsula

''HOW LONG?'' KIIN ASKED. HER VOICE WAS THIN, broken.

"Ten days."

"Ten days!"

"Soul Caller said that your spirit left you to follow your son. He was not sure you would come back to us."

Kiin struggled to focus her eyes. The woman speaking beside her—what was her name? Small Plant Woman. "But I am here in the ulaq, sitting."

"You were like a woman sleeping, with eyes open, doing as I asked you to do, but with no understanding of what was around you."

Kiin pushed herself slowly to her feet and walked in unsteady steps from one side of the ulaq to the other. "It is morning?" she asked Small Plant Woman.

"Yes."

"Would you let me take your ik and follow them?"

Small Plant Woman stood up, wrapped an arm around Kiin's shoulders, and walked her back to a place beside the oil lamp. "Kiin," she said softly, "if I thought you could find them, I would let you go. But you cannot. You do not know where they went."

"They went back to the Walrus village."

"That is a long way. Too far for one woman to go alone."

"I came this far alone."

"And you almost died, you and your son."

Kiin felt the tightness of tears in her chest, building up until she could no longer hold them back. She sank to her knees and covered her face with both hands.

Small Plant Woman hovered beside her, patting her back, stroking her hair as though Kiin were a child. She put her arms around Kiin and rocked her, sang a lullaby, a First Men's song, something Kiin had once sung to Shuku.

For two days, Kiin did what Small Plant Woman told her, digging roots, finding berries, catching fish, gathering sea urchins. The sorrow in her chest seemed to slow her mind, as though she walked always in fog, the gray hiding the sun, the earth, and all things beautiful.

The night of the second day, Eagle came to her, the man glancing often at his wife, as though he found the words he needed to say by looking into Small Plant Woman's eyes.

He spoke first of hunting, as though Kiin were a man, then

of sewing, as though he were a woman, until even Kiin's sorrow could not hold back her smile.

At last he said, "I will take you to your family."

Kiin looked up at him, lips parted, but could find no words.

"I do not know where the trader and his wife took your son, but if I take you back to your husband at the Traders' Beach, then perhaps he will help you find the boy."

Again Kiin opened her mouth to speak, but could not decide what to say. She had thought often in the past two days of returning to Samiq, but what if, in finding Shuku, the Raven had traveled to the Traders' Beach, had found Takha, taken him as well, or worse—had fought Samiq and killed him as he had killed Amgigh?

Tears came to her eyes, and she could not blink them away. I cannot stay here, she told herself. The Ugyuun do not need another woman to feed.

Kiin licked her lips and swallowed, rubbed one cheek against her shoulder. "When?"

Eagle shrugged. "Tomorrow, if the sky is good. Small Plant Woman, you want to come? You and Kiin could paddle your ik; I will go in my ikyak."

Small Plant Woman looked up from her sewing. "Yes," she said. "We will go together to find Kiin's husband and her other son." She reached over to pat Kiin's shoulder. "Then your tears will be for happiness."

SEVENTY-FIVE

THE RIVER PEOPLE

The Kuskokwim River, Alaska

RAVEN GLANCED AT LEMMING TAIL. MOUSE peeked out from the neck opening of Lemming Tail's parka, and the Ugyuun baby was a bulge that curled around Lemming Tail's side.

"You are Kiin; Mouse is Shuku; the Ugyuun baby is Takha," he said.

"The Ugyuun is Shuku," Lemming Tail replied. "He looks much like Shuku, only bigger."

Raven shrugged and asked, "Is he much bigger than Mouse?"

"Some, but what two babies are the same size?"

Raven nodded, thrust his paddle deep into the water, and directed the trading ik toward the mouth of the river. The water where sea met river churned, and Raven braced himself with knees widespread as he paddled.

"The current is strong," Lemming Tail said.

"Paddle. I told you it would not be easy," said Raven.

Lemming Tail pushed forward onto her knees so she could drive the paddle more deeply into the water. When they entered the river, the current was as strong as their paddling.

"We should walk," Lemming Tail finally called out.

"White Fox, Birds Sings, and I had no trouble."

The woman made no answer, only pulled her paddle up out of the river water and set it across the top of the ik.

"Paddle!" Raven bellowed.

"Let me out. I will walk."

Raven roared out his anger. "There, see? A place with sand. We will leave the ik there. Then we will walk."

Lemming Tail put her paddle back into the water and, thrusting it against the mud of the river bottom, helped Raven push the ik into shallow water.

Raven was about to climb out of the ik when a voice came: "Saghani, be careful." In the thick willow and alder brush of the riverbank, Raven saw Dyenen. The old man pointed to a welling of clear water in light-colored sand at the edge of the bank.

"See how the water comes up there? It is from below where there are spirits that would draw a man down."

Lemming Tail stared at the old man, her eyes following the red and blue embroidery that marked the shoulders and arms of his white fur parka.

"This is Kiin?" the old man asked, speaking in the River tongue.

"Yes," Raven said, but kept his head down as he searched among his supply packs.

Dyenen leaned over, carefully chose a place to set one foot, and reached to grab the bow of the ik. He pulled it close to the bank and offered a hand to Lemming Tail. She looked back at Raven, then climbed from the ik, clutching Dyenen's hand.

"Your son?" Dyenen asked and pointed with long brown fingers to Mouse.

"He asks if Mouse is your son," Raven said.

"He is Takha," Lemming Tail answered.

"Takha," Raven said, "though we sometimes call him Mouse."

Dyenen laughed. "Good. A child with two names is a child loved."

"The other son nurses," said Raven and gestured toward the bulge in Lemming Tail's parka.

Dyenen pointed toward a path that ran just inside the trees. Lemming Tail pushed through brush until she was there, then she waited, watching through the spaces between trees and shrubs until Dyenen and Raven had pulled the ik out of the river and tied it in place.

"It will hold until I can send men down to bring the packs," Dyenen said.

"It is good you are here," Raven answered. In the Walrus tongue he said to Lemming Tail, "Dyenen's men will come for our packs. Thank him. It would have taken me a long time to unload all the packs and carry them to the village."

"I would have been the one to carry them," Lemming Tail said.

Raven leaned over and whispered into her ear, "You are Kiin. Kiin does not complain."

"Is there anything you want to take now?" Dyenen asked.

"This only," Raven said and reached into the ik, untied a pack. He pulled out the lynx skin medicine bag Dyenen had given him.

"I can carry something," Lemming Tail said.

"Here." Raven handed her a pack of food. She set it on her head, balanced it with one hand, the other arm around Shuku strapped under her parka.

Dyenen held out his hands, but Raven said, "Your men will carry. Show us the way."

Dyenen and Raven pushed ahead through the trees, leaving Lemming Tail to follow.

"He is old, but he is not ugly, and he is strong," Lemming Tail whispered to Mouse as he watched from her shoulder. She began to hum a song, something she had heard once, long ago, something about furs, food, and a village of many lodges.

After they had walked for a long time, Lemming Tail began to call out questions to Raven. "How much longer? How much farther?"

Raven did not answer her. Instead he directed his words to Dyenen. Raven hoped Dyenen did not sense the rudeness in Lemming Tail's voice. On their journey back from the Ugyuun village, she had been no problem, and Raven had let himself hope she had begun to change, for once appreciating the good things in her life.

When they had stopped at the Walrus village, Raven had been sure Lemming Tail would spend all her time with her friends, but to his surprise she had said she was tired. She needed sleep because she wanted to leave the next day. She told him she had said goodbye to all her friends and did not want to cry tears of parting twice.

Raven had shrugged and let her stay in the lodge. He had spent his time gathering supplies and trade goods, repairing the ik, and checking his harpoons and knives. His parka was torn, so he gave it to Lemming Tail to repair, expecting a sharp and angry reply to his request, but she had smiled and promised to sew it quickly.

Even so, they were two days in the village, days when Lemming Tail asked that no one be allowed to come into Raven's side of the lodge. She had much to do to be ready.

They had left in early morning, and Raven had not had to drag Lemming Tail from their bed, had not had to chide her for her slowness.

They had launched the ik with no one on the bench to offer songs or prayers, though as Raven took the first strong strokes with his paddle, he thought he saw those two old ones, Grandmother and Aunt, on the beach. He laughed. Why think such a thing? The two old women were so weak they seldom left their lodge.

And now he was finally here, and if Dyenen believed that Lemming Tail was Kiin, that the babies were Shuku and Takha, he, Raven, would have all the power any man could want.

As they broke into the clearing of the River village, Dyenen heard Lemming Tail draw in her breath. His chest tightened and he looked back at her, hoping her reaction was one of joy, not despair.

When several of his hunters had run into the village to tell of Saghani's approach, Dyenen had put on his finest parka. He had washed carefully and smoothed oil over his face, chest, and hands. Under his parka, he wore a necklace of bear claws and caribou bone, all from animals he had taken in his youth. What would be better to remind the spirits that he had been a skilled hunter than such a necklace?

For days, Dyenen had prayed; for nights he had lain awake trying to think of ways to please this new wife, a young woman with spirit powers of her own, a woman who might not be impressed with his position among the River People. After all, she was of the First Men and the Walrus. Why find any importance in another tribe? Had he not seen his own daughters turn down offers from men of other tribes, hunters who had much to give a good wife?

To please Kiin, Dyenen had had a man skilled with drawing and dyes paint pictures on Dyenen's lodge to tell the stories of Dyenen's life. He had asked several women of the village to make her a fine parka and leggings, and they had used caribou skins worked until they were so smooth and soft that Dyenen's calloused fingers could hardly tell he was touching them. He had made her a bed platform next to his, filled it with the softest fox and hare furs. He had made sure all the oil in his food cache was fresh, that there was much meat on the food platform he shared with two other men of the village. And he had told his four other wives that they would accept this new wife as a shaman, with the honor given to a shaman, for though she might not claim such an honor for herself, her carvings were proof of her powers.

Saghani had not lied. The woman was beautiful. Her eyes

slanted up from a small nose, her brows slanted also, like a bird's wings. Her hair was long and smooth, oiled until it shone. Her parka bulged with her babies, so he could not tell her shape, whether she was slim or thick, but even if she was too thin, if she bore him sons he did not care. Besides, her hands and feet were plump and well shaped. Would her body not be the same?

Dyenen looked at her and smiled. Kiin's eyes were wide, her mouth open, and after a few moments of staring, she began pointing and jabbering, asking many questions. Dyenen waited politely as Saghani answered her questions, sometimes in error, but Dyenen did not interrupt, reminding himself that Saghani still did not know he spoke the Walrus tongue. Dyenen was glad to hear Kiin speak the Walrus language so well. He had only a few words of the First Men tongue. He would ask her to teach him during the long winter evenings when they were together in his lodge. How else would a man learn the language? The First Men were not traders. Most seemed content to stay on their small islands, hunting sea animals. Even their stone knappers made knives and harpoon heads flaked only on one side, which meant they did not have the knowledge of heating the stone before they worked it, a knowledge that had belonged to the River tribes for as long as their storytellers could remember.

Then Raven was asking questions, drawing Dyenen from his thoughts.

"How many people in this village?" he asked.

"Twenty tens in summer," Dyenen answered, and waited as Raven told the woman Kiin what he had said.

The woman looked at Dyenen, did not hide her eyes in shyness or modesty, but looked into his face and smiled. Dyenen felt the fear in his heart leave as easily as if it were ice melted by sun.

That night they ate together, Dyenen and Lemming Tail and Raven. Raven watched Lemming Tail carefully, caught her eye if she did something considered by the River People to be impolite. Once she almost walked between Dyenen and the hearth fire, but Raven caught her and pulled her outside through the narrow entrance tunnel, saying over his shoulder to Dyenen as they left, "I should have told her the ways of your people. They are different from our own.''

Outside, Lemming Tail turned on him, drew back her lips, showed her teeth. ''I am a child that you drag me from the lodge?''

''You have rude ways,'' Raven said.

''You should have told me these things before,'' Lemming Tail said. ''I am not stupid.''

''Would you have listened?''

''Yes. I want to be a good wife to Dyenen.''

''Then listen now,'' Raven said. ''It is rude to walk between the fire and a man or woman sitting in the lodge.''

''They should keep their cooking fires outside like the Walrus People, like the First Men.''

''Do you listen or do you complain?''

''I listen.''

''Women do not eat the meat of a bear.'' Raven waited for Lemming Tail to speak, but she said nothing.

''Women do not touch a man's weapons.''

''That is no different from Walrus,'' Lemming Tail said.

''Good, then remember it. Women eat when a man is finished eating unless invited to eat with him.''

Lemming Tail nodded.

''Women live apart in a separate lodge during their bleeding times.''

''All these things the Walrus People do.''

''Good,'' said Raven. ''Then remember that the Walrus and the River were once one people. Their difference lies in language and in animals hunted.'' He laid one hand over his chest. ''In the heart, they are the same.''

Lemming Tail took a long breath. ''I will remember.''

''Good. Then come inside and be polite, and if he asks you to carve, remember what I told you. And remember what we have planned when we show him the babies.''

Lemming Tail lifted her chin and made a strange smile, something Raven would remember later that night.

When they had finished eating, Raven motioned for Lemming Tail to clear away the food. ''Where are his other wives?'' she whispered, but Raven, frowning, motioned for her to be quiet, and when she walked past him, Raven grabbed her ankle and squeezed hard, leaving the marks of his fingernails in her skin.

He and Dyenen spoke of things interesting to men, but as he spoke and listened, Raven watched Lemming Tail from the corners of his eyes, watched as she pawed through storage containers and into the fishskin baskets where food was stored.

Finally Lemming Tail sat quietly in the corner, her parka bulging with both boys. She sat in a manner that would please any husband, hands folded, legs tucked under her. Dyenen, looking at the woman, said to Raven, "So ask her if she will stay with me."

Raven turned around, said to Lemming Tail, "He asks if you will stay with him."

"Yes," she said.

"Say more," Raven said, lowering his voice to a whisper.

Lemming Tail leaned forward. "Why?"

"For politeness," Raven said. "The River People speak long in politeness."

Lemming Tail furrowed her forehead, then lifted one hand toward the poles that shaped the dome of the lodge and said, "All things here are good. The village is large. The food caches are full. The children smile; the women are fat. This lodge is the best of all lodges and all the lodges are good. This man here, Dyenen, is a good man. His face shows the powers the spirits have given him. His eyes show the kindness of his heart. His hands show the years he has spent as hunter. I am honored to be his wife."

For a moment Raven said nothing. Lemming Tail's words were such a surprise to him that his tongue seemed captive in his mouth. Then, fighting against a smile, Raven wondered whether this woman's mother might have been like Lemming Tail herself, sleeping with any man, so that Lemming Tail might be daughter to some River man who came to the Walrus to trade. Who could have spoken better?

So he turned and said to Dyenen what Lemming Tail had said to him, adding what he thought might help, and waiting to hear the old man's answer.

"I am glad," Dyenen said—simple words, spoken as though Dyenen were Walrus, not River. "I will take her, but first I must see the babies, and I want to watch her carve. Then she will be my wife."

SEVENTY-SIX

THE UGYUUN PEOPLE

The Alaska Peninsula

"I TOLD KIIN I WOULD TAKE HER TO HER HUS-band." Eagle spoke loudly so he could be heard above the babble of voices in the chief's ulaq.

"She would be dead if you had not found her," the chief said. "Both she and the child. Why risk the husband's anger that the child is gone? Surely he thinks both are dead."

"She says her husband will give me oil and meat, many sealskins."

"What does a woman know of a man's ways?"

A quiet voice came from the back, a woman's voice, and as though surprised that a woman would speak, the men were suddenly quiet. "If you do not take her back, she will go back herself. I know her. She will not stay. She is a strong woman. What woman could survive what she has survived, alone with only spirits on strange beaches?"

"What if she is cursed?" one of the men asked. "What if her own people threw her away and in finding her, Eagle brought her curse to us?"

"If she is cursed, it is better that she go back to the Traders' Beach. Then we will not have to worry."

"Small Plant Woman is right," said her husband. "I told you I will take her back, and I will. My wife and I will go together with ik and ikyak. It is better that way."

Several people nodded, but Small Plant Woman's father

stood, looked at his daughter, and raised his voice in many
doubts, one question following another. Small Plant Woman's
answers were firm and strong, until the old man had no more
reasons for his daughter and her husband to stay. "Go if you
must," he said. "It will be better to have her away from us."

Then Eagle and Small Plant Woman left the ulaq, returned
to their own ulaq, to Kiin, who waited for them, her hands
clasped tight against her lap.

"Tomorrow, we leave—if the sky is good," Eagle said.
"Sleep now, both of you. You will be tired after days of paddling."

Kiin could not sleep. Her thoughts were filled with longing for
Shuku and Takha, and with fear that Raven had gone to the Traders' Beach. She left her sleeping place and found her carving
tools. Taking a piece of wood, she carved a murre, something to
give to Small Plant Woman in gratitude for her kindness. For
who does not know that the murre in losing one egg lays another,
giving herself another chance for a bird child?

When Kiin had finished the murre, she went back to her
sleeping place, and she finally did sleep, but her dreams were
strange, of her mother, of Kayugh and Samiq living with the
Raven. She woke herself with cries of protest, and when morning came, she felt weary.

She worked hard to pack food and supplies for travel, but
once they had launched ik and ikyak and paddled out beyond
the pull of shore waves, Kiin's eyes seemed to dim, and her
thoughts twisted themselves into the paddling songs Eagle
sang. With each stroke of her paddle, Kiin told herself she was
moving closer to Samiq, closer to Takha, and so she kept
herself awake.

They went slowly, stopping early and starting late, and Kiin's
impatience grew as the days passed. Near the end of the third
day, they came to the mouth of the Traders' Bay. If she had
been alone, Kiin would have continued even in the dark toward her people's village, but Eagle spoke of rest, and the
need to wait, to spend a night in quietness as preparation for
again seeing husband and son.

"You will need the clear head that comes with morning,"
Eagle said. "And you will need patience to answer their many
questions."

Kiin agreed with him, but her spirit voice whispered: "Is the man afraid? Does he think Samiq will challenge him with knife or spear because of the loss of Shuku?" And the most disturbing question: "Do you think the Raven is there, on the Traders' Beach?"

He is not there, Kiin told himself. If he went to claim Takha or challenge Samiq, the fight would be over. The Raven would have returned to his own people. There will be no one on the Traders' Beach but my own people, my mother and father, my husband and his wife Three Fish. My son Takha.

During the journey from the Ugyuun village, Kiin had tried not to think of her sons, but when she was so close to the Traders' Beach, how could she keep her thoughts from Takha? She saw Takha as a baby, one who had not grown since the time she had left him, and that made her wonder whether or not he was alive. Was he in the Dancing Lights, still an infant, no longer growing as a child on earth grows?

And if he was alive, what would Samiq and Three Fish say about Shuku? If Samiq and Three Fish had kept Takha strong for her, what would Samiq think when he found that she had lost Shuku to the Raven?

The night was long, and again Kiin did not sleep, her thoughts like those of a woman dreaming, mixing together all the pieces of her life. But when the first light of the sun came after the short night, once she and Small Plant Woman were again in the ik, Kiin suddenly felt strong—stronger than she had felt since she had fallen on the bird cliffs.

Why think all things will be terrible? she asked herself. Why not believe Samiq and Three Fish will be glad to see me, that they will help me get Shuku back? So Kiin paddled with strength, and a song floated from her lips, keeping rhythm with her paddle until she saw the first smudge of smoke from her people's ulas. She smelled seal oil burning, and finally she lifted her paddle, pointed with the blade toward the mounds barely visible from the bay.

"The village," she said. She put all her strength into her eyes, watching the beach, scanning the ulas. Someone was there, near the water, a man with spear and spear thrower in his hand.

She watched for a time before she knew, then she shouted out to Small Plant Woman, "It is Samiq! It is Samiq!" And the words were like a burst of joy in Kiin's heart, like something light and good and bright.

Then Kiin leaned forward, pressed her feet against the bottom of the ik, as though she could make it come more quickly to the shore. She lifted her voice and called out, "Samiq! Samiq! Samiq!"

SEVENTY-SEVEN

THE FIRST MEN

Herendeen Bay, the Alaska Peninsula

SLOWLY SAMIQ TURNED. HE LIFTED ONE HAND TO shade his eyes, and he stood completely still, as though he were a carving that had come from Kiin's knife. Finally he shouted Kiin's name. He dropped his spear, pulled the spear thrower from his hand, and ran out into the water.

Then his arms were around Kiin, holding her to him, pressing her against his chest. He murmured her name, again and again, like a chant, like a prayer. Kiin felt the strong, hard beat of his heart through the layers of their parkas. This is real, she thought. It is not a dream. I am here with Samiq. The Raven did not kill him.

Kiin smoothed Samiq's hair back from his face and pushed him away to say, "You must let go or we will not be able to bring the ik ashore."

And so he released her to haul in the ik, waited until the women were out, then pulled it far up on the sand. Once again his arms were around Kiin, and Kiin did not care who saw— her father or mother, Kayugh or Big Teeth. She did not care what Eagle or Small Plant Woman thought. After a long time, Samiq lifted his face from the softness of Kiin's dark hair and said to Eagle, "She is my wife."

Eagle laughed, then motioned Small Plant Woman to his side and said, "My wife."

Samiq drew away from Kiin. "You and I, we are fortunate," he said to the Ugyuun man. He looked down at Kiin, and she saw the joy in his eyes, and the questions.

"How did you get here?" he asked. "How did you escape from the Walrus village?"

"I walked," Kiin answered.

"And Raven?" Samiq asked. "Is he dead?"

"No, but perhaps he thinks I am." Her heart again pounding, fear creeping into her throat, Kiin asked in a small voice, "Takha?"

Before Samiq could answer, there were many people on the beach—Big Teeth and Kayugh and First Snow; Crooked Nose and Blue Shell, Chagak and Red Berry. All were crowding around Kiin, all laughing, the women crying, Blue Shell and Kiin, mother and daughter, clasped tightly in each other's arms.

Samiq watched as Blue Shell explained Waxtal's banishment from the village, listened as Kiin tried to answer the many questions about her journey to the Traders' Beach.

Samiq saw Three Fish at the edge of the group, the woman with Many Whales strapped to her back, Takha slung on her hip. Samiq saw the uncertainty in her face, something like fear in her eyes. He went to her side, put one arm around her wide body. "You know you are always my wife," he said softly.

Three Fish looked up at him, and for a moment Samiq thought he saw the shine of tears in her eyes, but then he thought, no, for her eyes were clear and her lips were smiling.

"She will want to see Takha," Three Fish said.

"Yes, but he will not know her."

"Soon he will understand."

"Three Fish . . ."

She raised one hand, pressed her fingers lightly against Samiq's mouth. "Nothing has changed," she said. "Kiin has always been with us." Then Samiq watched as Three Fish pushed through the people around Kiin and stood with the babies.

"Takha," Kiin said softly, and her voice caught on tears.

Takha turned his head away, hid his face in the fur of Three Fish's parka, but Three Fish bent her head over the child, laid her face against his dark hair. "It is your mama," she said quietly. "Your mama. She wants to see you." Three Fish untied the sling that held Takha to her side, and Kiin clasped the child to her breast.

Three Fish went to stand beside Samiq, both listening as Kiin, swaying to rock Takha, continued to speak of her journey to the Traders' Beach.

Then Three Fish whispered to Samiq the question that had not yet come into his mind: "Where is Shuku?"

"I could give you all things I own," said Samiq, spreading his arms out in the circle of his ulaq. "But still it would not be enough for the return of my wife."

Eagle shook his head. "Your woman is a good woman. I do not ask what she is worth, and I am only sorry that I could not bring your son as well."

Samiq raised a bowl of broth to his lips, looked over the rim at the Ugyuun man who sat before him. He carried the unhealthy whiteness of the Ugyuun People, the look of someone recovering from sickness. Did the man speak the truth? Had Raven and the woman with him taken Shuku only by chance, or had the child been traded? Kiin believed Eagle. Samiq had only to look into her eyes to know that. But even if Eagle had traded Shuku, he had brought Kiin. Raven would have given much for Kiin, so the Ugyuun man was probably telling the truth. But why, having Shuku, had Raven not come to the Traders' Beach to seek Kiin? Unless he believed Kiin was dead.

The Ugyuun wife said Raven had not seen Kiin and had probably stolen the child because he did not want the Ugyuun baby that was first traded to him.

Then, as though the Ugyuun woman heard the doubt in Samiq's thoughts, she said, "It was by my carelessness that your son is lost. I left him alone for a few moments, and when I came back, Broken Tooth's son was there on the ulaq roof instead of Shuku." As she spoke, she moved in small steps toward her husband, until her legs were pressed up against his back. Kiin, too, came to stand next to Samiq, though Three

Fish remained beside the food cache, chopping hardened fat into dried berries.

"We should take nothing," the woman said.

But the Ugyuun man quickly said, "Only what your wife ate when she was with us."

"Mostly she was sick. Mostly she ate nothing," said the woman. "Besides, she has already given me a carving." She pulled at a thong around her neck and held up the murre carving that hung from the cord.

The Ugyuun man's face darkened, but he looked up at Samiq and said, "I ask nothing, only food and lodging for my wife and me for this night."

Then Samiq also believed what the man and his wife said. Why would a man who had traded away a baby ask nothing for the return of a wife?

"You will have oil and meat and fur seal skins," Samiq said. "You will have knives and baskets and floor mats. Every time you come this way, past the Traders' Beach, you will have a place to stay, you and those who come with you. In returning Kiin to us, you have become our brothers. If you will accept me as brother . . ."

The Ugyuun man smiled, and his woman also. "Brothers," he said, and, raising his bowl to his lips, he drank long.

In all the talking, the laughter, in the crowd of people that filled his ulaq, even through the pain Samiq felt over losing Shuku, Kiin was in his mind, her name like a song in his thoughts: Kiin in his arms, Kiin in his sleeping place.

He could see the signs of her illness. Her arms were thin, her face drawn, her hair dull. The scars from her fall on the egg cliffs were bright pink, her torn fingernails still not grown out, but he wanted to hold her, to allow his own strength to flow into her body. Yet how could he do anything but stay here with all these people, pretending to listen to what they said, trying to answer questions?

"You are happy?" It was his mother Chagak, her hands and arms cradling bowls of dried fish, smoked fish, and fresh sea urchins, shells cracked, spines knocked off.

"I am tired," Samiq said, and smiled to soften the words. She started to speak, but one of the men asked for food, and she was gone. Then Kayugh was talking, his voice loud to be heard above the other voices.

"Eagle and Small Plant Woman will stay in my ulaq," he said. "I ask for the honor because they have returned my daughter. Everyone should come. I have much food." Kayugh led the two from Samiq's ulaq, Chagak following, and soon all others, too, had left, even Three Fish.

For a time, Samiq busied himself picking up bowls, straightening floor mats. He looked up and saw Kiin watching him, smiling as a mother might smile at something done by her child, and then she was in his arms. Her warm breasts, still hard with milk for Shuku, were pressed against his chest. He moved his left hand up under the warmth of her long hair, up the curve of her back to her neck.

"My right hand," he said and held up the bent fingers so she could see.

"I do not care about your hand," Kiin said and pressed her belly against his man part. She laughed softly, and he scooped her into his arms, carried her into his sleeping place.

SEVENTY-EIGHT

QUIETLY, THREE FISH WENT TO EACH MAN AND woman in Kayugh's ulaq; quietly she asked them to listen to what she had to say.

When Three Fish came to Chagak, Chagak looked hard into the woman's face, tried to see if her eyes were filled with sorrow or anger, but she saw only worry. So she waited until Three Fish had spoken to everyone of the village, such a small group that Chagak's heart tightened in fear. How could they continue to live with so few hunters, so few women? But, she told herself, we have lived so far, and it does not hurt that our village is on the Traders' Beach.

Finally Three Fish began to speak. Her words were slow but loud, and still carried the heavy accent of the Whale Hunters. "I am only a woman," she said, "not even of your people, but I am the one who must speak because I am wife to Samiq, mother to Takha, and sister-wife to Kiin."

Chagak heard the words, but also, as though her eyes were opened for the first time, she saw the woman that Three Fish had become, gentled by being mother to three sons, strengthened by being wife to the alananasika.

"Kiin comes to us in joy because she returns to her people. She comes to us in sorrow because she has lost Shuku. I have been wife to Samiq three summers now. I know him. I know what he will do. He will go to the Walrus village. He will fight Raven for his son. Samiq is stronger now, and he has learned to use his knife well. He might kill Raven, but perhaps Raven will kill him. It is enough that we have lost one man to Raven. We cannot let Samiq go. He has three sons here, and we do not have enough hunters. If he is killed, how will we live?"

"How can we stop him?" Kayugh asked. "I am his father, but he is alananasika. Can I say to him, 'You must stay here. You must let a Walrus man raise your son as his own'? Can I treat Samiq as though he were a boy?"

Chagak heard the pain in her husband's words. The loss of one son was enough. To lose Samiq . . . the thought seemed to rip the soul from her chest.

"If all of us go to him, if all of us ask the same thing— that he stay here—would he stay?" asked Big Teeth.

His wife Crooked Nose shook her head. "You know he would not," she said.

No one spoke, and as the silence grew long, it seemed to Chagak that Three Fish shrank in on herself, grew smaller and smaller as though she were an old woman, losing her body in yearning for the next world. Then from the outside edge of the circle, Blue Shell stood. She waited until all eyes had turned to her.

In the oil lamp light, Blue Shell was almost the young woman Chagak remembered when Kayugh and his people first came to Shuganan's beach. Then Blue Shell had been the most beautiful woman Chagak had ever seen. Her belly had been full of her daughter Kiin. Her husband Gray Bird—Waxtal— had not yet beaten the joy and beauty from her. And now, after months of being wife to Big Teeth, the woman had lost her look of fear. She had enough to eat and no worry over beatings, no shame of having a husband who ate but did not hunt.

"I have a plan," Blue Shell said, and looked at her husband, Big Teeth, looked at her sister-wife Crooked Nose. "There has been time to hunt seals and time to gather roots. The traders will soon come to this beach." Blue Shell held out her hands, wrists together. "When the Walrus People come, sell me to them as slave."

Big Teeth jumped to his feet. "I will never sell you. Why should I do such a thing?"

Turning to face her husband, Blue Shell said, "I will find Shuku, and bring him back here, to us. I am strong. I can do such a thing. We have heard the story of Kiin's journey, how she walked from the Walrus People's bay."

"She almost died," Crooked Nose said.

"You are not young. You cannot walk that far," said First Snow.

"But we did not know Kiin was coming. If you know I come, you will bring your ikyak to get me. I will not have to walk as far as Kiin."

"I will never sell my wife as slave," Big Teeth said again.

"Do not tell me no," Blue Shell said. "Shuku is my grandson. Someday he will be a hunter. I am only an old woman, beyond the years of giving sons and daughters. Let me give this. To pay back for these months I have lived well, without beatings, without a husband who curses me with each breath."

And to Chagak it seemed as though Blue Shell had suddenly grown larger, as large as a hunter bringing in meat. If she succeeded, if she was able to bring Shuku back to them, then someday, when he was a hunter, would not every animal he brought in also belong to Blue Shell?

Then everyone was speaking, making plans, voices loud and soft in arguing and pleading. But the noise brought hope to Chagak's spirit, that Shuku would come back to them, that she would finally have her whole family here on the Traders' Beach.

In Samiq's sleeping place, Kiin and Samiq saw no one, heard no one but each other. Though Samiq's right hand was crippled, he used it to caress, stroking Kiin's breasts and belly while his left hand moved in slow circles in the soft flesh between her legs.

When Samiq finally took her, Kiin could not keep the tears inside her eyes. In the darkness she reached out to touch Samiq's face and found that he, too, cried, his cheeks and eyelashes wet. They moved together, and Kiin knew again the joy of being wife. And for a little time she did not feel the pain of losing Shuku.

Late that night, Three Fish returned to the ulaq. She took her son Many Whales from his carrying strap under her parka and put him in the cradle Samiq had made for him. She hung it from the rafters of her sleeping place. Takha was curled, rump up, in her sleeping robes. Sometime during the next moon, when he understood that Kiin was also his mother, he would go to Kiin's sleeping place, and would stay there until he had five, six summers and was old enough to sleep alone.

There was the sound of someone on the ulaq, then Small Knife's quick feet were on the climbing log.

"We are all here," Three Fish said, "all but Shuku. And soon he will come also." She looked for a moment toward Samiq's sleeping place, her eyes staring as though she could see through walls and curtains.

Small Knife looked also, smiled, and said, "It is good."

SEVENTY-NINE

THE RIVER PEOPLE

The Kuskokwim River, Alaska

"TAKE OFF YOUR PARKA. HE WANTS TO SEE you," Raven said.

Lemming Tail stood and slowly removed the parka, hands and arms swaying as though she were dancing. Raven turned his head away, but found himself drawn back by her teasing movements. He took a long breath. Lemming Tail was a poor wife in many ways, but he would miss her in his bed.

Raven glanced at Dyenen. The man sat with eyes half closed, hands limp in his lap. Lemming Tail moved her hands down to her legs. She kicked off her boots, slid off her leggings. She turned three times, wearing only her grass aprons front and back.

"Her legs," Dyenen said. He leaned toward Raven and pointed at the tattooed pattern of triangles and dots that covered her legs from knees to ankles. "It is custom among Walrus women to mark the legs?"

Raven held his hands out, palms up, "Among some. It adds beauty, does it not?"

The old man raised his eyebrows. "Does it add strength?" he asked. "Does it help in birth?"

The questions irritated Raven, and he said, "Who can say why women do such things? If a woman pleases a man, who should care?"

"I want a strong woman," Dyenen said.

Lemming Tail untied her aprons and let them drop to the floor. She stood with legs apart, hips thrust forward, but Dyenen did not seem to notice.

"In this you find no pleasure?" Raven asked.

Dyenen grinned at him, a boy's smile on an old man's face, and Raven began to laugh. He must remember Dyenen was trader here. Why expect compliments?

"She is good," Dyenen finally said.

Raven flipped one hand toward Lemming Tail, said to her, "Put on your clothes. Let him see the babies."

Before beginning her dance, Lemming Tail had laid the babies back in the darkness of the lodge. She turned toward them now, even as she retied her aprons and slipped on leggings and boots.

Raven had decided that in showing the babies, Lemming Tail should bring one child at a time, so Dyenen would not be as likely to see the differences between them. First she brought Mouse, the boy clinging to her. He wrapped his arms tightly around her neck, his legs around her body, even bent his feet in to hold on to his mother.

"This is . . ." Raven began, speaking in the River language.

"Takha," Lemming Tail said, her eyes holding Raven's eyes.

"Takha," Raven said.

Lemming Tail gave the baby to Dyenen. The old man took the boy, held him out at arm's length, then handed him back to her.

"Ask her to take off his parka and leggings," Dyenen said to Raven.

Raven flicked his fingers toward Lemming Tail. "Take off his clothes," he said to her.

Lemming Tail sat down and settled the boy on her lap, pulled his parka off and smoothed back his hair, removed his leggings, and set him on his sturdy legs. For a moment the baby stood, then fell back on his rump. He looked up at Dyenen, then broke into a smile and clapped his hands together. Dyenen squatted and held out his arms. The baby crawled to the old man and pulled himself up by clasping Dyenen's arm.

"So then, let us see the brother," Dyenen said to Raven.

For a moment Raven's eyes flicked to Lemming Tail, and she said to him, "I should first dress Mouse."

"She wants to dress this one first," Raven said to Dyenen, then began a conversation about salmon fishing and the summer's fish runs. The village was crowded with fish racks hung with red strips of drying salmon.

Dyenen finally held up one hand to stop the conversation and, rising to his feet, left the lodge, turning at the entrance tunnel to say, "I will be back soon."

Raven leaned forward to watch the old man crawl through the tunnel, then turned back to Lemming Tail and asked, "The Ugyuun baby, he sleeps?"

"I gave him the medicine you got from Grandmother and Aunt," she said. "He has been sleeping all day."

"Good," Raven said, and they waited in silence until Dyenen returned.

When the old man came into the lodge, he had his hands full of dried salmon. Each fish was split in half, the halves still joined at the tail. The flesh had been sliced crosswise five or six times but was held together by the skin. Dyenen handed a fish to Raven and one to Lemming Tail, then sat down and pulled away a bit of meat from the fish he had kept for himself.

Raven watched the old man and did as he did, ripping out

a chunk of meat and putting it into his mouth. The meat was dried at the edges but still moist in the center.

Dyenen nodded at Lemming Tail and said to Raven, "Have her bring out the other baby."

Raven motioned toward Lemming Tail, who had begun to eat her fish. She sighed, put down the fish, and went to the baby. She picked him up, held him out to Dyenen. "He sleeps," she said.

Raven said, "I am sorry that he is asleep. The traveling here must have made him tired."

Dyenen studied the child and moved his eyes to Raven. "He is called?"

"Shuku," Raven said.

"Shuku," Lemming Tail repeated.

"Take off his parka, let me see this boy," Dyenen said.

"Take off his clothes," Raven told Lemming Tail and frowned as the woman hesitated. Finally she laid the baby on the floor between them, held Mouse back with one hand as he leaned forward to poke at the sleeping baby's face.

She pulled off Shuku's leggings and parka.

"His clothes are different," Dyenen said to Raven.

"A gift from a trader," Raven told him, then said in the Walrus tongue to Lemming Tail, "It was a fine trade you made for Shuku's parka."

Lemming Tail nodded her understanding but kept her head lowered. She finished undressing Shuku and handed him to Dyenen.

"He is bigger," Dyenen said.

"Kiin says he eats more," Raven answered. "He is strong also. When he is awake." Raven laughed and leaned forward to lay a hand against the baby's head, but when he looked at the child's face, it was though some spirit squeezed his heart.

The boy was Shuku, Kiin's son!

For a moment Raven could not think, could not speak. Suddenly he was choking on the fish that was in his mouth, choking and coughing, until Lemming Tail left the baby and came to slap both hands against his back. Finally his throat was clear. Raven took a shuddering breath and stood.

Again he looked at the baby. It was Shuku, without a doubt. How had they come to have Shuku? Had Kiin returned to the Walrus village and given Lemming Tail her son? No, someone

would have told him. Had Shuku been found alive by one of
the Walrus hunters? No, again someone would have told him.
But what if Shuku had been found by one of the Ugyuun?
Perhaps before they left that village, the Ugyuun father had
decided to keep his own son and had given them the found
child, Shuku, instead.

No, Raven thought. Kiin must be alive. She must have been
with the Ugyuun People. Somehow Lemming Tail had found
out and taken Shuku ... Why had she not told him? But
Raven knew the answer to his own question. Lemming Tail
was not stupid. She would have known he would trade her to
the Ugyuun for Kiin. So why take Shuku at all? Why risk
Raven's anger? Did she think Shuku would carry the spirit
powers of his mother, enough power to blind Raven's eyes,
to ensure safety with the River People?

"Strange spirits," Dyenen muttered, pointing at Raven's
throat and chest.

"So," said Raven, his voice weak from the choking. He
cleared his throat and asked, "These babies, this woman, you
like?"

Dyenen sat very still. Finally he said, "All things are good,
but I want to see her carve."

While Lemming Tail dressed Shuku, Raven asked Dyenen,
"Did your men bring my packs? Kiin's carving tools are
there."

Dyenen pointed to the far side of the lodge. "Your packs
are under the caribou skins. My wives know they are yours."

Raven sorted through the packs until he found the one that
contained the knives he had packed: a woman's knife with a
dulled blade for smoothing, a crooked knife with a small blade
for details, a burin, and a pointed drill. He had been careful
to pack old knives. Kiin had been carving for a long time. Her
knives should look well used.

He also picked up a basket, something that had belonged to
Kiin. The basket was full of wood and ivory and also held a
few carvings she had already begun to shape. He took the
basket and tools to Lemming Tail and set them beside her.
She held both boys on her lap. Mouse was nursing, but Shuku
still slept. Raven fixed his eyes on Shuku.

The sight of the boy's face made Raven uneasy. What spirits
were working here? How could something like this happen?

He had many questions for Lemming Tail. The woman had better have good answers.

"Carve," he had said to her.

"The babies eat," Lemming Tail answered.

"Mouse eats," Raven said and took the child from her. The boy reached for his mother and began to whimper, his mouth stretching wide as his cries rose into a howl.

"I will take him," Dyenen said.

Raven handed him the baby. Dyenen took a small piece of fish, placed it on Mouse's tongue. The baby closed his mouth, opened his eyes in surprise. He stopped crying, stuck his hands into his mouth, took out the fish, looked at it, then sucked it off his fingers.

Raven watched as Lemming Tail took the carving knives from Kiin's basket. Her hands trembled, and Raven hoped Dyenen did not notice. But why worry? Even the real Kiin, having to carve to earn a husband, would be afraid.

Lemming Tail sorted through the pieces of ivory, and with each movement of her hands, Raven's chest tightened. Sweat prickled under his arms. He had the pieces arranged in order. If Lemming Tail was not careful, she would spoil their plans.

But no, she pulled out the right piece—a long sliver of walrus tusk, barely shaped, brown and discolored on one side. For a moment she hesitated, the crooked knife poised above the tusk. Then she sliced away a thin curl of ivory.

Raven had made the woman practice this during evenings they camped. It was not difficult to do, requiring only a steadiness of hands and patience, but Lemming Tail was not a woman of patience, and Raven had endured her complaints. He reminded himself of that whining as he watched her work. He needed to push away remembrances of nights spent together, to push away regrets that he would never again have the woman under him in the sleeping robes.

Lemming Tail blinked twice at him, and Raven leaned in front of Dyenen to block his view. Raven spoke to the baby that played in Dyenen's lap. They had not counted on Mouse to help distract the man, but the child made things easier, and by the time Raven was again settled beside the old man, allowing Dyenen a clear view of Lemming Tail, she had a different piece of ivory in her hand, one that Kiin herself had shaped, the beginning of seal or sea lion.

Lemming Tail kept her head bent over the work. Her hair was loose from her dancing, and it fell around her face and over her hands so that much of what she was doing was difficult to see. Finally, she again looked at Raven, again blinked twice. Raven stood, stretched, said to Dyenen, "We should walk. We need to go outside, see the stars."

Dyenen shook his head. "I want to watch," he said.

And when Lemming Tail looked up at Raven with questioning eyes, he could only shake his head and hope that she could think of some way to make the switch. The difference between this piece of ivory and the next was too great to risk changing the pieces while the old man was in the lodge. For a long time Lemming Tail remained with her head down, until again Raven said to Dyenen, "You see she does carve, though you cannot expect the woman to finish one carving in an evening."

"So we will watch for the night," Dyenen said.

Lemming Tail looked up at Raven, and Raven said to her, "Dyenen says he will watch for the night. However long it takes you."

"Tell him I need to feed my son—my sons," Lemming Tail said.

"She needs to feed the babies," Raven told the old man.

"Why?" Dyenen asked. He wrapped his hands around Mouse and bounced him on his lap. Mouse giggled. "This one eats fish," Dyenen said. "The other one sleeps."

"He says they are not hungry," Raven told Lemming Tail.

Lemming Tail set down her carving tools and cupped her breasts in her hands. "I ache from too much milk," she said.

Raven merely pointed, said nothing.

Dyenen threw back his head, mumbled something Raven did not understand, and handed Mouse to Lemming Tail. Lemming Tail gathered the baby to her and scooted away from the men, leaning back against one of Raven's trade packs.

"So we shall walk?" Raven asked and felt the lift of his

heart as the old man pushed himself to his feet.

"And we will talk as trader to trader?" the old man asked.

"Yes," Raven answered and led the way from the lodge out into the cool night air.

EIGHTY

LEMMING TAIL NURSED MOUSE AND AT THE SAME time tried to rouse Shuku from his heavy sleep.

"What did you give me, old woman?" she said aloud. "He sleeps too much. The old man, he will know something is wrong." She leaned over Shuku. The boy's breathing was so shallow that for a moment she was afraid he did not breathe at all. But then she probed the soft skin of his neck and felt the beating of his heart. She sighed her relief, picked up the child and coaxed his lips around her nipple, pressed her breast until a trickle of milk leaked into his mouth.

"Eat, baby, eat," she said, and finally, Shuku began to suck.

She scooted with both boys in her lap over to her carving tools. She hid the shaped ivory in the bottom of the basket and took out a third piece. The head and eyes of a seal looked out at her. She used the blunted woman's knife to smooth the ivory, gently pressing the edge of the blade down the chest.

"This is not so difficult, Kiin," she said. "You made us believe you had special spirit powers. Ha! I can carve as well as you." But her knife slipped and gouged the ivory, and Lemming Tail closed her mouth, bit her bottom lip, and worked more slowly.

"She is beautiful as I told you," Raven said.

"Yes, Saghani, but the one child. He sleeps too much. Is he sick?"

"No, he is bigger and stronger than Takha." Raven looked up, his eyes drawn by the many fine lodges of the River village. The old man began to speak again, and though Raven told himself to listen, listen carefully, his mind wandered. The shock of knowing that Shuku was Shuku seemed to settle over his thoughts like a layer of fog.

"Saghani . . . Saghani?" The old man's hand moved close to Raven's arm, hovered there as though he would touch him to get his attention.

"I am sorry," Raven said. "I did not hear you. My mind wanders. It is not an easy decision I have made to give up this woman and her sons. She is worth much to our people."

Dyenen nodded, but said nothing. He directed their steps in a circle around the village, slowing when they came to full food caches or meat-drying racks.

When he finally spoke, Dyenen said, "It is a good place for children to live."

"Yes."

"A woman would find many friends and never be hungry."

"Yes."

"We agree, also, that when I die, the two sons go back to the Walrus People, and the woman, she does what she wants. But whatever sons she gives me, they stay here with the River People."

"Yes."

"So then, the trade is set."

"And you will tell me the secrets of your animal calling, the chants and prayers and times of fasting," Raven said. "You will tell me how to call spirits so their voices can be heard in my village and their presence felt in the walls of my lodge."

"All things are not as they seem," Dyenen said. "We see stars each night, but who knows what they are? Some men say they are the fires of the dead, others that they are the spirits who created this earth. The women call the stars one thing, the hunters another. When I agreed to the trading, I agreed to tell you what to do. I cannot say what the spirits will do."

"What man does not understand that?" Raven said, again finding himself annoyed at the old man's many words.

"We should return to the lodge," Dyenen said.

"When will you teach me?"

"Tomorrow we begin."

Raven nodded. "How long will it take?"

Dyenen started back toward his lodge. At the entrance tunnel he looked up at Raven. "Four days here with me, and after that, the rest of your life."

Raven said nothing. Four days here. He would have to keep the old man away from Lemming Tail and the babies. They could not expect Shuku to sleep for four days.

Inside the lodge, Lemming Tail was smoothing the carving with a bit of lava rock. She held up the ivory, turned it so the men could see. "It is something done quickly, but still . . ." she said, and Raven translated her words.

"Especially for something done quickly," Dyenen said, "it is good."

He offered Raven more food, but Raven shook his head. Dyenen took a piece of fish, ate it, and went to the babies, leaning over them. Shuku still slept but Mouse was awake, his hands busy as he went from one thing to another. Finally the boy crawled over to the old man, pulled himself up, and looked into Dyenen's face. Dyenen chuckled and put Mouse on his lap. He spoke to Mouse for a long time in the River language before finally setting him down close to his mother.

Dyenen went to Shuku, picked up the sleeping child, stroked his face, arms, and legs, and laid him again on the fur robe where he had been sleeping. Then Dyenen left the lodge, saying nothing to Raven or Lemming Tail.

Lemming Tail lifted her eyes to Raven. Raven shrugged. "He says he will train me for four days, then the trade will be made. You will stay?"

Lemming Tail made a slow smile. "I will stay."

Raven pointed at Shuku. "Where did you get him?" he asked.

"From the Ugyuun," she said and glanced toward the entrance tunnel.

Raven squatted on his haunches and bent his head to see into the tunnel. Dyenen was not there. "He is gone," Raven said.

Lemming Tail bit her lips.

"He may be outside," Raven said and moved to sit close beside her. "Speak quietly."

"But he does not understand the Walrus language," Lemming Tail said.

"Never judge another by what you are."

Lemming Tail laughed. "So, that is your wisdom?" she asked. "How else can we judge? What else do I know but myself?"

Anger, as sharp as a needle, thrust up inside Raven's chest. He clasped Lemming Tail's wrist, held her hand still.

"I am carving," she said.

Raven's lips curled in a smirk, and Lemming Tail, her face coloring, looked away.

"What happened to the Ugyuun baby?" Raven asked, his words nearly a whisper.

"I exchanged baby for baby," Lemming Tail said. "Shuku was sitting outside on a lodge. I saw him and switched."

"And did not tell me it was Shuku?"

"I did not know it was Shuku. He was wrapped in a parka with a hood. I was afraid someone would see me, so I moved quickly. I took one baby from under my parka and put the other in. We were a long way in the ik before I looked at his face."

"Where is Kiin?"

"How should I know? You were the one who told me you found her ik. You were the one who said she was dead. She said she was going to the River People to find you."

"You should not have made her leave the lodge."

"It was not me," Lemming Tail said, and snapped her wrist from Raven's grasp. She held it up, pointed to the red marks his fingers had left on her skin.

"You deserve more than that," Raven said.

"You have given me more than that," Lemming Tail answered, her words changing from whisper to shout. "You are selling me here to an old man, to live with people I do not know. The whole village smells like fish. The dogs—they could hurt Mouse."

"Come back with me to the Walrus village," said Raven, and his lips curled when Lemming Tail turned away. "Then do not pretend you are being punished," he said. "Kiin was punished. For nothing. She was a good wife. A strong woman. She would have given me many sons. You are sure you did not see her at the Ugyuun village?"

"I told you I did not!"

"Then how did Shuku get there?"

"Maybe it is not Shuku, just some child who looks like him."

"Two children who look exactly alike? Not even Shuku and his brother Takha looked that much alike."

Lemming Tail shrugged. "All First Men children look alike."

"I will return to the Ugyuun when I leave here," Raven said his words so quietly that Lemming Tail leaned toward him, tilted her head.

"You said?"

Raven pointed at Shuku. "I said, 'How much medicine did you give him?' "

Lemming Tail looked at him with raised eyebrows. "What you told me to give him. You were the one who got the medicine from Grandmother and Aunt. Did you tell them it was for a baby?"

Raven closed his eyes, let a long breath out through his nose. "How could I tell them it was for a baby? They would have asked questions."

"You should have told them Mouse was not sleeping."

'It was better not to mention babies to them. Who knows what they see in their dreams?"

"If we gave him too much, will it hurt him?" Lemming Tail asked.

"Only make him sleep," Raven answered, though he did not know. Why give Lemming Tail one more thing to worry about, another reason for anger?

"How long?"

"For tonight," Raven said. "That is all. Long enough so that the old man will not notice so much difference between the two boys. They should be more alike. The Ugyuun baby was about the same size as Mouse."

"And you think the old man would not have noticed that the child was cursed by some spirit? Then what would I do? His anger would be at you, but I would be the one to face it."

"You are good at lies," Raven said.

"Mouse is big. Each day he grows. He will soon be the same as Shuku."

"It is not only his size," Raven said. "Shuku will talk sooner. Shuku already walks."

"You think all babies do things at the same time?"

"You think the old man . . ."

The noise of someone at the entrance tunnel made Raven stop. It was one of Dyenen's wives, his youngest. A new baby in a carrying basket was strapped to her back. "My husband says you are to go now to the traders' lodge to spend the night. You and the woman. You are to come back here in the morning." She looked at Lemming Tail, narrowed her eyes.

Lemming Tail raised the carving in her left hand, turned the carving, and lifted her head. She smiled, then looked at Raven, pointed at the woman. "What did she say?"

"That we are to go to another lodge, a place to stay for the night."

"It is comfortable here," Lemming Tail said.

"The trade is not yet complete. You cannot stay with Dyenen."

"The old man will stay here?"

"It is his lodge."

"It is the best in the village."

"Yes."

"Then I will stay here."

Raven shrugged. "Why should I care? You are the one who will carve for him tonight. You are the one he will ask about the babies."

Lemming Tail was still for a moment, then she put the carving in her basket, gathered up her tools and a pack. She held the pack out to Dyenen's wife, then pointed at her two babies.

"I cannot carry it all," she said.

"She is asking for your help," Raven said to Dyenen's wife, and waited as the woman reluctantly took the pack. They followed her to the traders' lodge. Raven closed his ears to Lemming Tail's whining complaints about the smallness of the lodge, the smoke of the hearth fire, and the mosquitoes that hummed in the dark corners away from the smoke.

Dyenen waited until he saw Raven and the woman leave. That she was Raven's wife he had no doubt. There was an easy way between them, questions answered with one or two words, a rise of an eyebrow or a nod of the head. It was not unusual for a man to trade his wife, especially for the powers that Raven assumed he would acquire. But two sons? Two sons who came from the same birth? No.

Dyenen snorted out a quick breath of laughter. Raven was

a fool. Anyone could see the babies were not his. Mouse looked much like the wife, but the other looked like neither. The boys were not even brothers, he was sure. They were about six, eight moons apart in age. Dyenen had not been blessed by sons, but he had many daughters. Boy or girl, babies grew in much the same way—sitting, standing, crawling, walking. Mouse—Takha—crawled, and he was a strong boy, one any man would be glad to call son. The sleeping baby, the one called Shuku, he could walk. The feet of his leggings were worn, one foot with a hole at the toe.

The old man laughed again. Still, a good woman—one who carved—and two boy children. It was not a terrible trade, especially considering what he would give Saghani in exchange.

The chants were sacred, but those most sacred he could not give. A man must find those for himself, seeking and praying and fasting.

"Besides," Dyenen whispered, "things of the soul cannot be traded for packs of dried meat, seal oil, or embroidered parkas. When a man finally comes to that place of respecting the spirits, trade goods hold little importance in his life."

So he would give Saghani a few chants, a song he had himself bought in trade from another shaman, a little knowledge about animals, and the secret of the voices. Those few things were worth a strong woman, one who carved and who might give him sons.

EIGHTY-ONE

ON THE FIRST DAY, RAVEN LEARNED CHANTS AND songs. On the second, he listened to old men of the village tell him the many things they had learned about animals during their years of hunting. Both days he spent much time listening to Dyenen say few things in many words. But this third day was the day Raven had waited for. This day Dyenen would teach him to call the voices.

Though it was morning, clouds kept the day dark. Inside Dyenen's lodge, even the hearth fire did not pull the damp chill from the air, but Raven gathered his feather cloak more tightly around his shoulders and did not complain.

Dyenen wore leggings and loincloth, no parka, no robe. His chest and belly were white compared to his dark, weathered face. His only ornament was an amulet made of fishskin and decorated with the black-and-gray feathers of a flicker.

Dyenen gestured for Raven to sit beside him. Raven sat.

"Close your eyes," Dyenen said.

Raven closed his eyes.

"Be still and listen," Dyenen said.

In the silence Raven held his breath, waiting, listening. Then the voices came—soft and loud, old and young, male and female. Some spoke in one language, some in another, so that Raven would not have been surprised to open his eyes to a lodge full of people. But when Dyenen told him to look, the lodge was empty, though Raven was sure he could feel the fullness of spirits pressing against him from all sides.

The lodge walls shook, once, twice, then Dyenen turned to Raven and said, "They are gone."

Raven's breath came in short, quick gasps, and his arms trembled as much as the lodge walls. A man who had the power to call spirits could own all things on earth.

"Bring them back," Raven whispered.

The old man laughed.

"You cannot?"

"I can whenever I want," Dyenen said.

"Is there danger of a curse?"

"Only if you deserve it, Saghani."

Raven waited for a moment, then said, "I have done nothing that deserves a curse."

"Saghani," Dyenen said, "all men deserve a curse. All men have hurt other men. All men have done things in carelessness. All men have acted in selfishness. What man thinks of anyone besides himself when his belly is empty?"

"Why is it so terrible for a man to want a full belly?" Raven asked.

"Saghani," Dyenen said, "most men have so many bellies to fill."

Raven sighed. More words. "Will you call the spirits back?" he asked.

"Listen," Dyenen said. He cupped both hands to his ears and nodded, then Raven, too, heard the voice, a quiet voice, the voice of a child, a voice that spoke in the River language. "I am Shuku."

Raven's throat tightened and his bowels began to ache. "Call other voices, different spirits," he told Dyenen, his words as tight and dry as his throat.

"I am Shuku," the voice said again. "Why do you say Mouse is my brother?"

"What spirit is that?" Raven asked, taking a long breath, making his words loud as though he were not afraid.

"What voice do you think?" Dyenen asked.

How close was Dyenen to the spirits? Did spirits come and go at his bidding?

Dyenen said, "Here, feel." He grasped Raven's hand and set it on his throat, then the old man spoke words of politeness, as though the two had just met. Raven felt the vibration of the words in the man's throat.

The Shuku voice came again. It called from the smokehole, as though the child knelt at the top of the caribou skin lodge. At first Raven thought only of Shuku's words, but then he realized that his hand, still at Dyenen's throat, again felt the vibration of words, that the voice of Shuku was coming from the throat of the old man.

Relief, then anger flooded through him, until a thin bubble of laughter rose up and broke out over all.

"It is a trick," Raven whispered.

"It is a trick," Dyenen said. "Trick for trick."

Raven laughed, laughed so that his belly ached, and his eyes squeezed out tears.

"The medicine bag was the true power," Dyenen said.

But Raven, wiping his eyes, only said, "Teach me."

"It will take practice, long days alone."

"I have already pledged myself to fasting, to vision quests."

"This is not the same."

"It is more difficult," Raven answered.

"No," said Dyenen. "It is more difficult to fast, to pray. Listen. When a man speaks, he lets his throat open wide so words can come out. To do as I do, you must tighten the throat, pinch it down so the words come out slowly. The mouth is almost closed, and the tongue, draw it back. It does not move, except for the very tip. Here''—he laid one hand around his neck—''it is very tight. The farther away you want the voice to sound, the tighter you must be.''

Again the old man placed Raven's hand at his throat and spoke in a voice that was thin and far away. ''Feel?'' he asked. ''Now you try.''

Raven moved his hand to his own throat, narrowed his mouth, pulled his tongue back, and let his words come slowly.

Dyenen cocked his head and listened. ''No,'' he said, ''but you are close. If you continue to work, you will be able to make the voices. Today and tomorrow we will practice together.''

''And you will teach me to move the lodge walls?'' Raven asked.

Dyenen chortled, flipped up a floor mat where he sat. Raven saw four strings, knotted together, joined like the rays of a spider's web. Dyenen slipped his hand under the knot and pulled. The lodge walls shook gently. ''The strings connect to the lodgepoles here behind me.''

Again Raven laughed. ''Another trick. What is greater than the power of that? So a man sees what he does not see and believes what is not true.''

''Sometimes it is necessary,'' Dyenen said.

''Some men would not think so,'' Raven answered.

''And you?''

''I believe anything that brings me power is necessary,'' said Raven.

EIGHTY-TWO

THE FIRST MEN

Herendeen Bay, the Alaska
Peninsula

THE TRADERS CAME, FROM FIRST MEN VILLAGES
and the lodges of the Walrus People, from the shores of the
Great River and the inland tribes of the Caribou People. They
came, filling the beach with their trade goods, filling the sky
with their voices.

First Snow spoke to each group of Walrus People, asked
which village they were from, what shaman they called their
own. Finally he found men from Raven's village. There were
three men, one woman with them. Chagak remembered them,
especially the tall one, Ice Hunter, who had stopped Samiq in
his fight against Raven. Seeing Ice Hunter, Chagak's fears for
Blue Shell lifted. He was a good man, fair, even in dealing
with traders from other tribes.

She hovered near when First Snow met with the men, she
and Three Fish working together, offering bowls of warm
broth to the traders as they sat with their trade goods, for the
wind blew in from the water, cold and carrying a mist that
soaked through all things.

"A handful of shell beads for your food," one trader
called out, and Three Fish dipped a bowl into the cooking
skin Chagak carried, handed the trader the broth, and took
the beads.

Chagak stood with the cooking skin, as near to First Snow
as she could get, listening to whatever words the wind did not
catch away.

"A good woman I bought from the Ugyuun," Chagak
heard First Snow say.

Ice Hunter mumbled a question that Chagak could not hear, but she heard a portion of First Snow's answer—"... you know they cannot feed ..."—then nothing more as Three Fish came to dip out another bowl.

"How much?" Ice Hunter asked.

Chagak knew First Snow would not give a quick answer. The trading might take all day, and she could not stand and listen forever. There was too much to do. So when no more traders wanted food, she and Three Fish returned to the ulas, each to her own work, Three Fish to Samiq's ulaq, where Kiin was watching Takha and Many Whales.

In Kayugh's ulaq, Chagak took out sinew and needles, but could not seem to make her fingers work. The stitches she made were like the stitches of a child, as bad as what Wren would do, and finally she put away her sewing and went to Big Teeth's ulaq. Both Crooked Nose and Blue Shell were there, both women working, sewing, talking, laughing, as though the men were only out hunting and not trading away a wife as slave.

Big Teeth came to Kayugh and motioned with his hand for Kayugh to follow him. The two walked away from the village, up from the clatter of trading and into a thicket of trees, where the leaves, moving in the wind, would disguise their voices.

"They will take her?" Kayugh asked.

"Yes," Big Teeth said. "They did not want to, but once First Snow brought her out, once they saw her ..."

Kayugh laid his hand against the man's shoulder. How many times on hunts had Big Teeth's quickness and his strength kept Kayugh safe? How many times had Kayugh done the same for Big Teeth? Yet now Kayugh could find no words. How could words explain the bond between hunting partners? Finally, he curled his right hand into a fist, pressed it against his chest, and said to Big Teeth, "Here, like a spear ..."

Big Teeth nodded. "I do not want to let her go," he said, and his voice broke like water on rock.

"Let her do this. Each time you go out to hunt, do you think she wants to see you go? Do you think you are less because you have a strong wife? You are the one who made her strong. Do not forget what she was when she was wife to Waxtal.''

Big Teeth squatted on his heels, reached down to shift sand through his fingers. ''They offered two bellies of oil,'' he said.

Kayugh opened his mouth to say, ''Good trade,'' but then thought, How can a man place value on a good wife? What are two bellies of oil compared to the heat of a woman's skin, compared to the fire that snaps in her eyes?

''Save them,'' Kayugh said. ''If we have to, we will buy her back.''

''I thought I might give them to the wind spirits, to ask their protection.''

Kayugh shrugged. ''Do what you think is the right thing. She is your wife. You know what is best.''

''First Snow says Ice Hunter will leave tomorrow.''

''They want her tonight?''

''Yes, but First Snow told them they could not have her until they were leaving. I will have her one more night. She will not sleep on this beach with traders.''

''You have decided when you will meet her?''

Big Teeth held up one finger. ''I will go for her at the next full moon. If I do not find her, I will go to the Walrus village and buy her back, even if it takes all I have.''

Kayugh said nothing, only looked into Big Teeth's eyes, brother to brother.

Too much sorrow, Kiin thought. She had returned to find Takha all she hoped he would be—strong, full of laughter— and Three Fish wiser, gentler, a true sister. But she had lost Shuku. She had returned to find her father gone, banished from the tribe, her mother happy as wife to Big Teeth. But now her mother would be sold as slave. And what hope did an old woman have? No man would want her as wife. She would be used for the hardest work, and would receive little to eat.

''For one moon, only that,'' Blue Shell said to her, then reached out, the two falling into an embrace.

Kiin clutched her mother tightly and held back a sob. Blue Shell pulled away, looked into Kiin's face, lifted a hand to smooth away a tear on Kiin's cheek.

''Daughter, let me do this for you. There is so much I did not do,'' Blue Shell said. ''I let your father beat you . . . .'' She choked on the words, then took a long breath. "I was afraid. Let me show you I have courage. Let me show myself . . ."

Kiin nodded. "I wish I could go instead," she said.

"They know you."

"Perhaps they will also know you."

Blue Shell smiled, shook her head. "No, I am only a gray-hair. Someone to prepare food and sew parkas. They will not know me. But I must go now. I have this night to spend with my husband." Blue Shell turned and walked to the climbing log. She looked back at her daughter. "I only hope I will be as strong as you are," she said.

Kiin reached out her hand, and Blue Shell did also. The two were apart the width of the ulaq, but it seemed that their fingers touched.

EIGHTY-THREE

THE RIVER PEOPLE

The Kuskokwim River, Alaska

DYENEN STOOD AND WATCHED THE IK AS IT started downriver. An easy journey to the sea, Dyenen thought. But the journey to the Walrus village? Not easy for a man alone in an ik. Ah, why worry? If Saghani died, he died.

Dyenen felt uncomfortable knowing how many of his tricks he had shared with the man. Saghani saw no value in the herb medicines, and the tricks were not meant to deceive, only to convince the people that the medicines had power. But Saghani—what would he do with such knowledge?

Of course, if the Walrus People felt fear instead of wonder, the voices would cease to carry power, and the tricks would be used only to entertain children and make men and women forget for a time the harshness of life.

Dyenen turned and walked back to his lodge. His new wife

was there with Mouse and Shuku. He had asked her to carve a bird for him to wear as an amulet near his heart. He was an old man. The end of his life was coming. He needed something to remind his spirit to look up, to fly when it was released from his body.

But before that time came, this woman would give him a son. Her powers were strong, even if both boys were not her own.

Dyenen entered his lodge, settled himself against a backrest of woven willow branches. He had told his other wives to stay away for the six days normally given a new bride. Young men might go out to a quiet place along the river, but he was old and had grown accustomed to the comforts of his lodge. He would spend the six days with Kiin, here.

Kiin was beautiful, and Dyenen found himself anxious to take her into his bed. But when he walked into the lodge, she did not greet him, and even now her eyes were on the ivory she held in her hands.

"You have finished the bird?" Dyenen asked, speaking the Walrus tongue.

The woman looked up at him, her eyes round, as though he had startled her. "You speak Walrus," she said.

"Do not tell Saghani," said Dyenen and smiled.

The woman also smiled, but then she looked down at the carving in her hands and frowned. "It takes a long time to carve some things," she said.

"Your seal, you carved it in one evening," said Dyenen.

"A bird is not as easy—the wings. How would you carve a wing?"

Dyenen heard the edge in her voice, the tears closing her throat. He left his backrest and squatted beside her. "Put down the knife," he said, his voice like the voice of someone talking to a child. "Why do you cry? Do you want to go back with Saghani?"

The woman lowered her head until her chin rested against her chest. "No."

"You do not want to be my wife?"

The woman's eyes were suddenly wide. "I am glad to be your wife," she said.

"You are afraid because I know one of the babies does not belong to you."

The woman scooted back away from him.

"You think I am a fool? You think I cannot see?" Dyenen asked.

"I did have two sons," the woman said. "Born together." She pointed at Mouse. "One died. In my sorrow, Raven—Saghani—brought me Shuku in trade."

"Will you give me a son?" Dyenen asked.

"I am good at making sons."

"You have others?"

"Someday I will," the woman said, and a smile lifted one corner of her mouth. She looked at the babies. They slept. She stood up and untied the string of her aprons. They fell to the floor. "It is a good day for sons," she said, and leaned forward to cup Dyenen's face in her hands. "Let us try now."

Lemming Tail smiled. The old man's snores shook the lodge. She had satisfied him. If she could lure him into bed each night, he would soon be too tired to worry about her carving.

Shuku began to whimper, and Lemming Tail slid from her sleeping robes to nurse him. He ate too much, this child. Maybe if she did not nurse him so often, he would not grow so fast. Then Mouse would catch up with him. She took Shuku to Dyenen's place near the hearth fire and leaned against his willow backrest. Shuku, eyes closed, found her nipple and began to suck, the ivory ikyak pendant that Kiin had carved for him clasped in his hand.

Lemming Tail pulled the pendant from his fingers. She had first noticed the pendant when Kiin returned to the Walrus village. It held some power of protection, Lemming Tail knew.

"It should belong to Mouse," Lemming Tail whispered to Shuku. "He needs it more than you do."

She let Shuku nurse until he fell asleep, then she returned him to his sleeping robes. She woke up Mouse and fed him, too, and as he nursed, she sewed the ikyak pendant to his parka.

PART THREE

LATE SUMMER
7037 B.C.

EIGHTY-FOUR

THE WALRUS PEOPLE

Chagvan Bay, Alaska

BLUE SHELL LAY ON THE GRASS MATS AND waited. One of the children whimpered in his sleep, and the hunter Chin Hairs mumbled and turned, rustling the sleeping furs on the bed platform. Blue Shell heard the soft snores that told of Day Girl's sleeping, but she waited a little longer.

When she had first come to this Walrus lodge and the woman Day Girl had asked her name, Blue Shell had told Ice Hunter to say, "Asxahmaagikug." And though Day Girl did not know what that First Men word meant, she had nodded her acceptance. Blue Shell had chosen the name herself, in the manner of men celebrating or remembering. A new name to add to what had been, something that carried its own spirit and would say what could not be said in another way. So now she was Asxahmaagikug.

Asxahmaagikug—I am lonesome—Asxahmaagikug.

Blue Shell worked hard and without the surliness of many slaves, and so received nearly enough to eat. And though she had worn her old suk, Crooked Nose had cleverly lined it with ground squirrel skins and sewn many things in the seams and hidden pouches—a woman's knife, needles, fishhooks, kelp line, burins—tools and supplies Blue Shell might need on the return journey to the Traders' Beach with Shuku.

But now Blue Shell knew it would not be with Shuku. The child was not in the Walrus village, and for a long time, Blue Shell could find out nothing about him, so that in the nights when she was lying on her bed and finally had time for thoughts of her own, her heart grew cold in dread. The child must be dead.

She listened carefully. Everyone was asleep, she was sure. She crept from the lodge, from her place near the entrance tunnel. She went outside into the darkness of the night, stood and looked for the moon. It was in the far western sky. Nearly full, yes. Soon she would slip away, walk the night along the beach. But she would meet her husband with empty arms and would have nothing to tell her daughter when she returned to the First Men village, nothing to show for a moon of work among the Walrus People.

Still, she had a few more days. Even this morning, she had found out something that Kiin might be able to use in deciding what had happened to her son.

She had been digging clams with five of the Walrus women, she and Day Girl working side by side. The woman called Shale Thrower had mentioned someone named Lemming Tail. Blue Shell knew Lemming Tail was the one who had been Kiin's sister-wife. But Shale Thrower spoke quickly, in the Walrus language, and though Blue Shell was learning many of their words—and had already known a few from Waxtal's conversations with traders—she could not understand what they said.

Where was Lemming Tail? If she were dead, the Walrus women would not speak her name.

"Lemming Tail?" Blue Shell had asked, raising the name into a question. "Who Lemming Tail?"

Three of the women continued digging as though Blue Shell had not spoken. Another coughed out a short, tittering laugh. But Shale Thrower, a woman of many words and—as far as Blue Shell could tell—little sense, said, "Everyone knows Lemming Tail is Raven's wife. But sometimes someone asks a foolish question. Sometimes a woman embarrasses herself by letting others know how stupid she is."

Blue Shell understood many of Shale Thrower's words, but more than that she understood the meanness behind the words, the taunting in Shale Thrower's voice. Blue Shell opened her mouth to speak, but remembered that she was slave, had been slave for many years, according to what the Walrus People knew. So she lowered her head and kept her mouth shut. Then she realized she had learned nothing she did not already know.

So again she spoke, this time spreading her hands. She pretended to look at the village and beach, then asked, "Lemming Tail? Where?"

This time Day Girl answered. "With Raven on a trading trip to the River People."

"Why bother to tell her? She cannot understand you," said Shale Thrower. "Besides, why should it matter to her? She is a slave."

"I do not know why your husband bought her," another woman said to Day Girl.

Day Girl started to answer, but before her words came out, Shale Thrower said, "He needed someone good in his bed."

The other women laughed, and Blue Shell pretended she did not understand, but Day Girl threw her carrying net of clams to the ground and strode off in long steps up the bench. Blue Shell picked up the carrying net while one of the other women spoke in angry words to Shale Thrower.

Blue Shell, head bent, shoulders hunched, continued to dig, and one by one the Walrus women left the beach until only Blue Shell and Shale Thrower were left. Shale Thrower moved close to Blue Shell and spoke in slow words, each sound drawn out so that Blue Shell had to hide her laughter at the foolishness of the woman.

"Asxahmaagikug," she said, "Lemming Tail went on a trading trip with her husband Raven. They have not yet come back."

"Where?" Blue Shell asked.

Shale Thrower seemed surprised at the question but answered, "To the River People." She raised one hand and pointed north. "They live far there. Three days, four days." She shrugged. "Many days."

"They come back?"

"How should I know?" Shale Thrower said. "Do I have the power to see the future? Ask Grandmother or Aunt. They know all things."

"Grandmother, Aunt," Blue Shell said and straightened slowly. Her back ached from the long time spent digging. She faced the village and pointed to the lodge where she thought the two old women lived.

"Yes," Shale Thrower said, then began a long story of the old women. Soon Shale Thrower was speaking so quickly that

Blue Shell could no longer understand most of what she said, so Blue Shell went back to her digging, and nodded sometimes to make Shale Thrower believe she was listening.

Now in the moonlight Blue Shell walked to the old women's lodge. She had heard Kiin speak of them once, and there had been fear and anger in her daughter's voice. But Blue Shell knew the Walrus People considered them to be shamans, with power for knowing what most people did not know. She skirted the lodges, staying in the night shadows, and when she finally came to the sisters' lodge, she waited, suddenly afraid to scratch at the grass door flap.

Then she heard a voice calling, "Asxahmaagikug, we wait for you. Will you be outside all night?"

So Blue Shell crawled in through the door, stood up, and faced the sisters. Each woman sat with a death mat across her lap.

"You have come with your questions," one of the women said, and Blue Shell suddenly realized that they spoke in her own language. The First Men words came to her ears as something beautiful.

"Do not be surprised," the other woman said. "We are First Men, married into this tribe of Walrus People."

"It is good to hear words spoken in the true way," Blue Shell said.

One of the sisters laughed. "No one language is the true way," she said. "The true way is something not heard with the ears, but here. . . ." She pressed a closed fist against her heart.

"You have come to ask about Lemming Tail," the other sister said. "She is gone. She will not be back. Raven has traded her."

The words were cold in Blue Shell's heart. "You know all things?" Blue Shell asked.

"We know very little, but more than other people know."

Again, one of the sisters laughed, but it was a gentle laugh so that Blue Shell knew that they did not intend to make fun of her. "Raven is your chief?" Blue Shell asked.

"You know Raven?" the sisters asked, their two voices blending as one.

Blue Shell lowered her eyes. "No," she said. "But I have heard the women speak of him."

One of the old women shrugged. "Some say he is chief of this village, but Ice Hunter is her son." She tilted her head toward her sister. "He is our chief."

Blue Shell nodded, then slowly, choosing her words carefully, she said, "The women told me that Raven has three sons, but that one is dead."

"He has no sons," one of the old women said. "Not now."

"What happened to Lemming Tail's son?"

"You know of Lemming Tail's son?"

"I have heard . . ."

"He is traded, he and Lemming Tail." The old woman paused, bent in the dim light toward the mat she was weaving. She cleared her throat and said, "Lemming Tail and her son Mouse and the son by Raven's wife Kiin, the child he named Shuku, are all traded."

At the woman's words, Blue Shell could not keep her hands still. They twisted themselves into her suk. "Why?" she asked softly, hardly aware that she had spoken the word.

The sisters acted as though she had said nothing, resumed their weaving as though she were not there. But I am not here, Blue Shell reminded herself. I am a slave.

She stood and thanked the sisters, though they made no response, and then she left the lodge. But as she wove her way into the shadows of the village, back toward the lodge of Chin Hairs and Day Girl, she heard someone call her. She turned back and saw one of the sisters. The old woman came close, clasped Blue Shell's arm, and pulled so that Blue Shell had to lean down toward the old woman's mouth.

"Kiin," the old woman said, "she is well?"

"She is dead," Blue Shell said, as Kiin had told her to say.

"Takha?"

"He is dead."

The words burned on Blue Shell's tongue.

EIGHTY-FIVE

THE NIGHT OF THE FULL MOON, BLUE SHELL AGAIN crept from Chin Hairs' lodge. This time she carried her small bag of belongings, the few things that were hers. She stopped first at the drying racks, where she took several handfuls of meat. She looked out toward the water, at the left side of the bay. She would walk that beach, keeping low and close to the beach grass.

During full moon many of the Walrus People were out, fishing and repairing ikyan as though it were day, so she would have to be careful. Once out of the bay, there would be no one—except Big Teeth coming for her, to take her back to her own people. The ache that had seemed to become a part of her body lifted, and she felt only the excitement of hope, the joy of being again with her daughter, and with Takha, with all the people of her village.

She crept from the shadows of the lodges, out past the ikyak racks. She moved as though she, too, were a shadow, walking carefully, slowly.

She heard voices on the beach, men talking, laughing. They were a strange people, these Walrus, living by moonlight as if they were the animals they told stories of—wolves, bears, caribou. Using night and day as one. Sleeping, eating only by need.

She was well past the village then, walking the curve of the bay, nearing the mouth where bay joined sea, where beach sand gave way to gravel and rock. Then she heard a man singing, and as though Kiin's spirit whispered the name into her ears, Blue Shell knew it was Raven.

She crouched in the tall grass, and, peering out, saw that he paddled a trading ik and that he was alone. He moved his paddle to the bay side of the ik and turned toward the beach. Raven was coming ashore.

Blue Shell's breath came hard into her throat. She was suddenly unable to move, as though her feet had grown into the

388

ground. When Raven stepped from the ik, she was able to rise to her hands and feet. She scurried more deeply into the grass and lay still.

She heard Raven's voice again, raised as though the man spoke to someone, and she peeked out through the grass, moved her head until she could see him sitting on his heels beside his ik. Then she lay where she was and watched.

Raven's throat was raw from practicing, but still he spoke. The voice came from the ik's bow. He spoke again and the voice came from a rock on the beach, then from a clump of grass at the edge of the tide mark. He began a chant, but the words came out in his own voice, so he started again.

This time he tightened his throat until it seemed as though his words were coming from a narrow tunnel behind his tongue. He nodded his head in satisfaction as the voice came to him from the high ryegrass at the back of the beach.

The grass moved. Wolf? he thought, trying to see in the darkness. No, not wolf, but something. Bear? No, too small for a bear. Perhaps a half-grown cub, he thought. He leaned back slowly, reached into the ik, and brought out spear and throwing board. He fitted his hand into the throwing board, looked down as he set the butt of the spear against the board's hook. But when he looked again, whatever had been there was gone, lost in the shadows.

Raven moved his head back and forth, using the clearer night vision that comes from the corners of the eyes, but still there was nothing. Spirit? he asked himself. It was true he did not yet know what powers he could draw with his voices. He spoke again, narrowing his throat so the words came from the grass. Again, he was sure he saw movement.

"If you are spirit, show yourself," he finally called out, using his own voice. "If you are spirit, tell me what you have come to tell me." He waited, but there was nothing.

He had thought to spend time here in the moonlight, to practice his voices before returning to the village, but how could he if some animal was hiding in the grass?

He looked across the water at the village, saw beach fires, and knew that men were awake. He did not want to go to them yet. Let them awake in the morning and see him in the village. Let them wonder when he had come. Let them find some mystery in what he did.

But now that there was a spirit on this beach he could not stay. In anger he flexed his throwing arm, in anger he drew back his spear. He let it fly from the thrower toward the darkness in the grass. He heard it hit, and with the hit came a sound like a sudden hiss of wind, then nothing, no cry, no scream.

"It was a spirit," Raven said, his voice a whisper. He watched the grass, saw no movement, heard nothing. Still, no one knew what might anger a spirit. Almost he went to retrieve his spear; almost he stayed to practice his voices. But then in his mind he saw himself coming toward the men on the beach in his ik, coming out of the darkness. Who could not see the mystery in that? Why should he wait until morning?

And so he pushed his ik back into the water, leaving his spear. If he had hit some spirit, why further risk that spirit's anger? He would send some boy tomorrow to retrieve the spear.

Raven paddled in long easy strokes. The bay was calm. He could smell the beach fire's thick acrid smoke—seal bones burning—and see the reflections of the flames on the water. He called to the men, lifted his paddle, and carefully, in his trader's ik, stood. He opened his mouth to call out his name, and across the water heard the men call out, heard them as they lifted his name, almost in a chant.

He sat down, and with three strong strokes moved his ik ashore.

"Where are your trade goods?" one of the men asked.

"Here," Raven said, pressing a hand to his chest. "Dyenen, mighty shaman of the River People, has shared the knowledge of his power with me. I spent many days in fasting and prayer to earn the power for myself."

"It is seldom anyone sees you fast," said Shale Thrower's husband.

Several men laughed, but Raven held back an angry retort. Instead, he tightened his throat, brought a voice from the beach fire. "Who are you to question a shaman's spirit powers?"

The men drew back, looked in wonder first at the fire, then at Raven. For a time they were silent, then they all began to speak at once. Words of praise, fear, and honor. Raven thought of Lemming Tail, Shuku, and Mouse. He smiled and whispered, "Good trade."

EIGHTY-SIX

THE WHALE HUNTERS

The Bering Sea

THEY PASSED THE TRADERS' BEACH AT NIGHT, IN the darkness after the full moon had set. Kukutux could see her husband's ikyak moving behind the women's ik, could hear his voice as he whispered angry words against the chief of that small village at the back of the long, two-armed bay. They could not see the village from the sea, but Kukutux felt a difference in the air as they passed, as though the voices of the people's prayers brought some softness to the wind. Soon she was too busy with her paddle, fighting the chop of the water where the bay emptied into the sea, to notice any difference made by prayers.

Then they were back again into the regular swells of the North Sea. Kukutux pushed the salt-stiffened hair from her eyes and wished she had been allowed to stay in the Whale Hunter village with the old ones. Theirs would be a good life this year. With few mouths to feed and the oil and meat Hard Rock had left them, they would not starve.

"Do you see the men?" Speckled Basket asked.

"Only Waxtal," Kukutux said. "He is behind us." And she wondered how Speckled Basket expected her to see anything in the dark. "I think they are far ahead," said Kukutux.

"They made us come and now will not wait for us," said She Cries, her voice a whine that made Kukutux's ears ache.

"They complain about our slowness," said Speckled Basket, "yet they knew we could not keep up with them in our iks. Even a hunter cannot paddle an ik as quickly as an ikyak."

"We should turn and go back," said She Cries.

Kukutux ground her teeth to keep from answering the

woman. Who was stupid enough to think they could go back?
Two moons they had been traveling.

Each day was full of complaints, full of anger. But the complaints were against the husbands, not Waxtal. He was the one
who would take the curse from the Whale Hunters. Why blame
him?

But the longer Kukutux was wife to the man, the more she
wondered about his powers. He had carved the tusk, but carving seemed to be the only thing he knew. He did not hunt; he
did not make weapons; he did not fish.

He prayed and sometimes even fasted. But usually he ate
enough for two hunters, and often during the times he claimed
to pray, Kukutux knew he slept. Still, why question a man
who spoke to spirits? What if his claims were true? What if
he did have great power? Then her doubts would not only
anger her husband but the spirits as well.

The battle against Samiq and the Seal Hunters will prove
Waxtal's powers, Kukutux thought. But she could not keep
fears and worries from entering her mind.

How could an old man like Waxtal kill a young man, a
hunter, like Samiq?

Answering her own question, Kukutux reminded herself that
not all power was that of muscle and bone. Waxtal's strength
was an inside strength that came from his carvings.

She took a long breath. Her shoulders ached, and her hands
were so tight on the paddle she did not know if her fingers
would ever straighten again. But the months in the ik had
seemed to strengthen her left arm, had even loosened her elbow so she could with effort hold the arm straight.

What if Waxtal was killed? Kukutux shuddered—she was
away from her own village, far from the island she knew. If
she was left without a husband, would the other Whale Hunters provide for her?

Yes, said Kukutux, and tried not to remember the stories
she had heard about times long ago, when widows had been
allowed to starve during hard winters so hunters and mothers
could live.

Besides, Kukutux thought, why would Hard Rock make
Waxtal fight? Better that one of the young Whale Hunters
should fight Samiq, better that a Whale Hunter should break
the curse. Perhaps Hard Rock himself would fight. The man

who broke the curse would be able to claim leadership of the Whale Hunter village. Who could deny such a man the honor of being alananasika? Would Hard Rock take the chance of losing that honor to someone else?

Kukutux pulled her paddle from the water, laid it across the ik, and flexed her shoulders. Waxtal had promised that once they passed the Traders' Bay—soon, in a day or so—they would come to a village of First Men called Ugyuun. There they would stay, Waxtal had promised, for one day and a night, a long rest before going on the eight, ten days it would take to reach the Walrus village. Waxtal had said that he and the Whale Hunters would be welcome at the Walrus village, that Waxtal's daughter—wife to the Walrus shaman—would share her lodge and food.

Kukutux took her mind from the ache of her arms and instead thought of the smell of meat cooking, the flavor of bitterroot and seal oil, the taste of sea urchins, their rich orange eggs raw from the shell. She dreamed of days spent weaving and sewing, of digging clams. She remembered the warmth and quiet of a ulaq, oil lamps burning, and was glad Waxtal did not want to be a trader forever. How terrible to always paddle an ik, days and days. How much better to be safe in her husband's ulaq, to fill her eyes with things known and understood.

EIGHTY-SEVEN

THE WALRUS PEOPLE

Chagvan Bay, Alaska

FIRST, THERE HAD BEEN NO PAIN, ONLY A SUDDEN thrust against her back and the realization that she could not move. In her surprise, Blue Shell could not even call out, but she had seen the man, seen his feather cape, and knew that he was Raven. He was alone and for some reason had thrown his spear at her. She waited, knowing he would come to see what he had done.

Instead he was again in his ik, pushing it off from shore. She lifted her voice, called out to him, but he did not seem to hear. With one arm she reached back, clasped the spear. Her blood was sticky on the shaft. She pulled, but could not move the spear. Then the pain came. She cried out, called to people long dead, her mother, her father. She called to her daughter Kiin, far away now at the Traders' Beach, and to her own husband Big Teeth, a man of laughter and gentle ways.

The pain drew dreams, and for a time Blue Shell was lost in strange worlds. She slept but did not sleep; she flew with her dreams to places only birds could go, then came back to find herself bound to the earth by Raven's spear.

Finally again she heard the sound of a paddle. Certain it was Raven, again she tried to call out. This time her voice was strong. He would hear her. If he would just take the spear from her back, she would return to the village, work hard for them . . . but no, she was supposed to meet her father . . . no, her husband, Big Teeth. To tell him . . . to tell him . . . there was something she must tell him.

Her eyes closed, but she forced them open. She called out until her mouth could no longer make itself form words. She was too tired, pain burned her back, and the spear seemed to press her farther and farther into the earth. She slept, then a voice was calling.

"I am called Asxahmaagikug," Blue Shell whispered. "I am slave . . ." Someone was beside her, trying to turn her. She opened her eyes. Big Teeth. She raised one hand, but could not reach far enough to wipe away his tears.

"Why?" he asked her. "Why?"

For a moment Blue Shell did not understand his question, but then she felt his hand on the spear.

"No," she whispered. The pain came again, cut into her body like the blade of a knife. The earth was suddenly soft beneath her, and she clutched for Big Teeth, calling out with all her strength, "The River, the River, the River . . ."

Then the pain was gone, and the world was a new world, shining, and she opened her eyes wide to see it.

EIGHTY-EIGHT

BIG TEETH PICKED UP THE SPEAR. HE STUDIED THE markings, then, speaking aloud, he said, "Raven." The word was a whisper, then rose into a shout, a scream: "Raven! Raven! It is not enough that you killed Amgigh? You must also kill my wife?"

He lifted his voice into a long and mournful cry, then he knelt beside Blue Shell, stroked her hair, her face. For a long time he did not move, did not speak. Finally, he covered his face with his hands and wept.

When the sun broke into the eastern sky, a thin line of red over the rise of the land, Big Teeth went to his ikyak and brought back a sealskin from his pack of supplies. He laid it over Blue Shell. He gathered stones from the beach and covered her.

Then he tied Raven's spear to the deck of his ikyak and pushed the craft into the bay. He paddled toward the Walrus village.

Raven went into his side of Grass Ears' lodge. The lamp was cold, the oil in it thick and partially congealed. There was no smell of food cooking, no sound of women's voices. He set his pack on the floor, then called to Grass Ears' wives, asking them to come and light the oil lamp, to bring food.

One came and with her woman's knife trimmed the lamp's wick. She lit the oil, and her sister brought dried fish and a few fresh sea urchins.

Raven cracked open the sea urchins and used his thumbnail to scoop out the eggs. He opened his mouth to ask for water, but Grass Ears' wives had already returned to their own side of the lodge. Raven stood, reached up, and pulled down a water skin. It was nearly empty. The other bladders, usually clustered together like small white moons at the top of the lodge, were also empty. Did the women of this village expect their shaman to get his own water?

He untied the bladders and carried them to the women, then, without speaking, returned to his half of the lodge. He would have to get a wife. A man could not live without a woman to sew his parka, to prepare his food, to warm his bed and bring his water.

He opened another sea urchin. But who? There were no beautiful women left in the village. All had husbands of their own. There was the young daughter of Chin Hairs, but she had not yet had her first bleeding. Besides, he wanted a widow. Someone who already knew how best to please a husband. He sighed. The only widows in the village were those of Lemming Tail's oldest brother. And what woman would marry the man who had killed her husband?

Of course, he had killed Kiin's husband. . . . And now, Raven wondered if the woman was alive, back with the one she called Samiq, or if she was dead, lost somewhere in the North Sea. In a few days he would go back to the Ugyuun village. If Kiin was alive, he would find her.

The curtain that separated Raven's side of the lodge from Grass Ears' moved, and Raven waited for Grass Ears' wives to bring in his water. They were slow. A tight feeling of anger began to push its way into his chest. What should he expect? he asked himself. Grass Ears demanded so little from his wives that they had never learned to serve well.

"You took a long time," he said without looking up from the sea urchin he was eating.

"I came to return your spear."

The words were in the First Men language, and the voice was hard. Raven looked up. He curled his lips, ground his teeth. Who was this man who came into his lodge, spoke without politeness?

"Who are you?" Raven demanded. He stood up, and without turning his back on the man, took two quick steps to his weapons corner. He clasped a walrus harpoon with his left hand, a throwing spear with his right.

"I am Big Teeth of the First Men, husband to Blue Shell, the woman you killed with your spear."

Raven glanced at the spear in the man's hands, knew it was

the spear he had thrown into the grass that early morning.
There was blood on the andesite point.

"I did not invite you to my lodge," Raven said. "I did
not kill your wife. I do not even know you. I do not know
her."

Then Ice Hunter was in the lodge, ripping aside the dividing
curtain.

From the sides of his eyes, Raven could see Grass Ears
huddled against the far wall, his wives behind him.

"I called my sons," Ice Hunter said to Raven in the Walrus
tongue. "Who is this man?"

"He says he is of the First Men."

Ice Hunter, a sleeve knife in one hand, a spear in the other,
pointed the knife toward Big Teeth and asked, "The spear?
Whose blood?"

"He says I used it to kill his wife," Raven answered.

Big Teeth, as though he did not see Ice Hunter, as though
he did not hear the man's voice, held the spear up in one hand
and asked Raven, "This is your spear?"

Ice Hunter studied the spear. With a quick jerk of his chin
he pointed at the markings on the shaft and looked at Raven.
"It is yours?" he asked.

"Yes, it is my spear," Raven said.

"Whose blood?" Ice Hunter said again, then, turning to Big
Teeth, asked in the First Men language, "Where was your
wife? Why should Raven kill her?"

"I do not know why he killed her," Big Teeth answered,
"but she is dead. I found her this morning with a spear
through her back. This spear."

"You were hunting here or trading?" Ice Hunter asked.

"My woman was stolen and sold as slave. I have been
looking for her. She was named Asxahmaagikug."

"Asxahmaagikug is Chin Hairs' slave. If someone killed
her, perhaps it was Chin Hairs."

"Is this Chin Hairs' spear?" Big Teeth asked. "I came to
this village, asked the men who were at the ikyak racks whose
spear this was and which lodge he lived in. They told me it
belonged to a shaman named Raven. They told me this was
Raven's lodge. Did they lie?"

"It is his spear," said Ice Hunter.

"I did not kill the woman," Raven said, and his anger at

all things in that day came together to make him shout the words. He had thrown the spear at a spirit. But who could say what a spirit would do? Perhaps it changed itself into the woman that Chin Hairs had bought. Perhaps she was someone who would bring harm to the Walrus People. If so, then the best thing had happened. Why blame him?

This First Men hunter would probably expect him to give some kind of payment, probably enough to buy himself another wife. The man was a fool if he thought Raven would use his trade goods to pay for a dead slave.

Then Ice Hunter said, "Stay here and do not kill one another. I will go get Chin Hairs."

Big Teeth gave a short nod, but did not take his eyes from Raven. The two men waited, each with weapons in his hands, each watching the other, until Ice Hunter returned with Chin Hairs.

"He says Asxahmaagikug was gone this morning," Ice Hunter said. "He says he has not seen her since last night."

"I did not kill your slave," Raven said to Chin Hairs. "I will not pay for her."

"This man says he is her husband," Ice Hunter said to Chin Hairs and pointed at Big Teeth.

"Your shaman killed my woman," Big Teeth said.

"If you did not kill her," Ice Hunter said to Raven, "why does he have your spear? Why is there blood on the spearpoint?"

"I returned last night from my trip to the River People," Raven said. "I took my ik ashore, not far from here, to pray, to sing, to ask protection for this village. There was a wolf on the beach. In the darkness I threw my spear. At a wolf. Perhaps you did not truly know your wife. Perhaps she was animal, not woman. If so, it is better that she is dead."

For a long time, Big Teeth stared at the man. Then finally he lowered Raven's spear, set it against the lodge wall. He closed his eyes and shook his head. "She was not wolf; she was woman."

"If you killed her, you owe me two seal bellies of oil," Chin Hairs said to Raven.

Raven pointed at Big Teeth. "If she was stolen from her husband, and you took her as slave," Raven said to Chin Hairs, "you owe him more than that."

Chin Hairs said something under his breath, then turned and left the lodge.

"I will give you the oil," Raven told Big Teeth.

Big Teeth opened his mouth to speak, then shook his head, turned away.

"I do not say that the woman is worth only two seal bellies of oil, but it is better than nothing," Raven said. "She has children?"

"A daughter," Big Teeth said.

"Take the oil for her."

Big Teeth waited as Raven pulled out two seal bellies of oil from his food cache. "You will take them?" Raven asked.

Big Teeth nodded.

"Tell the daughter the woman was a wolf. I had no choice."

"I will tell her," Big Teeth said.

Raven handed him the oil, and Big Teeth tucked one belly under each arm. The First Men hunter closed his eyes. When he opened them, Raven saw his tears.

"Take this," said Raven. From his own neck, he took a rope of round, hollow beads made from salmon spine bones. He slipped it over Big Teeth's head. "It was given to me by a shaman of the River People. I was there learning from him. The necklace has power."

Then Big Teeth left the lodge. Ice Hunter walked with him to the edge of the water, helped him tie the bellies of oil inside his ikyak.

"I am sorry about all things," Ice Hunter said to Big Teeth.

Big Teeth cleared his throat, leaned over to stroke his ikyak, then, looking up at Ice Hunter, he said, "There was another woman, also sold as slave. She does not belong to me, but her father once came to our village looking for her. She had two sons. Her name is Kiin."

Ice Hunter closed his eyes, rubbed one hand over his face. "I am sorry," he said. "She also is dead, and her sons. She was out in her ik. Something happened. She drowned."

"If I see her father," Big Teeth said, "I will tell him." He lifted his hand to the necklace Raven had given him.

"Raven is a shaman," Ice Hunter said. "He cares much about power. My sons say he traded his wife Lemming Tail and her son Mouse to the River People shaman so the man would teach him. The necklace is worth more than it looks.''

Big Teeth did not answer. He pushed his ikyak into the water and settled himself inside, then paddled away. He went back to where he had left Blue Shell's body, to the grave of stones. ''The boy is gone,'' he whispered to her. ''Ice Hunter says he is dead.''

For a long time Big Teeth sat beside the grave, but finally he walked to his ikyak. Then he turned, took off the necklace Raven had given him, and carried it back to the grave. He dropped it among the stones that covered his wife's body.

He was in his ikyak, almost to the mouth of the bay, when the wind spoke—one word, Blue Shell's last word, ''River.''

EIGHTY-NINE

THE RIVER PEOPLE

The Kuskokwim River, Alaska

''YOU DO NOT CARVE, DO YOU?'' DYENEN ASKED the woman.

She smiled and lifted her apron, spread her legs, and held her arms out to him.

''I am an old man. You think you can make me forget by luring me into sleeping robes? I have four other wives who please me more than you do.''

The woman thrust out her lower lip. ''I carve,'' she said and with a wide sweep of her hand indicated the pieces of wood and ivory that were lined along one wall of the lodge. ''Look, animals,'' she said. ''Wolves and seals and sea lions. Two walruses and four birds.''

''You did not carve them,'' Dyenen answered and left the lodge.

He walked the paths of his village. In the tall lodge, the one owned by Two Hands' woman, there had been death: a new girl baby and a three-summers boy. The infant had had her breath stolen in the night; the boy had died from choking on meat.

Two Hands did not blame Dyenen. Both children were dead when brought to the shaman. What could he have done?

In the next lodge, an old man had died. Once he had been a great hunter. He had been strong even in old age, but a sudden flying pain in his shoulder had weakened him, and in six, seven days he had died. Dyenen's chants could not hold death away.

In a lodge at the edge of the village a young mother had died. No one knew why. She was repairing a fish trap in the river, then she was dead. Her sister had died also, only three days later, a pain in her side growing so strong that she could not bear to stay in the world of the sun. Her husband said he had heard her dead sister calling her in the night.

Dyenen could not remember so many unexplainable deaths in such a short time. What good was a shaman if he could not protect his people? No one was starving, no one was breaking taboos, yet people were dying. And what had changed in the village; what new thing had come that might cause that dying? Nothing except the woman Kiin.

A small voice, like one of the voices Dyenen kept in his throat, came into his mind. It spoke from the far corner of his thoughts in the thin voice of a child. "Raven lied. The woman he gave you is not Kiin. The children he gave you are not Kiin's children. You traded the safety of this village for the hope of a son. For yourself. Your own selfishness. You have had all things in life—good wives, a strong village, a good lodge, enough food, beautiful daughters, the respect of men in your own village and in villages far from the river. You have had all things except a son. Yet you could not be happy with what you had."

Dyenen, walking between the lodges, answered the voice in anger: "Is it wrong for a man to want a son? A son hunts. He brings meat for the village and children are fed. Is a man terrible because he longs for a son? Besides, I have powers. I have learned much. I need someone to teach so the knowledge I have gathered will not be forgotten."

"You have taught someone already," the voice said, and it

spoke in the Walrus language, in the harsh and strange sounds of that tongue.

"He learned little. He did not understand what was important," Dyenen said.

"Then you did not choose wisely."

"How can a man know what is in the heart of another man?"

"Your son would be different?"

"He would have my blood."

Then the voice was silent. But Dyenen's anger grew until his chest ached with the fullness of it. He went back to the lodge, found his new wife there feeding one of the babies. The ivory bird was lying beside her, no closer to being finished than it had been the day before.

A man sees what he wants to see, Dyenen told himself.

"Do not lie to me," Dyenen said. "I have ways of knowing the truth. You have heard me speak to spirits. You have seen them move this lodge. You have heard their voices. If you do not tell me the truth, I will call all the spirits here tonight. They will stay with you. I cannot say what they will do to you while I am gone."

The woman's face blanched, and she held her hands out to him like a child asking to be held.

"Who are you?" Dyenen asked.

"I am Kiin," she said, but her voice was small.

"Who are you?" Dyenen asked again.

"Kiin."

"You lie!"

"I am Kiin!"

"No! Take your babies and leave our village. Go back to Saghani."

"I do not know the way," the woman said. She wrapped her arms around the boy in her lap.

"You cannot stay unless you tell me who you are," Dyenen said.

Finally the woman said, "Kiin is dead. When Raven promised her to you, he did not know she was dead. I was his other wife." She lifted her chin, set her lips into a hard, thin line, then said, "I was his first wife—more important than Kiin—so he gave me instead."

"And these boys, are either of these her sons?" Dyenen asked. He pointed at Mouse and Shuku.

For a long moment, the woman looked at the boys, Mouse nursing at her breast, the older, stronger Shuku standing, taking quick steps from one side of the lodge to the other. "One of her sons is dead," she said. "I told you that before. The other boy Raven brought you." She lifted her chin toward Shuku. "He is my son. This," she said and lifted Mouse from her breast, "is Kiin's son. He is the one who should be trained as shaman. He carries his mother's powers." She fingered the ivory ikyak carving that was sewn on the baby's parka. "See? His amulet is one of his mother's carvings."

"Mouse looks like you," said Dyenen. "He looks as if he is your son."

"Kiin was my younger sister," the woman said. "I look like her; she looked like me."

It is possible, Dyenen thought. Men often marry sisters. Besides, the boys were his now. They had found a place inside his heart. He did not want to give them up, and the woman seemed to be a good mother to them.

Dyenen thought about his village, about the lies Raven had told him. The woman was not Kiin, and yet they had called her Kiin, and so had misused the power of that name. They had insulted a woman who was a gifted carver, had called the anger of her spirits—the spirit of her soul, the spirit of her name. It was no wonder people had died.

If he fasted and prayed, if he told the dead Kiin he would honor her with chants and songs, he would honor her son and her sister, in that way he might be able to lift the curse from his village and still keep the two boys.

"What do they call you?" he asked the woman.

"I am Lemming Tail," she answered.

"Lemming Tail," Dyenen said. "I will keep you as wife, and I will keep your sons."

NINETY

THE WHALE HUNTERS

The Alaska Peninsula

KUKUTUX WATCHED AS THE IKYAN TURNED TO-
ward shore. "The men go in," she told the other women.
Suddenly the iks were full of shuffling as women retied packs,
pulled up fishlines.

The women paddled until they came to the inlet where the
ikyan had turned, then moved their iks into shallow water. When
they came to the gravel beach where the men had landed, the
women paddled ashore, then carried water bladders and sealskins of dried fish up to the campsite the men had chosen.

Kukutux picked up the roll of sealskins she used to make a
shelter for Waxtal and herself. As she walked to Waxtal's ikyak,
she noticed tracks in the gravel, paths through the ryegrass.

She hurried to Waxtal's side. "There are people here," she
said, leaning close to her husband as he bent over the hull of
his ikyak.

"Get me sinew and awl," Waxtal told her as though she
had not spoken.

"There are people here, other people," Kukutux said again,
this time more loudly. "Is this the Ugyuun beach?"

"I told you I need sinew and awl," Waxtal said again,
raising his voice. He laid his hand over a thin cut in the ikyak
cover. The cut did not penetrate the sea lion hide, but it was
long, and might split if the ikyak bumped against rocks or
came into heavy seas.

Kukutux shook her head in irritation but went back for her
supply pack. She found awl and sinew, then returned to Waxtal.

Walking with head down, she nearly ran into Dying Seal.

404

"Kukutux!" he said, his voice holding both surprise and laughter.

Kukutux did not think of politeness, of apologies, but instead looked at Dying Seal and said, "There are people here. Other people." She pointed at the paths in the grass and the footprints in the sand.

"We are near a village," said Dying Seal. "Waxtal calls them Ugyuun. He says they are First Men."

"Then we have eight, ten days until we reach the Walrus village?" she asked.

Dying Seal shrugged. "Ask Waxtal."

Kukutux opened her mouth to ask another question, but Waxtal called to her, his voice angry, so she turned away from Dying Seal and went to her husband, handing him awl and sinew as he berated her. His words ran like rain over her head.

As if they were rain, Kukutux ignored them.

She is not a worthless woman, Waxtal thought as he looked at the shelter his wife had erected. It was good, watertight and with room enough for a man to stretch out full-length to sleep. But in many ways Kukutux angered him. The one time he had hit her, she had hit him back, hard. Since then he had let his anger out only in words. Sometimes words were not enough.

Waxtal was standing with Hard Rock and Dying Seal. The two men were discussing whale hunting. Waxtal curled his lip. What was whale hunting compared to ruling spirits? What was whale hunting compared to carving? Who, in their children's children's children's time, would remember the names of Hard Rock or Dying Seal? But they would look at Waxtal's tusks and remember him.

"You know these people?" Hard Rock asked, turning back to Waxtal.

"The Ugyuun?" Waxtal asked. "I have traded with them before," he said.

Hard Rock grunted, a sound that always irritated Waxtal. The man was stingy with words, as though his thoughts were too important to share with others. Hard Rock could blame Samiq for the curse on the Whale Hunter village, but as alananasika Hard Rock was responsible for what happened to his people. Perhaps he did not spend enough time fasting, enough

time apart from his wives. Perhaps the whales sensed his im-
purity and would not give themselves to Whale Hunter harpoons.

Waxtal pointed to the path that led to the Ugyuun village.
He stepped aside to allow Hard Rock and Dying Seal to lead,
but when the low mounds of the Ugyuun ulas came into view,
Hard Rock slowed his steps.

"You go first," he said to Waxtal.

Even Hard Rock sees me as leader, Waxtal thought. What
is alananasika compared to shaman?

Dying Seal pointed at the shabby ikyak racks, and Waxtal
turned his head to say, "They are a lazy people and do not
have much, but some of their women are beautiful."

Seeing three Ugyuun men behind the racks, another two
sitting atop a ulaq roof, all doing nothing, Waxtal nodded his
head, as if in agreement with his own thoughts. An old ulaq
had been left to rot, good rafters with bad, the roof and one
wall caved in. The ikyak racks were falling down, propped up
with sticks and rocks.

Waxtal called to the Ugyuun men, called and greeted them
with open hands. "We are from the Whale Hunter people. We
journey to trade with the Walrus tribe, but we need fresh meat.
Would you be willing to trade sea urchins for dried fish? Bird
meat for sealskins?"

The two men on the ulaq slid from the roof and joined those
on the beach. One man carried a bird spear in his hand. The
others kept their hands tucked up their sleeves.

The hair in Waxtal's armpits prickled.

"You said you knew them," Hard Rock whispered.

Dying Seal stepped forward, held his hands out, repeated
Waxtal's greeting.

The tallest of the Ugyuun men also held out his hands, and
the other Ugyuun men followed, one by one.

Waxtal took a long breath, then stepped forward, ahead of Dying Seal. "We come not as traders but to trade, and to ask if we
may spend the night on the beach there." He turned and pointed.

"You are welcome to stay, but we have little to trade," said
the tallest Ugyuun.

"Water?" asked Hard Rock.

"Yes, we have water."

"Sinew?" asked Dying Seal.

"Some. What do you offer in exchange?"

"Oil," Waxtal said and ignored the look of anger on Hard Rock's face. They had enough oil to get to the Walrus village. What did Waxtal care about oil beyond that? He would not return to the Whale Hunters' island with the rest of them. He and Kukutux would stay—and that would be two fewer people for Hard Rock to feed.

Perhaps if the Whale Hunters did not have enough oil for the return journey, they would choose to be part of Waxtal's village, giving him the power of shaman over more people. Or perhaps they would leave some of the children. He would be willing to take She Cries' stepdaughter as second wife. Most shamans had at least two wives. If they killed Samiq, the Whale Hunters would owe him a wife anyway, a wife and much more. And if they wanted something in exchange, he would give them Blue Shell. He almost smiled. An old woman for a young one.

"We will trade some of our oil," Hard Rock said. "And dried fish. Sealskins, a few. Whalebone harpoon heads and beads."

The man who seemed to be leader of the Ugyuun raised his eyebrows and looked quickly at the men beside him. Several of them nodded.

"We will go back and get what we have for trade," said Hard Rock. He and Dying Seal turned, but Waxtal, lifting his chin to point at the Ugyuun village, said, "I will go with them."

Waxtal knew that Hard Rock would not bring much oil, but he did not want to go back with them. Why be loaded with sealskins and dried fish? Why carry baskets and water bladders? Let Hard Rock and Dying Seal carry what must be carried. Waxtal was the trader. He would do what he was good at doing, and the Whale Hunters would have more than if he had let Hard Rock or Dying Seal speak.

He felt the anger in Hard Rock's stare, but turned his back on the man and followed the Ugyuun.

Inside one of the Ugyuun ulas, the men squatted on their haunches near an oil lamp. From the dim edges of the room, a woman came, a beautiful young woman, her suk one that Chagak herself might have made, so intricate was the stitching, so beautiful the feathers.

As Waxtal's eyes adjusted to the light, he studied the inside

of the ulaq. It was neat and well-ordered, something that surprised him. He had been once or twice in other Ugyuun ulas.
All things were usually jumbled together, and the smell of
rotting floor heather and the stink of old fish had been as heavy
as smoke. But this ulaq smelled of fresh heather, of ryegrass
newly woven, of meat cooking. The oil lamp wicks were
trimmed, and even from across the width of the ulaq, he could
see that the curtain over the food cache bulged with what was
inside.

"I am Eagle. This is my wife, Small Plant Woman," an
Ugyuun man said. "Welcome to my ulaq."

Waxtal nodded, then reached for a stick of dried meat from
a bowl the Ugyuun woman was holding before him. "Your
lodge is good," Waxtal said. "You have had a good summer
for hunting."

"It has been a good summer," the man said and smiled at
his wife. She placed one hand over her belly, and Waxtal
wondered if she carried a child. He lifted his eyes to the shoulder of her suk, to a piece of ivory sewn there. As soon as he
saw it, his stomach tightened and his mouth grew dry. The
carving was a murre, wings spread.

It was one of Kiin's. Who would not recognize her work?
Each carving was so . . . so . . . what could a man say? Complete. As though the knife knew what was necessary, what
lines, what curves—and then stopped there.

"So you will trade for water and fresh meat?" Eagle asked.

"Yes," said Waxtal. "We will trade for what we need and
also for other things." He lifted his hand to point at the carving. "That," he said. "What will you take for that?"

The woman cupped her hand over the carving, looked with
worried eyes at her husband.

"It is not for trade," Eagle said.

Waxtal cocked his head to one side, took another piece of
meat. "Then perhaps you will tell me where you got it. Perhaps I could find the carver and get one like it."

The Ugyuun man smiled, but said nothing.

"One belly of oil," Waxtal said.

"Seal belly or sea lion?"

"Sea lion."

The man raised his eyebrows at his wife, and for a few
moments their eyes held, as though they spoke without words.

Finally she said, "He is Whale Hunter, not Walrus."

Her husband nodded. "The carver is a woman," Eagle said. "She is of the First Men. She lives with her husband and son on the Traders' Beach, only two days from here."

"But," said the woman, "if you go to the Walrus People, do not tell them about her. She has enemies there."

"Enemies?" Waxtal asked, but the worried look came again into the woman's eyes, and she pressed her lips together and would say no more.

The knowledge was like sand against Waxtal's skin. Kiin—what father had a worse daughter? Already, she had left Raven and gone back to Samiq. How could he, Waxtal, now ask for Raven's help? But then a smile came slowly to Waxtal's face.

"The Walrus People do not know where she is?" he asked.

The Ugyuun woman shook her head.

"Do not worry," Waxtal said. "I will never tell them."

NINETY-ONE

THE FIRST MEN

Herendeen Bay, the Alaska Peninsula

KIIN SAW BIG TEETH WHEN HE WAS STILL OUT ON the bay. She lifted one hand, and he did also, but when he beached his ikyak, he pulled the craft ashore with his back turned toward her, and then found something in the hatch coaming to keep his hands and eyes busy.

Kiin waited for him to turn, but finally could wait no longer. She came to the man, hesitated, then laid one hand softly against his back.

"My mother?" she asked.

For a time it seemed as though he had not heard her, did not know she was standing beside him, but then he lifted his head and looked at her, and Kiin saw that his cheeks were wet with tears. "She is dead," he said, and his voice carried the sound of his crying.

Kiin had no words, nothing, and it suddenly seemed as though her chest were cold and hollow. "How can I live without my mother?" a little child-voice asked from within. "Who will take care of me?"

She began a mourning song, then realized she was singing one of her mother's lullabies instead.

"I am sorry. I am sorry," Big Teeth said over her singing. "If I had been there sooner, I might have saved her."

"And my son?" Kiin asked, and the question was so large, so heavy, that she felt she could not even breathe.

"He is with the River People. Raven traded him."

The world darkened, grew small, but then Kiin's spirit voice whispered quiet words, comforting her as a mother comforts a child. "He is not dead. You will find him. Samiq will find him. Mourn your mother, but do not mourn your son." Then the world came back—the rush and roar of the waves, the strength and cold of the wind, the sound of Big Teeth's voice, broken in sorrow.

"What happened to my mother?" Kiin whispered, and then, though she did not know how, Samiq was with her, and Three Fish, Chagak and Kayugh, and Crooked Nose, her strong arms holding Big Teeth close to her even as he spoke.

"The man Raven killed her," he said.

Anger filled Kiin's chest so that she could do nothing but scream, but finally her screams became words and she shouted, "Why, why, why?"

"She had left the village—to meet me," Big Teeth said. "She was hiding in the grass on a beach where Raven came to pray. He thought she was a wolf."

"A wolf?" Kiin said, and her voice rose up into something that was almost a laugh. Samiq reached for her, tucked her head against his shoulder.

"I buried her in the manner of Whale Hunters, on that beach, with prayers."

"I must go to her," Kiin said, and fought to break from Samiq's arms. "I must go." But Samiq would not release her.

"Your mother is here," Samiq said. "Be still and wait. She is here. Why go back to the Walrus People? She would not stay there. She followed Big Teeth's ikyak back to us. Be still and you will feel her spirit with us.''

So Kiin no longer fought, but let her husband take her back to the ulaq, to Takha, who hugged her and patted her cheeks with his baby hands until he had coaxed a smile.

''I go now,'' Samiq said. ''If you want to come, then come. If not, stay.''

''There is ice forming in the bay,'' Kayugh said. He raised one hand to the sky. ''Snow maybe.''

''I cannot wait until spring,'' Samiq said. ''I do not know what kind of people have him. If they run out of food, they may let him starve—first before any of their own children.''

''You know that any man who takes a child as his own, though his wife did not bear it, treats that child as he treats his other children,'' Kayugh answered.

''That is the way of the First Men. The River People may be different.''

''You do not even know what the baby looks like,'' Kayugh said. He bent to pull a handful of grass from the ground and held up the blades one by one, let the wind carry each from his fingers.

''I will ask for the child traded by Raven of the Walrus People. I will offer everything I have. He is my son. I cannot let him be raised by River People who do not speak the sacred words of the First Men language, who do not know how to hunt seal or the whale, who cannot build ikyan.''

Kayugh looked away, out toward the bay. The sky was gray, and as the sun neared the western horizon, all things seemed dark.

''Tomorrow?'' Kayugh asked.

''The tide is best now,'' Samiq answered.

Kayugh nodded. ''I will get food. You get whatever you need to trade for the child.''

Samiq started up the beach toward his ulaq.

''You should have a carrying strap,'' Kayugh called after him. ''Something to hold the child under your parka on our journey back.''

His father's words seemed to put strength into Samiq's legs, and he went more quickly.

The ulaq was full of the mourning songs of women. Crooked Nose and Kiin were at the center of the group, both women with eyes closed, faces wet with tears. Samiq beckoned to Three Fish, and the woman came to him, listened as he whispered what he would do. Her eyes were round in fear, and she opened her mouth, wide and square so that Samiq knew she would soon begin to wail, but he clamped his hand over her face, spoke to her in the stern way of father to child.

"Do not cry. I will be back, with Shuku. Do not tell Kiin until you have to. Fifteen, twenty days I will return. Now get what I need—oil, a small basket of Kiin's carvings, a carrying strap for Shuku, dried meat and fish, my hunter's lamp."

He did not wait for her, but went into his sleeping place, took his harpoons and several knives, an extra parka, and the pack of supplies he always carried when he went hunting.

He stopped to press his cheek to Three Fish's face, to speak for a moment to Small Knife, to hold Takha and Many Whales. He lifted the small ivory ikyak Takha wore at his neck, the half ikyak like the one Shuku also wore, and, glancing at Kiin, took the necklace. "I will bring it back," he whispered to Takha, then looked once more at Kiin. Her eyes were closed, her mouth moving with the words of mourning. Her pain was a knife in his heart.

Samiq left the ulaq and went to the beach, waited for his father. Then the two left together, paddled out into the gray of the coming night.

NINETY-TWO

THE WALRUS HUNTERS

Chagvan Bay, Alaska

WAXTAL OPENED HIS MOUTH AND LAUGHED. THE story was an old one, and he had heard it before, but why tell

Raven that? Let the man have joy in small things.

Raven narrowed his eyes and stared at him. "I know you," he said. "You have been here before—to trade." Raven spoke in the Walrus tongue, and Waxtal was glad Hard Rock, who sat with them in Raven's lodge, did not understand.

Five men were gathered, Raven and Waxtal sitting on the bed platform, the others—two Walrus hunters and Hard Rock—standing. There seemed to be no woman in the lodge, and Raven had offered no food.

"I have traded here and in other Walrus villages," Waxtal said.

Raven sat quietly for a moment, nodding his head, watching Waxtal so that Waxtal had to force himself to sit still, to wait. Finally the man smiled and said, "So, you have come to trade, you and these Whale Hunters. What do they have that is worth so much?"

"Harpoon heads and spearpoints," Waxtal said. "Some that are new, others that have been used to kill whales. They hold much power." He noticed that Raven and the two men with him, a young man with a scar that ran from the corner of one eye to his chin, and an older man, large and tall, leaned forward. The younger man reached out one hand for the basket that held the points, but Waxtal drew the basket back, settled it between his legs.

"We have women," Waxtal also said. He looked around the lodge, let his eyes linger on the food rotting on the floor, on the legging skins jumbled in a heap on the bed platform, and on the oil lamp, the wick sending up curls of black smoke.

"I am in mourning," Raven said, and at his words Waxtal felt the sudden lifting of his heart, the beginning of joy.

"For your wife," Waxtal said. He thought Raven would show surprise, but the man only pointed at the basket of harpoon heads.

Waxtal handed him the basket and waited as Raven looked at each, laying them on a fur seal skin spread out beside them.

"So is it your wife you mourn?" Waxtal asked.

"Yes," Raven said but did not look up.

"We have women. Good Whale Hunter women. They make strong sons."

"It is too soon," Raven said, "but perhaps you will allow

me one for tonight. There is a chance I may decide to take her as wife.''

''There is another woman I know about,'' Waxtal said, his words deliberately slow. ''You might like her. She is not with us, but I know where she is.''

Raven made no sign that he heard Waxtal's words, but Waxtal said, ''She is beautiful, and there is one strange thing about her. She carves. She has spirit powers, some men say.'' He tossed a seal carving into the basket of harpoon heads. The carving was one of Kiin's—a tiny wooden seal that Waxtal had bought in trade from an Ugyuun man.

Raven clasped the carving in his hand, looked up at Waxtal, his eyes so hard and bright they were like knives piercing Waxtal's skin.

''Where did you get this?''

''Her name is Kiin,'' Waxtal said.

''Where did you get this?''

''You know her?''

Raven jumped from the bed platform, spilling the harpoon heads to the floor. He gripped the front of Waxtal's suk, pulled Waxtal to his feet, and began to speak in the Walrus tongue, his words too quick for Waxtal to understand.

Waxtal used both hands to shove the man away, then backed from him to stand beside Hard Rock. Hard Rock stood with a knife in his hand, blade out, but Waxtal grasped Hard Rock's wrist. ''He is not angry with me,'' Waxtal said. ''I have just told him what Samiq did to me. He is angry with Samiq.''

Waxtal released Hard Rock's hand and said to Raven in the Walrus tongue, ''I know where she is. I know and I will tell you how to get her. But I am a trader. I give nothing without receiving something in return.''

''What do you want?'' Raven asked.

''You see that I did not come here alone,'' said Waxtal. ''I have brought many men with me.'' He laid his hand on Hard Rock's shoulder. ''They are Whale Hunters. They have come to seek revenge against the man who cursed their island.'' He paused so Raven would understand the importance of his next words. ''He is the same man who stole Kiin.''

Raven's eyes narrowed.

"The trade is this," Waxtal said. "I will help you if you help us."

Raven shook his head, laughed. "And you are happy with that?" he asked. "You want nothing for yourself?"

"I have all I need."

"No man is content with what he has," Raven answered. "There is always something a man wants that is just beyond his grasp." Raven laughed. "Otherwise there would be no traders."

"You are too wise," Waxtal said.

"And so?"

"And so, you are right. There is something I want."

"And this something, is it here at my village?"

Waxtal squatted on his haunches, giving Raven the advantage of standing, looking down at him. "For years I have fasted and prayed and called on the spirits," Waxtal said. "For years I have sought to strengthen my people by teaching them to respect the spirit world. I am close to becoming a shaman."

"You know I am shaman of this village?" Raven asked.

"Who does not know?" Waxtal answered, looking up at the man.

"You ask to know the secrets of my shaman powers?"

"Yes."

Raven threw back his head and laughed. Waxtal felt the heat of that laughter burn red across his face. Almost, he left Raven's lodge. But then Raven strode to the far wall of the lodge. He took down the skin of an animal Waxtal did not know. He threw it to Waxtal. The skin was whole and heavy, plump with packs of something stored inside.

"That is a medicine skin. It is the source of my power," Raven said. "A River People shaman gave it to me. When you pray, hold it up so the spirits will know you honor them."

"You give it too easily," Waxtal said. "Why should I believe what you say?"

"Try it. If it gives you power, then you will know I tell the truth. Tonight in this lodge I will let you stay alone. Pray. If nothing happens, then do not tell me about the woman. If it does, it will be a fair trade."

"And your hunters will help us fight this man who has stolen your woman?"

"Yes, they will do what I ask," Raven said.

"Then it is a trade," Waxtal said and smoothed his hands over the thick fur of the medicine skin.

They made other trades—oil for harpoon heads, walrus hides for whalebone, sealskins for fur seal pelts. Then Raven did as he had promised. He left Waxtal alone in the lodge. Raven stayed on Grass Ears' side of the lodge, asking Grass Ears and his wives to let him have the whole lodge for only this night. Grass Ears, clutching the oil belly Raven had given him in return, left, and Raven settled himself to wait, eating from the food in Grass Ears' cache until he was too full to eat more. Then sitting down, his legs beneath him, his hands clasped, he said a short prayer to call spirits that might help him.

When he heard Waxtal's thin voice rise in a chant, Raven lifted his own voice to call from the peak of the lodge, to call in a small high voice something in the River People language. Then he called in another voice from the dividing curtain, something in the Walrus tongue.

Waxtal's chants stopped, and soon he was babbling, a mixture of laughter and boastings. Now and again through the night, Raven made the voices come from the lodge, and each time he heard Waxtal respond with fervent chants, Raven hid his laughter behind cupped hands.

NINETY-THREE

THE RIVER PEOPLE

The Kuskokwim River, Alaska

THEY WERE NOT TRADERS. WHY WOULD TRADERS brave snow and new ice? They had ikyan, not iks, and they carried themselves like hunters. They did not speak the River language.

The older man was tall, and if you did not look at his parka, sewn in the manner of the Walrus People, or his boots, made like the seal flipper boots of the First Men, you would think he was Caribou, with his long legs, his light skin, the sharp bones of his face.

The younger man was of a people Dyenen did not know. He was wide-shouldered, short-legged, a man whose body spoke of strength even in the way he walked. He, too, wore strange clothes, half Walrus, half First Men.

The goods they brought to trade were of fine quality, but there was not much, though the young one had a knife—a blade of black obsidian and a handle wrapped with something that looked like hair. That, Dyenen thought, I would give much oil to have.

It would be good if they wanted dogs, Dyenen thought. He had many dogs, trained to carry a pack, but though some Walrus People had dogs, most seemed to think their ikyan were enough.

"Walrus?" Dyenen asked. "Speak Walrus?"

The older man threw up his hands, spoke to the younger.

Dyenen used his hands to make the sign known among traders for the Walrus tribe. If these two men wore Walrus clothing, they must speak the language. But the men made no reply.

"Go get Lemming Tail," he said to his third wife, the woman hovering near, offering meat, oil, dried berries to the men as they squatted on their haunches inside Dyenen's lodge.

The woman dipped her head in acknowledgment, put the bowls of food where the men could reach them, and left the lodge.

When she returned, Lemming Tail was with her, carrying two babies. The traders looked at her, and the younger man stretched one hand out toward the children. Dyenen shook his head. What hunter noticed babies?

"Lemming Tail," Dyenen said to his wife, "these men, see whether your language is their language."

The woman sat down, settled the babies in her lap, and spoke to the two. Dyenen listened to her words. He would pretend with them as he had done with Saghani. A man could learn much more by listening than by speaking.

The older man said a few words, enough for Dyenen to

understand that he came from the place called Traders' Beach,
that he was of the First Men and new to trading. The young
man with him was his son. Though the two did not look alike,
Dyenen saw a resemblance in the way each man used his
hands, the way each held his head, though the younger man
kept his right hand hidden, drawn up into the sleeve of his
parka. The one time Dyenen had opportunity to see the hand,
he studied it carefully, saw the long scar across the top of the
wrist, the clawed curl of the fingers. The scar was clear and
thin, as though the cut had been made with a knife, and Dyenen felt the sudden chill of fear. Was the man a fighter?
Someone who challenged men?

Then the two men spoke together in a language that Dyenen
thought was the First Men tongue. He listened, and though he
did not understand the words, he recognized the feelings under
them—anger, sorrow. Finally the younger man looked at Dyenen, met Dyenen's eyes with his eyes.

"Tell him to look well, look long," the father told Lemming Tail. "Tell him to look also at me and see that we come
with no deceit. We have come to ask for something that your
people may not want to give. But it is ours, stolen from us."

Dyenen listened to the man, and then listened again as Lemming Tail used River words—her knowledge of that language
not perfect, but improving each day—to tell him what had
been said.

"You speak well, Lemming Tail," Dyenen said to her.

She laughed. "I like to talk, and your women here do not
know Walrus. But you should speak to these traders yourself.
You speak Walrus."

"Not as well as you," he answered.

She cocked her head at him, made a slow smile. "You do
not want them to know you understand," she said.

The woman was smart. In many ways it would be easier if
she were not—but if she gave him a son, he would be glad
for that intelligence. Many times he had seen stupid women
have stupid sons.

"I think they are First Men," Dyenen said. "Speak to them
in the First Men tongue. Raven said you and your sister Kiin
were First Men."

"Raven lied," Lemming Tail said softly. "I am Walrus."

Dyenen looked at her with narrowed eyes, but Lemming

Tail turned to the traders, lifted her hands in invitation for their questions.

"You are not River," the older of the two said.

"I am Walrus," Lemming Tail answered. Mouse reached up, clasped a handful of his mother's hair.

"What is your name?"

Lemming Tail looked at Dyenen. "Do I tell them my name?" she asked. She pulled her hair from Mouse's grasp.

"Tell them you are Utsula' C'ezghot. It is a good name for you," he said.

"I do not lie," Lemming Tail said. "Raven lies," and she shook her head against the name Dyenen had given her. Then she turned to the men and said, "I am Lemming Tail."

"Do you know a woman of the First Men called Kiin?" the older trader asked.

The woman's forehead crinkled, and she clenched her hands over the babies in her lap.

Dyenen leaned forward onto the balls of his feet. "Kiin?" Dyenen asked.

"Yes."

"Ask them how they know her."

"She is dead," Lemming Tail answered. "I cannot say her name."

"You have said it before. Ask."

Lemming Tail thrust out her lip at Dyenen, but with eyes lowered told the two men, "The woman you ask about is dead."

The father lifted his head, looked for a moment at his son, and said, "I know she is dead."

"Then why do you ask for her?"

"He was her husband," the man said, pointing with his chin at his son.

She looked at Dyenen. "They lie," she said in the River language.

"Why do you say that?" Dyenen asked her.

"She was my sister. Before Raven took her as wife, he killed her first husband in a knife fight."

"This one has been wounded with a knife."

"How do you know?"

"Look at his right hand."

The woman watched the man for a time. "He keeps it hidden," she finally hissed at Dyenen. "You think I would not know my own sister's husband?"

"It does not matter," Dyenen said. "Ask him why he has come."

"My husband asks why you are here," Lemming Tail said.

"To claim Kiin's son." The trader again pointed his chin at the young man beside him. "And his son—Shuku."

Lemming Tail gasped. "The woman's son is also dead," she said, her words quick and falling over one another.

"Ask him why he thinks we have Kiin's son," Dyenen said, but Lemming Tail did not seem to hear him. She babbled to herself in the Walrus tongue, words that made no sense. "Ask him!"

"You ask him!" Lemming Tail screeched back. "I will say something wrong." Mouse reached up with both hands and grabbed his mother's hair, held tight. Shuku began to cry.

Then Dyenen spoke, his voice loud so he could be heard above Shuku's crying. "These are River children," he said, speaking in the Walrus language. He turned his head toward Shuku and Mouse. "We do not have Kiin's son."

For a long time Kayugh studied the old man. For a long time he held the old man's stare without blinking. Finally, the old one raised his voice above the crying and said, "I am called Dyenen."

Lemming Tail moved to stand behind Dyenen. She jiggled the babies in her arms until they stopped crying, then Kayugh said, "I am Kayugh of the First Men. This is my son Samiq."

Kayugh turned to Samiq, said to him in the First Men language, "The old one is named Dyenen. He claims they do not have your son."

"Raven brought my son here," Samiq said, and Kayugh translated the words slowly in Walrus to the old man.

"Why, if Kiin was Samiq's wife, did Raven have her and her son?" the old man asked.

Kayugh grasped Samiq's right wrist and held the hand up so the old man could see the scar. "Raven did this, then stole Kiin and her two sons. When Kiin and one son died, he decided to trade her other son. He also traded the woman who caused Kiin's death—Lemming Tail."

"Lemming Tail claims to be Kiin's sister," the old man said.

Kayugh shook his head. "No, she is not."

The old man turned to Lemming Tail, his eyes angry. "This is true?" he asked. "You killed Kiin?"

Lemming Tail said, "I did not kill her. I only sent her away."

"And she died," Dyenen said.

Lemming Tail did not answer.

"Which child is your son?" Dyenen asked Samiq.

Kayugh said, "The one who wears an amulet like this." He held out his hand, and Samiq reached over, placed the ivory ikyak in Kayugh's open palm.

Dyenen gestured to Lemming Tail. "Turn the babies so we can see their faces," he said.

Lemming Tail shook her head, but Dyenen said, "Do it now or I will call Two Hands and Weasel. You know they stand just outside the door."

Slowly Lemming Tail turned the babies; slowly she raised her head and looked with hatred at Kayugh.

"That one," Kayugh said and pointed to the carving sewn on the smaller child's parka.

"No!" screamed Lemming Tail. "He is my son. I sewed the amulet on his parka to give him power."

"Give me the babies," Dyenen said, but Lemming Tail ran to the door of the lodge.

Then two River men were also in the lodge, blocking Lemming Tail's escape.

"Take the babies," Dyenen said to the men. "Bring them here to me, then put Lemming Tail in the women's lodge and do not let her leave."

Lemming Tail herself brought the babies to Dyenen and asked in a quiet voice to be allowed to stay.

"You have caused too much trouble already," Dyenen said, then he flicked his fingers at the River men. Lemming Tail tried to grab the babies from Dyenen's arms, but the River men dragged her away, screaming. One of the men finally put his hand over her mouth, picked her up, and carried her from the lodge.

In the silence, Samiq said, "The child without the amulet, he is Shuku."

"You are sure?" Kayugh asked. "You saw him last almost

a year ago. Babies change as they grow.''

"He is my son," Samiq answered.

For a long time Kayugh studied the child, then said to the old man, "This one."

"You are sure?" Dyenen asked.

"Yes."

"He is one of two sons born together?"

Kayugh looked into the old man's eyes. "Yes," he finally said.

"I am shaman of this village," said Dyenen. "I do not have a son. I have many daughters, but no sons. I was told this boy's father did not want him. I would not have taken him otherwise."

"I am sorry," Kayugh said.

"I will not keep your son," said Dyenen, "but I gave much for him in trade."

"All we have is yours," Kayugh said.

"No," Dyenen said. "I want no trade goods, but take the woman Lemming Tail. That is all I ask. This other child, Mouse, will be my son, but you take her."

"I have a good wife," Kayugh said.

"Then give Lemming Tail back to the Walrus."

"What does he ask?" Samiq asked his father. "I will give everything I have. I will stay here and hunt one summer with the River People and give them all I take in. I will teach them to build ikyan, to hunt whales."

"Do not offer too much," Kayugh said. "He asks only that we take the woman Lemming Tail."

"We will take her," Samiq said.

NINETY-FOUR

LEMMING TAIL STRUGGLED AGAINST THE HANDS that held her. She was not a fool. The First Men hunters thought Mouse was Kiin's son. They would take him away. Dyenen in his anger would let them.

The River hunters opened the door flap of the women's lodge and threw her inside. She fell on the floor, scraped an elbow against the stones of the cooking hearth. She stood up, straightened her parka, and turned her back on the other women in the lodge. They stared at her in rudeness.

All things had been hers. As wife to Raven she had had honor, a good lodge, the respect of the other women in the village. Then Kiin had come. Kiin and her sons. The woman had been second wife, but her carvings had made her too important. Kiin had received the gifts and honor due Lemming Tail.

Then Kiin died, and again Lemming Tail was the honored one, not as wife to Raven, but for her place as Dyenen's wife. What were Raven's powers compared to Dyenen's? Yet now Kiin reached out from the dead to again take Lemming Tail's honor and her son Mouse as well. Now because of Kiin she was Utsula' C'ezghot, a liar, and yet she had done only what her husband had forced her to do.

Lemming Tail scanned the walls of the women's lodge. There were no weapons, nothing Lemming Tail could use against the men who held her prisoner. The lodge was for women in their bleeding times, so their blood would not curse their husbands' weapons and clothing. Today there were three women here—a girl only a few moons past her first bleeding, an old woman who would not have many more summers in this lodge, and a mother nursing a small girl child. Though usually the women in the lodge spoke with much laughter and loudness, now the women were silent.

The noise of the girl child suckling made Lemming Tail's own milk begin to flow. She slipped her hands into her parka, wiped her breasts, and began to cry. Kiin. Lemming Tail remembered the first time she saw the woman. Kiin's belly had been big with her unborn sons, her face peeling from the salt of long days in a trader's ik. Even then, Lemming Tail had known that Kiin brought evil to their village. Grandmother and Aunt, they, too, had known the evil Kiin brought. But where others saw evil, Raven saw power.

Power! Lemming Tail thought. Death!

Who could doubt that Kiin's evil spirit was here with the River People? Lemming Tail crouched beside the fire, stirred the ashes with a charred stick lying on the hearth stones.

The women watched her now, but tonight they would sleep. Dyenen was an old man. She was stronger than he was. She would take Mouse, and he would not be able to stop her.

Kayugh and Samiq slept that night in the traders' lodge, with Shuku tucked between them. Samiq pulled the boy close to his side, rejoiced at the heat of the boy's small body.

Shuku had cried at first, frightened to be alone with them, but when they spoke to him in the First Men language, he seemed to grow calm, and soon he was playing small games with Samiq. Finally, when the sky was dark in the short night, the boy climbed into Samiq's lap and fell asleep, his head against Samiq's chest.

"Kiin will be glad," Kayugh said, and Samiq fell asleep with those words in his heart.

Lemming Tail waited until the other women were asleep, then, creeping on her hands and knees, made her way to the lodge door. She peered outside. The men who had guarded the lodge were gone.

The River People—what fools! Did they think she was stupid, that she would let them take her son?

She kept to the shadows between the lodges, avoided the dogs curled together in front of each lodge door. When she came to Dyenen's lodge, she stopped. Would Mouse be here, or would one of Dyenen's wives have him in another lodge? Best to check here first, she thought.

Dyenen's dogs lifted their heads, growled. Lemming Tail's heart beat hard. She did not like dogs, but she knew these, had fed them each day since coming to the River village.

She spoke to them in a quiet voice and let the female, mother to most of the others, sniff her hand. The dogs quieted and let her slip past them into the lodge.

Once inside, she dropped to her hands and knees. The lodge was dark except for the glow of red from hearth coals. She saw Dyenen, wrapped in his sleeping robes, then let her eyes follow the curve of the walls as she searched for Mouse. She listened for the small baby sounds that he sometimes made in his sleep.

In the quietness Dyenen said, "You think I would keep the babies here with me?"

The voice coming so suddenly made Lemming Tail jump, and she scooted back toward the door.

"You will not find them," Dyenen said. "You do not know who has them."

Lemming Tail took a long breath. "Why let those First Men take Mouse?" she asked. "I have been a good wife to you. I will give you more sons. Perhaps I already carry your son in my belly."

"I have had enough of your lies," Dyenen said. "Your lies have cursed this village and brought death to my people."

Lemming Tail sat back on her heels. She could see Dyenen like a shadow in his bedding of furs. He rose up on one elbow.

"Then tell me where Mouse is and I will leave," she said to him.

"You cannot leave," Dyenen said. "I have given you to the traders. You and Shuku."

Fear grew large in Lemming Tail's chest. He had given her to the traders! "Let them take Shuku," she said, "but let me stay here with you and Mouse. I have promised to give you a son. You must allow me to keep that promise."

"You promised me a son," Dyenen said. "I have chosen Mouse."

"He does not belong to you," Lemming Tail said. "He does not even belong to Raven, though Raven does not know that. Give him to me, and I will take him back to his true father."

"He is mine," said Dyenen. "Leave my lodge. Leave my village. I will not try to stop you, but you cannot have Mouse."

He turned his back to her.

Lemming Tail took long slow breaths and searched the lodge walls for some weapon she could use against the man, something to make him tell her where Mouse was. But all the weapons were behind Dyenen's sleeping place. Lemming Tail's eyes filled with tears of anger, and the hearth coals blurred into balls of red and orange. Gritting her teeth, she pulled a caribou skin from the floor, twisted it into a tight roll, then held the end in the coals until it caught fire. She walked slowly to Dyenen's bed, the twisted skin flaming before her.

The old man sat up, gasped.

"Tell me where Mouse is!" Lemming Tail shouted. She lowered the flame until it was only a handbreadth above his head.

Dyenen moved his eyes to look up at the flame. "In the tall lodge at the far edge of the village. You know the hunter. Gives Meat. His wife is Fish Watcher."

Lemming Tail hesitated, and Dyenen said, "I do not lie. He is there."

Lemming Tail meant to throw the caribou skin onto the hearth, into the circle of stones, but as she turned, Dyenen pushed her, shoving hard. She fell on the burning hide. The fire licked at her face and arms, and she rolled, flinging the skin away from herself. It fell on the bedding furs that were wrapped around Dyenen's legs. Dyenen beat at the flames with his hands.

Lemming Tail jumped to her feet, started toward the old man, then stopped. She watched for a moment, a smile forming slowly on her face, then she ran from the lodge.

She heard Dyenen scream, and she stopped, but then turned toward Fish Watcher's lodge.

Let the old man burn, she thought. He will never take Mouse away from me.

The noise came first as a part of Samiq's dreams, but then Kayugh was calling him. Samiq wrapped his son in a sleeping pelt and laid him against the wall of the lodge farthest from the entrance tunnel.

"What is it?" he asked his father and waited as Kayugh crawled outside, waited until he heard Kayugh call him.

"Should I leave the child?"

"No," Kayugh answered. "There is a fire, several of the lodges. It might spread. Bring water bladders."

Samiq turned back, gathered Shuku into his arms, pulled the carrying strap from his packs, and fastened it to hold Shuku in place on his back. Then he untied the water bladders from the lodgepoles and followed his father.

In the darkness, the flames seemed too bright for his eyes. "It is the old man's lodge," Kayugh called to him.

But Samiq was watching the other men. Some slapped at the flames with hides; others slit open water bladders and threw them at the base of the fire. Samiq did the same, but the flames seemed to gather strength and spread.

"Is Dyenen safe?" Samiq called out, but no one answered him, and Samiq realized no one understood his First Men words.

"Dyenen! Dyenen!" he cried out, until one of the women pointed at Dyenen's lodge and spoke, her words mingling with tears.

Then in the flames, Samiq saw someone move. Unfastening Shuku's carrying strap, he handed the boy to Kayugh. Samiq took a water bladder from a woman standing near, slit it with his sleeve knife, and poured the water over his head and the front of his parka. He ran through the flames, moving quickly, feeling the burn of coals and hot earth on his bare feet. He drew in breath, and it was as though the fire spread its long fingers into his chest. Finally he reached the one in the flames. It was Dyenen, his hair burned from his head, his skin black, the red of raw flesh bright where his charred skin had split.

The old man clutched an empty water bladder. The stink of his burned skin curled through the smoke into Samiq's nostrils, but he picked him up, closed his ears to Dyenen's groans as he carried him out of the flames.

Someone spread out a soft furred blanket, and Samiq laid Dyenen on it. Samiq moved his arms away carefully, but even so, the old man's skin pulled from his body, clinging to Samiq's parka. Samiq walked away and retched. When his stomach was empty and he had caught his breath, he went back to Dyenen, pushed his way past the circle of hunters who surrounded him, the women who already lifted voices in mourning cries. Kayugh was also in the circle of men, the boy Shuku clinging to him.

One of the River men spoke and pointed. In the distance Samiq heard a woman scream, once, then many times. Finally the screaming stopped, and from blackened lips Dyenen spoke to Kayugh. Kayugh answered, speaking in the Walrus language, then gestured for Samiq to come.

"Dyenen says the woman Lemming Tail started the fire," Kayugh said. "The screams you just heard were her screams. Dyenen said the River men killed her. He is sorry we will not have her for trade. He wants us to take Mouse. He says his people will kill the boy if he stays here."

"We will take him," Samiq said.

Dyenen called out, speaking in the River language, and those gathered near moved away, making room for five women. Beside the women was a girl of perhaps seven summers, and in her arms was a baby, new.

"His daughters," Kayugh said. He stood, but Dyenen reached out for him, and Kayugh leaned close, Shuku in his arms.

Dyenen spoke, his voice a whisper.

Kayugh turned to Samiq. "He says he has no sons," Kayugh said.

"Tell him he has two sons," Samiq said. "Tell him we will raise both boys as his."

Kayugh made the promise, speaking in the Walrus tongue, then Dyenen spoke to one of his daughters. She came to Kayugh, lifted her hands, and placed something over the baby's head. Samiq looked down, saw it was the cord of a shaman's amulet, blackened by fire. The girl spoke, but the words were River. Then she called to another woman. The woman brought Mouse, put the crying child into Samiq's arms, and gestured for the men to leave.

They went back to the traders' lodge, gathered their supplies, chewed meat until it was soft, and fed the children. Then with Mouse strapped to Kayugh's back, Shuku to Samiq's, they went to the river, walking in a wide circle around the mourners.

Finally they were in their ikyan, sliding over the forming ice to the center of the river, where the water was cold and clean. The wind blew the smoke from their eyes. And when they had cleared the rough waters where river joined sea, Samiq let himself reach back to pat Shuku's head, let himself rejoice in his son.

NINETY-FIVE

FOUR PEOPLE DIED THAT NIGHT. THE GREAT SHAman Dyenen. The child Cub, son of Makes Rain. The old woman Greets Dawn. And the Walrus woman Dyenen had named Utsula' C'ezghot.

Her death was in payment. Since she had come to their village, too many had died. She had set the fire that killed Dyenen. Makes Rain himself had seen her.

Now that their shaman was gone, how would the village live? Who would call the caribou when it was time for the hunt? Who would call the salmon to come into the rivers? Who knew how to speak to spirits when someone was sick?

When the four days of mourning had ended, when Dyenen's knowing spirit had left the village and was on its journey to the Above World, Stick Walking called the men to his lodge. Stick Walking was an old man, older even than Dyenen. He claimed no spirit powers, but he was known for his wisdom. What more did a man ask for in old age than that? What more than wisdom and the respect of his children and his children's children?

Stick Walking called four men to his lodge, four men, each with a special gift from the spirits—carver, storyteller, dancer, singer.

The men sat for a time without speaking. There was no woman to bring food, no hospitality of small words and laughter. Finally Stick Walking said, "We have lost our shaman. I am thinking that his power was taken by Saghani, that shaman of the Walrus. I am thinking that with his own power gone, our shaman could not protect himself against the Walrus woman."

There was a mumble of agreement, then the carver asked, "Her carvings have been destroyed? All things that held her power?"

"All things," Stick Walking said. "Even her clothes. Even her bed furs."

"But still the son of Makes Rain died," said the storyteller. "Still the old woman died."

"Who knows why they died?" the singer said. "It might not be from the power of the Walrus."

But no other man spoke to agree with him. Instead the storyteller said, "Saghani is a man of lies. We should not have allowed our shaman to keep the woman. Our shaman traded a medicine skin. Makes Rain saw Saghani with it. No one should do such a thing. The spirits give powers to the ones they choose. Not even a shaman should trade a medicine skin.

"By now Saghani has his children back, and if we had not killed the woman, those two who called themselves traders, they would have stolen her also."

"They told us they were First Men," the singer said.

"Have you ever seen First Men dressed as they were dressed, with Walrus parkas? With caribou skin leggings?" asked the storyteller.

"They wore seal flipper boots."

The storyteller made a sound of rudeness through his nose. "So they went to a First Men village, bought the boots in trade."

The dancer, a quiet man, placed several sticks into the hearth fire at the center of the lodge, then looked up at the others. "They claimed to be traders, yet came in sheathed boats like sea hunters," he said. "They claimed to be First Men, but how often has any man in this village seen a First Men trader? They stay in their own islands. They do not come to us."

"The young one," said Stick Walking, "his knife was something any man would want."

"I saw it," said the carver. "The blade is obsidian. First Men's spearheads, even the points on their harpoons, are obsidian, but it was too good, the craftmanship too fine, to have been made by the First Men."

The singer lifted his hands and said nothing more.

Then Stick Walking stood. Speaking with the authority earned by living many years, he said, "I am thinking that the two men are not traders. They are hunters. They are not First Men. They belong to the Walrus. They were sent by Saghani to bring back the babies and the woman, especially the boy with the carving on his parka. Did you not see that the younger Walrus hunter also carried such a carving?"

"But why, if these children had special powers, would Saghani bring them?" asked the singer. "Why not bring others who had no spirit gifts?"

"He wanted the spirit powers our shaman had promised him," said the storyteller. "You think our shaman would not know if the wrong children had been given?"

"But if he would know about the children," replied the singer, "he should also know that the men Saghani sent were lying."

"By then our shaman had traded away his power," said the dancer.

"The women say he gave the children to them, those First Men or Walrus, whatever they are," said the singer. "The women said the young man promised to raise the boys knowing our shaman as father, honoring the ways of the River People."

"Women hear what they want to hear," said the storyteller. "The man had a good face, a strong body. The women did not look beyond that."

Then the carver asked, "What then should we do? Is it best to offer prayers? Is it best to fast and burn meat? Or should we go to the Walrus and kill Saghani?"

A hiss seemed to circle the fire, as though each man breathed in the idea of killing.

"Kill," said the storyteller quietly.

"Kill," said the carver.

"If it means our village will be safe . . ." said the singer.

The dancer looked long at Stick Walking. "What do you say we should do?" he asked.

"Nothing good has come from this man Saghani," said Stick Walking. "I am thinking we must be sure he does not return to our village."

"How many hunters in this village would go?" asked the dancer.

"Five would go, we know this," said the carver.

"Eight tens of hunters we have," said Stick Walking, "but each man must decide for himself. Go each of you, talk to those hunters who are not so old, not so young. Tell them we will go to the Walrus and destroy as Saghani has destroyed."

NINETY-SIX

THE FIRST MEN

The Alaska Peninsula

"WE LOOKED FOR ONE SON AND BROUGHT BACK two," Kayugh said. He handed the boy called Mouse to Chagak. Her hands, from long years of holding babies, knew what to do, and so she took the child, settled him against her side. But her eyes were on Kiin and Samiq, on Three Fish and Small Knife, the four of them standing together with arms around each other, Shuku and Takha and Many Whales at the center of the circle, a family complete. She watched as Shuku and Takha reached for each other. With baby fingers they poked at each other's face, Takha clinging to his father, Shuku to his mother.

"What do you think?" Kayugh asked his wife. "Are we too old to raise a son?"

Chagak, her throat filled with tears, could give no answer, and so instead, she turned her eyes to the child she held, a fine fat boy, large-boned in the manner of the Walrus People, with clear dark eyes and much hair. She looked down at Wren, who stood beside her, and when her voice came again to her throat, she asked the girl, "Would you like a baby brother?"

Wren lifted her eyes to the boy, studied him solemnly, and finally asked, "Is Shuku my brother?"

"He is your nephew," Chagak said.

"Like Many Whales?"

"Like Many Whales."

"Like Takha?"

"Yes."

"Like Small Knife?" And in asking, Wren laughed, covering her mouth with one hand.

432

"Like Small Knife," Chagak answered, knowing the girl thought it funny to be aunt to a man who was already a hunter.

"I need a brother," Wren said. "A little brother."

"Good," said Kayugh. "You will help take care of him." Wren reached over to pat the baby's leg. "What is his name?"

Chagak raised her eyebrows and looked at her husband.

"We have to give him a name," Kayugh said. "We will think of one, but not today."

"He is Hunter," said Big Teeth. "Name him that."

Kayugh nodded, slowly said the name, as though he tasted the sound of it on his tongue. "It is good," Kayugh said. "We need hunters."

"Yes."

"I promised I would raise both boys to know they are sons of the old man Dyenen, shaman of the River People," Kayugh said. He looked at Big Teeth as he spoke, but his words were loud enough for Chagak to hear.

Chagak felt a sudden tightening of her chest, an ache that seemed to squeeze into her heart. Another son raised to honor a different village, a different way of living. Was Samiq not enough? What good had come from sending him to the Whale Hunters? If he had stayed with the First Men, in their own village, Amgigh would probably still be alive.

"If I raise Hunter as son through his childhood," Chagak said to the two men standing beside her, "I will not give him back to another tribe. I gave Samiq. I will not give another."

"He is Walrus," Kayugh said. "The River People do not want him, but I promised their shaman I would tell the boy about the powers of the man who would have been his father."

"Then we do not take him back to the River People?" Chagak asked.

"No."

"We do not take him to the Walrus?"

"He is ours."

Chagak let herself look into the boy's eyes. She stroked the smooth skin of his face and smiled at him. Slowly he smiled at her, laid his head against her. And Chagak heard the otter's voice singing, a high clear song: "A son to love. A son to raise." And looking at Kiin, Chagak knew Kiin must be hearing the same song.

NINETY-SEVEN

SNOW MIGHT COME, THE WALRUS HUNTERS SAID,
and there would be ice on the bays. So Raven and Waxtal
promised much in trade goods and spiritual power to the men
who came with them. Even to the women who came, said
Waxtal, and gave his wife Kukutux no choice. Why return to
the Walrus village after the battle was won to bring back the
women? he asked. Why take the chance that ice and snow
would keep them apart?

So Raven and Waxtal—with the Whale Hunters and many
men from the Walrus village—paddled their ikyan toward the
Traders' Beach.

Six days later the River men left their village, fighting ice
and cold winds in their clumsy fishing boats on the four-day
journey to Saghani's village—thirty men, each hoping to kill
Saghani.

The River men arrived at the Walrus village on the fourth
night. The lodges glowed yellow from the oil lamps within.

"No dogs," the hunters whispered to one another, "no
dogs," and were surprised at the quietness of the village.

They had planned carefully, and started at the edge of the
village, splitting their number so that as they moved from
lodge to lodge, they pinched in toward the back of the village.
They came to Chin Hairs' lodge first, crept inside on feet that
had learned quiet ways from walking in the forest.

Chin Hairs had decided not to go with Raven. He, his wife,
and their children slept. They woke when the knives cut their
throats. They screamed out, but the River men cupped hands
over faces and no one heard.

Kiin held Shuku and Takha on her lap, rocked and sang. Samiq sat beside her, reached out to touch Shuku. The boy
opened his eyes for a moment, smiled, then closed them. "I
am too happy," Kiin said. But Samiq set two fingers against

434

her lips, pressed the words back into her mouth.

"It is a good thing," he said. "But do not tempt the spirits to take what we have."

Kiin's inside voice repeated what Samiq said, then reminded Kiin of her dead brother Qakan, of her father Waxtal who must also be dead. Why draw their spirits with words?

Kiin handed Shuku to Samiq, picked up Takha. They put the boys into Kiin's sleeping place and stood for a time watching. Then Three Fish was with them, also watching, her son still nursing at her breast, the baby folded into her arms.

Samiq leaned down to whisper to Kiin, "Tonight I must spend with Three Fish," and Kiin nodded, did not allow herself to regret that she must share her husband. Three Fish had been mother to Takha, wife to Samiq, when Kiin could not. Many Whales would know Kiin as his mother, and to Kiin he was also son.

The long-ago taunts of Kiin's brother Qakan came to her ears, the many times he had told her that she would never be wife, never be mother. Now she had four sons, because Small Knife also was hers.

She went into the main room of the ulaq, sat with sealskins for sewing on her lap. She began to hum, a song coming to her as often happened when she was happy, something without words. She laid down her sewing and climbed up the log to the ulaq roof, then sat outside in the chill of the wind, without parka, without leggings, wearing only her aprons.

The wind was like water against her skin, clean and cold. The roof hole of each ulaq glowed with the soft light of lamps within, but darkness hid the beach and the water of the bay. In the hills wolves howled, a noise that took Kiin back to the months she had spent in the Walrus village. She shivered and turned to go inside, but then heard a whisper, something brought to her ears from across the water.

She looked toward the sound, tried to see but could not, listened but heard nothing more.

"The word was a Walrus word," Kiin's spirit said, the voice clear in her mind.

Kiin stood still for a moment, heard nothing, said to her spirit, "It was only the wolves. Their songs always take me to the Walrus People."

But then Kiin heard another word, and she knew the voice.

The Raven. She moved slowly, down in through the lighted roof hole, but once inside she jumped from the climbing log, ran to Three Fish's sleeping place, called out to Samiq, her voice a whisper but somehow loud in the ulaq, so that Many Whales began to cry, and then Takha and Shuku.

"Samiq," she called, "there are people coming. Walrus. I heard their voices. The Raven is coming. I will hide. I will go to the hills. I will take our sons."

Then Samiq was with her, arms tight around her, as if he could protect her from spears, from knives, with only his flesh. "No," he said. "You are my wife. The Raven cannot stand against me."

Small Knife also came from his sleeping place, the young man rubbing his eyes with his fists. Samiq handed him a short throwing spear. "Go, get my father, get Big Teeth. Tell them the Walrus men have come to us. Tell them Raven has come."

The boy left the ulaq, and Kiin wished she could go with him, wished she, not Samiq, could fight the Raven.

"I will not go back," she said, and when no one seemed to hear her, she said again, "I will not go back. I am here with my sons, with my own people. I will not go back."

Samiq looked at her, held her eyes with his. Then he lifted the shell bead necklace he wore. "Long ago," he said, "I made this for you. You gave it back to me as a pledge. Now I return it to you."

Samiq placed the necklace in her hands. The beads were warm from his skin, and it seemed for the first time that Kiin saw Samiq's true strength. Not the width of his shoulders or hard muscles under his skin, but the power that came from his spirit.

Woman of the Sky and Woman of the Sun stood in the center of the circle, River hunters around them. Each hunter carried a knife or throwing lance, the weapons tipped with blood.

"You think you need all those weapons against two old women?" Woman of the Sky asked.

The men made no reply, but Woman of the Sun turned to her sister, said in the First Men tongue, "They are River, look at their clothing. They do not understand you."

One of the men stepped toward them, said awkwardly in Walrus, "Where be your men?"

"You know they are dead," Woman of the Sky said. "But someday they will take revenge."

"Where be one called Saghani?" the River man asked.

"I do not know a Saghani," Woman of the Sky said.

The man grabbed the old woman's arm, twisted it behind her back.

"You think you must hurt an old woman?" Woman of the Sky asked. "You think you are powerful because you are stronger than me? There is strength you do not understand."

The River man released her, and she rubbed her arm, then said, "I do not lie. There is no man here called Saghani."

The River man turned to one of the hunters beside him, spoke rapidly in the River tongue. Finally the man said to Woman of the Sky, "Raven. The man Raven. He say he shaman."

"He is not here," she said. "He is on a trading trip. I cannot say where. Who knows at which village a trader might be found?"

For a moment the man stared at her, then said, "Let him be alive. Let him find his people dead. You two old womans, you tell Raven we watch him. Someday River People find him. Kill him. Feed him to dogs like we did his wife."

Then he pushed Woman of the Sky aside and left the lodge. The others followed.

Woman of the Sky and Woman of the Sun sat down. Each picked up a death mat; each began to weave.

"Do we have enough?" Woman of the Sun asked.

Woman of the Sky looked over her shoulder at the death mats piled against the wall. "Almost," she said.

Samiq, Kayugh, and Big Teeth stood on the beach, called to the men in their ikyan, in the darkness, in the silence. From the tops of the ulas, Small Knife and First Snow waited, spears and spear throwers in their right hands, knives in their left. In each ulaq, the women waited, the children slept.

"Come to us now," Samiq called. "I am alananasika. If you have come to trade, you are welcome. If you come, Raven, to fight, then come in the morning. Or does the night hide your shame?"

Kayugh laid one hand on his son's arm, tightened his fingers, and Samiq knew his father warned against foolish words spoken in anger.

No one answered. There was no sound, and Samiq thought Kiin had been wrong. Perhaps she had heard nothing but the sound of wind bringing old words spoken long ago. Then a voice came, a man speaking, and for a moment Samiq thought he was in a dream, hearing someone long dead, but then Kayugh said, "It is not Raven. It is Waxtal."

"Are these spirits then?" Big Teeth asked.

Kayugh and Samiq did not answer the man, only listened as Waxtal called out, "Hunters of the First Men, you sent me from your village into storms, to die. You thought I was dead these many moons, but see, I live. I will have revenge for my life, for the one who took my wife, who took my daughter, who took my ulaq, my food, all things that were mine.

"If you could see through this darkness, you would see that I bring many men. If I ask, they will destroy your village. They will kill your women and children. If I ask, they will do this. But I am a good man. I have the favor of the spirits. Your village, your women and children, will be spared—if I am given my wife Blue Shell and my daughter Kiin and the life of the man who would have me dead. Give me Samiq; give me Blue Shell; give me Kiin."

"Waxtal lies," Big Teeth said. "He has no men with him. Some way he lived through the winter, and now he comes in the night to make us think he has great power."

Big Teeth cupped a hand around his mouth, called out to Waxtal, "Your wife Blue Shell is dead."

For a time Waxtal did not speak, then Samiq heard laughter, and Waxtal said, "Already the spirits avenge me. Then I will take Chagak. Woman for woman. Tell Kayugh he can keep his daughter, the small one, Wren. I do not need her."

"You will not have my wife, nor any of my daughters!" Kayugh said. "Not Red Berry, not Wren, not Kiin, not Three Fish."

"He is alone," Big Teeth said. "Return to your ulas. I will stay outside and watch until morning. He cannot throw a spear far enough to hit me from the water, and I will not let him come on the beach."

But Samiq, while waiting, had lifted prayers to the Mystery, that Creating Spirit. He felt the power of that One surround him, and suddenly he knew that Waxtal spoke the truth. He had brought others with him. Samiq felt the hard, warring spirits of hunters, the strong, flowing spirits of women, and, to his surprise, the smaller spirits of children and babies.

"He does not lie," Samiq said to Kayugh and Big Teeth. "He has brought many with him, even women, even children."

"Why?" Big Teeth asked.

"Who can understand Waxtal?" said Samiq.

"Who are they?" Kayugh asked. "Are they First Men? Are they Walrus?"

As if in answer to Kayugh's question, Samiq heard another voice: "Samiq, I will fight you for the woman Kiin. Last time I took your hand; this time I will take your life."

A rush of blood pumped into Samiq's arms and legs. "It is Raven," he said to his father. "Somehow he knows Kiin is here."

"You told me you were ready to fight him," Kayugh said.

Samiq heard the confidence in his father's voice and so called out to Raven, "I will fight you. If I win, Kiin stays here and Waxtal leaves us."

"It is fair," Raven said.

Samiq heard the murmur of protest, Waxtal's high, thin voice, but then there was silence, and in the silence Samiq again felt the spirits of those with Waxtal, remembered the sounds and tastes and smells of the Whale Hunter village.

"They are Whale Hunters," Samiq said to Kayugh. "Waxtal has brought the Whale Hunters."

"No, Samiq," his father said. "Why would Whale Hunters come here? He has found Raven, brought him and some of the Walrus People."

Over the water, Samiq heard the thin wail of a baby's cry, then Waxtal's voice, in anger, scolding the child's mother. "Whale Hunters," Samiq said again. "Somehow he has brought them here."

He cupped his left hand around his mouth, called out, "Dying Seal, Hard Rock, Crooked Bird!"

At first there was no answer, then Crooked Bird's voice came, "You, Samiq, did you think you could kill us with your curse? We are Whale Hunters. Our power is greater than yours. You are nothing. We have come to kill you and break the curse you left on our island.''

"You know I did not curse your island," Samiq said. "If my powers were that great, you would be fools to try to kill me. But you have women with you. Children. They are welcome, and any hunter who comes as friend. We have food and oil and a good beach. Together we can be a strong village. Together we can hunt and teach our sons to hunt. Who can say why a mountain grows angry and destroys a village? Perhaps it is not something men can understand. But we must go on; we must hunt and eat and live.''

"You are the fool, Samiq," Crooked Bird said.

Then Raven called out: "Samiq, I do not care what these Whale Hunters do. If they fight or do not fight. I have come for Kiin. You cannot change my mind with words.''

"I said I would fight you," Samiq called out. "In the morning, on this beach.''

"On the beach, now," Raven said.

"We cannot see," Samiq answered.

"Light fires. I will wait.''

"Come when you are ready," Samiq called and went back to his ulaq, to his wives and children, to his weapons, while Kayugh and Big Teeth gathered seal bones and oil, wood and grass, and started two fires, one on each end of the flat place where the men would fight.

"Grass Ears and his wives, Chin Hairs and his children, Shale Thrower and her husband, two Whale Hunter women," Woman of the Sky said.

"There are many more," said her sister, but Woman of the Sky did not answer. Each woman carried death mats doubled over her forearms, the mats heavy enough to make the women bend forward as they walked.

"The children?" Woman of the Sky asked.

"Some were killed, and all the men, half of the women.''

Woman of the Sky looked at Ice Hunter's lodge. "My son's wife?" she asked, her voice a whisper.

"She is alive. She is with the children. But Bird Sings' wife is dead.''

"Who takes care of her baby?''

"Her sister. Be glad that your son and grandsons are safe.''

"They are with Raven," Woman of the Sky answered. "They are not safe."

"They will come back to us," Woman of the Sun said.

Her sister straightened against the weight of the death mats. "It was because of the babies—Kiin's sons."

"They are both alive," said Woman of the Sun. "I told her to give one to the wind spirits, but she would not. She said Takha was dead, but he was not. I knew. When the babies were small, we could have taken one. It would not have been difficult."

"It is always difficult to take a life."

"To save so many?"

"I have never convinced myself that we should be the ones to make that choice. So do not blame yourself," Woman of the Sky said. "I also knew Takha was alive."

"How did you know?" Woman of the Sun asked. "You do not have dreams."

"No, I do not have dreams. But I know you. I know what I see in your eyes, and I knew that Kiin's sons were alive."

"The one was evil. He should have died."

"No, sister," said Woman of the Sky. "He was not evil. In that, your dreams are wrong. Evil uses what it can to cause pain. The evil is in Raven. If anyone should be dead, it is he. If Kiin's babies had died, the evil would have come to us some other way. Why else these?" she asked and lifted her arms, pointed with her chin to the death mats she carried.

Kukutux sat with the other women in the ik. From the water, the village was only a darkness on the shore, but as the fires caught and the flames rose, she could see the mounds of the ulas, could see the people gathered on each ulaq roof. Kukutux hunched her shoulders, and the cramp that pulled at her back muscles eased.

I should have stayed with She Cries and Many Babies in the Walrus village, she told herself. I need to spend days on the beach; I need to sew and weave, dig clams and gather sea urchins.

But Waxtal had wanted her to see the village where he would be chief, and he did not want to go back to the Walrus village to get her once the battle was won.

Kukutux shook her head. This was no village—four, five

ulas, a few drying racks, and a handful of hunters. But it was not much worse than the Whale Hunter village, she thought. And the ulas were in good repair; the people, what she could see of them, looked strong and healthy.

"There is no curse here," she whispered.

But Samiq was here. She had heard his voice, and she remembered him—the Seal Hunter man who had come to their village, who had called so many whales. Had Hard Rock forgotten that? Had he forgotten the whales the young man brought them? The village had never been stronger. The curse had come when Hard Rock made Samiq stop hunting, when he gave him boy's work to do instead of honoring him as a man. Perhaps the curse was as much Hard Rock's as Samiq's.

She kept the ik well back from the beach, she and the women with her, so the fire would not show the First Men that they waited.

Raven would fight, Hard Rock had agreed. Then if Samiq was not dead, Hard Rock would fight, then another hunter, and another, until Samiq died and the curse was lifted from the Whale Hunters.

But, Kukutux thought, what if there is no curse?

NINETY-EIGHT

HE CAME IN BLACK FEATHER CLOAK, A KNIFE IN each hand, hair flowing like water over his shoulders. He was a tall man, but thin. One of Samiq's arms was as thick as two of Raven's, but Samiq could not keep his eyes from the man's hands, each whole and strong, each gripping a long-bladed knife.

Two strong hands, said some voice in Samiq's mind. Two strong hands against your weakness. Samiq shook his head to clear the doubt and untied the straightening bone from his forefinger. He placed Amgigh's knife in his right hand and tightened his fingers on the handle.

"You, Raven of the Walrus, you have two knives," Samiq called. He waited for some voice to translate his words, but Raven answered with no translation.

"Get another knife," he said and laughed. "I will wait. The fight must be fair."

Samiq heard the taunting in his words and with sinking heart understood that Raven knew about his hand. He turned to the men gathered near him on the beach, to those who stood in the orange light of the beach fires, and stretched out his left arm, asking for a knife. His father offered his knife, one also made by Amgigh, but then Small Knife came from the ulas. Lifting his knife from the scabbard that hung from his neck, Small Knife said, "Father, you are a man of two people. Let your strength come from two tribes."

Kayugh nodded and stepped back, and Samiq accepted Small Knife's weapon. It was a short knife. The blade, thrusting out from the space between his thumb and forefinger, was no longer than Samiq's thumb, and the handle tucked easily into the palm of the hand. The andesite blade was crudely made, but the point was as sharp as the end of a whale harpoon.

Samiq turned to face Raven, but Small Knife caught his arm, turned him back, and said, "Wait. It will be better this way." He moved the knife so the blade pointed down from Samiq's fist. "To thrust," Small Knife said and made a downward motion with his hand.

"Yes," Samiq said. "Yes." And he turned again to Raven.

Raven threw off his cloak, stretched himself tall, and waited. Samiq slipped out of his parka. The night wind was cold against Samiq's skin, but he felt only the hardness of the knives in his hands. He held his right hand out, blade up, kept his left hand down at his side.

"You said the fight must be fair," Samiq said to Raven.

"You complain about your hand?" Raven asked. "I do not force you to fight. Give me Kiin. I will leave."

"The fight is not fair because I have strength earned in prayer, in fasting."

"You think I do not pray?" Raven asked.

"A man who seeks that Spirit greater than himself does not need a knife to prove his power."

"Fool!" said Raven. "No one is greater than I am!"

"You say your power is equal to the power of the spirits?" asked Samiq.

"Yes," said Raven. "I call spirits. They do what I ask. You do not see them, but there are spirits in the fires, spirits hovering in the darkness. Listen."

Suddenly a voice called from beyond the fires, a cry like a woman mourning.

"Already your grandmother's spirit mourns your death," Raven said.

A second voice came from the fire behind Samiq. "There is no hope for you, Samiq," the voice said. "Soon you will be with me in the spirit world."

Almost, Samiq turned, but a quietness came to him, an assurance of his own strength.

A third voice spoke, and this time Samiq watched Raven, watched carefully how the man held his head. He watched his mouth, the stiffness of his lips. It is a trick, Samiq thought. Only that—a trick.

Samiq spoke as if there had been no voices.

"Kiin is my wife," he said. "She will stay here with me."

"She is worth your life?"

"Yes," Samiq said, "and she is also worth yours."

"You have learned then to fight with knives?"

"I fight with more than knives," Samiq said. He held up the knife in his right hand. "This blade cries for your blood," he told Raven. "With this blade you killed my brother—a blade he himself made. Since that day, this knife in all its spirit thoughts has wanted nothing else but to taste your blood."

"Your many words only show you are afraid of my knives," said Raven. He stepped forward, swung his blade in an arc toward Samiq's belly. Samiq jumped back, made a sound of disgust low in his throat.

Samiq took three quick steps, turning his body sideways to give Raven's blade less chance to strike. When Raven advanced, Samiq slashed with his left hand, drawing blood on his first attack, a thin cut along the bone of Raven's right forearm.

Raven leaped back, and Samiq jumped forward again, blocking Raven's right arm with his left, arm against arm, bone against bone. Then he slashed in toward Raven's belly with his right hand, with the long black stone of Amgigh's obsidian blade. Again Samiq drew blood, and this time, as the wound opened across Raven's belly, Samiq heard the hiss of breath from those standing near.

"You are slow," Samiq said and moved in again to draw blood, this time from a cut across Raven's cheek.

Raven did not flinch. Instead he came forward to meet Samiq's thrust and to slash with his right hand, a long stroke that caught Samiq's side, the blade going through skin to grate along Samiq's ribs. But Samiq ignored the pain and tried to slash Raven's neck. Raven spun, turning so quickly that Samiq's knife met only air. In the turn, Raven thrust toward Samiq's shoulder with the blade in his left hand, but Samiq let himself fall, and, in falling, tangled Raven's feet with his own. Raven landed heavily on his belly, and his left-hand knife was thrust to the hilt into the beach sand.

Raven pulled out his knife, then both men were again on their feet, both with bodies marked by blood, both with sides heaving as they drew in long breaths of air.

"You have learned much," Raven said and paused as though to give Samiq time for words, but Samiq said nothing. Then Raven, knees bent into a crouch, said, "There is more to power than strong arms and good knives, Seal Hunter." He lifted his voice, called out toward the darkness, the words in the Walrus tongue.

Samiq saw the ikyan he had known were there, not only the long, clumsy ikyan of the Walrus Hunters, but the fine, sleek ikyan built by Whale Hunters.

"You think you could run from such a people, Seal Hunter?" Raven asked.

But Kayugh's voice rose above Raven's: "Samiq, think only of this fight, of these knives."

Then a voice came from the ikyan, a voice Samiq knew: Hard Rock. "Die now. Die quickly, Whale Killer," Hard Rock said, using Samiq's Whale Hunter name. "My revenge will not come so easily as Raven's. You will wish for the quick cut of the knife if you wait to die by my hand."

Kayugh's voice came again: "Samiq!"

But the warning came late, and before Samiq could raise

his own knives, Raven's blade had slashed Samiq's right arm, and his left-hand knife was at Samiq's neck.

Samiq gathered his strength, thrust the man away before he could cut again, then, with his own left hand, caught Raven across the chest, but it was a shallow cut that drew little blood.

Both men circled, and Raven began to chant, something in words Samiq did not understand.

Another voice came, a woman's voice, loud, from the First Men ulas: "Raven, you won the last fight by my power, by the power of my carvings." Kiin came and stood beside one of the beach fires, her sons in her arms. The fire lit her face, the faces of her sons. "Raven," she called, "this time my power stands on the side of Samiq, my husband, father to Shuku and Takha."

Samiq saw the surprise on Raven's face and knew that Raven had thought Takha was dead, that Shuku was with the River People.

Others from Samiq's village came, women and children, each carrying carvings, and they set the carvings at Kiin's feet, a circle of animals and men, a circle of spirits caught in ivory, in wood. And in the shadows of the fire each carving seemed to move.

Samiq watched his wife, and fear drained his strength as she stood with both sons. Why show Raven what he would gain in this fight, why give him more to fight for? But then Kiin looked at Samiq, her eyes bold, and he understood that this was Kiin's strength—her sons, her carvings. She gave that strength to him. Kiin would not show Raven Shuku and Takha if she thought Raven would win.

The pain of Samiq's wounds was suddenly gone. "You are dead," he said to Raven and lunged forward. Raven stepped aside, raising his left arm to cut as Samiq moved by, but Samiq spun and turned, plunging Small Knife's short blade into Raven's neck.

Samiq jumped away and stood, the fingers of his right hand still gripping the baleen-wrapped handle of Amgigh's knife.

Samiq held up the knife and called out, "Kiin does not belong to you, Raven. Her power is her own. If you want such power, you must find it in your own prayers, in your own visions."

Then Raven turned, picked up his feather cloak, and pushed

past the men of his village, past Ice Hunter and his sons, and went to his ik. Ice Hunter walked toward him, but Raven waved him away, then dragged the ik out into the water. Raven climbed in and picked up his paddle, then moved with the ik into darkness.

"See, Raven," said Samiq in a quiet voice. "Even a tiny blade is greater than you are."

Waxtal watched as Raven's ik slipped between the ikyan of the Whale Hunters. Hard Rock called to the man. Raven turned but then slumped into the bottom of his ik, and Waxtal saw that his eyes were fixed and staring, the eyes of a man already dead.

Large wet flakes of snow began to fall from the dark sky. At first Waxtal thought they were ash, like the ash that had fallen the night Aka and Okmok erupted. But then the snow was on his face, cold, wet. A bird swooped down into Raven's ik and flew out again. "A raven," he heard the carved tusk murmur. But what raven flew at night over water?

Waxtal set his paddle to follow the shaman's drifting ik. Raven no longer needed his cloak, his amulet. Why not take them? They should belong to another shaman, someone who would use their power wisely.

But then Hard Rock called out: "You have fought one, now fight another."

Waxtal waited to hear Samiq's answer, but Samiq said nothing.

The sky was beginning to lighten, and even though the fires had burned down to coals, Waxtal could see the beach more clearly. Kiin stood beside Samiq, her twin sons in her arms. Samiq's Whale Hunter wife was also there with her baby and with Small Knife.

Hard Rock moved into shallow water, then, gesturing for his hunters to follow, he beached his ikyak. Waxtal waited. Why get close to the fighting when his own power was in prayer, in the calling of spirits? He reached into his ik, pulled out the animal skin Raven had given him. "The man was a fool to give me this much of his power," Waxtal said to his tusks. "Now I have the power I earned by my carving, and the power I bought in trade from Raven."

Waxtal waited for the carved tusk to speak, but whatever

answer it gave was lost in the loud anger of Hard Rock's voice as he called to Ice Hunter and his sons, "What will you do, Walrus men? Will you fight for the honor of your people, or shall I fight?"

"My people do not measure their honor by men killed, or the power of knives over flesh," Ice Hunter answered. "I will not fight, but my sons are grown. Each must speak for himself."

Ice Hunter's sons turned their backs on Samiq, stood by their ikyan at the edge of the water. "We have no argument with this man or his wife," the son with the scar said.

"Then I will fight him myself," said Hard Rock.

Samiq stepped away from his wives, went forward to meet Hard Rock. But Kayugh, coming from the shadows, pushed ahead of him. "My son did not curse your village," Kayugh said. "Would he have called the mountains' anger to his own people as well as yours? Do not forget our village was destroyed as well."

"You, Kayugh, did you lose all your hunters? Did your children die? Your women?"

"We lived because we chose to leave our island. You did not make that choice. Now you blame another for what has happened to you."

"I blame a man who brought a curse to us, and I will kill that man."

"You will fight me before you fight my son."

Hard Rock laughed, and during his laughter Samiq stepped forward to stand beside his father. "I will fight him," Samiq said in a quiet voice, words spoken only to Kayugh.

"You are tired," Kayugh said.

"I will fight. If I die, I die."

Kayugh lowered his head, waited for long moments, but finally stepped away.

"One knife?" Hard Rock asked.

Samiq held up Amgigh's obsidian blade. "One knife," Samiq said.

Then again Samiq was circling with knife blade held forward, but from the sides of his eyes, he saw someone move, saw someone come into the circle of scuffed sand. He turned his head, thinking another of the Whale Hunters had come to help Hard Rock in the kill, but then he saw that it was Small

Knife, and his heart twisted in fear for the boy.

"It is my fight. Stay away!" Samiq called to him.

"I will do nothing unless he does," Small Knife said, and pointed his spear at a man who stood behind one of the beach fires. It was Crooked Bird. He held spear and spear thrower lifted in his right hand.

"Hard Rock, you must have your hunters fight your battles?" Samiq asked.

Then Ice Hunter and his sons, men of the Walrus, were beside Small Knife, weapons ready. "No curse is broken by cheating," Ice Hunter called out.

Dying Seal came forward. He laid his weapons at his feet. "We came only to end the curse on our people," he said, "not to bring that curse to others."

"Crooked Bird, you are a fool," Hard Rock called out. "I am strong enough to take him. Why doubt?"

"There is no curse. There should be no fight," Kayugh said.

But Hard Rock answered, "Seal Hunter, you have not seen my island. We die still, even though the mountains' anger has lifted. How can you say there is no curse?"

"And if there is a curse," Kayugh answered, "how do you know it is because of my son?"

"We had no problems before he came."

"You had a different chief then, a man who respected the spirits. Perhaps the curse is something you yourself brought to your people."

Hard Rock threw down his knife. Samiq watched as the man walked away, as he went to Crooked Bird, spoke to the man in hard, yelling words. Samiq turned his back, joined Kayugh and Small Knife, Ice Hunter and Dying Seal.

In his weariness, Samiq said nothing, only stood, trying to keep his legs and arms steady against the shaking spirits that had entered his body. So when Small Knife's quiet groan mingled into the words of those beside him, Samiq did not even turn toward his son. But seeing the horror come suddenly into Kayugh's eyes, Samiq understood and caught his son as he fell, a spear in Small Knife's back.

Small Knife's weight carried Samiq to his knees, and he cradled the boy across his lap, speaking words and promises he could never keep, until he realized that the boy's spirit had already left, pushed from his body as soon as the spear hit.

Samiq looked back at Hard Rock, at Crooked Bird. Hard Rock stood with spear thrower in hand, and Crooked Bird was saying, ''Your spear took Small Knife. Samiq still lives.''

Ice Hunter threw his spear. It took Crooked Bird in the throat. Another spear flew, and both Crooked Bird and Hard Rock were on the ground, lying in their own blood. Samiq looked up, saw that Dying Seal had thrown the second spear.

For a moment no one moved, then Samiq lowered his head to Small Knife's body, and his sorrow came out in long, choking sobs.

NINETY-NINE

WAXTAL WATCHED FROM HIS IKYAK AS SMALL Knife fell, waited without breathing for Hard Rock's second throw, but instead two spears came, one and another, and Waxtal knew that Hard Rock and Crooked Bird were dead. So now who could say what the Walrus men and the Whale Hunters would do? They had come because Waxtal had persuaded them to come, but now with both the Walrus shaman and the Whale Hunters' alananasika dead, would they say he, Waxtal, was to blame? Would they try to kill him in revenge?

Waxtal's heart beat so quickly that it made his hands shake, and he could barely paddle his ikyak. Still he managed to turn the craft. He headed toward the mouth of the Traders' Bay, paddling quickly until he was out again on the sea.

The voice came to him, the carved tusk speaking. ''There are many ways a man can die,'' said the tusk. ''You are in danger. Do as I tell you, Waxtal.''

Strength came into Waxtal's arms; power again filled his chest, and he knew that he was stronger than Samiq, than the man who held a dead boy in his arms and wept like a woman.

So Waxtal turned his ikyak as the tusk told him, turned it toward the Walrus village, kept it close to shore, and that night, when it was time again to sleep, the tusk directed him to a safe beach.

Kukutux and the Whale Hunter women sang mourning songs as they followed Ice Hunter and his sons back to the Walrus village. Kukutux knew she must tell Many Babies of Hard Rock's death. Women must tell women, and who could expect Hard Rock's other wives to do so? Their sorrow was too great.

She also mourned Hard Rock. The man had tried to do what he thought was best for his people. And Crooked Bird—though he was always one to do things in wrong ways—was a man who had lived each day, feeling the sun, the cold, the wind, seeing stars on clear nights and hearing the voice of the grass, the words spoken by the sea.

Kukutux sighed and thrust her paddle into the water. They had wrapped the men's bodies and tied them across the tops of ikyan, Hard Rock on Dying Seal's ikyak, Crooked Bird on Wind Chaser's. They would do their mourning in the Walrus village. They would find a place for burial and honor their dead.

Ice Hunter had said they could spend the winter with the Walrus People. Since Raven was dead, some of the women could live in his lodge, and Walrus families would make room for the others.

They were out of the Traders' Bay and into the sea, their boats sped by a wind pushing strong from the west, when Kukutux realized that Waxtal was not with them. She shrugged her shoulders and did not let herself worry. He would know they had returned to the Walrus village. She would wait for him there. Better that he was not with them now; better that she did not have to listen to his anger, to his whining.

Samiq had survived Raven's knife, had killed the man whose spirit powers were supposed to be so great. He had survived Crooked Bird's spear. Perhaps the man was not evil but good. Perhaps the evil was in something or someone else. But who could expect Waxtal to see such a thing when Waxtal wanted what belonged to Samiq?

* * *

Ten days they traveled, in snow and wind and ice. On the tenth day, toward the night, they came to the Walrus village. It was a village of mourning—lodges burned, hunters, women, and children dead.

For the first time, Kukutux saw the strange old women, those two sisters, Grandmother and Aunt, and she listened as they spoke to Ice Hunter, as they spoke in voices cut with sorrow.

Ice Hunter told the Whale Hunters, in their First Men language, about the raid made by the River People, the killing brought by Raven's lies. And together, the people mourned.

ONE HUNDRED

SMOKE DRIFTED UP INTO THE GRAY SKY FROM the six First Men ulas. Snow covered the beach and hills. The sixth ulaq was new—built a little apart from the others.

It must be Dying Seal's, Kukutux thought, for his wife and many children. She sat forward in her place in the women's ik so she could see the ikyak racks. Had Waxtal, perhaps afraid to go to the Walrus village, returned here to the Seal Hunters? But no, she did not see his ikyak, and there was little chance that he was out with the hunters. He would be eating or sleeping, expecting others to do his share of the work. She took a long breath and dipped her paddle into the water, helped Ice Hunter's wife direct the ik toward shore.

Eight Walrus men had come with Ice Hunter: his sons White Fox and Bird Sings, and six other hunters. Many women came, both Walrus and Whale Hunter, and all the remaining Whale Hunter men. Some, Kukutux knew, planned to return to the Whale Hunter island next spring, but others, like Dying Seal, said they would stay as hunters in the First Men village here on the Traders' Beach.

In the ik with Kukutux were Ice Hunter's wife, and She Cries' stepdaughter, the widow Pogy, and the two Walrus women, Grandmother and Aunt. The two old women sat in the middle of the ik, fur seal skins in their laps. During the days traveling from the Walrus village, they had been rubbing oil into the scraped sides of the pelts.

"Baby blankets," Grandmother had said. And her small brown face had crinkled into a smile.

Ice Hunter was the first to beach his ik, dragging it up over the ridges of ice that ringed the shore. He was greeted by the chief of the Seal Hunter village, Samiq, and an older man who stood beside him. Other men were also on the beach, their women with them, children playing nearby. It was good to see a village that was growing, a village where people laughed and smiled and were fat from full food caches.

For a long time, Ice Hunter spoke to Samiq. Then Samiq called to the people on the beach, and Ice Hunter gestured for the Walrus men to land their ikyan. The women, too, came in their iks, and Samiq spoke to all, Ice Hunter repeating his words in the Walrus tongue.

Samiq's welcome found its way into Kukutux's heart so that it lifted the tiredness from her arms, the burn of sun on water from her eyes. This village would be their own, a place to grow strong children.

Kukutux recognized Three Fish standing among the Seal Hunter women, a baby strapped to her back—Three Fish, that one Kukutux had thought long dead, alive here with the Seal Hunters, a wife, a mother.

Then Ice Hunter was directing the women to unpack their iks, and women, children, and men were given places in the First Men ulas until new ulas could be built.

"And if we build in the manner of the Walrus lodges?" Ice Hunter's oldest son asked.

"Each man should do what is best for himself and his family," Samiq replied. Then smiles came, and laughter.

It is good, Kukutux thought. It is good, and she did not let herself think about Waxtal, about a husband who might come and take her away from the Seal Hunter village.

For nearly a month, Waxtal had listened to the words of the carved tusk, listened as a boy listens to his father. The tusk knew the waters here. Why not? Waxtal asked himself. It had once lived in that sea, had been part of an animal that swam in that water. The tusk directed Waxtal to caves and hot springs, to open waters where he could catch fish.

On this night of full moon, they came to a long spit of gravel that extended into the sea, something Waxtal did not recognize, though he knew he had been in this place before. He remembered it without a beach, only the mountains rising straight from the water, cliffs full of birds. But the spit extended out like a giant oar from the land, snow on the blade of that oar, with enough space for a man to stand and walk, enough space for several ulas.

"Here, Waxtal, a place for a man to pray," the tusk said. "A place for vision fasts, a place for the spirits to show you how to kill a man who needs killing."

So Waxtal paddled his ikyak onto the spit, dragged it up into the snow, and cleared a place to sit. Then he wrapped himself in warm fur seal pelts, sat down, and began to pray.

His first prayers were curses on Samiq and the First Men, on his dead wife Blue Shell and on Kiin. As he prayed, he rejoiced in his own power, the strength that had brought walrus to the Whale Hunters, the vision that had drawn those people with him to the Traders' Beach. And finally, within his rejoicing, he slept.

That same night Samiq held Kiin close to him. Though he mourned Small Knife, his joy in Kiin lifted a portion of his sorrow, let him see each new day with hope.

"They are good people, those who have come to us," Kiin whispered.

Samiq pressed his face into her hair.

"I will give you another son," Kiin said. "We can give him the name of your Whale Hunter son now in the Dancing Lights. We can draw the strength of that good name back to us. And you can give me a daughter, someone who will have the name used by my mother."

Samiq could find no words to hold the joy of that hope, and so he tightened his arms around Kiin's strong body, let his hands speak for him.

Waxtal awoke from his sleep cold, and looking down saw that he sat in water. Night had brought high tide, a full moon drawing the sea. As his eyes followed the path made by the moon's light,

Waxtal saw his ikyak on the waves, moving away from him.

He called out to the ikyak, to that brother he had made with his own hands, called out to the tusk that bore the marks of his own knife, but they went on without him. Then, coming from the ikyak, he heard the voice of the carved tusk. It laughed. It laughed.

Waxtal called until the water reached his shoulders, then across the waves there came a bird, a raven, its voice harsh and loud, and as though the cold of the water gave Waxtal sudden understanding, he knew the bird's call was a rejoicing. Joy over food that would soon be his—the body of a man, fresh liver, soft eyes.

Waxtal swung his arms at the bird, but the raven only flew circles, waiting. Curses came into Waxtal's mouth, and he spat them out, dark as blood. He cursed all things: people and animals, water and sky, mountains and grass. Finally, the sea numbed him and he could no longer speak.

The curses settled themselves in his throat, and they were so thick, there was no room for breath.

Aunt came to Kukutux in the night, crawled into the sleeping place that Kukutux shared with the Seal Hunter woman Red Berry. Aunt shook her awake and pulled her into the main room of the ulaq, over to the lamp where several wicks still burned. The old woman said, "Your husband, he is dead."

For a moment Kukutux said nothing, thought nothing. The old woman repeated the words, and finally Kukutux understood.

"Waxtal," Aunt said, "the sea has claimed him."

"I have no tears for him," said Kukutux.

"There are men here who would take you as wife—White Fox or the First Men hunter First Snow."

"I have a moon of mourning," Kukutux answered.

The old woman shrugged. "A moon passes quickly."

"Yes." For a time Kukutux said nothing else, but Aunt waited as if she knew Kukutux had questions to ask.

"This is called the Traders' Beach," Kukutux finally said.

"Yes."

"Do all traders come here?"

"Most."

"They come only in spring, only in summer?"

"No, Ice Hunter says they sometimes come before winter, when men are filling caches. It is a good time to make trades."

"Then I will wait. There is one who may come. . . ."

"Owl," the old woman said.

Kukutux's breath stopped at the roof of her mouth. "You know him?"

"I will," said the old woman and gave a low chuckle.

"Good," said Kukutux.

"Yes, it is good," said Aunt, then reached over to pinch out the lamp wicks and went back to her sleeping place.

In the darkness Kukutux climbed from the ulaq and sat outside in the wind. She clasped the blue and gold beads at her neck and sang a song, something quiet and happy, a song of calling. And the wind took it, carrying her words far.

To a trader's ik.

EPILOGUE

WINTER
7036 B.C.

CHAGAK TIGHTENED HER ARMS AROUND TAKHA and Shuku. Almost, she could believe she held Amgigh and Samiq. Why did something so long ago seem so close, as though she could reach back at will to days long past?

She closed her eyes and listened to the evening sounds of the ulaq—the scrape of Kayugh's lava rock against a spear shaft, Samiq's voice as he spoke to Owl, the clatter of wood dishes as Three Fish, Kiin, and Kukutux put away food. They all carried the sorrow of Small Knife's death, but with each moon it was better. Who could not feel joy when so many babies had been given them—Shuku and Takha, Many Whales and Hunter, and the new baby that Kiin carried in her belly.

"So tell your grandsons a story, Grandmother," Kiin said and sat down beside Chagak.

Chagak laughed in her surprise, but who could know what Kiin would ask next? Her joy in being wife and mother seemed to shine out from her face and glow through her words. Each day brought a new idea, some way to make the ulaq stronger, the food better, clothing more beautiful. And now she wanted a story.

"A story . . ." said Chagak. She smiled at Kiin and at Samiq, at the others sitting in Kayugh's ulaq. She pressed her cheek against the top of Shuku's head and closed her eyes. Songs, prayers, and women's chants came into her mind, but no stories.

"I do not know any stories," she finally said.

Then the otter's voice came, a teasing voice that spoke in Chagak's mind. "Ah, little grandmother," said the otter, "everyone has a story, and all of us are storytellers."

Chagak looked up into the shadows that shifted and moved

459

above the oil lamp, then she tilted her head as though she listened to something others did not hear. Finally she spoke, and her words were in the strong, clear voice of a storyteller.

"Six days," she said. "The hunters had been gone six days, and during that time there had been a storm—rain and a roaring that seemed to come from within the mountains, and waves that swept the beaches bare . . ."

AUTHOR'S NOTES

ONE OF THE JOYS THAT HAS ACCOMPANIED THE publication of my novels has been the opportunity to travel as a guest lecturer. Because time does not permit me to meet all my readers, I have decided to use these author's notes to answer the questions I am asked most frequently by lecture audiences: where I get my story ideas; how I developed the "voice" or writing style for each novel; what portions of the novels are symbolic; and why I use an inner voice with some of my characters.

I am sure most authors are asked where they get their ideas, and I am equally sure most authors have many more story ideas than I do. (I seem to have one good story idea about every two years.) Fortunately for me, story ideas abound in Native American legends, myths, and traditions, and I have borrowed from these in developing my characters and story lines. *Brother Wind,* being the last of a trilogy, is of course founded on the legends and stories used as a basis for its predecessors, *Mother Earth Father Sky* and *My Sister the Moon.*

These legends include the Aleut sea otter legend, the moon myths of the Pueblo and Osage, the Aleut Raven's marriage story, the Inuit oral histories of a mother hiding the son of an enemy, blue ice men legends, Ojibway twin sons stories, tiger legends from the Orient (which have counterparts in Aleut whale-hunting traditions), Aleut Shuganan and "Outside Men" stories, various creation legends, and the raven-trickster legends. In addition, *Brother Wind* is also based on a Native story from the Northwest about a one-handed man and a beautiful woman who save their tribe from marauding warriors, and also on Athabascan raven and porcupine traditions.

The "voices" (sometimes called writing styles) I have developed for this trilogy are based on the rhythms and voice patterns of spoken Native American languages. These patterns are quite different from those of spoken English, and especially inconsistent with polysyllabic English words. Native rhythm patterns (let me insert here that there are thousands of Native American languages and I have studied only a handful) are often a basic unaccent-unaccent-accent (for those of you who are poets, an anapestic rhythm), while English is often (but, of course, not entirely) a pattern of accent-unaccent, accent-unaccent (trochee).

The voices I developed for this trilogy pull their language rhythms from this basic anapestic pattern and from the energy which makes oral storytelling a form of theater art.

In the tradition of Native American storytellers, this trilogy is filled with symbolism, from the names of the characters to weapons to sky conditions. All animals, birds, and fish in the trilogy are allegorical according to their habits or to Native legends. In approaching Native American art forms, it is essential to remember that the women and men who live according to Native traditions see life itself as an allegory of the spiritual world.

For each novel in this trilogy, I developed an "inner voice." In *Mother Earth Father Sky* it is Chagak's otter voice; in *My Sister the Moon* it is Kiin's spirit voice; and in *Brother Wind* it is the voice of the carved tusk that speaks to Waxtal. My intention is a circle of voices which defines the experience of the artist. The artistic vision begins in Nature (otter), is internalized (spirit), and is given expression (carved tusk).

Let me say here that in spite of my fascination with symbols, research, and voice, it seems to me that the best literature—from Homer to Shakespeare to Twain—the truly excellent work that survives both time and political clime is that which tells a good story. Native American storytellers knew this very well. Theirs is a fine standard of wisdom.

Let me answer one question about *Brother Wind* before it is asked: Yes, many of the best Native American storytellers and well-known shamans were masters of ventriloquism.

Last in this mini-session of questions and answers: Yes, I have begun research for a second trilogy which will continue the saga of the First Men. Please plan to join me in this next journey!

—SUE HARRISON
Pickford, Michigan